BECOMING
the SON

An Autobiography of Jesus

D1509806

C.D. BAKER

Note: References from the *Holy Bible* are author's paraphrases and not intended to be direct quotations from any copyrighted translation.

ISBN: 1477491147
ISBN 13: 9781477491140

OTHER BOOKS BY
C. D. BAKER

Novels:
The Seduction of Eva Volk
The List
Swords of Heaven
The Journey of Souls Series featuring:
    Crusade of Tears
    Quest of Hope
    Pilgrims of Promise

Inpirational Books
40 Loaves
101 Cups of Water

www.cdbaker.com

BECOMING the SON

An Autobiography of Jesus

Author's Edition

BY

C.D. BAKER

DEDICATION

For Irene Loux Baker, my mother and devoted Follower of Jesus Christ

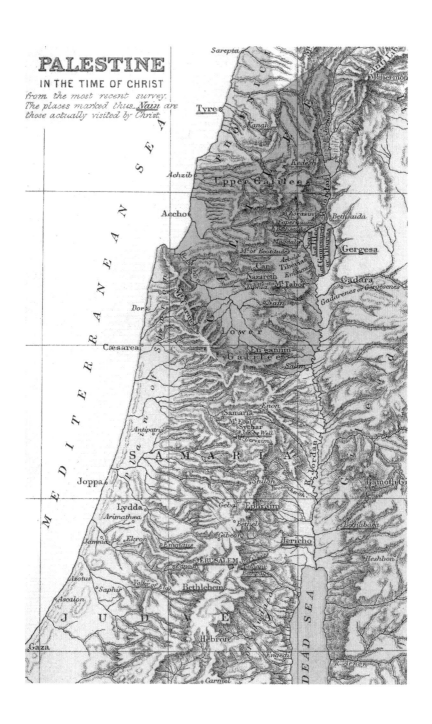

PALESTINE

IN THE TIME OF CHRIST

from the most recent survey.
The places marked thus Nain are
those actually visited by Christ.

TABLE OF CONTENTS

PREFACE

One of the great joys of fiction and film is the 'suspension of belief,' that is, the permission we give ourselves to let go of how we see the world so that we are free to enjoy—and consider—possibilities. However, 'suspension of belief' can be very challenging when it comes to a Jesus novel. This is understandable because many of us uniquely value what we believe about Jesus Christ and are reluctant to loosen our grip. (Readers who are interested in more about the approach to this novel may want to turn to the 'Author's Postscript' located at the very end of the book.) Nevertheless, I invite you to step boldly into the story that follows so that you might delight in fresh possibilities of who Jesus of Nazareth *could have been*.

Those last three words are important because I wrote this novel with the following standard in view: *The events in this story either happened according to the biblical record, or could have happened according to clues in the biblical texts, the historical record, or reasoned observation.* I hope you will forgive what errors you may discover, but you'll not be encountering a Jesus of fantasy who was secretly married to Mary Magdalene etc., etc. Instead, you will experience the Jesus of the Gospels, though in ways you might not expect.

SHALOM

My name is *Adlai bar Ammitai,* scribe of the Sadducees and I am a liar. To be clear, I am not a liar like the market cheat who says, 'this fish was caught this morning' when the thing had floated overnight in a tub. No, I am a liar of a different sort and I will explain shortly. First, I am bursting to tell you of something wondrous that happened just before sunset on the fourteenth day of *Iyar* [1]--a month after *Yeshua* [2] of Nazareth was crucified.

I was walking with some others toward the synagogue in Capernaum when a man rounded a corner, dancing. I am generous to use the word 'dancing,' but he seemed happy enough and so I smiled, believing him to be one of those cheerful madmen whom I sometimes envy. With me were four women and a centurion's young slave named Brennus—the very same Gaul whom the Rabbi had once healed. Amused, we paused to watch until one of the women mumbled, *"Yeshua?"*

I worried for her. Like so many others she was desperate to believe the rumor that the Master had come out of his grave. Excited witnesses had come to Capernaum and insisted that *Yeshua* had risen--but if this were true, why had he not yet appeared to us?

The Gaul suddenly bolted past me. The others followed. Brennus arrived first and hurled himself into the man's arms.

What is this? I thought.

---

1 The Jewish calendar was based on a lunar system, each of its twelve months beginning at the new moon. For this reason, Hebrew calendar references tend to overlap the Roman solar calendar of which most readers will be familiar. For example, in this case the 14th day of the Jewish month of Iyar is equivalent to the Roman, May 7.th

2 *Yeshua* is Hebrew/Aramaic for 'Jesus.' Note that Jesus' primary language was Aramaic, not the ancient Hebrew of Moses, David, etc. A language related to Hebrew, Aramaic was further divided into regional dialects, Jesus having spoken Galilean Aramaic, a dialect considered distinct from that spoken in Judea.

One of the women fell at his feet. I narrowed my gaze and watched warily as the man knelt down and cupped her chin with his two hands. He kissed her face and her forehead, and then whispered something in her ear.

The impetuous Gaul shouted back at me, "It is he, it is Jesus! He lives!" *Can it be?* Wary, I lifted my chin and crossed the cobbled street.

When I arrived, the man lightly pulled away the many arms wrapped round him and he faced me with a kindly expression. "*Shalom,*[3] Adlai."

At the sound of his voice I lost my own, for the voice I heard was *his* voice; the smile was *his* smile, and the eyes... Then *Yeshua* laid his hand on my shoulder. I remember well how his hand had weight and warmth. I felt power fill me, and my body trembled.

I have but two words for all of this and they came from that confounded Gaul: 'He lives.' Two words. *Two words* to proclaim all things forever changed?

Imagine containing the sea with two spoons

or gathering the deserts under two bushels

or collecting the stars beneath two tents?

No. These two words are not enough.But would many words be more able to capture the incomprehensible glory of that moment?

No.

Not even if they filled the libraries of Alexandria and Pergamum.

For words can only contain a portion of the truth, and as you surely know, truth is only Truth when it is whole. Thus it is said that words lie, and this is why I confessed to you that I—a first hand witness—am a liar.[4]

---

3 *Shalom* is a Jewish greeting, meaning 'peace' in its most profoundly sacred, holistic sense.

4 As linguists and epistemologists continue to consider how language works, they are discovering that Fyodor Tyutchev's famous quote, 'a thought once uttered is a lie,' may be relevant, after all. Language is a study of its own and well worth the reader's consideration.

A scribe can never be more. Such is my warning for all that is to come. *Selah.*[5]

Still muted with wonder, I followed this man and the others. He led us beyond the edge of the city and to the stony shore of his beloved lake, called by some as 'Chinnereth' or by others as 'Gennesaret' (or which the Gentiles know as the 'Sea of Galilee') where he helped us build a small fire. As he held his hands to the growing flames, my stunned gaze filled the shadowed holes in both his wrists. I looked up and our eyes met.

If I would forget everything else about this man I would never forget his eyes. Indeed, they were nothing like those of ordinary men. They did not simply sparkle or fade according to mood or circumstance. When he was happy they could make the rivers sing for joy; when he was angry they could pierce Roman armor. Yet, when he needed rest it was as if their effect could be withdrawn so that he might lose himself in a crowd. From their bottomless pupils they could reveal the heart of another—which is why so many turned their faces away from him. Indeed, it was his eyes—even more than his melodious voice—that heaped so much meaning atop the backs of his words.

"Do you believe, Adlai?" he asked, suddenly.

I felt his eyes warm my spirit. Did I? I stared at him and filled my lungs with breath. My heart pounded, my spirit lifted. Oh yes...I believed! Unable to speak, I nodded.

He smiled and toyed with a burning twig. "I am happy for us both, Adlai."

I began to weep as he then turned to the others. "So you wish to hear my story..."

"From your youth," blurted Brennus.

The Master then drew a long, restful breath and looked upwards to peer at the stars. One of them arced wildly westward. He faced the tranquil sea now boasting a silky, silver pathway to a rising moon. "The Spirit

---

5 '*Selah*' is a Hebrew/Aramaic equivalent to 'Amen,' or 'Let it be so.'

will soon choose good men to write down much of what has happened. This will be an important way that she will guide you in all truth until I return.[6] However, men are men and so what they record can only be a kernel of all that has been. Even now you are only able to bear some of what I could tell you. Indeed, my life among you has been so full that all the scrolls of the earth could not contain more than a small measure of what was!"[7]

Yeshua then looked at each of us. "Therefore, in the days to come it will be good for men and women to loosen the spirit of their minds to what *could have been*.[8] May they allow the Spirit to enliven their imaginations so that all might better realize the depth of my love."[9]

He tossed his twig into the fire and stared at the flames now licking the small stack of wood before us. Finally, he said, "Do you understand that I was like you in every way except one?[10] For most of my life I did not fully understand this truth, but it was at the heart of all of my joys and all of my struggles. So it may be with you."

---

6 The author chooses to reference the Holy Spirit as 'she' but respects the unfamiliarity of modern readers with this choice. The word for 'Spirit' in Jesus' native Aramaic was '*Ruach*,' a grammatically feminine word. Therefore, Jesus, himself, would have referred to the Spirit as 'she.' Early translations such as the Sinaitic Palimpsest from the 4th century were careful to use 'she.' However, grammar does not prove the point. The Greek translations freely used a neuter word '*pneuma*' for the Spirit and therefore 'it' as the pronoun. But when the Greek was translated into other languages including English, neither Aramaic nor Greek was followed. Instead, the translators chose the word 'he' for reasons that included patriarchal assumptions about the nature of God.

Importantly, Genesis 1:27 clearly states that the Godhead includes both male and female qualities. Therefore, the Scriptures describe God in the imagery of both genders. Examples of female imagery include Isaiah 46:3, 66:9,13; Deut. 32:18, and Luke 13: 33-35. Much more could be written and the interested reader is encouraged to research this issue. The concern is that by ignoring the feminine aspects of God, we do ourselves a great disservice. Indeed, the role of the Spirit as companion, helper, comforter, nurturer etc. are surely expressions of feminine love from a God who is both male and female. Thus, the author has chosen to recognize this truth in his choice of pronoun.

7 See John 21:25

8 The American 18th century theologian Jonathan Edwards considered the imagination to be an important faculty with which to experience God more fully, referring to it as the 'spirit of the mind.'

9 See Ephesians 3:18-20

10 See Hebrews 2:17; 4:15

I watched him carefully as his face then slowly turned once more from one of us to the next. I prepared myself to follow his every gesture; I inclined my ears to capture his slightest change of tone; my lips were readied to whisper his words behind him. Then *Yeshua*—this Jesus of Nazareth—began to tell his story.

PART I

"But who do you say that I am?

MARK 8:29

CHAPTER I

MARY, THE STORY BEARER

Like most fourteen-year-olds my mother thought she would have a happy life, one spared from sorrow. So, forty days after my birth, young Mary carried me into the Temple with a smile and a song. Confident of the good to come, she made her way through the courtyard laughing alongside my quiet father, Joseph.

Somewhere near the Portico of Solomon, an old prophet named Simeon found us. He knew who I was and he was excited. He asked my mother if he might hold me, and she gladly agreed. With me clutched tightly against his breast, Simeon wept for joy and praised the Lord. When he was finished, he handed me back to Mary and proceeded to bless us. My mother liked that. He went on to speak of things to come, but then his face suddenly fell. Trembling, he slowly took my mother's hand and touched it to his lips. He then prophesied sadly that a sword would pierce her soul.[11] Shaken, my mother could not answer. No longer smiling, she quickly turned her face to Joseph and begged him to hurry us away.

For the year that followed, Mary said nothing of Simeon's prophecy. Instead, she kept herself busy with the comforting distractions of cooking, weaving, and chatter by Bethlehem's well. However, all the while she desperately tried to believe that the old man's words were of what *might* be and not necessarily of what *must* be.

---

11 Adapted from Luke 2:25-35

The prophecy did not disturb Joseph, however, for he had been wary of the world's snares from the very beginning. So while Mary struggled, Joseph spent those months working the same way as when he first arrived-- with two hands on his tools and one eye spying shadows. Perhaps it was an odd relief then, when an angel finally shouted to him from a dream in the deep dark of a Bethlehem night...

Joseph leapt from his bed and snatched his clothing. "Mary...Mary, wake up. Get the boy!"

My startled mother sat up. "Why?"

"The King wants to kill him. Soldiers are coming."

"How do you..."

"Just believe me, Mary! Now get dressed and wrap him up!"

Without delay, my mother gathered me into a bundle and snuffed the lamps. She and Joseph grabbed their few belongings and tied them fast to our donkey. Anxious, they rushed through the unlit streets of Bethlehem.[12]

"What's happening, husband?" Mary whispered.

"An angel warned me that Herod's soldiers are coming to slay every boy under two."

"But..."

"Those fool star-gazers from the East. They must have told him..." Leaving the sleeping village of Bethlehem behind, Joseph rushed us over dark goat trails toward the valley highway that lay ahead. When we reached the broad road, he led us behind a large rock for a brief rest. It was then when Mary began to weep.

But she did not weep for me.

She wept for the little ones in the village and for Joseph. Mary believed that I was to be the One, so what could Herod's soldiers do to me? But no angel had promised anything for these children, or for Joseph. So Mary wept for them.

But she also wept for herself. She now understood that Simeon's prophecy was of what must be; her life would not be spared from sorrow.

---

12 See Matthew 2:3

Also note, the author's research led him to speculate that Jesus' birth could be plausibly identified as the 10th day of Tishri, (15 September) 5 BC, during a chronicled total eclipse. However, he makes no claim to this date other than its reasonableness.

Joseph, however, did not weep at all. He was angry, for he knew that Herod's soldiers would be merciless. His mind filled with images of them tramping through Bethlehem at dawn with swords drawn. He stepped on to the highway and cocked his ear for any sound of jangling metal. He placed his big hands flat on the earth to feel for boots or horses pounding the earth. He was perspired and his breath was short and rapid. He stood and when he did, Mary saw him turn white, even under starlight. He muttered something, stared at my mother and finally turned his head back to Bethlehem. "Stay here with the boy."

"But..."

"Just stay here. If...if I don't come back you must hurry on. *HaShem*[13] will protect you both."

Have I told you yet that among men, Joseph was a good man?

Panting, my father found the house of Bethlehem's rabbi. He beat on the door, wildly, and when the rabbi answered, Joseph wheezed his warning. "Herod is sending soldiers to kill the youngest boys of Bethlehem..."

The rabbi was bleary-eyed and annoyed. "You're mad."

"No! No, it's true. He fears a rival..."

The rabbi slammed his door.

Joseph pounded again.

The door opened and Joseph fell to his knees, begging for the man to scatter the little ones into the wilderness.

The rabbi slammed the door once more.

Finally, Joseph pounded the door so furiously that lamps were lit in all the houses of the street. The rabbi answered with a loud oath. "Get out!"

"You know me! Listen to me..."

"Leave!" With that the door was slammed shut for a third time.

Joseph then sat in the dust, wailing, and tossing dirt over his head. He shouted at the people now gaping from their houses. One by one they

---

13 *HaShem* is a Hebrew word meaning, "The Name" (the prefix, 'ha,' means 'the') and was a common way of referring to God without disrespecting his name by uttering it. The actual name of God was written as YHWH but was considered too holy to say out loud. Therefore, other words were used to refer to him in terms of various titles that often applied his many roles. The author will usually substitute the more familiar English reference of 'Lord' and even 'God,' but it is important to recognize the historical Jewish way of referencing the Divine in their speech.

closed their doors. But a simple shepherd listened—one who had heard the angels sing at my birth almost two years before. This one believed and he took Joseph's hand and kissed it.

When Joseph returned to us he was panicked and filled with dread. "Go, go, go! Only one of them believed. May the Lord have mercy on the rest."

He snatched me up in one of his thick arms and with his free hand he took a stick to our donkey. "Get! Get, you beast!" He shouted at my mother. "Run!" I think he would have struck her if she had stumbled. And so we raced to the night-blackened highway and deep into the wilderness of Judea.

Long after sunrise we passed by Hebron. Refusing to stop, Joseph pushed, carried, and drove us farther and farther into barren lands until we finally collapsed for the night in the city of Beersheba. Still fearing Herod's reach, Joseph awakened us early to flee ever deeper into the desolation of the Idumean desert. Exhausted, we eventually turned southwest toward Gaza and days later took a brief rest among the Jews of Pelusium where Joseph's fear began to ease. Finally he led us to the blessed tributaries of the Nile where we all breathed easier in the lush regions of Alexandria.

After a week's rest in cool shade and among refreshing springs, Joseph led us farther south where he discovered the reedy shores of Lake Mariut some distance south of Alexandria. The lake was beautiful and filled with peace. Joseph and Mary paused to survey the waters. "Here, husband?"

Joseph nodded with satisfaction. We had found a home…and we thought that we were safe.

But the struggle of my becoming had just begun.

My relieved parents enjoyed a sweet taste of *shalom* for about two years along that gently riffled lake. Joseph found work building various structures for a community of prayerful Jewesses known as the Therapeutae.

While he was hard at work with his mallet, chisels, and saw, Mary set up housekeeping as she tended my newly arrived baby sister whom she named after her own sister, Salome.[14]

We were very happy there. In fact, my parents soon became famous for singing and for dancing along the clay shoreline—and for being caught making love out-of-doors. Let me say here that many years later Joseph bragged about that particular incident, and I remember laughing as my mother feigned shyness, even as her eyes revealed the delight of a mischievous kitten!

As for me, I loved to hide in the summer shade of the fruit groves where I stuffed my mouth with fallen dates or figs so that I wouldn't make a sound. There I would watch for my mother with wide eyes, and when she found me she'd kiss my face clean. Mary laughed whenever she told me about that. She also said that my face was so often smudged with sticky fig paste that the sisters nicknamed me 'Figgy Cheeks.'

And it seemed that my father had a way of making funny faces at my baby sister, Salome, who then became famous for her loud chortling. It didn't take long for the Elder Mother to nickname us, 'The Giggling Galileans.'

As I said, we were happy in that place.

But joy is all too often spoiled and ours was quickly snatched away. The Evil Hunter—Satan—that spiteful, mocking profanity of all things good—finally found us and when he did, he was the one who laughed.

On an October evening a star appeared in the east as a foreboding storm was darkening the horizon to the north. Flocks of birds were gathering and a lone rider galloped along a far shore.[15] My mother—who was then about

---

14 The Therapeutae were gender-segregated monastic style communities of Jews and Jewesses who lived in the region of Alexandria and beyond. Their lives of devotion are referenced by the Jewish philosopher/historian, Philo (20BC – 50AD).

15 Images from Revelation 19:11, 17; Revelation 22:16

seventeen years old—was heavy with her third child and weeping at the water's edge.

The sudden trumpeting of seven water birds startled her.[16] She looked up and saw the Elder Mother of the Therapeutae walking toward her. Mary stood, slowly, and set my baby sister[17]Salome on her hip.

"What troubles you, Mary?"

The sound of thunder rolled over us. My mother was pale as death and could not form her words.

"Child?"

My mother hesitated. "I fear that I'm too weak to protect my son."

"Figgy Cheeks? Protect him from what?" The Elder Mother stroked my hair.

Mary was desperate for comfort but was reluctant to share anything about what came to be called our 'Story.' She finally answered slowly, "The Beast."

"The beast? What beast?"

Mother answered in a low whisper, "Satan…"

The woman gasped and quickly withdrew deep within her linen shawl. "Do not speak the name…"

Mary bit her lip and clutched my hand.

The Elder Mother recovered slowly. "Oh, child…what is happening here?"

"He followed us." Mary wanted to cry for fear. "This morning I found my son staring across the lake. His eyes were filled with a terrible nothingness. When I touched him, the heat of his skin turned my fingertips blue-white as if they were being frozen by fire. I was so afraid…"

The Elder Mother stared at Mary, blankly.

Waiting, my mother's eyes swelled and she finally blurted, "You must think that I'm mad." She lifted her chin.

The old woman raised a hand. "Shh, my child. Be still. I do not think you are mad. But tell me, why would the Beast chase a harmless boy to Alexandria?"

---

16 Revelation 8:2

17 Jesus siblings are referenced in various locations of the Gospel accounts. The author respectfully acknowledges the position of some who argue that references to 'brothers' and 'sisters' should be interpreted as 'cousins' in order to sustain a belief in Mary as an eternal virgin.

Again, Mary hesitated. "Because of who he is."

"Who is he?"

My mother set my sister on the ground and knelt awkwardly by my side. "You will not believe."

The Elder Mother stroked Mary's head, gently. "I will listen."

Emboldened by the woman's kindness, Mary looked up. "He is the Son of the Most High, heir to the throne of David, a light to the Gentiles, a glory to Israel…"[18]

"Stop." The Elder withdrew her hand.

"Who told you these things?"

"Gabriel, some shepherds in Judea…a priest named Simeon, a Temple prophetess named *Anna bat Phanuel*…and my cousin, Elizab…"[19]

The Elder Mother was now deeply troubled. "I know Anna well; I cannot think that she would say this. Gabriel? Shepherds? Do you hear yourself?"

Mary stood, her face drawn tight. "I speak truly. Jesus is the promised king."

A gust of wind blew my mother's headdress into the reeds along with the old woman's. The Elder retrieved both shawls and stared at them, thinking. "Child…"

"I'm not a child." My mother took her scarf from the woman and pulled it over her head. "And I am not mad."

The woman stared at Mary and then bent low to look into my face. "He is…about three years old?"

Mary stepped between the woman and me. "I think we should leave."

"Do not be angry with me, Mary, wife of Joseph. But you must understand how these words frighten me. I'm worried for you."

Mary picked Salome off the clay shore and set her on her hip. She took my hand. "I didn't mean to frighten you, but I have spoken the truth. You need not worry for any of us…"

The Elder Mother stiffened. "Be still." Her voice was suddenly hard as Greek granite.

Mary took a breath.

"You say this boy is the One?"

My mother nodded, bravely.

---

18 See Luke 1:32; Luke 2:32

19 See Luke 1 and 2.

"That is a bold claim for a poor woman of Galilee. Tell me why should I believe you?"

Mary faced the Elder Mother squarely. "I told you why but you do not believe."

"Who could believe such a story?"

Mary turned to leave. "Those to whom the arm of the Lord is revealed." [20]

"Stop." The Elder's tone was still sharp. The old woman turned to me and studied me as if she were measuring the depth of every pore and the breadth of every hair. She looked at Mary. "I would like to hear more of your story."

"To make me the fool?"

"No, dear Mary, to consider what you say."

My mother faltered. She had kept our Story close to her heart for years but her fears had grown and she needed to share it with someone besides Joseph. [21] Mary squeezed my hand and looked at the Elder Mother warily. She knew that this woman was a wise and faithful Jewess who loved my Father.

But what would the woman think?

Who wouldn't think me mad...or a liar? Mary thought.

"All's well, Mary, wife of Joseph." The woman took my mother's hand. "Now, tell me your story."

---

20 Isaiah 53:1
21 Luke 2:19

CHAPTER II

OUT OF EGYPT

The sky was black with clouds when Mary finished. Thunder rumbled ever more loudly. The waters of the lake were frothy. Mary's Story had shaken the Elder Mother. The old woman stood, slowly and with a slight tremble. "Boy, look at me." The woman laid a hand on my head…but then pulled it away with a cry. Stunned, she stared at her palm as if it had been scorched by fire. She stared at me for a long moment before turning to the stirred waters of Lake Mariut. Another round of thunder rolled through the second heaven. The Elder Mother then sang a groaning lamentation:

> "There is a Terror stalking the cosmos.
> Darkness, It swallows light like a gaping cavern;
> Beast, Its blasphemies scorch the wind.[22]
> Seducer, Its temptations are sweet as Passover figs;
> Its heart covets glory,
> Its mouth is filled with deceits,
> Its hands pour out the pollutions of Miasma[23]

---

22 Rev 17 also note I John 3:8…'for this purpose the Son of God was manifested, that he might destroy the works of the devil.'

23 Reference from Greek mythology that regarded evil as pollution

And its prey is peace."[24]

She returned her gaze to Mary, thinking. She later said that she was wondering whether my mother was like Eve—seduced and in alliance with the Serpent—or also like Eve—given to nurture the seed of promise.

Anxious and confused, the old woman then bent to her knees and lifted her arms toward the third Heaven.[25] She began to pray loudly and in a strange tongue. A brief, swirling gust lifted the linen shawl off her white hair and laid it gently on her shoulders. The woman pulled it into place and began to pray once more. But, again, as soon as she spoke the wind blew her shawl off her head. She then fell silent and the wind stopped. She paused, her face now misshapen by the agony of her prayers.

The woman then covered her head once more and lay prostrate on the earth, arms stretched forward and her fingers clawing the clay. She prayed again, this time with great force and ever more loudly against a wind that abruptly began to howl.

Frightened, my mother gathered up Salome and me. A startled flock of pink-legged flamingos flapped desperately away from their cover. The reeds along the shore bent low; the waters of the lake began to roll heavily against a yielding shoreline. But at last the wind stopped and the suffering woman became silent. The sky fell quiet; the lake became calm and the reeds stood tall and still once more. Exhausted, the Elder turned to Mary. Peace had come upon her.

She had been given to believe.

Now smiling, she took my mother's hand in hers and sang:
'When his soul has endured the end of suffering,
He will see the light of life
And be at peace.' *Selah.*

When she finished, the Elder Mother led us quickly along the lake-shore and deep into a palm grove where the sisters lived in a series of

---

24 In this time it was believed that humans had a three-fold design…Eyes and Heart relate to inward reactions/desires; mouth and ears relate to the world via language; hands and feet relate as active performers.

Opposed to the whole person is the presence of Evil that seeks to pollute God's order and ultimately destroy Shalom…that is embodied in Jesus.

25 The home of God and his angels was considered the 'third heaven.'

small huts built for solitude and prayer. In the center of the grove was a lamp-lit gathering room where the women would meet on the Sabbath to share simple meals around a round, olivewood table. The Mother summoned her sisters to that place and soon we were all seated on comfortable mats. Excited, the old woman spoke to them and they, too, were quickly given to believe.

The sisters hurried to Mary's side and began to pray and sing over her and me. My mother would speak of this moment often, for in that circle of prayer she had felt the Spirit enfold her again, even as she did as Life Giver on that dawn in the month of *Tebheth* (December, dear Brennus) nine months before my birth. As they prayed over her, she also saw Gabriel standing with us, smiling like he had in Nazareth on that month before her chilly wedding in the early *Adar* (*Februarius*) rain.

My mother was safe.

And happy once again.

Within days, the sisters served my mother as midwives at the birth of my brother, James. And when my mother was able, she quietly served the Therapeutae by weaving or sewing or salting fish. In exchange, they taught her much about the world and the Scriptures.

Every Sabbath our family was invited to lounge at the sisters' round-table to sing, to eat, and to pray. I loved the short-legged table of the Therapeutae. It was warped and stained by spills—it served with no glory of its own, but as a circle it welcomed all to recline alongside the other as neither lord nor servant, better or lesser, but rather friend by friend. I felt secure in the peace of its welcome and I held fast to its image as my first memory.

"Woman, it's time to go home," Joseph announced one evening.

Mary set her bowl of fruit down and faced her husband. "How do you know?"

"An angel came to me in a dream."

"And?"

"And he commanded me to take us to Nazareth. He told me not to tarry in Judea for it's still not safe there...but Galilee is ready for us."[26]

Mary set down her bowl of sliced eggs and onions, then surveyed the room she had come to love. "You're certain?"

Joseph nodded.

Mary walked beneath the herbs hanging above the door and drew their scent deeply through her nose. She didn't want to leave her house, the lake, or the sisters. She felt safe there. She glanced at James and Salome, and cast a long look at me. "Then we must go."

The Therapeutae were saddened to hear the news but their Elder Mother had already expected us to leave, and so in the weeks before she had the sisters make gifts for us. They presented my mother with a tiny scroll on which they had written the Elder Mother's song. She wept as they sang the words to her:

"After the suffering of his soul,

He will see the good light of life;

His offspring shall prosper; the will of the Lord will multiply in his hand,

And he will be at peace."[27]

For Joseph they made a leather *tefillin*[28] so that he might wrap his thick arm more tightly when he prayed.

For my little sister Salome (now two years old) they sewed a little robe hemmed by tiny lake shells.

For my baby brother James they weaved a fine blanket.

For me they sewed a *tallit*—a prayer shawl woven from half-bleached lamb's wool that was sheared from the finest of their fold. In accordance with the law, they had patiently tied the violet-blue *tzitzith* at its corners in exactly 613 knots.[29] I should say here that my mother kept my shawl for me until the day that I first beheld Jerusalem. From then on I would spend

---

26 Matthew 2:19

27 Inspired by Isaiah 53

28 *Tefillin* were worn either on the arm or forehead. Those worn on the forehead (also known as phylacteries) consisted of a little box into which were inserted tiny scrolls with specific references from the Scriptures.

29 The *tzitzith* were fringes on the prayer shawl. They were tied in 613 knots that represented the number of Jewish laws

many hours with it draped over my head as I prayed. As I did, the shawl's four corners would fall into my hands as familiar friends and their fringes would yield to the roll of my fingers. By the time of my trial not a single knot remained.

Yes, our time with the Therapeutae was much blessed. And why not?

They wept when they needed to weep;

they laughed often;

they danced when they were able to dance;

and they prayed without ceasing.

Such is a life that brings joy to our Father.

It was good that the sisters had strengthened my mother in that place, for the Beast followed us out of Egypt with a vengeance. Truly, we had no sooner lost sight of Lake Mariut than Mary felt its heated breath once more. "We must hurry, Joseph."

Somewhere in the Egyptian desert our donkey began to foam at the mouth. He collapsed suddenly and writhed in the dust until he died. Leaning over the poor beast, Mary understood. "*Satana* is here." But it was then that she first knew that seeds of doubt had begun to sprout in her husband's eyes.

"Joseph?"

The man looked away; his deeply buried doubts about the Story of my birth had begun to take root.

"Joseph?"

He looked to one side. Despite his dreams, he had recently been tempted by whispers of my mother's madness from men he had worked with in Alexandria.

"Joseph?"

Joseph was a good man but like all men he was made of dust.[30] He stared at Mary sadly but took her hand in love. "I am here."

---

30 See Psalms 103:14

When we arrived in Pelusium, Joseph summoned a rabbi to pray with my mother against the Evil One. But the rabbi, like all the Jews of that dusty place, believed nothing and so the power of the Thing increased.

Joseph hurried us on our journey but Mary's struggle had only begun. In Gaza she grew weak, in Judea she begged to rest. By the time we crossed into Perea she had begun to stumble and eventually she could barely walk. Truly, even lionesses grow weary. Near Scythopolis Joseph finally bartered some of my spice-gifts given by the stargazers for a young donkey that delivered her into Galilee. My mother later named the gentle beast, 'Noah,' which, as you must know, means 'rest.'

When we finally arrived in Nazareth, Mary fell into her sister Salome's arms. There, nestled within the fourteen limestone hills that rimmed the village, she poured out her sufferings to her and also to Joseph's brother— Cleopas of Cana—and to Cleopas' wife, Miriam. These three believed Mary and their belief strengthened her mightily.

In time I heard her singing and I was glad.

Of all the seasons, my mother loved the grape harvest the most. She loved the music and the dancing, the laughter and the cool breezes. And she very much loved the feeling of grapes squishing beneath her feet! So, on a beautiful day during the Roman month of September--soon after my fifth birthday--she was dancing in Nazareth's winepress with her friend, Hannah.

I clapped in rhythm with a tambourine player. "Dance, mother, dance!" She looked at me, laughing. "Come, come," she panted.

I looked from side to side, then pulled off my sandals and climbed into the sweet-smelling mash.

"Take our hands!" laughed Hannah.

The three of us held hands and jumped up and down atop that grape-stained rock. We sang some old songs, loudly and badly. "Louder!" cried Joseph from the side.

Mary's eyes twinkled as they met his. She laughed.

"Jesus, you too," Joseph shouted.

My mother, Hannah and I then sang so loudly that we thought all of heaven could hear us:

'Go your way,
    eat bread with joy,
drink wine with a happy heart!
Go forth to dance with them
Who make faces shine and
    make the weary, merry!'
And may the Lord God of Israel be forever praised.[31]

As we sang, Hannah lifted her feet high and flung them about like a child does with a cloth doll. My mother squatted and stamped her feet in wild bursts, squirting juice high into the air. Already covered in mash, Hannah then slipped and fell on to her broad rump, tripping my mother who yanked me with her into the slurp.

We all squealed. I lay laughing in the purple juice alongside my giggling mother and her howling friend. I smile now as I tell you of it.

A voice then growled above the grumbles of the harvesters. "Get out of there."

My mother turned her face. "Esther?" she tittered. With a few grunts and more giggles, she, Hannah and I climbed out of the press and began sliding grape mash off our clothing.

Esther, the neglected wife of Nazareth's cruel olive merchant, came close. "You've no right," she hissed. Others joined her and scowled at my mother.

Mary took a breath. "And you've no joy." She slung a handful of mash back into the press.

"You've no shame! If you did, you'd have paid for your sins...like anybody else. But no, not even a simple village dinner. And here you are dancing and laughing..."

"Which of my sins are you asking about?"

The woman pointed at me. "Him."

Seeing the fury in Esther's eyes, I retreated and stood by Joseph. The harvesters and musicians fell silent. All eyes fastened onto my mother.

Esther leaned into Mary. "You are a whore...an unrepentant whore."

---

31 Inspired by Ecclesiastes 9:7 and Jeremiah 31:4, Psalms 104:15

Before my mother could answer, Hannah pushed a handful of mash into Esther's face and shoved her to the ground. "You and your hags spend too much time in gossip! But if it's gossip that you like, maybe you should follow your husband in the streets of Jerusalem!"

"Enough, Hannah," said Mary. She reached her hand toward Esther's to help her stand.

The woman glared. "Whore..." she hissed. She slapped my mother's hand away and then fixed her fury on me. *"Mamzer!"*

Now Mary's face hardened. She placed her fists on her hips and leaned into Esther's face. "Say what you will about me, but do not speak to my son again...ever."

All of these things saddened Joseph. The incident at the press had not been the first confrontation between his wife and the other women, and he knew that as long as Mary denied her fornication it would not be the last. As a man, no one had ever bothered to challenge him, of course. Everyone knew that Mary, like all women, was responsible for her virtue. But it was exactly that point...Mary's virtue...that had been secretly bothering Joseph for some time.

That night he invited me to sit with him atop Nazareth's watchtower. There he sang gentle songs to me beneath the rush-covered roof as he took his turn at guarding olive groves and the figs from thieves. His voice was deep and comforting like the full sounds that fill an empty cistern:

> 'I am a little sparrow alone upon the roof top
> But the Lord shall remember me
> For I am worth more than the sparrow,
> And far more than the kings of the earth.
> The Lord shall heed the cry of the little ones;
> He will hear the chirp of the lonely,
> His mercy will endure forever and ever,
> And we will praise him, *Selah.*'[32]

I leaned against his thick shoulders. "I love you, *Abba.*[33]" I felt the man tremble.

He whispered that he loved me too.

---

32 Inspired by Psalms 102

33 Aramaic for 'father' in a familiar sense, comfortable sense

I snuggled against him, knowing nothing of the smoldering struggle that lay deep within the man. I felt safe with Joseph and I felt blessed to call him 'father.' If only I would have known then how much the man suffered on my account.

CHAPTER III

THE QUEST OF THE BEAST

"Are you ready, Joseph?" Mary asked.

"Ready?"

"He's past his fifth year. I've taught him what I'm to teach him...and more. Now you..."

"I don't know, woman." Joseph shook his head. He knew that I—like all boys my age—would be released from my mother's soft embrace and placed within the callused hands of my father for instruction. "I don't know if I'm able."

Mary took his hand. "You are a good man, husband." She hesitated. "But I understand."

"How? How do you understand?"

Mary was surprised at his tone. "Because I, too, sometimes wonder what all this means..."

Joseph silenced her with a wave of his hand. "We have other children who are caught up in all of the village trouble...and worse than that are these night terrors that come over Jesus. If Satan is prowling about like you say, then what if he attacks the others? Is the hand of *El Shaddai*[34] on *them*?" He shook his head. "And how am I supposed to raise this...this 'Son of Promise' as you call him? What do I know about these things? I'm a simple

_____

34 Hebrew word meaning 'The Almighty God.' Note that the ancient prefix, 'El,' refers to the deity, the words that follow are descriptors.

man, woman. I don't know about kingdoms and messiahs and prophets! What if I fail!"

Mary clutched her hands to her heart. "What if *we* fail? Oh, Joseph..."

"How do you know that he *will* be who you say he's to be? Maybe he can only be that *if* ..."

"No..."

"No? What if we never fled to Egypt? What if we never left Egypt? What if he falls from a scaffold? What if our prayers are weak and Darkness overcomes him?"

Mary stammered. "But...but the Lord will protect him..."

"But what if *we* sin? What if *I* sin? Aren't the sins of the father visited on his children?" Joseph wrung his thick hands. He paused and took a deep breath. "But..."

"Say it."

Joseph walked away.

On a cool *Kislew* [35] night in Nazareth, I awoke from my sleep with my nostrils burning from the smell of some sulfurous breath. I choked. *"Ama! Ama!"* I could barely wheeze her name, and no one could hear. My eyes strained to see, but utter darkness had filled the house. I searched desperately for the light beyond the blowing cloth that covered our window high above. But on this night the moon was blotted out, not for a brief rest like it had been on the night of my birth, but by thick clouds held in place by the merciless grasp of the Prince of the Air.

I didn't know it yet, but the Beast had come for me.

Barely able to breathe, my ears filled with a chatter of wicked whispers hissing, '*Y e ssss h u a, Y e ssssh uaaaa...*' I then felt as if I was being dragged into some outer darkness where images of slaughtered infants began to wing around me. Their voices accused me in a single chorus: '*Yeshua*, you

---

35 November

have sent innocent lambs down to Sheol; you have abandoned our souls to Hades so that you might have life!'[36]

But then I heard my mother calling my name. Her voice was calm and controlled. "Jesus, my son. Jesus, I'm here."

I could not see her but her voice soothed me. She began to sing:

"My strength comes from *El Shaddai*...

My strength comes from *El Elyon*.[37]

My mouth scoffs at my enemies

And I rejoice in my victory..."[38]

At the sound of '*El*,' I felt my body filling with life and I burrowed into my mother's bosom. *"Ama!"* [39]

Mary held me firmly. Now in a defiant voice, she spoke to Heaven. "You have given your angels charge over my son.[40] Lord, send your hosts."

I heard a roar. Mary heard it, too, and at that moment our eyes were opened to see a fresh host of Light-soldiers fill the room. That's when my mother planted her feet hard upon the earth and lifted me with a resounding cry. "*Satana*! My son—my Jesus—*shall* reign over Israel![41]"

Still afraid, I clung to my mother and together we huddled as a wind suddenly blew dust and chaff off our floor and over us. I felt the house quaking; I felt my mother's heart pounding against my ear. Finally the cloth covering the window was torn from its place and the house fell still.

Mother released her breath, warily, and began to stroke my hair. She then kissed her fingertip and touched it to the cleft in my chin that matched her own. Peace slowly settled over me. The moon had been set free and silver moonlight now broke through the little window above.

And I knew that the Beast had fled.

For a season.

---

36 Reconfiguration of parts of Psalms 16:10, Acts 2:27

37 Hebrew for 'God Most High'

38 Adaptation of I Sam 2:1 per Luke's Magnificat

39 Aramaic for mother

40 From Psalms 91:11

41 See Luke 1:33

"You refuse to remember, Joseph." Lying in her bed, Mary pushed Joseph away. Eight months had passed since my night of terror but now James was having nightmares and Salome had fallen ill. My mother was fearful that the Beast was among us.

"I remember things that are good to remember." Joseph's tone had a bite.

"If you care for me, husband, then try to understand my fear."

"Remembering it gives it power," grumbled Joseph in a hoarse whisper.

"Forgetting gives it more. You're too much like your father. You can't just ignore things and have them go away."

"That's not fair, Mary. I don't ignore the gossips, do I?"

My mother fell silent before answering, "You defend me. You're a good man and for that I'm grateful. But you were never happy about any of this..."

"Happy? It's not easy to be happy in this life. I just want us to stop thinking about these things." His voice began to rise.

"How can I not? I can feel its eyes lingering near again. It's always watching. Sometimes I smell its breath like I did in Pelusium."

"Pelusium was a strange place..."

"You are doubting, aren't you?"

"Why do you say that? I have not forgotten my dreams."

"Yes, of course, you and your dreams. You never just believe *me*. Your own brother believes our Story..." Now my mother's voice was rising.

Joseph objected. "I never said that I didn't believe you! I know what the angels said in my dreams. I was there with the shepherds and the Magi...I do believe that Evil opposes us..."

"But I still see something in your eyes when you look at me."

I could hear Joseph take a deep breath. "We've told only a few, but rumors are spreading from my relatives in Bethlehem. I don't know how to answer them. It's becoming difficult to be here..."

"Maybe we should go back to Lake Mariut..."

"No."

"And why not? I felt safe there. The rumors won't follow us..."

"We will not go to Egypt," said Joseph. *"Hashem's* Spirit is here in Nazareth—despite the Gentiles and their cursed new bathhouse.[42] *This* is the Lord's land, woman. Not Egypt. Evil must be overcome here, in Israel. You said yourself that your son will crush the Serpent's head..."

"Then you must teach him to do that."

Joseph chafed. "Teach him to defeat Satan?" I heard the man stand up. "You married a plain man, Mary, a plain man. If that's not good enough for your son then I'm sorry for you both."

Mary sobbed quietly and for a long time, and she was still sobbing when Joseph finally returned to our room. But the man had barely lain down when my mother asked him a surprising question. *"My* son, Husband? Is Jesus not also *your* son?"

I remained uneasy for months after my parents' argument, especially because of my mother's last question to Joseph. Why would he have called me her son but not his own? Some of the village boys had already accused me of being the son of a Roman soldier, or a passing merchant. Some called me a *mamzer.* [43] All of this confused me. *Why is anyone wondering who my father is?* And so I was happy when my grandfather came for a Sabbath visit just past my sixth birthday.

Grandfather Heli was a wise old man with strong hands and a lively step.[44] One of his eyes was milky blue and the green one strained to see

---

42 These baths were recently discovered in Nazareth, per author's research on site in February 2011. It should be noted that dating has not been absolutely confirmed at this writing. However, this discovery strongly suggests the presence of Gentiles in Nazareth during the lifetime of Jesus. It should be further noted, that Galilee was often derided for the many Gentiles who had found their way into its villages.

43 A *mamzer* was a bastard child conceived out of the norms of identity. This was most common in regard to a child of mixed Jewish and Gentile origin, but was sometimes even applied to a child conceived with someone of a different village or an unapproved household.

44 Luke 3:23 cites Heli as Joseph's 'father', but this same reference is also understood to mean 'father-in-law,' especially if Mary was an heiress to Heli.

shadows. Most of his teeth were gone but he loved to smile, anyway. His breath was terrible, but his heart was tender and he was filled with wisdom. He had taught my mother and her sister all he knew of the Scriptures. Love and Light followed him everywhere.

Whenever Heli arrived at Joseph's house, the first thing he did was seek out a grandchild. When he caught one of us he'd lift us very close to his face so that he could better see and hear us. We never liked the shower of spittle he sprayed in our faces, but we loved how he loved us.

"So, what's wrong?" he said to me.

I shrugged.

He reached into his purse and pulled out some raisins that he had just finished drying from the recent harvest. He handed them to me. I took them and stuffed them into my face.

Heli laughed and bent low. "I see why they used to call you 'Figgy Cheeks!'"

Heli took my hand and the two of us walked through the streets of Nazareth, careful not to go beyond the distance that the Sabbath allowed. We ended up in an olive grove. "Sit with me, boy." He dropped his bottom hard on the grass. "First, let me test you: what is the *second* greatest commandment?"

"'Love your neighbor as yourself.'"[45]

Heli smiled. "Good. Now, you may speak about whatever you like."

I began to ramble on about this and that. My grandfather listened, carefully, cupping his ear close to my mouth and nodding, often. He then opened his purse and shared some more raisins. I finally stopped speaking of things about which I cared little, and I faced the ground, anxiously. "I heard *Abba* tell *Ama* that I was *her* son. And then she asked him if I wasn't also *his* son and he didn't answer."

Heli shifted. "Have you asked your father about it?"

I shook my head. "Am I a *mamzer*, grandfather? Am I unclean?"

His eyes moistened. "He's the one who named you."

I waited.

"Do you ever think that you are special in some way?"

I thought about that. I had a growing sense that something was different about me but what it was I didn't know. "I heard my mother tell her friend that the Evil One wants to kill me."

---

45 Leviticus 19:18

Grandfather's mouth dropped, then he stroked my head with a trembling hand. "Why do you think you lived in Egypt?"

I didn't know.

"Because the old King Herod was afraid of you."

"Why?"

Heli looked directly at me. "Because you are born to be a king."

"What? How do you know that?"

"Your mother told me."

I thought for a moment. "And how does she know? And why didn't she tell me? And does my father know?"

"The angel, Gabriel, told her...and the Spirit of *HaShem* told others, too."

My heart began to race and I began circling the olive tree that we were sitting beneath. "Some in the village think *Ama* is mad."

Heli reached for me and held me still. "Your mother is *not* mad." He embraced me. "Your mother loves you; your father loves you. Let that be enough for now."

"But why wouldn't *Abba* say that I was his son?"

Heli paused. "By now you must know what makes a man a father."

I answered what Joseph had already taught me about a man's seed and a woman's womb.[46]

"Yes, but did he tell you that there are two ways to be a father. One is by seed and *one is by law*."

I listened, suspiciously, as he went on to talk about kinship and adoption and the meaning of family. When he was finished I asked, "Is Joseph my father in *both* ways?"

Heli filled his mouth with raisins.

"Is he?"

The old man stood and I knew something was wrong. "I want to be *Yeshua bar Yosef* in *every* way!" I shouted.

My grandfather's face twitched and his hand began to stroke his white beard. *What is it?* I thought. "Grandfather?" I felt my belly fluttering.

"Come, boy. It's time to get you home. You need to have a talk with your father."

---

46 The predominant view of procreation identified the male 'seed' as the source of new life; the female womb was understood as a repository that provided subsistence and nurture for the developing child. With this in mind, it may be interesting to consider how claims of a virgin birth might relate to Genesis 3:15 where God indicates that the *seed of a woman* will crush the serpent's head.

CHAPTER IV

JOSEPH

"You must," said Mary.

Joseph kept planing a long plank.

"Did you hear me?"

"Yes."

"You've kept a distance from him ever since my father talked with him. That was many months ago."

Joseph kept planing.

From my hiding place in the courtyard I watched my father stop and wipe his face. My mother took his hand.

"It is time," Mary said.

Joseph set his plane aside and took a breath. "Jesus...I know where you are. Come out."

I crept from my cover.

"Come with me."

My breath quickened as I followed Joseph out of the village and to the watchtower where he loved to spend time alone. I climbed the ladder behind him to the railed platform above.

"My son," Joseph began. "You had quite a talk with your grandfather."

I was happy that he had said, 'my son.'

Joseph leaned on the rail and looked over the groves. "The harvest was good this year." He stuck his head out beyond the cover of the tower roof. "I think a storm is coming." He then rubbed his heavy-bearded jaw with one of his thick hands and, after some delay, turned to me. "Jesus, you wonder if I'm your father."

I nodded.

"I am."

I smiled at the man and leaned into him, hoping to be embraced. But Joseph's hands fell on me lightly and his body felt tight. He moved to a corner of the watchtower floor and bade me sit close. I obeyed, wondering why he seemed so nervous.

"Jesus, you know that I love you." His voice sounded strained. "Now, the time has come for me to tell you who you are." He took a breath. "My father once told me that knowing who you are is very important."

I took a deep breath.

"You must know who you are so you'll know what to become. This is true for all men. Knowing who you are directs your path. The boy who knows he's a prince will walk like a king. Do you understand?"

Even a mere boy could see that the man was struggling. I nodded.

"It's also important to know who you are not."

Those words spread a cold chill over my skin.

"You are *not* a child of sin; you are *not* a child of some Roman soldier; you are *not* a *mamzer*. You are *not* unclean."

I waited, hands clenched into tight fists.

"Listen." Joseph licked his lips. "You *are* very much like other boys." He began to falter. "After I was betrothed to your mother I learned that she was with child. Your grandfather was furious with her, but I assured him that we had never...come together in that way. You understand?"

"Yes."

He took a very deep breath. "Your grandfather and I both assumed that your mother must have been with another man, but an angel came to me in a dream and told me that I should not think that because the child she was carrying was given to her by the Spirit of *Elohim*. The same angel told your mother the same thing."

My mind whirled. I didn't understand.

Joseph waited for me to settle. "Do you have any questions about that?"

I looked at Joseph. *Do I have any questions!* I was so confused that I couldn't answer. But I was also troubled by the way Joseph had said these things. So I asked him, "Do you believe your dream, *Abba*? Do you believe *Ama*?"

I wished that he wouldn't have hesitated.

"Well, yes." He then hurried to tell me more, including the startling announcement that I was the promised Messiah.[47]

What? What! My mind spun. *Messiah? How? Me? But...*

Then I heard the words, 'King Herod' and 'Bethlehem.' "Stop." This was all too much. I suddenly wanted to run away but instead I blurted, "Did he murder the children there?"

Joseph nodded.

I felt sick. I bent over as my vision filled my mind with dark images. "How many?"

"I think about a dozen..."

I vomited. I regretted ever asking my grandfather about my parents' words, or ever wondering about the gossip in the village.

Joseph handed me a rag. "This is not easy." He waited as I wiped my face and sat on the ground. He then stooped in front of me and took my shoulder. "Do you want to ask me anything?"

Do I want to ask you anything? What do you think! My mind reeled as I gaped at him. Finally I asked, "Do you believe *all* of this?"

He dodged my eyes and stood. "Yes," he said. "I had a dream."

I thought his voice sounded weak and so my throat thickened; I felt tears rushing to my eyes. *Does he really believe?* I wiped my eyes and stood, waiting for him to say more. But Joseph kept his face turned toward the fields and away from me. I heard thunder and I looked around the tower's roof and into the dome above.[48] A warm breeze immediately brought the sweet scent of coming rain. I wiped my nose and breathed of it, deeply. The smell comforted me, and my mind quieted.

I stood by my silent father and closed my eyes. All of my prior thoughts faded away and a pleasant succession of images and sounds eased their way into my young mind. I saw a soft light slow down to allow a formless void to appear out of what had been nothing. The void then filled with deep waters and it was all held in place by a voice in song...a voice that I thought could have been my own voice if I were a man. [49]

---

47 Luke 1:32

48 In these times, people believed in a three-tier universe. The first tier, or 'heaven' was the atmosphere in which they breathed; the second heaven was the sky and stars that fit over the earth like a dome, and the third Heaven was the realm of God.

49 See John 1. It is interesting to consider Genesis 1 in the light of John 1.

The light slowed yet more and I saw a splendid scattering of water and I saw mountains and forests rise up; colors for which I had no name entered this world and I could *taste* them. And then the strange name of '*El Abba*' came to me like a gentle whisper.[50] *HaShem as Abba?* I thought. *"El Abba...*
El Abba?"

I left my father's side and climbed down the ladder. Walking some distance away, I raised my face to receive the first drops of a fresh rain. As they splashed lightly on my face I felt warm and wonderful. *El Abba?* I repeated the words out loud and felt my spirit lighten, and so I said them again, and then again. *"El Abba. El Abba!"*

And peace settled over me.

A few months later, I awakened to find my father angrily tossing through a variety of tools scattered between boards, stones, and some baskets strewn just outside our doorway.

"Where's my oak mallet?"

I didn't know.

Then he noticed that his favorite chisel was also missing. "Jesus?" he barked. "Were you playing with my tools again?"

"No."

"Was your sister? What about James?"

I shrugged.

"Mary!"

My mother came out of the door holding my youngest brother, Joses, on her hip.

"Have you seen my mallet and chisel...my favorites, the ones from my father?"

"No." Mary looked around. "Maybe if you kept your tools in one place you wouldn't lose them."

"I didn't lose them!"

---

50 Aramaic for 'God as Father' in a familiar sense.

Salome peeked her head out of the door. She was caring for a little bird that my father had found earlier that morning. *"Abba,* I saw that woman looking at your tools."

Joseph whirled about. "What woman?"

"The one that has the *mamzer."*

Joseph grumbled. "The woman's name is Rachel."

Rachel was a sickly, mysterious woman who had appeared in Nazareth without a husband but heavy with child and seeking mercy. Rabbi Isaiah had collected gifts from the village and provided her a house from which she made baskets to sell in Sepphoris. Most now thought that she was a sorceress and some no longer believed that her child was of Roman rape—as Rachel had claimed—but rather a daughter of seduction. Many wanted her tested for adultery with bitter water.[51]

"Are you sure?" asked Joseph.

Salome nodded.

Mary asked Joseph what he was going to do. "I'm going to ask her about it," he said, scowling.

"But it's not safe for you to speak with her...or decent."

Joseph folded his arms. He was angry and suddenly cared little for the rabbis' concerns.

"Fine then. But wait." Mary turned into our house and returned with an amulet. "Put this around your neck."

Joseph did. We had all heard the rumors that Rachel had the Evil Eye.[52] In fact, most were certain of it ever since the day she stared silently at two bickering women at the well who then died within a week.

Grumbling, Joseph walked hastily through the village and toward the woman's house that stood near the edge. I secretly followed and hid behind a millstone as Joseph paused at the woman's door. The house was a crumbling pile of plastered stone with a poor roof. Joseph hesitated and then pounded on the door. As he waited for it to open I sneaked to the back of the house where I climbed atop a sturdy bushel and peaked through a hole in the woman's wall.

"Who's there?" Rachel said.

---

51 A woman accused of adultery could be forced to drink a terrible mixture made primarily of dust from the Temple floor. If she fell ill she was considered guilty.

52 The 'Evil Eye' was a widespread belief that some had a magical power to inflict harm or to steal well-being with a look. Many methods of self-protection were adopted all over the ancient world including various amulets, gestures, and so forth. The apostle Paul would later deal with this issue in the Galatian church. (See Galatians 3)

I heard Joseph's muffled voice from the far side of Rachel's door.

"What do you want?" She was frightened.

I watched her hurry about, thinking she looked like a skeleton wrapped within a threadbare robe. Her hair was uncovered and wild. She quickly put her baby daughter atop some blankets. "Come back another time."

My eyes scanned her floor. There I saw Joseph's tools peaking out from beneath some straw.

Joseph pounded on the door again.

Rachel took a deep breath and finally opened it. "Yes?"

"I am Joseph, your neighbor."

"I know."

I saw my father tilt his head past the woman to gawk into her house. Seeing nothing he looked at her, staring for a long moment. I could see his weathered face suddenly soften. "Uh…my wife…we were wondering if you needed anything?"

Rachel didn't move.

Joseph then spotted the child on the blanket. From my peephole I could see his eyes swell. "Is your child well? You look too thin to feed her."

"My child is fine."

Joseph nodded. "What is her name?"

I could see Rachel stiffen. "What does it matter to you?"

Joseph said nothing.

"What did you say you wanted?"

Joseph leaned his stout body forward, interested to see the child better. "My wife would like to share some food with you. We have some extra meal and some fruit. Could I bring some to you?"

"Then why did your wife not come? You should not be talking to me."

Joseph faltered. "Uh…she is sick."

"You do not need to feed me."

Joseph looked past the woman once more. "May I see your child?"

Rachel hesitated but Joseph stepped past the woman and entered the house, leaving the door partially open. He squatted in front of the baby girl. "She is thin, Rachel. Please, let us give you some food."

Uneasy, the woman hurried around Joseph to open the door wider. As she did her bare foot caught the handle of the mallet and the tool slid from the shadows. My father saw it and then his eyes fell on his chisel, as well. Joseph stood and stared at his tools lying on the woman's floor. I could see Rachel catch her breath.

I waited.

CHAPTER V

LOVE AND LOSS

My father bent over and picked up his mallet and his chisel. He looked at them as if they were children of his own. He turned to Rachel, thinking. After a long moment he said, "These are fine tools."

The gentleness in his voice surprised the woman. Trembling, she nodded.

Joseph hefted them in his hands. "Yes, these are very fine. I have ones just like them."

I could not see Rachel's face but I could see that she was staring at the ground. Her baby stirred and she quickly picked her up.

Joseph set his tools down. "What's your baby's name?"

"Susanna." The woman's voice cracked.

"That's an unusual name."

"Yes."

I watched Joseph lay a thick finger lightly against Susanna's soft cheek. "She is a beautiful child, Rachel. I like her red hair. But she is too thin. My wife will bring food to you."

Rachel's shoulders sagged with the weight of shame. Her voice fell to a whisper. "Thank you."

Joseph took a deep breath and then picked his tools up once more. "I like these very much."

I could see Rachel's body tighten.

"Would you sell them to me?"

"What?"

"Would you sell them to me?"

Rachel turned away from my father. "I...I cannot..."

Joseph waited.

She walked toward the back wall from which I was watching. I could now see her face, plainly. It was drawn and haggard. My throat filled with a lump.

"I...I took them from you. They are yours." She bit her lip.

Joseph did not answer.

Then Rachel turned and fell before Joseph. "Will you forgive me? I took them from your door. I was going to sell them..."

Joseph knelt in front of her. "Rachel, I forgive you."

My chin quivered. I knew even then that lesser men would have dragged the woman out of her house by her hair; they would have kicked her through the village and shouted at her violently until throwing her at the feet of the Elders. Instead, my callused, thick-muscled father now knelt before this broken woman like a gentle bear soothing a cub.

Relieved, Rachel began to sob. Joseph could not touch her, of course, for it would not be right. But he quietly comforted her. "The Lord is merciful and fair, *HaShem* is compassionate. Blessed be the name of the Lord." [53]

As he spoke, I heard another voice whisper '*El Abba*' as it had before. I looked behind me but saw nothing. *What's happening?* I sat against the cracked plaster wall. I closed my eyes and listened to the thumping within my chest.

What's happening? I wrestled with this question for the rest of my sixth year and into my seventh. I did not understand, but whenever I would even think the words, '*El Abba*,' I would be excited, or I'd feel warm all over. But on an afternoon in the Roman month of *Martias* that followed, I set those thoughts aside to weep with Salome and my brother James in the

---

53 From Psalm 116:5

doorway of our little house. A physician named Eli was finishing a prayer for our baby sister, Assia, whom my mother held tightly. Alongside sat my mother's friend, Hannah, who had brought a collection of dried plants—hyssop, rosemary, palm and rue—in case the physician had forgotten. But the man would use none of it, nor did he use any of the remedies he left hanging on his donkey.

"A curse on you, scribe!" shouted Joseph as he trailed the man out of our house. "The best of your kind will lay cold in Sheol."[54]

"It's less than two hours before the Sabbath. I told you this would be a problem when you dragged me from my door."

I watched Joseph grit his teeth. "She is my little girl." He unwound the *tefillin* from his arm and threw it aside.

Rabbi Isaiah was standing in the street reading through a long *Targum* as he searched for some way to challenge the physician's claim. "Good sir, it seems to me that you would not be guilty of *malakha*[55]..."

"Pull the hair from your ears, old man. If I administer my medicine now, the *effect* will occur during *Shabbat* and that will be *my* sin." The physician knew the prescriptions of the Law better than most, but he knew them according to the rigid demands of the House of Shammai.

Isaiah struggled and began reciting the various prohibitions against Sabbath work: "So you see, this is no untying, or planting, or reaping, or weaving, or threshing, or..."

"You have no need to instruct me, Rabbi. I could tell you nearly forty such things..."

"But...I believe it is permitted to save a life..."

"You interpret too liberally, Rabbi."

Isaiah shook his head. "The medicine could work *now*. Our Lord is able to protect *Shabbat*..."

"Able? Of course he is able." Eli threw a fine blanket atop his donkey. "We, on the other hand, are able to present ourselves before him as a righteous and holy people. Is this not what you teach, Rabbi? If this is true, then how much more is it true on the eve of Sabbath?"

"Wouldn't you lift your wife from a well if she fell in on *Shabbat*!" Isaiah was now angry.

---

54 Adapted from a comment in an ancient Jewish commentary that discredited physicians.

55 Means 'work' or more specifically, a forbidden activity.

"Perhaps your wife draws water on *Shabbat*, but my wife would not. And if she did, it would be the Lord's will that she sink to the bottom."

Isaiah stiffened. "It would not be the Lord's will that she sink, and it is *not* the Lord's will that you walk away from this poor child."

"No? Return your eyes to the Scriptures," growled the doctor. "Then come and see me."

I watched Joseph curl his lip and I wondered, *Is the scribe right? How could the Law be wrong?*

Isaiah would not retreat. "No. This is not what the Lord…"

"Enough!" The scribe bent close to the rabbi and finally revealed his heart. "Hear me. Sabbath or no Sabbath, I am unable to bring the Lord's healing to this house."

Isaiah waited. We drew closer.

Eli took a firm hold on his robe and turned a hard eye against my suffering father. "I feel Evil is here, I sense a darkness. The child suffers because of this family's sin and for that I have no remedy."

I thought Joseph might lunge at the man and choke him dead in the street.

Sensing the same, the physician raised his hand. "'If you will do right in the sight of the Lord your God and give ear to his commandments, he will not put diseases on you.'"[56]

Joseph did lunge and he caught Eli by the throat. The man cried out, gurgling and rasping until Hannah and my sister ran into the street.

"No, Joseph!" begged Hannah.

My father turned and set his jaw. But when he saw the sudden horror in little Salome's eyes he closed his and released the scribe with a push.

Gasping, the scribe shouted to all now gathering in the street that Joseph was a wicked man and that our house was a house of demons. When he finally collected himself he continued to torture my father. "I will see to it that the guild makes you suffer. Now, pay me what you promised or I will see that you get no more work in the city." [57]

Joseph chafed but he wanted no more trouble. He plunged trembling fingers into his purse and retrieved two *denarii*. "Leave us!"

Eli clutched his cloak. "We agreed on six."

"You physicians would steal the dowry of a sick widow."

---

56 Adapted Exodus 15:26

57 Scribes were not permitted to be paid for services, but they could ask for a 'gift'

"Builder, you prove my charge: 'He who sins against his Maker will be defiant toward the physician.'"[58]

Joseph threw two more *denarii*[59] into the dust. "That's all. I should have hired a Gentile."

I followed behind as Joseph kicked open the door to our little house and pressed his face against a wall to hide his tears. Isaiah tried to comfort him. "The Law of the Lord is not that scribe's law of tears and sorrows. His life is a warehouse of rules and a thimble of mercies, woe to him!"

"What does it matter now? My daughter will die." Joseph gathered himself with a deep breath. He turned and looked at me, oddly. Our eyes met and I knew he was searching me for something.

"*Abba?*" I said.

He turned away.

Joseph's look troubled me. I had an idea of what he was thinking—but if I truly was who my parents said I was, then who was I? *What does it mean to be the Son of the Most High?* I remembered hearing Rabbi Isaiah once teach that healing flowed from the throne of David. I wrung my hands. *But is it possible that the Story is not true? Could things have been mixed up? And didn't Joseph seem unsure?*

Saying nothing, I followed Joseph to my mother's side. She was sitting on the floor and cradling Assia on her lap. Mary's cheeks were stained with tears. Salome climbed over the floor to sit by her and stroke Assia's hair.

My mother looked at me knowingly. Her swollen eyes were filled with pain. "The ways of *Avi'ad*[60] are not our ways," she said, bravely. "Blessed be his holy name." She wiped the tears from her face and offered me a gentle smile. "Jesus, come close."

I obeyed.

Joseph suddenly blurted, "Maybe I should find the one they call the Circle Drawer. He's healing people in Cana this week." His voice was desperate.

"If you think that's best."

---

58 Sirach 38:15

59 A *denarius* (plural, *denarii*) was a Roman silver coin worth about a day's wage for the average worker.

60 Hebrew name for 'God as Everlasting Father'

Joseph then looked at me, again. He opened his mouth to speak when Mary interrupted. "Perhaps in the fullness of time?"

What did that mean? I wondered.

Joseph looked like a man being torn in half. I pitied him and I felt sick for him. He so loved Assia; he called her his 'little treasure,' and he had been sure to sing her to sleep every night. Now he stood over her, helpless, turning away from all of us to bury his face in his hands.

Mary then laid an amulet on Assia's blanket to protect her from prowling spirits. She asked Hannah if she had another. Hannah did. In fact, Hannah had several amulets with her and so my mother carefully set seven charms on the blanket.

Joseph was perspiring. "You fear the…Beast, don't you?"

Mary could barely look at her husband. "I know that the Lord is mighty…but…" Her voice faltered and her chin quivered. "But…but forgive me, my faith fails me." She started to sob.

Joseph bent down and wrapped his arms around her tenderly. He kissed her on the cheek. "Mary, dear Mary. I have not seen such faith in all of Israel." He wiped his eyes. "Yes, woman, the Lord is mighty…but we are not. Blessed be the name of the Lord."

Mary took one of his hands firmly in hers and kissed it. "Let the Lord be our strength and our salvation…"[61]she choked. "Blessed be the name of the Lord."

Isaiah then came to my parents' side and bade me kneel by him. I did. He looked at me carefully, as if he could discover something within me that could help. Uncertain, he simply said, "Jesus…pray with me." He raised his hands upward, as did I. He began to pray in loud groans and when he finished, everyone turned their faces toward me, expectantly.

But I was confused and frightened. What was I to do? And I was filled with grief when I thought that the Beast had come for Assia because of me. I wondered if that's what they all thought.

And what would they do if I failed them?

I fixed my eyes on Assia who was now laboring to breathe. *But who am I? What do I do?* I felt sick.

My mother then spoke, gently. "Jesus? What troubles you?"

I knew that what troubled me was also troubling her but I had no answer; I had no words for her. *What do they want from me?* I clenched my

---

61 From Psalms 118:14

teeth. *I'm just a boy; I'm just Yeshua bar Yosef of Nazareth…or am I more? Am I? What would that mean?*

Mary then laid a soft hand of mercy on my head. At her touch I knew that she had released me from the moment. I looked into her face and I saw such peace as I had never seen before. Her quiet surrender to all that was beyond herself prompted awe within me. I immediately tried pushing against my own confusion.

The Circle Drawer, I thought. I had once seen the Circle Drawer in Nain where he laid his hands atop a sick boy and drew disease away from the boy's belly. *Perhaps if I'm someone special like him…who knows?*

I laid a hand on Assia's body. At the touch my breath left my lungs and a cold darkness quickly came over me, swallowing me into some black void. I took my hand away and the moment I did, air rushed into my lungs and I returned from the sinking abyss, blinking.

"Jesus?"

I turned my face away from my mother and toward Heaven, but found myself simply staring at the underside of the roof. I felt suddenly distant from this supposed Father of mine but I was determined to try again. This time I laid both my hands on Assia and when I did my ears filled with roaring sounds and my belly cramped. I retched and gagged; my nostrils filled with rancid odors. I felt as if my inward parts were beginning to roast. The skin on my palms felt afire but I held them fast to my sister. I clenched my jaw.

And then I knew one thing for sure…Evil was among us. "No! Get out of this house!" At the sound of my command a powerful wind blew through the uncovered window high above, filling the room with a swirling gust that blew Isaiah's shawl off his head. I felt strength fill my limbs and I pressed my hands yet firmer.

Assia stopped crying.

"Who?" murmured sister Salome. "Who must get out?"

Mary knew.

The stench left my nostrils. My palms quickly cooled; my lungs released stale air. My ears cleared. I saw three mighty warriors in shimmering armor standing on three sides of us. My face lit with joy.

And then I heard a low moan from my mother. I looked into Mary's face, and then lowered my eyes toward Assia. Stunned, I fell backward to the ground. My little sister had died.

And I heard the Beast, laughing.

CHAPTER VI

LIFE

In the days that followed, my mother was filled with such sadness that the memory of it still weighs on my heart. I can only speak of it briefly.

Assia's body was washed within an hour of her death and was anointed with some of the spices given to me at my birth. Assia was then shrouded before the Sabbath lamps were lit and kept in the storeroom by our beds until the sacred day had ended. At first light my brothers and I then helped Joseph open a tomb. Assia would lie alongside the shrouded remains of another poor child who had died just two days before. Knowing that my dear sister's remains would not lie alone was a comfort to my mother.

When all was ready, the village Elders summoned several women to lead our procession with loud lamentations. Joseph carried little Assia's body behind them with dear Mary leaning hard upon his breast. I followed with little brother, Joses, and with Salome and James on either side. Behind us four flautists played as Nazareth's mourner sang a psalm.

Once we neared the opened tomb I felt a deep rage rise within me. Though only seven years old I knew then that death was an enemy. *Truly*, I thought, *the Lord must hate death, for I surely do!*

But where was he? Where is '*El-Abba*?'

Had he forsaken us?

Had he forsaken Assia?

I heard Joseph weeping bitterly as he carried Assia into her tomb. He laid her upon a bed of sweet-smelling dried herbs, and as he did, Rabbi Isaiah prayed for the mercies of Heaven to bring us peace. Then Joseph rolled the heavy stone against the tiny vault, moaning something about leaving his dear daughter to the care of the good earth.[62]

When the stone was set my mother rocked on her knees and cried out,

"I was feeble and utterly crushed;

I groaned in anguish of heart.

Yet my sighing is not hidden from you.'[63]

Blessed be the name of the Lord."

Isaiah was moved by Mary's faithfulness. I saw him wipe his eyes. He then reminded us of the Lord's love for his people and of the coming gift of resurrection. But I was not comforted.

Was I the cause of all this misery?

If I was who my mother said I was, why was I not able to save my sister? How could I be the One?

My mother noticed my struggle and called me to her side. I fell against her and wept. She held me tightly and began to sing softly: "*HaShem* is with her; she will not fall; your Father in Heaven will help her when that day breaks."[64]

My Father in Heaven? I pulled away, saying nothing but wanting to say, *Look at Joseph, mother, can't you see the questions in his face? I have them, too.* I then thought of the words, '*El Abba,*' but this time I felt no excitement; no warmth filled my limbs.

Mary reached for my hand once more and I received it, dutifully. "My son, the Lord's ways are not our ways." Her face was swollen with grief. "Be still and know that he is God."[65]

---

62 According to author's interview with Amer Nicolas at Nazareth Village in February, 2011, excavations of first century tombs have revealed round stones standing at the entrances to small tombs. Typically, a person was buried in a tomb until the flesh had left her bones. Later, the bones were removed and gathered into a stone box called an ossuary.

63 Adapted from Psalms 38

64 Adapted from Psalms 46:5

65 From Psalms 46:10

Rabbi Isaiah helped our family through the difficult weeks that followed. I say 'difficult' because they were filled with grief and anger, and for me they were also filled with confusion. One warm afternoon he saw me waiting for my parents outside our door. "Boy, how's your mother? Is she still weeping for your sister?"

"Yes, but not as much as before. Grandfather says that she's a woman of great faith."

The old man wrinkled his nose. "Faith is given to comfort sorrow, not replace it." He reached into his robe and retrieved two dried figs. He handed me one. "And you?"

I bit into the fig. "What about me?"

"Do you still grieve your sister?"

I couldn't swallow. "Yes. I always will."

The old man stared at me. I could see pity in his face and so I knew exactly what he was thinking. "Well, you must let sorrow live for its season." He put his fig in his mouth. "But it's not your fault..." He lost his words and stared at me blankly.

My chin quivered.

Isaiah then scratched his chin. "What about your father?"

"He works very hard."

Isaiah nodded. "Does he not cry?"

"No. Only that first day."

The sound of my parents' voices turned our heads. The rabbi greeted them with a kiss. "I've come to see how you are doing."

Joseph answered, coldly. "How do you think we are doing?" Mary touched his arm, lightly, and has face softened. "Thank you, Rabbi. We are well enough."

Isaiah nodded, then pointed to a stick in Joseph's hand. "What's that?"

My father bounced the stick on his hand. "Watch." He began to draw in the dust. "I will build us a new house, Rabbi. And you will bless it." Joseph's voice was firm. He pressed the point of the stick hard against the earth and scratched a wide rectangle with many rooms.No one said a word until he was finished. "There," he said, proudly. "I built one like this in Sepphoris. It's wonderful."

Isaiah raised a brow. My mother walked from one side to the other until finally saying, "Do...do you think it's a little too big?"

Joseph darkened.

"Maybe just a little?" Mary glanced at Isaiah. She knew that in a village like Nazareth it would not be good for Joseph to seem the better man. But she also knew how it was that Joseph would find rest from the pain of Assia.

Disappointed, Joseph looked at my mother and the rabbi, then rubbed his jaw. He studied his plan one more time. "I thought you'd like it." No one spoke as the man squatted and poked the drawing with his stick. Finally, he stood and surveyed the streets of the village. "Maybe you're right...this time." He forced a smile. "Yes, yes. You're right, Mary. Who do I think I am?" He bent over and then slowly brushed away his dream to settle for his place. When finished, he stared blankly at his blank canvas of dust.

I wanted to weep for him.

Joseph paced around a bit, scratched his head a few times, squatted, paced some more, and finally held the point of his stick against the ground. "Ready?"

We waited.

Joseph began to sketch a rectangle that enclosed an inner courtyard and some rooms. "There and there...and that...yes, of course, one of those..."

I watched the man begin to smile. His hand moved skillfully like the hand of the artisan he was. Finally he folded his arms, proudly. "There. What do you think of that?"

I wanted to cry out that his house was wonderful, but my mother was biting her lip. *Oh no*, I thought.

Joseph raised his eyebrows as he waited for Mary to answer. Finally, she said, "Husband...do we really need such a large courtyard?"

Rabbi Isaiah faded back a step as Joseph collapsed his brows. For all his goodness, Joseph could be stubborn. He raised his chin. "Yes, woman, we do. We need a courtyard *exactly* like this."

Mary looked to Isaiah who turned away, quickly.

Joseph sounded suddenly desperate. "Judas has a big one; John of Jacob does too...his is even bigger than this. And your father..."

Mary took his arm. "No. It's wonderful, husband, wonderful."

Relieved, Isaiah winked at me.

"Are you sure? I want it ten strides long and five wide. I really don't think it will be too much." Joseph was suddenly beaming.

My mother began to walk around it. "Yes, yes. It's wonderful."

Joseph grinned and began pointing his stick. "Look, here's a sleeping room, storage, and a workshop to the side."

Mary smiled—and when my mother smiled the world came alive. Joseph began to chatter on, wildly. "And a stable on the far end, and..."

"I love it." Mary kissed his hands. "Husband, build your house!"

For the next weeks, Joseph and his helpers worked hard at preparing the plot of land he had bought near the edge of the village, not far from the vineyard and away from the Gentiles. Once cleared of wild olives and brush, he then began digging and dragging stones from the village quarry to be stacked as fine walls for our new house. I remember him driving wooden wedges into the quarry stone and me soaking the wedges to crack the stone away. Most of all, however, I remember how my father sang during those wonderful days; he was so very happy.

Joseph was soon teaching me how to strip bark with the adze and how to hammer bronze nails into hard wood without bending them. I also learned how a carpenter was measured by his faithfulness to the plane, the square and the clamp, and how a worker was to be fairly paid. Before long I was smearing mud and straw into mortar joints, and limestone on the outer walls, and carrying thatch to the rooftop. I was grateful that he seemed to hold nothing against me for Assia's death.

The day that the house was finished, Joseph smiled such a smile as I would never forget. Mother prepared a special meal and our relatives from Cana came. Rabbi Isaiah then blessed it as 'good,' and so it was.

A sturdy wooden door welcomed guests into a small room where they could wash their feet. From there they entered into the inviting courtyard of comfortable seats and shade that served as both a place for guests and for women's work.

Of course, the house was a target for the village gossips. Many believed that Joseph's insistence on a courtyard was because of his 'fornicator's dishonor' and Mary's shamelessness. Others said it was so he could hide his mad wife from others. It seemed to me that Joseph was wise to protect my mother in a place where she was able to bear the contempt of others honorably.[66]

As for me, I loved the courtyard, too. It was a pleasant place to play with my brothers and sisters before our meals, and to be away from the probing eyes of others. I liked dipping my hands into the cool waters of the

---

66 Simply put, a primary role of Jewish women was to preserve the family's honor; the male's role was to promote the family's honor.

cistern Joseph soon added. But the rooftop of Joseph's house was where I most loved to be. In accordance with the Law, a low parapet extended above the thick-thatched rafters to guard the edges. I would lean against that parapet for hours, for this was a place to look upward and wonder about what lies beyond the second heaven.

"I need to go to Sepphoris and pay the guild fee," announced Joseph. He had just returned from the Feast of Tabernacles. "And they won't take anything but Tyrian shekels."

"Then I will come with you. You don't do well with moneychangers."

Joseph shrugged one of those yielding shrugs that I had begun to notice. "Fine."

"And we'll bring the children."

"Why?"

"They should see what the world looks like."

The next day Salome and I walked alongside our parents as we began the two-hour journey to the prospering city and the moneychangers who were waiting. Now you must understand that my father had a good eye for plumb but no nose for business. Unlike the reputable guilds of the Alexandrian Jews, Joseph's guild was run by a Herodian cheat—a pretend-Jew named *Ezra bar Ezra*. My mother called him Ezra the Asp and all manner of names that had to do with serpents.

"He wants to cheat you," my mother said. "So, remember that one Tyrian shekel is the same as four *denarii* or sixteen *sesterces*..."

Joseph grumbled.

"What coins did you bring?"

"A mixture."

Mother bit her lip. "Please tell me you didn't bring those little copper mites."

Joseph shrugged.

The four of us walked in silence for a time. The morning was hot, unusually hot for the end of September. But the walk through the valley was always pleasant enough and made more bearable by the generosity of travelers returning late from the joys of the feast in Jerusalem. I made a few friends of some other children and we dashed about along the edges of the roadway, throwing stones and chasing one another.

I was told that one of the boys, *Menahem bar Jonathon* from Nain—a village an hour's walk or so south of Nazareth—could race like the wind. I studied him. *If I'm the 'Son of the Most High,' shouldn't I be able to win every race?* I thought. I smiled. "Let's see."

I called to the boy and challenged him to race me. He laughed and gathered his friends, then pointed to a bush about the distance of a Roman *stadia*—two hundred paces for a man. I removed my sandals and Menahem removed his. We took our places behind a line in the sand, and when a thrown stone hit the ground, Menahem and I sprinted forward like two young gazelles.

I can still feel how it felt as my feet pounded the hard earth! My legs and arms churned forward; my breath heaved in and out of my chest. I could feel the rhythm of Menahem just behind me. I felt as if I was one with the wind. I lowered my head. *Faster, faster.*

Menahem's elbow then brushed mine once, and then again. *Faster, harder.* Suddenly I no longer felt one with the wind. Desperate for air I stretched my mouth open; my lungs sucked hard. My limbs began to ache. Menahem began to move ahead.

So I prayed! Ha! Yes, yes, I laugh about it even now!

Menahem then pulled away from me and moved directly in front so that his heels kicked dust and tiny stones into my legs. I leaned forward, straining with every bit of strength I had.

And then it was over.

I had lost. And I was not happy about it.

As the other children gathered around the proud Menahem, my sister took pity on me and tugged on my tunic. "You ran really fast," she said.

I sat down to catch my breath and could only shake my head.

CHAPTER VII

SEPPHORIS

"Where are your sandals, Jesus?" My mother was annoyed.

I looked at my feet, blankly, and then over my shoulder at the roadway. "I…I don't know."

"You don't know? How could you not know?"

I shrugged. "I guess I left them where I raced."

"How many times is this?"

Joseph shook his head. "You'll have to work for the money…again."

I looked back once more and scratched my head. I then looked at Salome who was covering her mouth so I wouldn't see her laughing. My mother continued scolding me when several lepers from the city recognized Joseph and ran to him, begging. By their size and movement I could see that the wrapped figures were two men, three women, and a child. [67]

My mother quickly handed Joseph the food he always brought for them. He greeted the lepers kindly and they called him by name. He placed a generous portion of salted mutton, some raisins and fig cakes in their bags

---

67 It should be noted that there is some disagreement as to the actual nature of the skin disease referred to as leprosy in the Bible. It may not have been the flesh-rotting disease made famous in the film, 'Ben Hur,' but rather a reference to any variety of skin disorders such as a stubborn rash or psoriasis, etc. Nevertheless, anyone suffering skin problems was considered unclean and exiled from normal community life until they experienced a full recovery.

that they extended toward us on long poles. "Be blessed, my friends. May the *shalom* of our Father fill you."

I watched the lepers hurry away as others cried out at them, "Get away. Unclean!" I felt sad for them and began to run after them. My parents shouted for me to stop but I couldn't. My feet carried me closer and closer. The child leper must have heard me and so she turned around.

"Stop," she said. Her voice was gentle.

Something within urged me to come closer...to see into her eyes.

"Please. No closer. You can do nothing."

I slowed until I could see her eyes within her wrappings. They were tender and moist. I shuffled just a little closer so that I could see more deeply into her. When I did, I gasped, for what I saw was a cloud of dark filth looming over a tiny lamp. The lamp was struggling to cast its light. I blinked. Oh, how I wanted to drive out that darkness! I clenched my fists and prayed for the Lord to wash her clean and make her whole...

"Why do you care?" she asked, shyly.

"Why do I care?" I wasn't sure. Did I need to know? What kind of question was that?

"What's your name?"

"Jesus."

"I will remember you, Jesus." She turned away.

I called after her. "What's your name?"

Still walking, she answered, "I am called, 'Unclean.'"

I could think of little else except the leper-girl, and so as we entered Sepphoris I did not marvel at the new colonnades that now lined the white-paved streets. Artisans and craftsmen like my father had been very busy and the city was becoming the jewel of Galilee. What I cared about was the little wretch outside the walls.

"Jesus," said Joseph. "Look around you. Just five years ago this place was put to the torch by that monster Varus. He slaughtered all the Jews to be sure that he killed the rebels among them."

I raised my head to see scaffolding everywhere.

Joseph pointed to the new construction. "Sometimes I wonder if I should work in this place. It's full of Romans and Greeks, but even worse, the city is becoming the boast of Herodians." He looked at me. "Remember, any friend of Herod is a false Jew."

Joseph stopped to buy some sage tea, flatbread and pieces of honey-comb from a merchant he knew. He then led us to the shade of a heavy-leafed fig where he rolled out a blanket for us.

I settled by my soon-snoring mother, marveling at the sounds and the color around me. Everywhere I looked, profane images of Caesar Augustus appeared. I saw his likeness as a statue on one corner and in a fresco on the next. I turned to find his face staring at me from a painting, and he mocked the world from within a framed mosaic being carried on the backs of two grunting slaves. I felt compassion for the slaves and pity for Caesar the Fool. Then I remembered something from my mother's instruction: '*You shall not make for yourself images...*'[68]

The vendors of a nearby bazaar were loud, chanting their prices for fish or fresh-picked pomegranates or breads or spices. One of them had a monkey dancing in his stall. I stood to watch him and I laughed at the way he played with the shoppers. "Look, Salome!"

The two of us giggled as the monkey then leapt atop the fine headdress of a Roman woman. The woman screamed and flailed her arms but the monkey dodged about, chattering happily until he snatched a silver brooch off her shoulder and dashed away. The whole of the bazaar howled with laughter, but my face was abruptly turned by a shriek. I searched out the street that lay to one side of us and there I saw a Roman soldier dragging a woman. She cried out again as he stopped to strike her once, then again, and then a third time. He shoved her into the arms of another soldier. Frightened for her, I looked at Joseph. "Can't you help her?"

"How can I help?" His voice fell away.

I returned my face to the street. The poor woman was gone, overpowered and taken into a dark alley behind a merchant's stall. A flood of feeling filled my belly. Eight-year old boys of Nazareth knew something about these things. Joseph told me that women were nothing more than bodies of pleasure for some men. I groaned for her and I took a few steps into the street, but Joseph caught me by the shoulders. I strained against his firm grip but his powerful hands tightened. A sharp pain stabbed my loins and I shuddered.

Joseph turned my face away and knelt in front of me. I could see that he was ashamed of being powerless against the forces that ruled us. "It's not your fault," he said.

---

68 From Deuteronomy 5:8

"What's not my fault?"

He pointed in the direction of the alley. "What's happening to that woman is not your fault."

I nodded. Was he telling me this for his sake? So I answered. "It's not your fault, either."

Joseph grunted. "The day will come, Jesus, when our oppressors will be thrown out of Israel."

I was surprised. I had never heard Joseph speak that way before. I wondered if all Galileans might be rebels after all! Joseph stood and as he did the sudden tramping of feet turned both our heads. Marching around a corner came a well-ordered company of Romans soldiers. I heard Joseph suck in a fearful breath. But I was excited. I had seen a few soldiers here and there, but never this. So I watched in awe as they marched closer in tight ranks. Their helmets gleamed, their leather armor was well fitted, and their sheathed swords rocked evenly off their hips. I thought they looked invincible.

Joseph was nervous but dared not move. However, he quickly told me that if I counted them they'd be about a hundred men. "It's called a 'Century.'" He stared at the ensign being carried in the front. "This one's garrisoned in Syria." He fell silent. The soldiers then tramped in front of us as if we did not exist. They followed their centurion with eyes fixed forward, each indifferent to the world around him. I knew that with one word they could slaughter us all, and so did everyone standing still and breathless around me. I felt the hair on my head tingle.

None of us moved until the soldiers arrived at a marketplace about a quarter *stadia* away[69] where they were ordered to break ranks. Joseph took a breath and shook his head. Everyone around us sighed in relief. My mother took my hand and pulled me close.

But I was still fascinated. I watched the soldiers remove their helmets and throw themselves on the ground in the shade of the marketplace. I then noticed how carefully the ensign bearer leaned his staff against a wall. It was as if the wooden pole and scrap of cloth had some sort of power that he feared.

Joseph leaned over to me and pointed to the ensign. "'Third Legion Gallica, Sixth.' They served Varus when he crushed this city." He looked for Salome and motioned to my mother. "Now, we should get to our business."

---

69 One *stadia* is 200 yards

As he gathered my mother and sister behind me, I noticed how passers-by kept a great distance from the soldiers. I understood why, of course. But then I saw a woman walk toward the ensign very slowly. When she came within a few strides, she stopped and stared at it for a long moment. Her legs then buckled beneath her and she fell to her hands. Curious, I pointed her out to my father. "One look at the flag and she fell down."

"The ensign is a symbol to her."

I wrinkled my nose. "But it's only wood and cloth...how can it make her fall down?"

Joseph was busy hurrying my mother. "It can't."

"But..."

He took a moment. "I heard an Elder in the synagogue teach the story of Moses lifting up an image of a snake in the wilderness. All who looked at it were healed. But the image had no power of its own; it was only a symbol of the Lord's power. He said that symbols are given power by belief."

"So the woman gives the ensign power by believing it has power?"

"Something like that."

"But if she didn't, its power would not be real?"

Joseph scratched his beard. "Not for her. But the power of Rome would still be real."

"So if she stopped believing, then the ensign wouldn't even be a symbol...it would just be a stick with a cloth."

My father shrugged. "I guess. You think too much." He took my mother's arm. "Time to go."

"Tell him no, Joseph." Mary's tone was patient but I was miserable. We had been inching forward in Sepphoris' suffocating moneychanger's line for the last hour and had finally arrived at the clerk's table. "Do not trust his scales."

The young clerk was surly and sweated. He had bits of food in his wiry, red beard. "Tell your woman to shut her mouth."

I chafed, but Joseph could only lower his eyes. His strong arms and hard fists were powerless in a place like this. My mother, on the other hand, faced the clerk proudly.

"Look away!" the man barked.

Mary did not. Nor did she provide him the pleasure of a reaction. Instead, she simply waited.

The man cursed. "I said, look away!"

Joseph's body tightened and Mary laid a calm hand on his arm. "Be about your business, husband." She smiled at the annoyed clerk and I marveled at her, again. My mother understood the power of longsuffering. Joseph reached into his purse nervously and began thumbing through a confusing variety of silver, bronze, and copper coins.

I should say here that Joseph was not a poor man; others in Nazareth had less and only a few had more. As a skilled builder he had been earning the equivalent of ten *denarii* a week, which is nearly twice what a common worker could earn. But he was no less a slave to the powers than anyone else. With the head tax, escalating transit tolls, tributes, a new workshop tax and the like, he lost more then half his income directly to Rome or to that grasping son of Herod the Great—Herod Antipas.

Added to that were the Temple tax and his tithe, so Joseph only kept about one third of what he earned. Of course, his third was still greater than the thirds of others and he had the confidence of Mary's eventual inheritance from her father. This is why there were some in Nazareth who wondered why Joseph was not more generous in his invitations for supper. After all, when an elder once whispered of Joseph's tithe, it soon became an easy way for the whole village to reckon his yearly earnings.

"Now give me my coins so I can get out of this place," said Joseph. He was not always a patient man.

The clerk was a thick-armed brute with a Judean accent and a cutting gaze. He said nothing as Joseph repeated the number of coins in the stacks he had built. He simply scooped some up and dumped them on his scale.

"No," barked Joseph. "I'll not settle for weight. My count is exact."

"My scales say otherwise." The clerk nodded to a soldier who was lounging in a corner.

Joseph shifted on his feet. "Your scales…they are off."

"Now how would you know that?"

"Because the count is right and if you look at my coins you'll see that none are shaved…"

"Hold your tongue or I'll turn you over to him." He tossed his head toward a soldier who quickly put a hand on his sword and took five long strides toward us.

Joseph looked at my mother with such a look that I nearly wept for him. His eyes told the tale of a beaten man. Saying nothing, Joseph then yielded to the moneychanger who mocked him with a sneer.

I looked behind me at the long line of other beaten men, men who suffered the abuses of corruption. I then turned to stare at the moneychanger and it occurred to me that here was a Jew in league with Rome to exploit other Jews. I remembered something Mary had recited just days before. I squeezed past Joseph's hips and spoke to the clerk. "You are a Jew?"

"Run away, boy, before I beat you." He spat at me.

To everyone's surprise—even my own—I then leapt atop his table on my bare feet. " 'Anyone who cheats his neighbor is unfaithful to the Lord.' "[70] The furious clerk swept me to the floor as the soldier rushed forward and drew his sword on my father. The room fell silent. A young scribe then stepped from the line, calmly gripping the edge of his cloak with one hand. In the other hand he held the leash to his Molossian—a wary, thick-necked dog with huge paws. The scribe calmly added what I had not remembered: " 'And he must add a fifth.' [71] Now, enough of this." He pressed his nose close to the clerk's and spoke with enough volume for all to hear. "Perhaps I should have a look at your scales?"

Murmurs of approval rose within the room. The clerk reddened. He threw all of Joseph's coins into a chest and quickly counted out his exchange. "There. Now get out."

The scribe followed us into the street where my mother bowed with respect; Joseph thanked him with his face fixed to the ground. He introduced himself as *Moses bar Simeon* of the famous Sadducean family of Kamith in Jerusalem. He had joined the Pharisees to study under the well-respected Rabbi Hillel.

As the man spoke to my father, I ran to the dog. The beast leaned away from me at first. Then I raised a hand toward him, slowly, and he sniffed

70 Leviticus 6:2
71 Leviticus 6:5

it. Before long I was scratching his massive head and he soon rolled over to expose his belly.

"Petrus," Moses said. "His name is 'Petrus.' He is superior in size to the racing hounds that the Romans boast about, and he's more loyal than most. He can be a bit suspicious but he has the courage of a lion." The scribe whistled and the dog rolled to his feet, then stood on his hind legs and set his huge front paws on his master's chest. The man let the broad-headed dog lick his face and beard.

Laughing, Moses released Petrus and then turned to me. He laid both hands on my shoulders and praised me for my knowledge of the Scriptures and for my courage. He turned to Joseph. "You've an uncommon boy."

I remember smiling proudly, but when I saw my father's face I noticed that he did not seem proud. In fact, I thought he seemed ashamed about something. Joseph looked away. The scribe then spoke to my mother and I turned my attention to him. I was taken by his cloak—a fine, striped garment of smooth cotton that fell well below his knees to exactly one hand's breath above the blue fringes of his tunic underneath. His presence was powerful, like the dog by his side. I was happy to know Moses, and he would soon mean much to me.

CHAPTER VIII

TOUCHING TRUTH

A man in the village hired me to build a threshing sled, which I was happy to do in order to pay off the cost of my new sandals. Joseph watched, but the task was easy for a boy of almost nine.

"Let me see how you fastened the boards." Joseph inspected my work and approved. "Now, don't carve the holes too wide," he said.

"I know." I didn't like being told to do what I already knew to do. Grumbling, I proceeded to chisel holes in the bottom of the boards, then soaked the wood in water before inserting sharp stones into the holes. My brother was now supervising with my father.

"Stop whining, James," I grumbled.

"I want to be the rider."

"You can't," I said. "You're not heavy enough to break chaff…and you're too weak to handle the donkey."

"I'm not weak!"

"Boys. Enough." Joseph wiped his face. I knew what was going to happen—he almost always yielded to James. Sensing victory, James begged Joseph to build a *heavier* yoke for the donkey that would pull him.

Joseph scratched his head. "Why a heavy one?"

"So it will obey me."

Joseph laughed and shook his hand through my brother's hair. He turned to me. "Should your brother be the rider?"

I looked at James. He was not yet six years old and was far too small to be a rider. "If you want to break the wheat from the chaff, father, you need a heavier rider and lighter yoke...not the other way around."

James scowled and threw a stone at me, just as our mother arrived.

"James!"

"What?"

"You know what."

My brother pouted. "You're always for *him*."

Joseph interrupted. "Mary. Just leave it be."

Ignoring my father, my mother walked toward James and knelt in front of him. "I love you, James. You know that, right?"

James faced the ground.

Mary pulled him close. "Well, I love *all* my children the same."

When she said those words I heard Joseph sigh. Surprised, I looked at him carefully and then I saw his eyes meet my mother's eyes as if he didn't believe what she had just said. I turned toward Mary and I saw her face fall, sadly. *What's the matter?* I thought.

I returned to my work but I noticed that my mother and Joseph were talking in hushed tones in a shaded corner of the courtyard. I set my sled aside and crept into the welcoming room of our new courtyard where I listened carefully while peeking above a low wall.

"I don't know, either," said Joseph. "But you are right to love all your children the same."

"But...does Jesus need something more? Are we to love him differently?"

"How can we not?" Joseph wrapped her in his powerful arms. "This is not easy for us."

The two stood quietly for a long moment before Joseph released her from his embrace. "I...I don't know what more to do with any of this." He wet a rag and wiped his face. "If you're right about Jesus, then I...we...can only do what we are able to do."

Mary sat on a basket. "Joseph...you do have doubts, don't you?"

My father didn't answer.

"I love you, husband, and I worry for you. You are a different man than the one I married."

Joseph's tone suddenly changed. "Different?"

"Yes. Even your brother sees it."

"What did he say?"

My mother hesitated.

"What did Cleopas tell you!"

"He said that you were really never the same after my conception with Jesus."

Joseph's face twitched a little. "He said that?"

Mary nodded.

"Do you agree with him?"

"I didn't notice then. You and I still laughed and danced. But..." she bit her lip. "But over these years I..."

Joseph faced her squarely. "You what?"

Mary answered, gently. "I see you becoming less happy and more restless."

Joseph stared at her, waiting for more.

Again, Mary hesitated. "Dear husband, tell me: do you doubt the angel's visits...to either of us?"

I strained to hear every word. *This again.* My belly churned.

Joseph turned his back. "I'm so tired..."

Pain filled my mother's face. "I beg you, tell me what's troubling you."

Joseph paced about, struggling within himself. Finally he faced her. "You mean besides struggling to believe it's all true? Besides feeling helpless in raising the boy who could be Israel's Messiah? Besides dealing with the gossips and the mockers? Besides... it's all too much for a man."

My mother's chin quivered.

Joseph then looked directly into her face and revealed yet another burden. "And what about this: how you think a man feels when his wife thinks she is his 'better'?"

Mary was stunned. "I...I never said that. I don't believe that. Why... how am I your better?"

"And how does a man feel when his own son is supposedly his better?"

Mary could only stare, but now the words stabbed me, too. I remembered Moses' recent praise of me at the moneychangers...of how it turned out I was the one who saved the family's honor and not Joseph. Why hadn't I thought about that? My heart sank for my father.

Mary's eyes filled with tears. I knew that she was feeling what I was feeling. She reached for his hand but he stepped back, slowly.

Joseph was quiet for a long moment. He then sighed. "Woman," he said with a suddenly softer tone. "Just listen to your Story and tell me how you think it makes *me* feel." He then turned away and left my mother clutching her heart.

I crouched close to the ground as my father walked past. I then peeked over the wall and watched my mother fold herself on the ground to pray in a soft song:

"Lord, comfort my husband.

May the peace of Jerusalem fill his soul and

May he prosper in your love.

May there be peace within his defenses

And prosperity inside his fortress;

Bless him with your presence once more.[72]

Listening to her sing calmed my spirit…and calm was something that I sorely needed. You see, by now my brother James had told his friends many of the details that he had heard from behind closed doors. His friends answered that our mother was either a liar or madwoman, and that our father was a poor, suffering soul who had no choice but to protect his wife.

They then pressed me. Shepherds? Magi? Choruses of angels? I had tried to avoid their questions but it seemed that the whole business was becoming great sport in Nazareth. Even my uncle, Zebedee, had become an outspoken skeptic of my mother. I was angry with him for that…but I was also confused because I had always respected Zebedee, even as I had always respected Joseph. How could I respect these men but dismiss their doubts?

Yet, when others repeated the Story back to me, I found it ringing oddly in my own ears. I would listen, blank-faced, as they began reciting the tale of a virgin who conceived without the seed of a man so that I…a simple village boy…could become the Son of Promise…the Messiah…the long awaited King of Israel…

What evidence was there? I could not even save my own sister.

What reason was there to believe any of it other than the word of Mary and the dreams of Joseph? I felt sick.

But then there were those whispers of *El Abba* that would find me from time to time.

---

72 Adapted Psalm 122:6-9

A year later we were finishing our meal of hummus, fish, olives and bread, just after the Sabbath sunset on a warm summer evening in late July. I had eaten little because I was suffering some sort of stomach distress for which my mother's friend, Hannah, had delivered a concoction of herbs.

"They have always weighed heavy on you," said Mary to Joseph. She shifted my little sister, Lydia, on her lap. "If you're right about my father selling, then you've no choice but to dig them up."

"But then what?"

Mary thought for a long moment. "Would you allow Jesus to decide? He is nearly ten years old and you said yourself how much he has grown in wisdom."[73]

Joseph looked at me. "Yes, but he is not yet a man."

Salome served me some bread so I shoved a piece into my mouth, suddenly realizing that they were talking about the coins supposedly given to me at my birth. I groaned, inwardly.

"These are birth gifts to him," said Mary.

Joseph shook his head. "They boast a graven image. We should never have kept them. But they are mine to protect until he is of proper age."

"You could give them to a banker?"

"How would a simple Jew from Galilee explain seven gold coins... *Parthian* coins at that?"

"So what will you do?"

"Dig them up."

"And then?"

"I don't know. But I'm telling you, if Heli sells..."

"We have some time..."

"No, we don't. I saw buyers walking all over his field yesterday. And you know your father."

Hearing them talk like this made me wonder if they were both mad. *Parthian gold coins buried in Grandfather's field? I'd have to touch them to believe.*

"Jesus?" Joseph saw me rolling my eyes.

---

73 Luke 2:40

"Yes, father?"

"What's the matter?"

"Uh…I don't feel well."

He narrowed his gaze. "And?"

"I…maybe you should let me see the coins sometime."

A week later Joseph and I dug up the coins under the cover of darkness. When we returned home my father dropped the seven coins into my opened hands. I stared in near disbelief as they clinked one atop the other. He then waited as I wrestled within myself. I wondered how could anybody deny my mother's Story with these? Of course, some might say they only prove some of it…

"Jesus?"

"Yes?"

Joseph looked at me, sternly. "No one in Nazareth can know about these. No one! And say nothing to James."

I nodded, but I was a little disappointed. I thought the coins might shut the mouths of some of our mockers. But Joseph was right; the coins invited danger so we hid them in the bottom of a large jar of oil in the storeroom guarded by our bedroom.

In the months that followed I spent many an evening thinking about my coins. When everyone was asleep, I would often climb over the others and quietly open the door of the storeroom. Lifting the lid off the jar, I would dip my hand through the oil to feel them on the bottom. Sometimes I'd lift one out and step into the courtyard where I'd hold it up to the moon.

Such a little thing, I thought one night. I held a coin close to my eye and studied it, marveling at the power of the ridiculous image of an emperor in a studded helmet with a wart on his forehead.[74] What was it? Nothing

---

74 Parthian emperor Phraates IV

more than metal mined from the earth by suffering slaves and melted into a yellow circle stamped with a pompous face.

Yet it troubled me, deeply.

Like my father, I was troubled to look upon a graven image, for as you know, such things are forbidden to Jews. But there was more—I was troubled by how the poor coveted coins and how the Temple hoarded them. I hated to hear how merchants cheat for them, how the Herodians murdered for them and how Caesar boasted about them. My grandfather once said that a man's bulging purse means more to him than his bulging loins, and to this day he said that women swoon more for the first than the latter.

So I knew that gold possesses the power to possess men. The coin I held had authority—and yet none of its own; its supposed power is granted by those who call it 'Master.'

Which is why its authority is 'supposed.'

Yet its temptation is great; its jingle sings a sorcerer's song.

But for me the coins, like the Story as a whole, caused yet another distress. Even with the gold in hand, I had been unable to wholly believe. Why? Because I was *unwilling* to believe. After all, a virgin mother, sages from the east, spices for a king, the throne of David,[75] 'A light for the Gentiles?'[76]

Such things were still not easy for me to accept.

But neither was Parthian gold that I could touch on the bottom of an oil jar in Nazareth. Therefore the coins assumed a new power—they urged me to consider my mother with greater confidence.

Still confused, I eventually chose to share the Story with my new teacher, Moses, the trusted scribe of Sepphoris who had helped us with the moneychanger some years before. I should say here that Joseph had talked Moses into beginning my education more then two years before the customary time. He had told Moses of my early training in Egypt with the Therapeutae, of my mother's deep instruction, and of what Joseph saw as 'uncommon wisdom' for a boy my age.

When I first told Moses of my mother's Story, I only mentioned parts of it and so he dismissed me as a bored youth with a strong imagination. So he pressed me harder in my studies to better occupy my mind. But he was secretly curious about what I had said and so he eventually asked about it

75 Luke 1:32
76 Luke 2:32

again. This time I told him more, ending with a confession of my nagging doubts.

He was not pleased to hear what I had told him this time. "Anyone who believes such a tale is treading close to blasphemy!" he said. So, over the next many months, he thought it best to exhaust me with the task of putting to my memory the six hundred and thirteen laws of the rabbis. Shocked that I was somehow able to rejoice in such learning, he then put me to the less pleasurable task of learning to read the Scriptures written in the common Greek by the Seventy. [77]

My lessons required so much attention that I gave no thought to the Story for a very long time, until Moses finally interrupted me one day to ask me about it once more. This I offered with some hesitation. Upon hearing what I said, he became enraged. "If your parents have truly told you this, they are blasphemers! Tell me that you are lying to me!"

"I…I am not…"

"Did your parents truly say these things?"

I nodded.

Moses growled.

I wondered if I should tell him the only part I had left out—the part about the gold. After all, that was the part that anyone could believe because it was the part that anyone could touch. So I did.

When I finished, Moses stared at me for a long, silent moment. "You want me to believe that you have seven Parthian gold coins hidden in your house, and that these were gifts from the East?"

I nodded.

He glared at me. "What am I to do with you?" He began to pace. "Enough of this. I will not insult your parents with your lies, but I will save you from yourself!"

---

77 Greek had become the common language of the eastern Mediterranean world. In the third century before Christ, Jews in Alexandria decided their sacred books should therefore be available to those who were not fluent in Hebrew. A legendary group of scholars called the 'Seventy' undertook the task of translating these texts from Hebrew into common Greek. Over time, this expanding collection became known as 'The Septuagint.' Scholars generally agree that Jesus often quoted from this Greek translation in his teaching.

CHAPTER IX

BELIEF

"Mary, I am sorry for you." My father's eyes were red. "I have no words."

My mother took his hand and sobbed. Her father--my dear grandfather, Heli--had been found dead in his bed.

I stood staring at my mother. Who had more love for another than she? Who gave of herself like she did? To see her suffer another loss was hard for me to watch. I walked to her and held her.

"He loved you, my son," she whispered.

I already missed my grandfather; I loved him more than most people knew. Leaning into my mother, I thought of his long beard and his milky eye; I remembered how his laughter made me happy.

For the next months, I threw myself into my studies as if I could imagine my grandfather looking over my shoulder. This was especially helpful because of my teacher's zeal. Moses had become so extreme that the moment I entered his door he reached for his oak staff. This he would hold over me as he listened to my recitations. Upon missing a word, he would strike me with such force that his dog, Petrus, would whimper and run to a corner.

One of his law students, *Yacob bar Joazar*—the seventeen year old son of a former High Priest—finally begged him to be merciful. But because of the things I had told the rabbi, he was certain that I had come under a spell from the Evil One and so he believed his rod *was* mercy. In fact, because Rabbi Moses loved me he took his rod all the harder to my hands. So I suffered for righteousness sake, and from my suffering I understood why my parents had been so careful about sharing the Story with others.

It is not good to offer that which will not be received.

Such was my life until the end of the Passover that followed my eleventh birthday.

"Boy," said Joseph. "What's wrong with your hands?"

I said nothing. I could see the concern in my father's face as he lifted a lamp in his workshop to better see in the failing light of day.

"Tell me." Joseph noticed that I was struggling to handle a board that I was chiseling. I wasn't sure how to answer him so I said nothing. He cared about me—but so did Moses—and I saw no reason to split the two men over a piece of oak.

Joseph dragged me into the courtyard where my mother was resting. "Mary, look." He grabbed my forearms and held my hands toward her face.

Mother took my hands in hers. "What happened?"

I did not wish to lie to her—for had she ever lied to me? I was suddenly jolted to imagine my mother ever lying to me. No, I could not imagine that. My mind began to spin and I stared into my mother's imploring eyes. They revealed her exhaustion in body and spirit.

"Jesus?"

I hesitated to answer. I was suddenly troubled by the way my mother looked under lamplight. I knew that she had not been feeling well since she had conceived again. And she was still mourning her father. All the while the others had been tugging on her cloak and Joseph needed a wife to be a wife. Yet I knew that something else was making her feet plod heavily to the well each day, and that same 'something' had stolen the bird-song from her voice. Even now she seemed distant and in the grip of some sort of dread.

"Jesus?" Mary again took my hands and kissed them. "You are suffering greatly for the things you learn, aren't you?"

I forced a smile and then turned to Joseph. "Thank you for hiring Rabbi Moses. I have learned much." My words were true, but not only because of the rabbi. During the past year I had noticed what seemed to be another voice behind my teacher's voice, one that filled his words with more--a voice that was awakening the whole of me.

Joseph was pleased. "Now, tell us something you learned today."

I thought for a moment as a soft breeze bent the small flames of the few lamps lighting the courtyard. "Rabbi Moses reminded me that in order to believe in the Lord one had to *stop* believing in His enemies. One could not serve both."

My parents approved, but my own words suddenly cut me. I thought of my mother's many enemies in Nazareth who didn't believe her Story. *Do I believe them or her?* At first, I didn't want to think about it at all. I was tired of the Story and the mocking whispers it invited; I was tired of my father's suffering on the Story's account.

But I quickly recalled the many times and places that Mary had gently tried to teach me more of myself. Whether alongside our first house or sit- ·ting together on the roof of our new one, walking to Japhia for wool, trudg- ing the dusty Sepphoris roadway, or standing in the courtyard not so long before, she had never wavered in her belief of who she claimed me to be. I looked at her again. Her green eyes were steady and sure. I could imagine why her enemies didn't believe her, but how could *I* not believe?

That's when the cut went deeper. I realized exactly what was taking the life from her--it was my unbelief. A chill ran over me. I stared at my mother, deeply troubled by this sudden awareness. *How do I not believe her? Is she a liar? Is she mad? And what of her enemies? Should I stand with them?*

As if she knew what I was thinking, Mary raised my hands to her face and kissed them. Her warm kiss felt suddenly more convincing than the cold touch of Parthian coins. My heart began to beat faster. *Mother cannot both love me and lie to me, and surely, she loves me.* I took a deep breath. *No, my mother is not a liar. But if she is not a liar, could she be mad?* I withdrew my hands, lightly, and struggled for a long moment. Another breeze bent the lamplight and then the wisdom of *Ecclesiastes* came to me:

'The words of the wise *invite grace,*'

But madness is the end of a fool who is devoured by his own lips.[78]

I stared into the love that was Mary's face; *Her words are wise; she is filled with grace*. Nothing in her life showed her to be the fool.

No. Mother is not mad.

Mother Mary waited silently as my spirit wrestled within. Floods of feeling washed through me as these words repeated themselves over and over: *My mother is not a liar and she is not mad.*

A sudden gust spun dust and dried herbs through the courtyard. I heard a whispering in the wind. *El Abba?* As if commanded, I saw a wonderful vision that appeared in the way that a beautiful song might look, or a fragrant horizon might smell. And when it was over my spirit was more content than I had ever remembered.

Filled with this strange peace, I turned to my patient mother. *If she is not a liar and is not mad, then she speaks the truth!* My heart raced to think of it! A light tingling tickled my belly. I smiled. Looking into my dear mother's green eyes, I suddenly *wanted* to believe.

And so I believed; it was a simple as that and yet as difficult at that.

My chin began to tremble. "Mother, I...I believe you. I am who you say that I am," These words no sooner left my lips than my spirit suddenly overflowed with rapturous joy. "*El Abba...HaShem* is my *Abba*!"

Mary's face filled and she trembled as she began to sing,

" 'Give thanks to the God of gods, for his abounding love endures;

There is no Lord but our Lord!

How priceless is your unfailing love." [79]

My face was abruptly lifted to the deepening dark of dusk. There I saw a star fall like lightning—and I was not afraid. [80] Instead, I smiled for I knew that Love had found me.

---

78 From Ecclesiastes 10

79 From Psalms 136:2, Psalms 36:7

80 From Luke 10:18

The joy that my mother and I shared that evening was not for us alone, for Rabbi Isaiah had believed the Story all along and he became delirious with delight when learning of my belief. For this unspoken reason, he encouraged Joseph to take his whole family to Jerusalem for the coming Passover.[81]

Joseph announced the good news to us and said that with good weather, with our donkey Noah, and with a light step we could make the journey in three days. Mary, however—though pleased to go—was uneasy about a 'light stepping' with six children. She reminded my father that our donkey was no Lycanoian [82]and that his step was never light.

"Fine, we'll take four days."

"Five?"

"Mary!"

She laughed. In fact, she could hardly contain her happiness at the thought of introducing all of us to her Bethany relatives—especially her aged cousin Elizabeth, (the widow of Zachariah) and Elizabeth's own son of promise, *Yohanan*.

I decided to take one of my coins with me to offer as my tithe. The night before we left I sewed it carefully in the hem of my robe and hoped no robber would find it. I also hoped that Joseph would not find it, for I doubted that he'd be pleased. Truly, the risk of a Parthian coin in the hand of simple Galileans was great. But images of poor children in the big city of Jerusalem filled my imagination and I knew that my Father's will would be to serve them...even against my father's will.

The next day we began our pilgrimage on a wonderful springtime morning. We were not alone, of course, for the Elders had also approved three other families for the journey and had assigned Israel the olive-merchant to be the 'eye' of our little caravan. This did not please Joseph in the slightest, for broad-girthed Israel was a miserable man with a merciless stride.

"Try to keep up, Joseph," Israel said at the third hour.

---

81 Passover was 28 March in 9AD. Luke 2:41 tells us that Joseph and Mary went to Jerusalem every year for Passover. However, the Law did not require every adult beyond 15 miles to come to do so. Villages often appointed representatives for those who remained behind.

82 Lycanoian donkeys were considered the very best of the times.

Joseph stopped and re-tucked his tunic into his belt. Loins girded, he set his jaw. " 'He who keeps close watch on my path fastens my feet in shackles.'"[83]

I raised my eyes with delight. I still laugh when I think about it!

Israel grumbled and wiped the sweat pouring over his round cheeks. "Just keep your family moving."

"'Then smooth a wide path beneath our feet so that our ankles do not turn.'"[84] Joseph smiled and winked at my mother and then at James.

We all laughed, loudly.

Israel growled. "I am the one to lead us into Jerusalem, builder. If your woman can't move faster I will have to leave you all behind."

Joseph raised his hand. "'Ah, Israel, you have made known to me the path of life; you fill me with the joy of your presence.'" [85]

The whole group from Nazareth howled.

"I will not be mocked! Find your own way." The man spun about, spilling a wallet of coins from his belt. Grumbling a few oaths, he strained over his belly to pick them up and then went his own way.

As you know, the road from Nazareth leads along a stony ridgeline south and into the valley of Jezreel where we walked under the watch of Megiddo with many other happy Jews. Joseph explained how the magnificent expanse now spread before us had been soaked by the blood of Israel's warriors from the days of the kings and prophets.

Excited by my father's teaching, I took some earth into my hand in remembrance of them. As my young hand squeezed the stony soil, my veins began to pulse. I felt the lifeblood of Israel's brave men of old pump through me; I felt the sorrow of her widows fill my throat, and the fear of her orphans made my limbs begin to shake. Surprised by these feelings, I dropped the dirt and stared at the stain it had left on my hand. *What was that?* I asked myself.

Stepping to the side of the ancient roadway, I blinked a few times and took a breath. Curious, I bent down and scooped up another handful of soil. The same feelings came over me but this time I did not fear them. Instead, I closed my eyes to understand them.

---

83 Word play on Job 33:11
84 From Psalms 18:36
85 From Psalms 16:11

In a few moments I opened my eyes to gaze far beyond myself into a horizon that had begun to open. I heard a song from somewhere just beyond my sight and my heart began to race as it had those few times before when my limbs felt warm. The song had a sweet fragrance and I drew it through my nostrils. I listened, carefully, and I began to hear the voice that had filled the words of my teacher.

My eyes opened wider and the blue of the sky filled them. There, in that valley, I felt the presence of *El Abba* again, and so I began to speak to him as if he were Joseph. I walked a short distance from the road and I began telling him of my life--of my confusion and my joy, of my fears and my happiness.

"Jesus!" My mother was calling. James yelled for me. "Jesus. Come on!"

"Coming." I felt my limbs cool and my heart slow, but I knew that my Father was still close. I squatted and spread the dirt from my hand back atop the earth from which it came. I whispered, "Be at peace."

I ran back to my mother and stayed close to my parents as we followed the road. We turned eastward through the center of the valley now blooming eagerly from the generous earth. With bald Mt. Gilboa in far sight, Salome and Lydia took their turn to race ahead. They ran into the fields of wildflowers with a happy crowd of other girls. I watched and smiled as they snatched yellow flowers and blue buds into their tender hands. And then I noticed an older boy make Salome laugh so hard that she fell into green grass...I liked to hear her laugh. His name was *Samuel bar Benjamin* of Cana.

We eventually found ourselves crossing the Jordan and turning south on the busy King's Highway that paralleled the river on its eastern side. Like most, Joseph refused to lead us by the more direct route that ran through Samaria. It seems that good Jews would rather face jackals and hyenas with tar knives and cudgels than the blasphemies of the Samaritans with a prayer! Of course, Joseph said that the heat of the King's Highway during Tabernacles sometimes reversed that sort of thinking!

With our Nazareth brethren out of sight we found ourselves now traveling with strangers for safety's sake. As you already know, to this day bandits fill the stony wadis all along the highway and are eager to pounce. Therefore, no Jew objected to finding protection amongst even Gentiles along that highway. To be sure, most of our fellow travelers were Jews.

Many were from the Diaspora—residents of the far-flung reaches of the Empire such as Ephesus in Phrygia, the busy port of Corinth, or the city of Neapolis near Rome. One was a young merry-maker from faraway Tarraco in Hispania. I liked him very much and I also liked the Gentile guards who accompanied him to protect the strongbox of Temple taxes that he had collected from the synagogues of his home.

Among the other Gentiles were Abyssinians who were trading between Judea and Syria, Babylonian merchants with their fine silk garments and nose rings, thin Nabataeans, and dark-skinned men from Ethiopia. Weighty profits were waiting for these Gentiles when Jerusalem swelled with the feasts. As he had told me in Sepphoris, my father reminded me to not fear the Gentiles, but rather to pity them. After all, *Elohim* had not chosen them to be his people.

Along the way an old Jew named Zebulon from the Babylonian city of Nisibis took an interest in me, insisting that I should know more about who we Jews were. He claimed that he was related to the great rabbi, Hillel, who had once walked from Babylon to Jerusalem with his family.

I smiled, politely.

"I have a brother in a fishing village called Bethsaida by the lake of Gennesaret. His name is Enoch and if you are ever there, seek him out." Zebulon then told me of the mysterious Ur of Abram and of the Land of the Two Rivers, of Nebuchadnezzar, of Daniel, of Jeremiah's lamentations, and of our people's glorious return to the land of promise. He told me that he chose not to live in Jerusalem because he so loved the pilgrimage. "On every journey to Jerusalem I'm able to remember the faithfulness of *El Yisrael,*"[86] he said. "It is in the remembering, Jesus, that we become who we are.

"Anyway, for more then ten years the Babylonians have spread rumors about a new king of the Jews who's been born in Judea. Maybe the Messiah is come!"

I felt a chill. What would this man say if I told him that the rumors *were* true?

Zebulon pointed into the sky. "The moon casts the light of *Torah* so that we can find a path in darkness," he said. "And the stars that follow the

---

86 Hebrew for 'God of Israel'

moon are like the many lessons we sons of Israel teach one another from the Prophets and the Writings.

"In this way we are shown our path under silver light until the Messiah comes. But when Messiah comes…ah…then the moon and the stars will set because he comes as the sun!"

"As the sun?" My ears were piqued. "I thought he would be a king?"

"Listen, boy…he comes as the Light, for it has always been light that gives life to Israel."

That confused me a little but my mind quickly returned me to the little leper girl outside of Sepphoris. I wondered if *I* could be the light to chase her darkness away.

CHAPTER X

UP TO JERUSALEM

Late on the third day, familiar voices called from behind. "Ho, Joseph! Mary!" It was my uncle, Cleopas—Joseph's younger brother, and his wife, Aunt Miriam. Delighted to have them join us, Joseph and my mother ran to them, as did we all.

"Ha, ha!" shouted Cleopas as he embraced my father. "This is a blessing!"

Their company made our steps very much lighter and brought good cheer to my mother. She loved Aunt Miriam dearly and had only ever spoken the name 'Cleopas' with a smile. Both had been kind to Mary from the day her conception of me was announced, so she often visited them at their house in Cana.

As for me, I loved my uncle like no other. It was true that he was a man of many virtues and few vices, but what drew me to him was his odd way of snorting when he was excited...and he was easily excited! A potter by trade, I would visit him as a small boy and he would let me plop wet, heavy lumps of clay on top of his wheel and then pedal a spin. He'd then snort and laugh as red clay flew all over his face and mine. I smile when I think of it, even now.

But there was more. I knew that he—and my aunt—believed everything that my mother had said. Knowing this made me feel even closer to them both. I wondered, however, if my uncle could ever convince my father to abandon the doubts that continued to grow deep within him.

"So boy," Cleopas said. "I'm told that you can recite the Law and the Prophets like no other."

"And the Writings."

He snorted. "We should have a contest."

"No," said my aunt. "You should show more respect than to use them for a contest!"

"There you have it, boy. The Law." He now snorted wildly.

I laughed with him and walked close by his side. Cleopas loved life with a heart as soft as the flat tails of the many sheep he owned. He did, indeed, own some of the best sheep in Galilee and it was not uncommon for rich Jews from as far as Caesarea Philippi and beyond to come and choose fine lambs from his folds for sacrifice. Since he had such remarkable animals, he usually herded dozens to Jerusalem several months before the feasts so that any injuries they suffered along the way would be healed. Thus, his lambs would be 'without spot or blemish,' and suitable for the Temple. For the next hours he taught me all that a man could know about sheep and shepherding.

On the fourth day of our journey the caravan crossed the Jordan and sang its way between the oases around Jericho, past Herod's monstrous palace, and up the gentle rise of the Jericho Road as it led us through the dry Judean desert of our forefathers.

Well before the day's end my father pointed to the eastern slopes of the Mount of Olives that were beginning to burst with color. Soon we were following an ascending curve where I began to feel the delight of my Father and the Spirit. Indeed, my Father's olive trees shaded his terraces in marvelous deep green and silver. Flowers and lush foliage waved lightly under his kind eye. There the Spirit's cool breezes began to refresh me, filling my nostrils with the scents of springtime. I smiled.

Soon, others filled my ears with songs of ascent:

"'I lift up my eyes up to the hills where my help is found.

My help comes from the Almighty,

Creator of heaven and of earth!

He who keeps Israel shall never slumber

and shall never sleep.

Blessed be the name of the Lord!'"[87]

And so we were almost in Jerusalem!

---

87 From Psalms 121

"Jesus?" said Uncle Cleopas.

"Yes?"

"Come with me and help me check on my sheep."

I followed Cleopas to his sheepfold and I looked in awe at his flock. They were beautiful creatures and my uncle loved them. I could not imagine a more kindly, brave, and devoted shepherd then he.

I followed Cleopas as he moved slowly amongst the animals and I could see that his eyes were searching. Then he stopped and pointed. "There. Do you see that one? I've a red cord around his neck."

"Yes. I see him. He is...perfect." The lamb was surely 'spotless and without blemish,' but he was somehow more than that, and I was in wonder of his beauty. I then thought of my Father above and these words came to me:

'We are the people of his pasture,

we are the sheep of his hand...'[88]

Cleopas interrupted me. "I have chosen him for you."

"For me?"

"Yes. He's my gift for your first sacrifice. When we come to take him you will lay your hand on his head and he will be yours."

I looked carefully at the lamb, and as I did the creature lifted his face from green grass to return my gaze. We stared at one another for a long moment and a lump filled my throat. "What shall I name him?"

"Name him?"

"Yes."

My uncle struggled. "He is just a lamb."

"Well, he's not *just* a lamb."

The lamb bleated and scampered away, butting another gently with his head. I followed his every move. "His purpose is to be a servant of the Lord. I will name him, 'Obadiah.'"

Cleopas shrugged and the two of us ran from the green meadow and up the roadway until we spotted Joseph struggling with Noah. "There, ha, look!" Joseph was leaning his shoulder hard against the animal's rump. My mother was rolling her eyes and shaking her head. Cleopas turned to me, howling. "I love the feasts!"

---

88 Psalms 95: 7

Before long, our group rounded the Mount's curve of descent. I could feel the excitement racing through my body. Joseph stopped us behind a screen of a budded shrub where I felt Cleopas' big hand suddenly cover my eyes from behind. I was surprised.

"Can you see, Jesus?"

"No. Nothing."

Cleopas snorted twice, then a third time.

I was excited, too. *Jehovah-Jireh,* City of David! I think I may have snorted, myself.

Joseph then laid a hand on my shoulder and sang with my mother, each in turn:

"I rejoiced with those who said to me, 'Let us go to the Lord's house.'
> Our feet are standing at your gates, O Jerusalem.

May those who love you be safe;
> May there be peace within your walls." [89]

Eyes still covered, I was led down the road a bit farther until Joseph and Cleopas turned my shoulders and eased me on to a flat ledge. I felt my father lay a heavy cloth over my head; it was the prayer shawl made for my manhood by the Therapeutae and kept safely by my mother through my childhood years. I thought of the sisters and their round table and their lake. I felt goodness fill me. My heart was beating; I could feel others pressing close around me. My mother began to softly sing:

"He will see the good light of life;
> His offspring shall prosper,
>> And the will of the Lord shall multiply in his hand."

It was then when Cleopas removed his hand from my face. I squinted for a moment. And then I saw. And I marveled.

And I wept.

From my vantage on the ledge I scanned the magnificent panorama that lay under my eyes. Before me was spread a blazing bronze cast of towers and walls, lit by a sun now hanging proudly in the western sky. Jerusalem...

---

89 Adapted from Psalms 122

the fortress of my Father's Kingdom! The city sprawled over the mounts of Zion and Moriah, Acra and Bezetha, dotting hillside and hollow with terraces, palaces, colonnades, and high towers that reached toward heaven. Jerusalem, O Jerusalem! She shined beneath me like a finely cut jewel, her stunning Temple gleaming with a white brilliance that filled me with wonder.

Cleopas stood beside me as I stretched my arms outward as if to embrace the glorious city; I wanted to feel her heartbeat; I wanted to be embraced by her. I sang, loudly:

"All who pass near clap their hands at you,
O Jerusalem; this is the city called the perfection of beauty
and the joy of the earth." [90]

A warm gust took the shawl off my head, gently. I picked it up and as I did I noticed Cleopas leaving me so that he could join my family along the roadway. I looked into their faces. They seemed peaceful and happy for me.

It was then that I heard the hewn rocks of Jerusalem's mighty walls and the stones of her surrounding hillsides begin to sing. I covered my head and turned to listen. Their song was beautiful; it was pure. It was *for me*! I did not fully understand it then, but they sang for me the Song of Truth. Their music echoed from hillside to wall to valley and height where the hillsides sang of sorrow, for sorrow is true—and of joy, for joy is likewise true; they sang of dread and of hope and of triumph—and of their redemption. For these things are all true within the will of my Father.

My spirit soared and I opened my arms. *El Abba* felt suddenly so close that it was as if he were standing by my side. I thought I could feel his breath in the breeze; I thought I could hear his voice over the song of the stones.

He had come to me and I was beginning to remember.

I fell to my knees. "Tell me what to do," I whispered. I looked to my parents. Oh how I loved them. They were still smiling at me, yet they now seemed suddenly apart from me—not torn away as if we no longer belonged to one another, but separated like a branch from its fruit. I reached an arm toward them, but they did not move.

So I stood and returned my eyes to my Father's city. I listened and I heard the mighty stones of the Temple begin to whine in pain, and the

---

90 From Lamentations 2:15

hills answer with calm assurance. The lonely rocks of the valleys' beds then clamored to be heard and the tiled rooftops echoed their impatience.

I raised my arms and shouted the words that I thought I could hear my Father saying: "*Shalom*, Jerusalem. In the fullness of time all will be well with you."

At that moment, the pebbles beneath my feet began to hum in such a way as I could feel their delight and I knew that hope was welcome...I knew that *I* was welcome.

I then filled my chest and I sang to them all a song of my own:
"Shout for joy, O heavens, rejoice, O earth;
Burst into song, O Mountains![91]
For the Lord reigns, let all the earth be glad;
Blessed be the name of Lord, forever;
May his Kingdom come."

We descended the mount quickly toward the Kidron Valley that separated us from Jerusalem's eastern wall. As we walked I lifted my nose to smell the musty air of the rocky valley. I turned my face into the mysteries of its shadowed depths and studied the rugged course of the muddy brook far below. Mary reminded all of us of how King Asa burned the idols here-[92]and about the day that King David crossed the polluted waters barefoot and weeping.[93] She told us of the terrible things that this tiny stream swept away from the Holy City when it became a torrent of winter rains. She then pointed to the many sepulchers beneath our feet and told of how they had been carefully whitewashed just weeks before the feast.

I would have stared longer into that place—I felt it drawing me. But Joseph commanded we keep moving. So we followed the wall toward the Water Gate on the south side where we entered. The heaving throng of people jostled us so badly that Joseph told me to watch out for Salome and

91 From Isaiah 49 and Psalms 97
92 See I Kings 15
93 See 2 Samuel 15

Lydia. "Your mother is tired and she has your brothers. And I don't have eyes in the back of my head. So we're trusting you!"

But I was tired, too, and I certainly didn't want to turn my eyes away from the exciting new sights around me. So I came up with a plan that my sisters later teased me about. In fact, in the years that followed they would tell others of it in order to prove how strange they thought I could be!

I took little Lydia by the hand, but I told Salome to walk behind me and shout out from time to time. "Say, 'I'm here,' and then I don't have to keep turning around." So as I reveled in the bustling color all around me, my sister would cry out, "This is Salome and I'm here! I'm here!" I still laugh about that.

Eventually, our company squeezed through the gate and into the Lower City where shouts of greeting and joyful chatter filled the air. Happy to be re-united, Jews from the far-flung edges of the empire were running to kiss one another. Black robed Jews from Babylon embraced Phoenician Jews in their striped drawers; Anatolians in their goats' hair cloaks ran to greet their Persian brethren adorned in silk.

We pressed our way past the Pool of Siloam and deeper into the poor neighborhoods that covered the slopes of Acra with modest little houses. The streets of this Lower City were named for their gates or the many loud bazaars that filled busy squares in the marvelous maze. We jostled our way along Fish Street for a time, then turned on Bread Street, then to Fig Bazaar, then Stranger's Street and so on. Whatever the street, the scene became ever more noisy. It was wonderful!

However, the push and pull of beast and man, and the complaints of my brothers soon had my mother ill-tempered. When she heard Salome crying out her name, Mary took hold of my ear and gave it a good twist.

"Ouch!"

"You think you're clever? That's not how you watch your sister. I should have kept them both with me. How would you feel if Salome got lost?"

Joseph finally gathered us in the shade of a merchant's booth and kissed my mother on the cheek. "We'll be there soon, woman, soon." He then led us into the wealthier streets of the Upper City that occupied Mount Zion and what you all must know as 'The City of David.' Here was an equally enthusiastic press of people, though dressed better and mixed with lavishly bejeweled Gentile visitors.

Mother felt out-of-place there, as did Aunt Miriam, but the rest of us were delighted to greet these proud Judeans! We answered them in our crude Galilean accents and then laughed loudly as they turned away.

Joseph led us along the white marble blocks of Tailors' and Silver Street. I marveled at the strength and beauty of the houses and public buildings. These were of cedar and marble, fine tile and designs that were pleasing to the eye. We eventually crossed the nearly impassable intersection of Theater and Market, then up Wool Street until we finally arrived at the door of a red-roofed house that occupied a comfortable place in the northern section of the Upper City.

My other grandfather—Joseph and Cleopas' father, *Jakob bar Matthan*[94]--had a cousin named Isaac who enjoyed a prosperous trade in metals. He had recently bought the house and dutifully shared from his good fortune. As we waited for the door to open, my mother said to me, "Isaac is the only successful relative of your father other than Cleopas. The rest are more like your grandfather. He lived in Bethlehem where you were born, Jesus."

Isaac's door opened. "Joseph! Cleopas! Come, come."

The man and his wife greeted us each with a kiss and we were soon resting comfortably in the courtyard. A servant served us cool drinks recently delivered from a pure-water well and some roasted nuts. After reading some Psalms and offering a prayer, Isaac then provided us with a delicious meal followed by some sticky honeycomb. It was a wonderful welcome to my Father's city.

---

94 Matthew 1:15. A word about the genealogies of Jesus: A son could have two lineages, a legal one and a blood one. In Jesus' case, the genealogy that Matthew seems to report is the legal line that follows Joseph, his legal father. This meant that Jesus was a rightful heir to Joseph's inheritance, et al. Luke, however, appears to report the blood line of Mary, having first recognized Joseph in his marital position as son-*in-law* to Jesus' maternal grandfather, Heli.

CHAPTER XI

OBADIAH

A few nights later...long after the trumpets had sounded the setting sun, I lay in bed with my three brothers and smiled. The sights of Jerusalem had been more than my mind could contain. The sheer size of the place and the noises and the smells had made me dizzy. It seemed that people filled every crevice, and not just my people, but Gentiles from every corner of Caesar's empire. I remembered the feeling of Isaiah's words: 'Joy of mine, pride of mine, Jerusalem...'[95]

The dawn to come would bring the Passover. *I* had been chosen to enter the Temple with Joseph to bring the sacrifice on behalf of our family. I had been spellbound by the Temple's magnificence earlier, but to be inside... to walk past gawking Gentiles and cross the Wall of Partition with my lamb, as they could not. To step boldly and freely into the Court of the Priests...oh, how glad I was to be a son of Abraham! My mind also filled with images of the supper that would follow. Isaac said that I was to be the one to bless the first cup of wine.

I suddenly wondered if Isaac knew anything of our Story. If he did, was he a believer? He seemed welcoming enough. And he did offer me the honor of the first cup. I smiled.

And there was more that kept me awake that night. *Yohanan bar Zachariah* (John to you, dear Brennus), and his mother, Elizabeth, would

95 Inspired from Isaiah 60

also be at Isaac's table. I had longed to meet John for many years, for he, too, was said to be a son of promise.

I had often wondered if he believed.

At cockcrow Joseph hurried me to Cleopas' sheepfold near the base of the Mount of Olives. We had almost arrived when I heard a sound like thunder run through Kidron. Joseph raised his hand and listened. "When the priest atop the pinnacle sees the sun crest over the mountains of Moab, he'll signal others to hammer a huge shield of bronze. The new day made official, the Levites will then open the Nicanor Gate that opens to the Court of Priests and the altar."

My heart raced with excitement. Joseph enjoyed my enthusiasm and wrapped a loving arm over my shoulders. He then proceeded to instruct me on the complicated rules affecting the Sabbath when a feast falls upon it like it had in this year.

My mind whirled. "But I'm not quite thirteen."

Joseph laughed. "We Galileans don't mind easing the rules just a bit!" [96]

In the dim light of dawn, one of the shepherds moved aside from the entrance to Cleopas' rented fold and I found my Obadiah resting atop folded legs near the pen's far side. I walked slowly to him and gently tethered a lead rope around his neck. I stood and he stood, and I laid my hand upon his head. He was mine.

Smiling proudly, Joseph then led us away from the mount, back through the Kidron Valley and to the eastern gate where we squeezed through a thickening crowd of men and sheep. We pressed our way toward

---

96 Galileans were famously more casual about ritual and rule keeping than were the Judeans, at least in the minds of the Judeans. Of particular interest, however, is the fact that Joseph is referred to by Matthew as a 'righteous' man--typically used to describe a person who is known for honoring the Law. Yet Joseph did *not* impose the Law on Mary when he first learned of her pregnancy (Matthew 1:19). No doubt Matthew recognized Joseph's greater righteousness in following the spirit of the Law over the letter.

the colonnades of Solomon's Portico and then hurried into the huge Court of the Gentiles. "Jesus, stay close."

I was nervous. I clutched my lamb's tether as I was jostled through the bustling courtyard until I finally lifted him into my arms. I then took my place alongside Joseph at a rather great distance from the twelve steps leading to the wide Susa Gate that separates the children of Abraham from those who were not.

Joseph was disappointed, for the priests had put us in the third and final division of the day. Our wait would be long and we would need to be patient as those who had gone before us offered their sacrifices.[97]

The hours passed slowly, yet I remained excited, as did my father. But by noon we had both grown weary of standing in the huge courtyard and we were especially annoyed with the ceaseless cries of priests selling lambs and doves in the courtyard, and of the profiteering moneychangers who occupied its edges. I took a long draught from my water-skin and shared some with the lamb. The animal was tired and anxious; I felt such compassion for him.

Finally, the Beautiful Gate was shoved open and our group poured into the Court of Women, only to now wait in front of the fifteen curved steps leading to the towering Nicanor Gate. From the other side—from within the Court of Priests where stood the altar and the Holy of Holies—we could hear trumpets and the singing of the *Hallel*. The smoke of sacrifice billowed into a cloud above our heads.

"Soon, my son."

I nodded. My heart was racing again.

"You do remember what I told you?"

I did. He had given me careful instructions about how to sacrifice the animal, and how the priest would collect its blood in two bowls and so forth. At last, the final massive gate was pushed open and I hoisted my lamb to my shoulders. The impatient third division now jostled and elbowed its way through the towering entrance, through the Court of Men, and into the priest's courtyard.

I struggled to see over the shoulders of others. I wanted to finally rest my eyes on the altar standing somewhere before me. But my eyes began to

---

97 An astonishing number of sacrifices were made at the major feasts. According to Josephus, the number of lambs slain at one Passover exceeded 200,000.

sting from the smoke that filled the whole courtyard and my nostrils burnt with the smells of burning fat and entrails.

"Jesus!" Joseph shouted. "Come, come." He was so proud.

With the lamb still on my aching shoulders, I moved toward the double row of blood-splattered priests where I'd wait my turn. But it was there when my thoughts turned to the deep-red blood that covered everything. It was smeared thick and sticky under my sandals. It hung on man and marble, everywhere congealing into droplets and blotches. It flowed sluggishly through the veins cut deep into the marble floor. I could smell blood and dung—life turned into death. It was a horrible stench and I suddenly wanted to vomit.

Joseph urged me closer so I shuffled forward. But now I was hesitant. I could plainly hear the priests' prayers being chanted. I could see their bloodied faces beneath their turbans; their beards were matted thick and even dripping. I turned my head from side to side. The whole court was filled with the sounds of trumpets and prayers, the roar of the altar's terrible flames and of bleating lambs.

My ears collected a song of sorrow; Death was all around me. The delight I saw in the faces of others confused me. Truly, this was nothing like the glorious images I had heard about. Instead, I asked myself, *What kind of joy comes from this bloody pit of death?* I felt an urge to turn away but I obediently followed my father's voice and inched ever more slowly toward the priest who would take my lamb.

Obadiah now squirmed on my shoulders. I could feel the heat of his belly on the nape of my neck. I then felt warm urine suddenly run through my shawl and under my tunic. A lump filled my throat as I tightened my grip around his legs. I knew he was terrified—lambs can smell death.

Finally, Joseph bade me step up to our priest. Knowing, Obadiah released his bowels and wet dung slid down my shoulder and arm. *What sort of glory is this?* I closed my eyes so that I would see no more. I wondered how it was that this greedy slaughterhouse purified anything? How was it that this stench and these rivers of blood bring joy to my Father?

At that moment I felt a sudden and deep hatred rise within me such as I had never felt before. I hated the evil corruption that the Serpent had spawned in my Father's good Creation; I hated death with all that was within me. Standing there, I remembered dear Assia and I vowed that I would somehow defeat this darkness and the many sorrows its deceits had delivered to the house of Israel.

But I also wondered about a Father who was thought to need this butchery.

I began to tremble but Joseph was smiling, proudly. I watched him speak into our priest's ear. The old man likewise smiled. "Put the lamb down, Jesus, and bring him to me," the priest said.

I nodded, sadly. I lowered Obadiah from my shoulders and set his feet on the floor. No sooner had he felt his footing than he lunged forward as if he might escape. My heart leapt with joy as I suddenly imagined him free! But the priest snagged him by the ear and jerked him backward. Ordering me to hold him firmly, the priest quickly inspected him by skillfully running his fingers through Obadiah's wool as he searched for broken bones. There were none, of course. Then he surveyed him for any blemish. "Good, very good."

Joseph was pleased. The priest then handed him the knife and he, in turn, gave it to me along with the same instructions he had given me along our journey. "At the third blast of the trumpets, draw your blade quick and deep."

The priest took Obadiah's tether from my hand indifferently and tied an end to a ring fixed in the marble slab. He then squatted in front of me and held a bowl in both of his hands beneath Obadiah's throat—one golden and one silver. I knew that once the bowls filled with blood he would pass them up a long row of other priests toward the one who would sling them into the fires of the altar.

I took a quaking breath and then obediently grabbed a handful of wool from the back of my lamb's head. I pulled his head backward to expose his throat to the sharp edge of my knife. The blood-covered priest nodded, approvingly. At any moment silver trumpets would sound their three-fold blast and I would slay my trembling sacrifice.

My heart pounded in my heaving chest. I knew that the color had left my face. I looked about anxiously to see hundreds of others poised for the trumpets. More thousands of men waited their turns behind me. I glanced at Joseph. His chest lifted. But my racing heart then chased my mind to consider differently what I was doing. To Joseph's surprise and the priest's, I lowered my blade and knelt by the lamb. I looked deeply into my Obadiah's wide eye where I saw my own reflection. A chill came over me.

There I was, a vision of myself in the lamb's eye even as he must have been in mine. All things around me quickly fell away. I looked yet deeper into his eye and there I saw a green pasture and a cool spring; I saw him nuzzling his resting mother and then frolic away under a kind sun. A shepherd walked slowly toward the spring and cupped a cool drink. He was strong but gentle; I knew by the way he moved that he loved peace. [98]

"Jesus!" Joseph's voice startled me.

The window of Obadiah's eye closed. "Yes? Yes, father?"

"Are you ready?"

My hand trembled. I turned my face to the Holy of Holies rising behind the angry altar and closed my eyes. I remembered a recitation from the prophet Isaiah:

'The wolf will live with the lamb...they will neither harm nor destroy on all my holy mountain, for the earth will be filled with the knowing of the Lord, even as the waters cover the sea.'[99]

My mind crowded with tumbling thoughts. *Have my people not learned enough from this bloodletting? When will it all be finished?* I stood and blurted, "Tell me, where is mercy in this place?"

The priest gawked. Before he could answer, the trumpets blasted and a great cry rose up around me as the others praised the Lord. Throats were cut; blood flowed.

I did nothing.

"Now!" shouted Joseph from behind.

The rising song of *Hallel* filled the court and the other priests sang, "'O, servants of Jehovah...'"

And the people answered, loudly, *'Hallelu Jah!'*

My priest scolded me. "Slay him!"

I said nothing; I did nothing. I listened for *El Abba* to tell me what to do.

Joseph shook me by the shoulder. "Do it, Jesus. Now!"

From behind, voices were rising against me. The impatient priest shouted, "Honor your father."

I answered with sudden confidence. "I *am* honoring him. My Father has already spoken: 'I desire loving mercy, not sacrifice.'"[100]

---

98 Allusion to Psalm 23

99 Isaiah 11, excerpted

100 Hosea 6:6

Baffled, the priest stood and looked sternly at Joseph. "You?"

Now Joseph could only stare.

The priest then answered my words quickly, likewise with Scripture: " 'Their burnt offerings and their sacrifices will be acceptable on my altar, for my house will be called a house of prayer...' "[101]

I wrapped myself around my lamb, raising my chin and answering with a hint of defiance: " 'What are your sacrifices to me? So says the Lord. I have more than enough of burnt offerings; I do not pleasure in the blood of bulls and lambs and goats!' " [102]

The exasperated priest turned to his waiting brethren who were whispering to one another. Finally, he turned squarely to Joseph. "Enough. I will finish this."

Joseph's jaw was clenched and he jerked me away from my Obadiah. With a grunt, the priest then grabbed hold of my lamb's head and with one swift motion, sliced his throat, cleanly.

Crying out, I fell to my knees and stared into Obadiah's eye as he tipped slowly forward toward the cups now catching his spurting blood. Gasping, my lamb then collapsed into the blood-tide covering the stone courtyard. I tried to comfort him with the press of my hands on his body. His eye fast faded. In mere moments it just stared back at me, blank and lifeless, all light gone, all life gone.

And I wept for him, loudly.

---

101 Isaiah 56:7

102 Isaiah 1:11

CHAPTER XII

SONS OF PROMISE

Joseph was outraged. After Obadiah was flayed and after his entrails and fat had been burned on the altar, he angrily shoved a pomegranate spit through the remaining carcass. He commanded that we each put an end of the spit on a shoulder and Joseph draped the lamb's bloody fleece over my other shoulder. It would be a gift to Isaac, our host.

We walked in silence, but once out of the Temple Joseph scolded me about my shaming of him and our family. I listened quietly and I understood. Honor, as you know, is what matters to a good Jew—that and purity—and Joseph was a good Jew. Yet I was a good Jew, too. I thought it not dishonoring to either of my fathers to look beyond what *had been* and toward what *was meant to be.*

I didn't know why I felt this way, but I did not believe that I had been disobedient to my Father. Indeed, it was a sense of obedience to him that had me pause to absorb the whole of what was happening...and to then doubt...

...and then to imagine something better.

Nevertheless, poor Joseph had not been given such sight and so he could only see shame in a son whom he now called disobedient, strident, and in one devastating moment in the shadow of the city's theater, wicked.

I later learned he was furious with himself for not keeping to our customs as precisely as some said he should, and he was furious with Cleopas

91

for talking him into letting me enter the Court of Men a few months before I was really a man.

And he was surely angry with me.

We walked on through the streets of Jerusalem. Believing he had spent his anger, I finally answered, gently. "Father, I'm sorry that you think me wicked, but I am not wicked."

Joseph said nothing.

"Yet I hope you will forgive me for making you think that I am."

Joseph stopped walking. He shifted the spit to his other shoulder, as did I...also switching the fleece. "Forgive you, Jesus?"

I nodded.

Joseph spat. "Who am *I* to forgive *you*, the Promised One?" His tone had a bite and I was saddened.

We walked on in silence but as we rounded a vacant corner Joseph stopped again. He was still agitated and barely able to speak. "Let me tell you something, Jesus. Listen well. I know what I *think* the angel said and I have accepted that for all these years. But it might have been nothing more than the simple dream of a wounded youth." He turned his face from me. "Zebedee thinks I dreamt what I wanted to believe. He may be right; I too often think of what I want to be and not of what is."

My heart sank. "So, father, who do you say that I am?"

To that, the man retched thirteen years and three months of suffering, ending with the most painful of all his doubts: "I don't know."

I bit my lip so hard that it began to bleed. A man ought not cry, I thought. But was I a man? Yet I was also suddenly angry. I mustered my courage. "This means that you believe that my mother—your wife—is a whore and either a liar or mad."

Joseph said nothing. It was as if the demons that had crowded his belly had finally exhausted him. His eyes reddened and he turned his face away.

I felt compassion for him but I pressed. "If you don't believe your wife, what do you say about the coins? Are they a dream at the bottom of a jar?"

He did not say another word. Instead he thrust his jaw forward and led me to the house of Isaac.

My mother was waiting happily in Isaac's courtyard with several other resting women, including my Aunt Miriam. They were laughing and enjoying a basket of sweet Passover figs and their host's expensive beer from Media.

Joseph and I delivered the carcass to two of the women who were charged with roasting it. They quickly hung the pomegranate spit on the two forked stakes standing on either side of a hot heap of wood and glowing ash.

"So, Jesus!" clapped my mother. "Tell us of the day! Your first sacrifice!" She giggled. I knew how excited she was for me and how good she felt to be resting comfortably at a feast in Jerusalem.

I groaned and forced a smile, then presented Isaac's wife with the lamb's fleece. I returned to my mother, but Joseph waved me away with his hand. I understood and I faded into a shaded corner.

Joseph took my mother by the elbow and hurried her into one of Isaac's storerooms where he spoke too loudly of the day's events. The other women were quick to shuffle within earshot of the doorway. My poor mother emerged from the storeroom sobbing with Joseph on her heels. As she rushed past me, she nodded sympathetically and then I heard her say to Joseph that 'the spear continued to pierce her soul.'[103] The prophet, Simeon, had pronounced this warning to her forty days after my birth.

As Mary disappeared into our upstairs bedchamber, a huddling group of women surrounded my Aunt Miriam. They had overheard enough of Joseph's words to raise many questions. My poor aunt tried her best to protect my family, but her spare answers were not enough. Soon she found herself drawn closer to the edges of our Story. I need not tell you that a hint of fornication and the words, 'Son of Promise' were enough for the women to run to tell their husbands, leaving Miriam alone to wring her hands.

In mere moments, the whole of Isaac's household began pouring from their rooms and into the courtyard, driving my poor mother in front of them. She and my siblings then flew to Joseph's side as Isaac stormed toward the man with a wagging finger.

"Tell me, Joseph. Tell me with your own lips the truth about this boy of yours. Who is he to you?"

Even as he cast a fixed eye at me, he set his own struggle aside and answered boldly. "He is my son." Yet, despite the clarity in his voice I knew

---

103 Luke 2:35

that something had changed. Yes, he stood against Isaac as the honorable head of our household. But I could feel in the depths of my being that his struggle had finally overwhelmed him; he needed to release me. For him I was either whom Mary said I was, or I was the son of another man. Either way, for Joseph I would now and forever be simply the son of Mary. Knowing this, I grieved for him and I vowed to love him all the more.

Joseph's stubborn reply furrowed Isaac's brows. "And you've no more to tell?" said Isaac. "Are you guilty of fornication? Or is this boy another man's seed?"

Joseph said nothing.

"And what is the silly claim about a son of promise? Whose promise?"

Joseph remained silent.

Red-faced, Isaac turned on my mother. "Woman?"

"You will speak only to me, Isaac," barked Joseph.

The old man growled. "Then neither of you will answer?"

Joseph said nothing.

"Are you afraid?"

Joseph said nothing.

"Answer me!"

Joseph said nothing. And I saw power in his silence.

"What do you mean, 'Son of Promise?'" Isaac shouted. I thought the old man might fall to the ground and beat the earth. But he was a shrewd man and he knew how to loosen Joseph's iron jaw. As if his heart had been suddenly touched from above, Isaac grabbed hold of his robes in feigned sorrow and bent low. "Joseph, I see now that I have treated you and the woman with disrespect on this holy day. Do you forgive me?"

Joseph squirmed. He cast an uncertain glance toward Mary and shuffled on his feet. How could he not forgive the man? He hesitated. Finally he said, "Yes, Isaac, I do."

"Ah, then I rejoice!" Isaac stood upright and laid a hand on his heart. "Surely, you must understand my shock of hearing that your dear wife claims Jesus to be…well, what was it that Miriam said? Jesus is Messiah?"

Joseph said nothing.

Isaac took Joseph by the shoulders and smiled, broadly. "If her words are true, then praise the God of Israel!" He turned to his guests, now numbering twenty-two. "Shall we not sing the *Hallel*!" Now the guests were shuffling and facing the stone slabs of his courtyard. "But what's this? What's this? You all look troubled."

He turned to Joseph. "Oh, dear nephew of mine, what am I to do? My other guests are now confused by Mary's claim." He began to groan. "Now am I a man most confounded in his own house. Please, dear Joseph, can you not find it in your heart to help us understand?"

Joseph stared at his sandals, paralyzed.

Mary stepped from his side. "My husband is an honorable man, Isaac."

"Woman, be silent. Your husband says he speaks for you." Isaac turned to Joseph. "Yes, this is best. So tell us then, Joseph, is it true that Mary spoke these things? Has she ever said that Jesus is a son of promise?"

"Yes."

Isaac tapped a finger on his chin. "Then if it is true that she said these things, are these things true? Is this Jesus...this boy who would not obey his own father in the Temple...some sort of prophet? Is he really the Messiah?" The man laughed, lightly.

Joseph said nothing.

Isaac then scowled and the circle gathered closer. The old man leaned close to Joseph's face so that their beards touched. "What say you?" he hissed.

I wanted to weep for my father. He backed up and looked from face to face. "I...I..." He finally settled his weary eyes on Mary. Hers were filled with tears; she held her clasped hands at her chin, anxiously. The honorable man then answered and he answered honorably, his eyes not moving from my mother's. "I say...I say that I would be happy for it to be true."

The circle gasped. Isaac stiffened. He clutched his robe with two fists. "Do you realize that this lie, this illusion...this madness that she claims makes any who believe to be blasphemers! Are you a blasphemer against the Most High, Joseph? Is she? Is Jesus? And what of your other children?"

Cleopas could remain silent no longer. He bravely burst from the circle. "Hear me, Isaac...hear me, all of you! I believe this woman, I believe every word she speaks." The people gasped. "Look at the boy." He pointed a shaking finger at me. "He is the Messiah!"

Isaac could bare no more. He fell to his knees and tore his fine robe, then tossed dust over his head as he wept to God. When he finished wailing and had beaten his breast to bruising he stood, now weeping false tears. He cleverly embraced Joseph and Cleopas. "On this Sabbath I will show compassion on whom I will show compassion; I will be merciful to whom I will be merciful. I only pray that your household will soon be set free from this…this madness, this confusion." He kissed my father and my uncle. "Enough of this. Come, come all of you into my upper chamber and recline with me, for soon the sun will be set and we shall remember what the Lord has done."

As the *shofar* sounded over the city, old Isaac began assigning places. But he would not look at either my mother or me, and neither would Joseph who was still reeling from the painful events of this hard day.

"No, Joseph, I cannot…I will not sit at this table." Mary withdrew into her guest room with my youngest sister, Lydia.

I knew that I was unwelcome at Isaac's table and I could see that my presence would be a distraction for the others who genuinely wanted to celebrate the goodness of my Father. So I also left the room and hurried down the stairs. I walked across the courtyard, pulled open Isaac's heavy door, and sat on the street with my back against the outside wall. In truth, I was happy to be away from the misery.

I had barely settled myself, however, when the kindly voice of an old woman turned my head upward.

"Are you Jesus, son of Mary?" She and a small company of five were standing in front of Isaac's door under torches. They were well dressed and joyful.

"I am." I stood.

The old woman smiled and embraced me. She was ancient and frail and shorter than me, yet I could feel strength in her arms. "I thought so. And why are you out here?"

I wasn't sure how to answer. "You must be my mother's cousin, Elizabeth."

"I am." She introduced three younger women, an elderly male cousin from her father's side, and then a youth. Laying a hand on the youth's shoulder she said, "So, Jesus, who do you think this might be?"

I knew it had to be *Yohanan*, the son of Zachariah about whom I had heard so much. He was a bit taller than me and had black eyes and black hair. He looked powerful and intense. "You are John!" He laughed and we embraced with a kiss on each cheek.

Strangely, when our cheeks touched, my ears filled with the cry of a lone crow. This unsettled me and I pulled away to study him. I thought him to be handsome…indeed, more pleasant to look upon than me, to be sure. He was strong and bold, yet distant. But why the sound of a crow…?

"I have heard of you, *Yeshua*. I know your Story well," John said.

The sounds of the crow faded. "And I know yours. But you might not want to talk about it in there." I tossed my head toward the door and smiled.

"Well then," interrupted Elizabeth. "Shall we go in? I smell the lamb roasting and we are late. An old woman travels slowly."

I hesitated.

"So, Jesus, this day was your first sacrifice?" She knocked on Isaac's door. "You and your father must be so pleased."

I said nothing.

"Today was John's as well. He bought a fine lamb from your uncle's fold. He was in the second division."

I nodded.

Isaac's wife threw open her husband's door with little grace. "Elizabeth. You are finally here."

I watched as the old woman, my cousin, and the others with them entered Isaac's door. As for me, I returned to my place on the street.

Long before the Passover supper had ended, John burst out of the house and sat down hard on the street beside me. He handed me a piece of unleavened bread. "This is from Salome."

I was hungry and gladly took it. "What happened?"

John grumbled, loudly. "A curse on this house."

I prayed over the bread quickly, then broke a piece off and put it in my mouth. "A curse?"

John's eyes flashed. "'May the Lord pay them back what they deserve, for what their hands have done.

Put a veil over their hearts, Lord,

and may your curse be on them!

Pursue them in anger and destroy them

From under your heavens!'"[104]

I bit off another piece of bread, chewed it, then swallowed. "I wouldn't judge them too harshly, John."

My cousin spat. "After I prayed the blessing of the first cup, everybody passed the bowl to wash our hands and that's when my mother asked Joseph whether Mary was ill. He shook his head but Cleopas complained, 'she is exiled from the table that celebrates the end of exile!' To which Isaac, that puffed up old cock, replied, 'This is a day of trouble, and of rebuke, and of blasphemy.'[105] So I said, 'What blasphemy?' The old man shrugged and turned away from me. I was not happy about that so I asked, 'What does this have to do with Mary?'

"Isaac then ordered me to 'say no more!' He then went about the business of the table, splashing the herbs in salt water, mumbling, then shoving them into his mouth and passing them on. Then, as the first dishes were being removed, my mother asked him about Mary again.

"Isaac ignored her and told your brother, James, to recite the Passover questions with your father. And just so you know, I don't like your brother very much."

Ha! Oh, that made me laugh!

"Then," John continued, "as the dishes were being returned by the women, my mother asked for Mary a third time. Isaac could not keep the cork in his mouth any longer, so he began to shout about your mother and her claim, and he cried words against you and your shaming of Joseph in the Temple. My mother who knows and believes the whole of your Story got up and left the table to find your mother. So I left, too."

I was sad.

"I tell you, *Yeshua*, that man is not worthy to be called a Jew. He acts like some Roman senator..."

---

104 Lamentations 3:64-66

105 From 2 Kings 19:3

"I think he truly loves the God of Abraham."

John grunted. After saying nothing for a time, he then muttered, "I'm sorry, *Yeshua*."

"For what?"

"I should never have offered the first cup of blessing. It was an honor prepared for you, not me."

"Don't be sorry. My grandfather, Heli, used to say 'all is as it is meant to be.' If that cup was for me I would have held it, but you held it and so it was meant for you. It was a good thing, John, for you come before me. Besides, you're thirteen...you're an official 'man.'" I laughed.

We then sat quietly. I remember looking right and left along Wool Street and imagining the many suppers being enjoyed. My eyes fell to some dancing shadows. I thought some woman must have moved across her candle-lit window with a bowl of sop or a plate of herbs or a basket of unleavened bread. Judging by the likely time, I guessed that for some the second serving of bread and herbs were being eaten. For others, boys were asking and answering the questions, and for yet others the time was come for another hand washing. For most the lamb had already been eaten, the third cup of wine had been passed, and the song of the fourth cup was about to be sung.

Then something occurred to me: my Obadiah, the Temple ceremonies—the whole of Passover—were supposed to be symbols through which Israel might believe in my Father's love. But did my people see his love... or had they come to believe in these things as symbols of something else? Had they claimed a power of their own?

I spoke of this to John and he listened, carefully. "Israel would do well to hear you. But she is not ready."

I nodded. "And neither am I."

CHAPTER XIII

CLIMBING STEPS

Eventually, John bade me to walk with him and so I did. We turned away from Wool Street and we spoke of many things. We first spoke of my day in the Temple. He was uneasy. "I sacrificed my lamb."

I thought about my Obadiah. "Yes, I understand. But how do you think that shows mercy?"

John stared at me, suddenly discomforted. "Mercy? Well...what would you do? Release the lambs? What about justice? I can tell you that it brought me no joy to see what sin requires. All that blood...and the innocent beast. But that's the way it is, so it must be done. And I don't blame your Father...he didn't send sin into this world, the woman invited it. And so we must all repent, for she is our mother as Adam is our father."

I remained silent. I was amazed at my cousin's zeal for righteousness. I knew he would be a mighty prophet just like the angel had told his mother.

"I've lived my whole life in Jerusalem, so every day I see Romans parading about, mocking us and turning rich Jews away from *Elohim*. I'm sick about the Jews who hate their own birthright," he said. "But, in spite of the blood, I suppose the Temple amazes you?"

"I have no words for it."

"I have plenty of words for it. First is shame."

"Shame?"

"It's a den of thieves, a false house built to honor that monster Old Herod and now his son, the fox."

I hadn't thought of it that way. I stopped walking. "But it's my Father's house."

"We're told to think so but Old Herod once placed a Roman eagle over the main gate. What Jew could walk beneath that? Many did. Shame on them. And he wouldn't remove it until the righteous amongst us rebelled. No, the Temple is an abomination, like Old Herod was and his son still is."

"Joseph said the design is faithful to Ezekiel..."

"Herod needed to appease us...like he did the Romans with his temple to the goddess Roma and to Caesar Augustus in Caesarea. Now his son appeases the Romans inside *this* Temple, too. Did you know that the Romans keep the Temple vestments under their own guard and our priests have to *ask* for them? What evil is this? The vestments belong to the Lord of Israel, not to Caesar!"[106]

I had known of this from the many complaints about it in Nazareth.

John then stopped walking and kicked a stone away. "'I saw men corrupting their way, unrighteousness had honored itself with high walls and iniquity sat upon towers.'[107] Promise me that when you are King, you will chase the serpents from that place and then break it down, stone by stone!"

Tear it down? I thought. *Is he blind?* "So why do you enter it at all? Why would you offer sacrifice in a 'den of thieves?' Why don't you wander out to the Salt Sea and live with the Pious Ones?"

John searched out my face. "My father served this Temple in ignorance, but he served it and so I would not defy it until now. But now that I have

---

106 In 6 AD the Roman army occupied Jerusalem, making Judea an official Roman province. The sacred vestments of Israel's High Priest were then kept in Roman custody and released on necessary occasions upon the request of the High Priest. This was a humiliating, symbolic reminder of who actually held religious power in Israel.

107 From *The Testament of Levi*, Chapter 2. It should be noted that an official Jewish canon had not been organized in Jesus' lifetime. So, Jesus and his contemporaries would have been influenced by a wide range of texts. Nevertheless, the first five books of the eventual Jewish Bible (Genesis through Deuteronomy) were considered the most sacred as they contained the Law and the very essence of Israel's foundations. Next in importance would have been the 'Writings' that consisted of various books of wisdom, chronicles of events, the Psalms, and others. The third general grouping was known as 'The Prophets,' and as might be expected, contained the words of Israel's renowned men of old. Within these last two categories would have been found a number of books that would not be ultimately included in the Jewish Bible, one such book was *The Testament of Levi* noted here.

become a man and have done as my father would have willed, I'm free. Yet I will not pierce my mother's heart. So I will come and I will watch Herod steal the glory of *El Shaddai* until the Spirit calls me to do differently."

I thought for a moment. " 'The Lord is slow to anger and abounds in love.'"[108]

John seemed suddenly annoyed. " 'The heavens proclaim him as righteous, for he is a God of justice. Arise, Lord, in your anger; rise up against my enemies. Awake, O Lord; decree justice!'"[109] He took a deep breath and relaxed a little. "But until the proper time is come, we must obey your Father. That's why you were wrong yesterday. You disobeyed."

I thought for a moment. "Did I?"

"Yes. Joseph was right to be angry. And a report of this will find the ears of the High Priest, Annas. That isn't a good thing for any of us."

"Which is the greater command to obey, John, to show mercy or to offer sacrifice?"

John thought for a moment. "Is not sacrifice, itself, God's mercy?"

I liked his answer.

"The people must repent, then mercy comes."

I did not like that answer as much. "Then mercy is not mercy."

"Who teaches you these things?"

It was a good question. The answer was not Moses. I had realized for some time that Moses' instruction was more like an opening of doorways than a filling of a jug. He would say a phrase and my mind would somehow finish the thought before he ended his sentence...as if I already knew. So I shrugged. But I looked closely at John and asked him, "Cousin, you want Israel to repent...to turn away from all her misdeeds. Tell me then, what is it that *you* repent of?"

John darkened. "Why do you ask such a question?"

"You are quick to throw stones at others."

"So it offends you when I say that you are disobedient."

"I'm not disobedient, John. But no, your charge doesn't offend me. I'm only asking if you repent as much as you expect others to repent." He turned away and I could see that my question troubled him, greatly. And then I wondered.

Of what had I ever repented...Of what had *I* turned from?

---

108 Numbers 14:18

109 Psalms 50:6, Psalms 7:6

John and I walked on, this time in silence for several blocks as we allowed our own thoughts to steep within the hush of the late hour. When we began to speak again, we spoke of angels and of demons, of what was, and of what was to come. And then John stopped and took me by the shoulders. "You are the Son of the Most High. My mother says there will be no boundary to your Kingdom."[110]

"And *my* mother says that you are to be the prophet of the Most High."[111]

We started walking again. "The *Yishiyim*—the Pious Ones—of the Salt Sea are right," John said. "This Temple is a false place and its priests are false priests. In their worship they don't sacrifice animals because they know that true sacrifice is our lives, not these animals that bring a profit for everyone. You are the King they wait for and I may be the Prophet."

I thought for a long moment. "Rabbi Isaiah told me about them. These *Yishiyim*…Essenes, the Greeks call them…claim that it was their Teacher of Righteousness who properly interpreted all truth. Now they strive to live in absolute purity so that the Messiah will be able to come."

"But they are expecting two Messiahs…a priest and a king, both announced by a prophet. I think that I'm the prophet and you're the king… unless you're the priest…" John then offered a confession of sorts. "I really don't know what any of this means." He stopped and stared at me beneath the lantern of a rich man's house. "I'm going to go to them. I'm told that they've calculated the prophecies of Daniel to mean that a terrible war between the Sons of Light and the Sons of Darkness is upon us. So certain are they that the King is here that their rules are more severe than ever and none of them are happy."

I smiled at my cousin. "That should suit you, then."

"Well, the prophets foretold of a blessing for *all* the earth but these Essenes think it's only for them. So who knows?" All of his prior confidence had drained away.

"But you do believe your mother's story?"

"I do. And so I know that something important is coming."

"Why?"

"Because my mother lives like a woman filled by God's Spirit. And so did my father, I am told. Do you doubt her?"[112]

---

110 Luke 1:32,33

111 Luke 1:76

112 Luke 1:41, Luke 1: 67

I hadn't thought much about that.

"Well?"

I didn't really know his mother except from what Mary had said. And I knew that my mother loved her very much.

"I have no reason *not* to believe her."

John narrowed his gaze at me, angrily. "Your words are weak. They are too clever."

"Well then, do *you* believe *my* mother?"

"Yes, I do, and for the same reason that I believe mine."

A warm breeze tumbled bits of straw by our feet. I watched them spin about and fly away. John's words had strength and wisdom. I knew then that he had been filled with the Spirit even as my mother had told me. "The witness of a righteous person is true," I said. "And so, yes, I believe both of our mothers." Hearing my own lips strengthened my belief and binding my belief with his made it stronger.

"Then take my hand, cousin," John said.

I grasped it firmly; his palm felt rough for a city boy and his grip was powerful. At the touch my sight went white and I saw a room of drunken men and jewel-laden women, dancers and silver plates. My ears filled with mockery and oaths. I gasped and released my hand. But young John had seen nothing; he had heard nothing. Instead he began to speak with greater force than a thirteen year old youth should have: "Let both our paths stay straight, let our lights shine brightly, and may our hearts please our Father until the wilderness we call 'Israel' is restored…however that may be!"

I returned to Isaac's house and slept under a blanket beneath the stars in the man's courtyard, not far from the steps leading into his *mikveh*. But I did not sleep well, for my bed was cold and hard. So I awakened before the sun rose and waited for the others, thinking and praying.

Soon after the sun had risen and the trumpets had sounded, my sister Salome came into the courtyard and ran into my arms. "I'm so sorry for you, Jesus."

I smiled. "Don't be sorry for me. I'm sorry that this has been such a hard pilgrimage for you."

"Father and Uncle Cleopas are very angry with each other. Mama says it would be better if we went home separately. Father wants to leave this morning."

I nodded.

"Will you go with us?"

I hadn't really thought about it. I wondered if it wouldn't be wise to keep some distance from Joseph. "What do you think?"

"I think you should go with Uncle Cleopas."

My mother now came out of the stairway along with Lydia and my brothers. She looked haggard and miserable. She had just hurried a spare breakfast of bread, *leban*[113], and yoghurt. The children were given some buttermilk and a blessing. But now James was whining and Joses was fighting with Judas. "Jesus, we are leaving." She wiped her face with a towel.

Joseph emerged along with the whole host of Isaac's guests. He couldn't wait to leave Isaac's house and the discomfort he had suffered there. "Mary, we'll find the others along the highway. I want to go...now."

The courtyard was tense as awkward farewells began. Joseph retrieved Noah from Isaac's stable and Elizabeth sought out my mother. She held her tightly, raining a shower of blessings over her. She then took hold of me and of her son, John. She prayed that my Father would pour out his Spirit upon us both. Then she hugged me, and as she did the joy of her heart filled my ears with a song and I smiled. Truly I tell you, Elizabeth was all that my mother had ever said she was, and I loved her.

John then faced me and we bade each other a sad farewell. I stood still and silent as he helped his aged mother creep toward Isaac's gate. I watched him offer our host a cold farewell. But just before his mother and he disappeared into the crowded street, John cast an odd look at me. His face was grim. He raised his hand and in another moment he and his mother were gone.

I watched John disappear, sadly. I took a swallow of Lydia's buttermilk and thought about my walk with him the night before. I remembered how tortured his face had become when I asked him about his own repentance. I wished I had said something more to John; I wished that I had given him a word of hope or told him more of my Father's kindness. I stared through

---

113 A type of yoghurt

the gate and suddenly thought that I should find him and tell him now. So I hurried past Isaac—who turned his head from me—and burst through his door. I pushed my way into the crowded street, bumping against this one and that one. I was jostled and pushed, even once tripping to the pavement. I tried jumping above the shoulders enclosing me in hopes of catching a glimpse of where they had gone. *Elizabeth is old and slow*, I thought. *They must still be close!* But it was not to be. I soon yielded and leaned against a wall. *I will see him again,* I thought.

It would not be for a very long time.

"Where is my family?" I asked Isaac when I returned.

"Gone."

"Gone?"

"Are you deaf?"

"But…"

"If you hurry…"

"And Cleopas?"

"Gone."

I gathered my shawl and blanket and gave Isaac as respectful a farewell as I could. "I'm sorry, uncle, that my being here took the joy from your feast."

He grumbled something.

"May *Elohim Avinu* [114]bless you." With that, I returned myself to the impassable streets of the neighborhood. Once again I shoved and elbowed my way down Wool Street, across Market, inching my way downhill toward the Lower City. By noon I found myself standing within sight of the Sushan Gate where a mass of people waited endlessly. Those ahead of me squeezed together as if passing through a funnel. I was thirsty and hungry. Blowing dust had my eyes watering. I wondered if my family was waiting on the other side of the valley. Joseph would be very angry with me and my

---

114 Hebrew for 'God the Father'

mother too, unless, of course, they had just kept going. After all, Salome may have told them that I was with Cleopas…

While waiting at the base of the city wall, I turned to survey the Temple rising just behind me, thinking about John's disdain for all that it had become. My eyes followed the steps leading to the Portico of Solomon and I remembered the day before. My heart grew heavy; I had been in my Father's House but my time there had been a terrible disappointment.

I felt uneasy about all that I was looking at and so I began to long for the green hills of Galilee. I suddenly remembered my tithe. The gold coin was still hidden in the seam of my clothing. Whatever troubles the Temple stirred in my heart, I would joyfully share this coin for the needs of Israel's suffering children.

So I left my unease on the street and I moved toward the Temple once more. This time, however, I approached the massive stairways with a lighter step…with a new purpose in view, and I was glad.

CHAPTER XIV

THE UNBROKEN COLT

I was walking within the double row of towering colonnades that supported the roof of Solomon's Portico when I heard a voice call my name. "Jesus? Jesus of Nazareth?" I turned to face a man whom I guessed to be about twenty years old or so. He was dressed in a fine robe and by his side was a young woman. I did not recognize him at first. "I..."

The young man laughed. "Jesus! I am Jakob! *Yakob bar Joazar*...I was a student of Rabbi Moses for a time in Sepphoris..."

"Ha!" I laughed. "Yes, yes, Yakob, of course. I'm sorry. The master misses you."

"Still? Is he well?"

"Yes. And Petrus still frightens the mice from Sepphoris with his bark." Jakob laughed.

"And you remember me?"

Jakob lowered his voice. "I remember your beatings and I remember the Story you told Moses. Sometime you must tell me if you believe it."

I did not answer.

"This is my new wife, Esther."

Esther was a bold fifteen-year-old. She wore bright colors and moved with a certain confidence that announced herself as a very different sort of woman, indeed. "Are you the one whom my father-in-law spoke of this morning?"

I was confused.

Jakob leaned toward me. "Are you?"

"Am I what?"

"Are you the same Jesus of Nazareth who refused to slay his lamb?"

I was astonished. "Yes. But...how..."

"I thought so." Jakob shook his head. "I'm not surprised...remember, I know you. My father was very upset about this. Do you remember who my father is?"

"Joazar, the High Priest who Archelaus mistakenly accused of being a 'seditious Jew.' Yes, I remember. The Romans came and replaced him with Annas."

"Exactly," Jakob said.

"We do not belong to the Romans."

"Yes, you are a Galilean. 'Troublesome rebels with a horrible accent,' my father always says." He lowered his voice. "You'll find sympathy amongst the Pharisees and their followers, but be careful how you speak to the rest. The Sadducees think moderate responses to the Romans are better. In any case, we all know what the Romans will do to Jerusalem if they suspect a rebellion. They have no patience for rebels. They just sent General Varus to crush the barbarians of *Germania*...your parents would remember him as the 'Arson of Sepphoris.'"

I nodded. "That earned him another kind of rebellion: my mother joined the women's boycott of Roman pottery!"

Esther clapped. "Yes. Good for her."

"You see? This is why we Judeans worry about you Galileans. The Romans can burn your towns and villages, execute your leaders—like that man from Gamala, and you all still think as you do. You need to be careful.

"But all of this is beside the point. What I was saying is that my father may not be the High Priest any longer but he still has ears in those circles. Your name occupied his breakfast."

"My name?"

"Yes. Annas' secretary learned of you from the gossip during the changing of the priests. He then scampered off and told about your own little rebellion and then the story found its way to my father's house."

"It was not a rebellion."

"No? It sounded like one to me. You're the first Jew to rebel against the Temple instead of against the Romans!"

I shook my head and proceeded to tell him the truth of that day.

"I understand, Jesus," said Jakob. "But that sort of thing threatens the whole system, and many want the way things are left undisturbed." He pointed to an assembly of well-dressed men. "I come here with my father as often as I can because the greatest teachers of Israel gather along those marble steps and talk. They travel here from Damascus and Alexandria, and even parts of Asia. From them I learn how Israel must understand its place in these times. You could learn from them, too."

I looked into the shadows of Solomon's Portico.

Jakob gestured toward the scholars. "Their faces change but never the conversation. My father is somewhere among them. He is old and his beard is white. He wears a purple turban. I think it would be important that he hear about your sacrifice from you, directly."

I was tired of talking about it.

Esther touched my arm. "Where is your family?"

"They've left for Nazareth."

"But why are you not with them?"

"I was going to find them when I remembered some other business I have here," I said. "I suppose they think that I'm with some relatives."

"Well, what about when they find out?" she pressed. "Your poor mother!"

I had been thinking about her but I was certain that my tithe was important enough to delay me. I answered like the youth that I was. "She knows that I'm old enough to find my way home."

Esther was not pleased. "She will be worried."

I lowered my eyes. "Yes. I know, but I fell behind and..."

"Well, if you want you can stay with us in my father's house tonight. My father really should meet you."

I thought for a long moment. If I hurried, I knew that I could deliver my tithe and still find the caravan. But as I glanced around the courtyard I felt an urge to remain. I didn't know why I felt that way, but the feeling was strong. I took a breath and thought about all that had happened. I was suddenly, though mysteriously, sure that *El Abba* wanted me to tarry in his house a little longer. I would trust my mother to him and do what I believed he wanted me to do. So I answered Jakob, "Yes. I'll stay with you."

"Good. My father will be pleased."

I then pointed to the teachers. "Tell me more about them."

Jakob surveyed the scholars. "See him, the one with the blue shawl and the silk cloak? He's one of the wealthiest men in Jerusalem…part of the Abtinas family who has the monopoly for all the wood and incense that the Temple buys. And there," he pointed to a young Sadducee with a black beard. "He's a Garmu…the family that provides the Temple shewbread. I like him. And do you see that Sadducee of middling years over there…the one drinking?"

"With the curly beard?"

"Yes. Stay clear of him. He is Caiaphas, the son-in-law of the High Priest. He's a man who holds truth by the throat with one hand and wields a heavy rod with the other."

"Like Annas?"

"Not exactly. Annas is more ambitious than righteous," he said. "But enough of priestly politics. Can we meet here in half an hour?"

I agreed to meet Jakob later, so I made my way to the Court of Women that housed the Temple treasury. There I carefully moved along the thirteen trumpets and crept carefully into the shadows where I tore the hem of my tunic and withdrew my coin. I then followed a secretive old woman into what was called the 'Chamber of the Silent,' [115]and quickly yielded my offering to the work of my Father.

As I heard the coin clink against other coins I closed my eyes to imagine hungry children being fed and naked children being clothed. I opened my eyes and slowly left the chamber, then looked at the trumpets in treasury. I hoped that the gifts poured into them served my Father well. But how many hands did the offerings of the people cling to before the poor were served?

I could only wonder.

So, I repositioned my *tallit* and made my way back to Solomon's Portico where I found Jakob standing alongside an old Sadducee with a purple

---

115 In this chamber, gifts for the education of the poor were made.

turban. I knew that it must be Jakob's father, Joazar. I approached the two, suddenly a little anxious.

Jakob was perspiring and he looked fearful as he walked toward me. He then whispered. "I wasn't sure you would come."

"So this is he!" blurted Joazar. His voice was commanding.

Jakob introduced me and the whole Portico suddenly hushed. Jakob finished by saying, "He's come to learn."

"Is that so?" Joazar grasped his robe with both hands and spoke loudly. "So you are Jesus of Nazareth, the Galilean who shamed his father and refused to slay his lamb?"

I waited.

He proceeded to announce every detail to the gathering scholars. I was not surprised that most of his story was wrong. After all, men's ears are curved. "So, what do you teachers think?" He narrowed his eyes. "Who should be punished, the father or the son?"

I took a deep breath. Many grumbled but none answered. I glanced to my left to see a severe looking Pharisee. I later learned that his name was Kish, a learned man from Tarsus. At his side was a boy he called Saul who was not more then two years from his mother's reach. I remember him because he had such odd eyes—one bulging and both crossed. I wasn't sure whether to pity him or fear him. No matter, the truth is that the pair of them made me anxious and I could barely think.

I finally turned my face to Joazar. "I have come to learn from you, Rabbi, for I have much to learn."

The man liked that. He nodded his approval. "Yes, yes, indeed you do." He put a finger by his cheek. "But never forget, the best way to teach is to ask. So, let me ask you: who should be punished?"

I turned my back on Kish and the boy, and thought for a moment. I then answered, "Is a groomsman to be punished because his colt rejects the bit?"

Joazar turned to the others and repeated my response. "Now, what say you to this?"

At first, the scholars seemed indifferent to the whole idea of engaging a boy...and especially one from some village in faraway Galilee. But it seemed that Joazar was intrigued with me. He insisted that the others provide some sort of answer to my question.

A few of the teachers left, but those who remained began a half-hearted discussion about groomsmen, colts and bits. Finally, Joazar presented their consensus. "We think not. The Lord made colts to be spirited and so the groomsman ought not suffer because of the design of *HaShem*."

I could feel my heart racing. A stiff wind blew my shawl onto my shoulders. I lifted it back over my head and thought, carefully. "Then, Rabbi, with respect, I ask you if the *colt* should be punished for doing according to his design?"

The old man looked at his son, Jakob, who went pale and bit his lip. But Joazar was amused at my sudden spirit and he put the question to his somewhat annoyed friends. As with before, out of respect for Joazar's unexpected interest in me, a discussion followed that grew to include words such as '*Elohim*' and 'rods of instruction' and even 'Moses.' Finally one of the teachers answered. "We think not. The Lord made colts to be free for a season and so the colt also ought not suffer because of God's design."

Joazar was pleased. He turned to me. "There it is."

Perspiring, I thanked him and as I did I glanced sideways at Kish who was scowling, but I also saw a rabbi smiling at me from the edges.

The smiling rabbi called out, "My son, I'm *Nicodemus bar Nehemiah* and I welcome you here. Now, I say that *HaShem's* hope is for the colt to learn to take the bit."

I liked this man at once. His voice was gentle, yet firm. I thought him to be the sort of man that would laugh easily were it not for the burden of knowledge that seemed to weigh on him. I answered. "Yes. It is so. Yet do you not think that instruction requires time and patience?" I took a breath, still anxious. "For this reason our Father is quick to forgive and slow to anger."

Suddenly pleased, the group murmured amongst themselves until a Sadducee in a yellow turban strolled into the Portico. "Who is this boy, Joazar, and why is he here?"

"He is a friend of my son. I find him to be an interesting distraction from the usual chatter."

A breeze sent dust racing around my sandals. I watched the brown swirl fly freely across the white marble and disappear into the courtyard. I licked my dry lips and I spoke out of turn. "My name is Jesus."

The Sadducee glared at me. "You are a Galilean. Horrible accent you people have. From where in Galilee?"

"Nazareth, Rabbi. I'm Jesus of Nazareth."

Red-faced, the Sadducee turned back to Joazar. "Do you know who this is?"

"Yes." Joazar moved closer to me as if to protect me.

"He's the one everyone's talking about!" He spun back to me and pointed at me with a trembling finger. "You're the one, aren't you?"

"I am."

"You're the one who shamed his father?"

"My father's shame is my Father's shame."

"What?"

I remained silent.

The old man stooped and stared into my face. His breath was stale with garlic and onions. "What does that mean?"

I thought for a long moment and answered slowly. "Rabbi, I speak of two fathers. A child of Israel can be a father according to seed, and also one according to law..."

"Enough! You need not teach me! And why do you speak of two fathers? You said that your father's shame is your father's shame. You mean to say that your father has somehow shamed himself?"

Jakob quickly stepped forward. "It's late." With that, he grabbed hold of my arm and walked me quickly away.

CHAPTER XV

WISDOM IN THE WIND

I was exhausted by my time in the Portico. There I had felt the strange, empowering presence of my Father and the Spirit. I had also felt fear, confusion...joy, and even moments of sheer ecstasy, and so I had been completely overwhelmed in mind, body, and spirit. The effect of so many feelings, thoughts, and impressions kept my tongue fastened during the supper that Joazar later provided. I listened to them, but I could say nothing to the patient rabbi or to my friend, Jakob. I could barely chew or swallow, and I hoped that they understood.

But when I lay in bed in Joazar's fine house, my weary self did not sleep. Instead, I began to think of my parents and my brothers and sisters. *Is Joseph still angry with me? Is he still ashamed? Is Ama worried? Does she even know that I'm missing?* So I soon climbed out of my bed and walked to a small window that overlooked a clutter of rooftops heavily shadowed under moonlight. *Oh, dear mother...do not fear for me. My Father wants me here...I know it. I can feel him...and I like knowing that I am doing as he wills.*

I hoped my mother would understand. I hoped she and Joseph would forgive me.

I finally fell into my bed where I lay troubled all the more. I recalled what was said at Joazar's dinner—and what was not said. My teacher, Moses, had once told Jakob the whole of my Story, but during dinner Jakob had told his father only parts of it—only those claims that would be interesting but not be shocking. He told his father that the angels had announced my birth, and that my mother believed that I had a special destiny—perhaps as a prophet or a wise teacher. This false claim excited the old man and so he happily prayed a blessing over me—a nice blessing to be sure. But I was not happy about it. I stared into the darkness. *How is it that part of my Story makes people happy, but when they hear all of it they become furious?*

There was another thing that kept me awake that night. When our meal was over, Joazar had instructed me to return to the Portico just after the morning sacrifice so that I might speak with the scholars again. I rolled to my side and groaned. *I don't want to be tested anymore. But how do I escape this?* I was afraid and yet, as with before, I somehow knew that this was my Father's business.

And so I prayed.

I prayed for Wisdom much of that long night—'for she is a breath of the power of God, a pure light of my Father's glory.'[116] I wanted her to fill my heart with love, my mind with truth, and my mouth with words. I wanted to keep silent about all things that should be kept silent, and to pronounce all things that should be pronounced. My heart's desire was to speak only that which my Father would give me to speak so that he and he alone would be glorified.

And then I slept a deep sleep in Joazar's fine house.

"I invited him," answered Joazar. He leaned on his cane alongside his son, Jakob, and peered into the face of Kish. "And you and that son of yours will treat him as my guest." He then introduced me to the many new faces gathered that morning.

I stood in the shade of Solomon's Portico in my nearly outgrown linen tunic that was covered by a fine wool coat that Jakob loaned me. Atop my head was the urine-stained *tallit* of the Therapeutae that I had quickly come to love. But when I looked about the gathering scholars I understood

---

116 Book of Wisdom 7:25

why Galileans thought themselves to be the lesser Jews. Their coats were of fine wool or even silk, all richly dyed in pomegranate crimson or saffron yellow or sea-snail blue. On their heads were silk turbans and magnificent shawls. Their sandals were not of crude camel hide and rush like mine, but rather of jackal and hyena. It was then when I remembered something my grandfather had once told me: what a man does with his feet means more than the hide of his sandals.

"Look, see around you, boy," said Joazar. "These are the learned men of the House of Israel. These are the guardians of the Law, the interpreters of the Prophets. Sadducees and Pharisees, they are the keepers of righteousness, *Selah*."

I bowed respectfully.

"And seated here are two of the Pharisees' greatest teachers. The smiling one is Hillel the Elder. Unless his breath fails him, he will attain the age of Moses by Tabernacles." I knew about Rabbi Hillel and I was thrilled to be in his presence. My teacher Moses shared often of the old man's wisdom and I could feel the love of his spirit move amongst the others.

Joazar turned his body. "And there, seated directly opposite Hillel— the one with the scowl—is Rabbi Shammai. He once chased a Gentile with a mallet!" Everyone laughed, even Shammai. It was good to hear laughter in that place. I knew of Shammai's severity but I saw no mallet, stick, or throwing stone anywhere near him and I was relieved.

I was then urged closer to the marble terraces so that the teachers would be able to better hear. "And that one...the young one in the very fine clothes, is named Joseph..." To my surprise and to that of Joazar, Rabbi Kish suddenly shouted, angrily, "Listen to me, this is the boy who refused to sacrifice his lamb. He should be driven away."

My hands fastened themselves tightly to the corners of my shawl and my lips moved quickly and silently: "Father...I am your servant, your son, but I have too little understanding of judgment and laws. Send Wisdom to me so that she may be at my side, for she knows and understands all things." [117]

A warm gust tossed the edges of my hair. I felt Wisdom in that wind and so I opened my eyes and smiled as others began to protest against me for the day before. "Good teachers, I answered this charge yesterday."

---

117 Adapted from *Book of Wisdom* 9

Kish grunted something but another stepped forward. He was Nicodemus, the kind-faced Pharisee whom I had seen the day before. "And so you did." He faced the others. "This matter is settled. The colt is set free." He faced me again. "Now, tell us, what can we teach you?"

I thought about Assia, my sister. I answered. "What is more important, Rabbi, the Law or mercy—the Sabbath or a life?" From the corner of my eye I saw Hillel lean forward waiting for someone to answer. Finally a Sadducee spoke. "The Law reveals mercy; the way of the Law gives life." His comment was met with some uncertainty.

I considered his answer and as I did my mind seemed to open like a portal to the edges of some mystery that I had brushed alongside from time to time in my young life. But this day...this day I felt the breath of the Spirit breathe me deeper inside this mystery...and far beyond. The effect was as if I remembered things I did not yet know. "Forgive me, Teacher," I finally said. "Did you not just say that the way of the Law brings life?"

"No!" shouted many. "*Elohim* alone gives life!"

I listened to the others and then answered, "So, to be clear, the Law does *not* give life?" This was followed by a great deal of beard stroking. I went on. "Truly, good teachers, I confess with all my heart that the Law is good, but as you say, the Law does not give life. So tell me then: why does *HaShem* give us the Law?"

Nicodemus stepped forward and raised his hands to heaven. "Love the Lord your God and keep his commandments so that you may live and multiply, and that the Lord may bless you and have compassion on you."[118] He then looked at me directly. "He delights in his unchanging love."[119] And so I answer you, Jesus: For *HaShem* so loves Israel that he gives us the Law."

I nodded. "Then, does not love rule the Law?"

The Portico fell utterly silent. I saw many of the teachers staring blankly in confusion, as if they had never considered these words before. But how could they not have seen my Father's love throughout the Scriptures? I was astounded. Could they not see his love in the beauty of a flower, or the tenderness of a touch, or a song?

How could they have forgotten that love rules *everything,* for my Father *is* love?

---

118 Adapted from Deuteronomy 30:16,3

119 Adapted from Micah 7:18

After releasing the doctors for their midday meal, Joazar and Jakob found a quiet café on a corner in upper Jerusalem, just below the mighty fortress of Antonia. Joazar ordered bread and oil, wine, cheese, and boiled eggs. The old man was weary but oddly joyful; Jakob was quiet. We ate in silence and then Joazar informed me that Rabbi Hillel wanted me to return and continue a conversation until the evening sacrifice. I agreed.

Jakob leaned toward his father. "Caiaphas will surely be there again. He will not understand how a youth from Galilee can hold the attention of these men."

Joazar chewed slowly. "Jesus, you are something other than a rebellious boy from faraway Galilee. Your questions are not questions from the son of a builder, nor are the answers you hide within your questions. Caiaphas, Kish, and many others will pay wary attention to you now…this is dangerous. But to not return would be to insult Rabbi Hillel." Joazar looked at Jakob. "And that I will never do."

The end of that day was not unlike the beginning of that day. I was told to stand in the center of an enlarging circle where I breathed in and out of the wisdom that came to me from the teachers and from Wisdom, herself— and from the mysteries that seemed to hover near.

After I had listened intently to the scholars, I was invited to ask questions and so I respectfully began to ask many, like why blood must be shed, or how a goat could actually carry away the sin of Israel. Most answered with very persuasive ideas about justice and readings from the Scriptures, all of which I considered very carefully. But my spirit was unsettled and so I asked Kish which a man might more easily love—acts of justice or of mercy. I then asked Shammai where the boundaries of God's Kingdom lie, and then I asked a Sadducee about liberty.

A Pharisee disagreed with the Sadducee, but in hushed tones. I then frightened Joazar with my excited agreement with the Pharisee that liberty is truly a gift from the Almighty and one that ought not ever be yielded. The Sadducees immediately hushed me and told me that I needed to be more mindful of the 'state of things' as they are. I answered that their counsel was good, but asked if it wasn't true that *HaShem is* and therefore he and his gifts—such as liberty—*are* the state of things as they should be.

To that the Portico fell silent.

Then, before the evening songs of the priests began, Caiaphas received a message from the High Priest Annas. He ordered me to return again on the next day. This time Joazar took the news badly.

"I prayed for you all the night," said Joazar as we climbed the steps into the Temple the next morning. "You must beware of the dangers that lurk in this place. Annas is a toy of the Romans, the Temple guards are false Jews, spies are everywhere and sedition is severely punished."

Sedition! What a troubling word. And why would such a word be used about me? "I don't understand."

"Only a few need to fear you, Jesus. Only a few."

"Who would fear a boy from Galilee?"

"Your questions have caused some to wonder if all of Galilee is smitten with notions of rebellion."

"Rebellion?"

"The leaders of the Temple are held responsible for all of Israel. The Romans know that Galilee lies in the shadow of Jerusalem."

"Jerusalem should cast light, not shadows."

Joazar stopped. "My son. I can see that Wisdom has blessed you and that knowledge has found you. I see in you a heart unlike any other I have ever known. If I see these things, then others do, as well." He leaned forward. "If you are wise and if your mind is keen, then you must know that such things cause others to fear. And fear, boy, bears terrible fruit."

Jakob had said nothing, but finally reminded me that his wife was still troubled for my mother. "She imagines that she and your father must be very worried. Are you sure that you should not hurry home?"

I, too, wondered about them. Had they yet realized that I was not with them? Had they returned to find me? Would they be able to find me? Or, would they wait in Nazareth?

"Jesus, are you listening?"

"Yes," *But I am a man, now.* I thought. *Joseph has released me by doubt; my mother should release me by belief.* Either way, I knew it would be better for the both of them to learn how to set me free. "I hope they are not worrying and I hope they don't come looking for me. Surely my mother knows that I need to be about my Father's business." [120]

Joazar stopped. "I don't understand. What business does your father have here?"

"My father's Father is my Father and I am to be in his house again, today."

Before long I was again standing within the colonnades of Solomon's Portico. This morning, Rabbi Hillel was seated just beyond the roof of the huge porch along with a handful of the other ancient teachers so that the morning sun could warm their old bones. Hillel's younger rival-friend, Shammai, was standing just within the shade but both were within easy earshot of my voice. Packed between them and all around me stood a very large assembly of other scholars. Caiaphas sat in the center of them, taking his turn at teaching. When I saw him I again remembered the words of Jakob: 'Stay clear of him; he holds truth by the throat…'

---

120 See Luke 2:48-49

CHAPTER XVI

TREASURE IN THE PORTICO

Joazar introduced me again, but he had barely finished when so many questions were shouted at me that I could hear none of them. Caiaphas angrily took charge from old Joazar, ordering silence. He proceeded to prowl about me, studying every inch of my person. I thought him to be a man who seemed frightened of that which he did not command. I knew then that it was Caiaphas who was turning the others against me.

"Tell me, boy…Jesus of Nazareth…what is the most important question a man should ask?"

A gentle breeze tossed the hair hanging beneath the edges of my shawl. I thought about the struggles of my family and so I answered. "I think a man should ask: 'Who am I?'"[121]

This stirred a great deal of discussion. So long did their debate last that I faded to the margins of the circle to look into the Court of the Gentiles. There my eyes followed the many visitors to the Temple, Gentiles who had come from every province of the Romans' empire to marvel at the spectacle of our new Temple that was still being built with patient excellence. Among them was a family of Greeks walking close by. I thought them to be rich and probably powerful. The husband's face was strong; his draping

---

121 This is an allusion to the time when Jesus will ask, 'who do you say that I am?' as in Mark 8:29 and other Gospels. It could be argued that this is the most important question of all time.

toga shimmered its fine quality under the sun. His wife was extraordinarily beautiful; she seemed to float atop the white marble. Her pink, silk garments followed her form in the way that takes a man's eye. I fixed my gaze on the soft skin of her uncovered face, fascinated by the frailty of her features. To be truthful I should say that her beauty captured me and I felt a strange sense of life suddenly stir my loins.

A squeal from one of her two children trailing behind turned my eyes. The children were happy and dressed in equal finery. They were attended by two female slaves—one a child-like Nubian with beautiful skin as black as an ebony figurine that I had once seen in Sepphoris. The other slave was older and very fair, and so I assumed she had been stolen from the northern reaches of the Empire.

The children and the slaves seemed content, even happy. The mother stopped and stooped to listen to something her giddy little boy was saying. She laughed and stroked his hair. She kissed his head and then smiled at her daughter. I knew that this Greek woman loved her children as much as any Jewish mother in Nazareth. The Nubian slave saw me watching. She smiled at me and waved her hand. Her unveiled smile warmed me and I waved at her. Yet I felt suddenly uncertain about it. After all, she was no daughter of Abraham.

I then heard my name. I turned about to see the bearded faces of the doctors waiting impatiently and so I returned to the center of the circle. Caiaphas was clutching his robes and he approached me like some orator might approach his pedestal. But before he could speak, old Hillel shocked the rest. "Caiaphas, stop and listen." This, of course, created an uncomfortable stir—but no one dared challenge Hillel. He then shocked them yet more by having me sit in the middle of them, as if I were a teacher in my own right. I reluctantly took my position in the center, even as the grumbling Elders took their places on the marble terraces.

Hillel remained standing at my side. "Now, young Jesus of Nazareth, tell us the second most important question a man should ask."

The answer came to me quickly: "Should he not ask: Who is my neighbor?"

Hillel approved and I noticed how that agitated Caiaphas. *Why does he fear me so? How can I show him respect?* "Teacher, may I ask a question of you?"

The man was suspicious. "Ask."

"Where is truth to be found?"

Suddenly pleased, Caiaphas feigned a great deal of thought. He came and sat by my side and proceeded to reveal his treasury of knowledge, first quoting from the Holy Writings and then lecturing us all in the impressive thought of the Greeks and the insights of young Philo—the Jewish philosopher from Alexandria. "So you see, boy, truth is found where it is understood…and few are they that know it."

My heart sagged for him. Even as a boy I could see that he was a knowledge-worshipper and so knew nothing of love, and on that account, knew nothing of truth.

Caiaphas then raised his chin. "But those who know it must protect it, for is not Israel safe when we, her teachers, are strong?" Content that he had once again placed truth firmly under his profound protection, he asked me, "So, boy, is not truth found in the grasp of its defenders?" He remained seated.

I answered him directly and from my seat. "Teacher, I do not understand your answer." I took a breath. "Is truth so small that it can be held like a helpless sparrow?" Caiaphas' face filled with such rage that I thought he might have me arrested. He stood and walked away from me.

A great murmur rode along the lips of the rest until a young lawyer stepped forward to speak. "Let me ask what the boy *should* have asked: '*What* is truth?'" He paused and posed like a street actor in Sepphoris. "Now I answer. Truth is that which forever abides in goodness."

Still seated, I scratched my head. "Rabbi, tell me what is good."

"The Law is good!" The teachers agreed.

"Then *who* is good?"

This, of course, prompted another rumble of voices. "He who keeps the Law is good. Any fool knows that," said someone.

I strung their arguments together in my mind and then asked, "So he who keeps the Law *is* truth?"

The teachers became uneasy. I pressed. "Can a man *be* truth?" This evoked a long debate among them that left us all unsatisfied, so I abandoned truth and returned to goodness. "Then let me ask this: is the Law good or is *Avi HaRachamim*—the Lord of Mercies—good?"

The lawyer answered patiently. "The good Lord has given us the good Law. Do not the Lord's blessings come to those who strive to do good things?"

My mind turned to the miserable wretches by the Pool of Siloam. "But I see much suffering. Do so few strive to do good?"

I saw many nodding before someone cried out, "The boy is right to ask. Israel is broken and dark. Shouldn't we seek to do what sets us apart from this evil? Wouldn't that make us more lovable in the sight of the Lord?"

This prompted much discussion until a Sadducee answered. "Israel broken and dark? No! Look around you. We already set ourselves apart from wickedness; The Law is kept in Jerusalem. The Lord is in his holy place and we are his righteous remnant. Some suffer for their sins, but look at you and look at me. What should we fear? We obey the Lord and thus abide in goodness and in truth. Is not he sufficient in all things for those who are pure and holy?"

The teachers argued as my mind went to the hungry and sick of Galilee, to the broken lepers outside of Jerusalem and to the filthy beggars of her streets. Was it the sins of the poor that kept them poor? Were those who mourned not to be blessed? Was my Father's storehouse only for these keepers of knowledge? *Do they have no knowledge of my Father? What about mercy? What about love?*

Finally, a gentle old Pharisee raised his hands over the others. "'Come, let us return to the Lord. He has torn us asunder but he will heal us; he has injured us but he will bind up our wounds.'"[122]He paused. "The Redeemer will surely come to Zion...[123]Is there no room for faith in this world of trouble?"

The day wore on. At mid-day the Elders ordered servants to bring us bread and wine, some salted fish and cheese. Hillel insisted that I remain in the very center of that hard place where I finally received a cup of watery wine from a young servant named Jonas who asked me in a whisper, "Tell me, young teacher, how is a man made free?"

It was a brave question for a servant to ask. I stood and laid an arm on his shoulder. "Tell me first, friend, how is it that we imprison ourselves?"

The servant bent low, "We desire, wrongly?"

I marveled. "You are wise."

Jonas then asked me, "Tell me, how do we overcome our sorrows?"

---

122 From Hosea 6:1

123 From Isaiah 59:20

"'The Redeemer will comfort those who mourn, he will bind up the brokenhearted and proclaim freedom to the prisoners.'"[124]

The servant smiled.

Hillel shuffled close to me and took my hands in his. Respect hushed the portico. "For two days I have listened in wonder. The Lord is faithful; he raises up hope in Zion. Blessed be the name of the Lord."

I then heard a voice from behind call my name; it was a woman's voice and so I turned. To my surprise I saw my mother and Joseph standing alongside a nearby column. They looked astonished, but not pleased. *They came back for me!* I thought. I was surprisingly annoyed. *I'm not a child.*

Before I could answer my mother, another question found me. "Tell us, boy, why should a man be loved?"

The question was frustrating. "Why should a man *not* be loved?" A murmur rolled the words 'Goyim,' 'Romans,' 'Greeks,' and 'Samaritans' about. For some unknown reason I then thought of poor Susanna, the red-haired *mamzer* in Nazareth. I pictured the many bruises she suffered and the mocking laughter that followed her daily. So I asked, "Should a man be loved because he is a man…or is he to be loved only if he belongs?"

To that someone shouted, "All men outside of Israel hate the Lord… would you love a man who hates the Lord? Do sinners deserve our love?"

Sadly, I moved my face from one to the other. "Teachers, tell me, who among you is then worthy of love?" I noticed my mother and Joseph moving closer.

A Sadducee standing near pointed his finger at me. "It is written in the Books of Moses that the Lord loves us,[125] but we are to love him by *serving* with all that is within us.[126]Therefore, if we sow good deeds we harvest love."

"Do you do enough to earn the Lord's love, Rabbi?"

The man raised his hands to heaven. "I am thankful that I am not like the tax collectors and the thieves, the drunkards and those who walk with harlots. I rejoice that I am not unclean as are the *goyim*." He lowered his arms and looked at me. "My son, *the Law* is love, and so I love by keeping the Law…and in keeping the Law I am therefore loved."

---

124 From Isaiah 61:1-3

125 From Deuteronomy 23:5

126 From Deuteronomy 11:13

The man had barely finished when I heard a groan. I looked at Hillel who took a seat and closed his eyes. Tears sagged over their edges like water about to crest the lip of a cistern. He held his hands over his heart. I knew then what he knew…the teachers around us knew little of love.

The shadows were now long across the courtyard. The day was about to end. The Temple choirs would soon be singing, the fire of the altar would be rising and blood would flow again. I saw my mother and my father waiting, now impatient. I knew that the time had come for me to return home. I thanked Joazar and the teachers for their patient kindness to me. I paid special respect to Hillel. I then thought of something that Moses had taught me about a mysterious inscription at the Greek temple in Delphi. I stooped atop the marble, saying, "I have been taught that all truth is summed up in this…" I leaned forward with my finger and began to draw in the dust covering a marble slab.

The scholars gathered around me as I drew the Greek letter, 'E. ' Those who read it silently did not understand. But Hillel shuffled forward and quickly smiled a wonderful, toothless smile. He repeated the sound of the letter, loudly, and when he did the others understood. For the sound of this letter in its own tongue is the same as to say in Hebrew, 'He Is.'

Hillel looked at the others. "*He is* the King of Glory; *He is* faithful; *He is* our help…"[127]

Joazar nodded. "*He is* our fortress; *He is* our rock; *He is* holy…"[128]

Nicodemus smiled and raised his arms. "*He is* good; *He is* our helper; *He is* our merciful God."[129]

The others then said in unison, "Blessed be the name of the Lord."

I looked about the Temple. Indeed, this place was thought to be the place where my Father 'is.' Yet I knew then that somehow this Temple—for all its glory and supposedly splendid death—was but a shadow; it did not contain the full measure of my Father's love. How could it? Nor was it to be the eternal throne of my Father's Kingdom. No, not this place, not here where Herod boasts of himself in the mighty stones upon stones, or where bloodshed does not cease.

It could not be so forever.

---

127 Psalms 24:10, Psalms 33:4, Psalms 33:20

128 Psalms 31:3, Psalms 92:15, Psalms 99:3

129 Psalms 118:1, Psalms 118:7, Psalms 145:8

And it will not be so.

My thoughts were interrupted by the kindly face of Nicodemus. "Jesus, boy of Nazareth, what is to become of you now?"

I thought about his question. I recalled the scripture where my Father told Moses, 'I AM who I AM.' [130]So I then asked myself what Nicodemus was really asking: *Who am I becoming?*

I breathed deeply of a fresh breeze wafting through the heavily shaded Portico. When I did I realized that in those moments in my young life when Wisdom came to me, or when the Spirit filled my mind...and in those places where mysteries seemed to find me, it was as if the whole of me was being opened to remember *something*...what, I did not yet know.

So I answered Nicodemus the best way I could. "Rabbi, is it not true that Israel shall become according to how she remembers?"

He nodded and quoted from the prophet Malachi. "'A book of remembrance was written for those who fear the Lord...'" [131]

"So it is with me."

130 Exodus 3:14
131 Malachi 3:16

CHAPTER XVII

LEAVING NAZARETH

More than four years passed, and they passed slowly as they do in youth, but most especially when they are silent years as these were. I say they were 'silent' because my family said little of my time in the Temple and even less about the nights of thrashing that followed. My mother knew—as did I—that the Terror had become ever more agitated with me since *that* Passover, and it pursued me into deep nights so that I awoke sweated and staring into empty air.

In these years my life had become one of watching and being watched. I would have rather it had been one of knowing and being known.

Mary had sympathy, of course, as did my sister, Lydia. Salome did as well, only now from a distance. Almost two years after our return from Jerusalem, she had been joyfully given in marriage to *Samuel bar Benjamin* of Cana at a wonderful wedding blessed with dance, fine wine, and much laughter. Joseph, however, had forbidden anyone to speak about the Beast, the angels, the Story...any of it, ever. Unable to understand and caught in that terrible place between belief and unbelief, the poor man wanted only to think of his work. The women submitted but my brothers obeyed gladly. My brothers, of course, no longer suspected me to be mad but rather had come to be certain of it and believed that my madness was exhausting our dear mother.

I had continued to study under Moses in Sepphoris, but the time had long passed when I should have apprenticed more carefully with Joseph. So

I began to spend more time learning from him. I quickly became skilled with the mallet and the awl, the grinding stone and the chisel. I shaped stone, mixed mortar, planed boards, and secured rafters with ease. I soon stacked heavy rocks with skill; I carved cedar for the wealthy in Sepphoris, pegged beams with an eye for plumb, and even repaired a leg for the scroll table in Nazareth's synagogue. I became known for the quality of my work. And why not? After all, I loved wood and stone and mortar—and what a man loves becomes his joy, and his joy perfects his workmanship.

So, by the end of my sixteenth year Joseph proudly laid a wood shaving behind my ear.[132] He was greatly relieved to finally know me in a way that he could understand. Now when he watched me heft timber, he no longer saw a youth with a special destiny; when he watched me break stone, I was not set apart from him in any way; when sawing wood I wasn't a source of doubt or confusion. No, he was happy to see Jesus the builder...a worker in wood with hands full of splinters, a worker in stone with rough calluses—a young man with sinewy arms and sturdy legs.

This Jesus was easier for the man to understand, and so *this* Jesus was easier for him to love. However, the more he loved *this* Jesus, the less he seemed to love the *other* Jesus.

And so his love confused me.

I wandered into Nazareth's latrine after a hard day's work where a shepherd was grumbling to a group of other tired men. "The Romans better be on their guard. If those barbarians in *Germania* could send Varus' head to Caesar in a sack, why can't we Jews send him a few heads from the garrison?"

"What happened?"

---

132 This was a sign of a master woodworker. However, it should be remembered that Joseph and presumably Jesus were more than carpenters. They were builders and as such would have also worked with stone, plaster, tile, and more.

Old Rabbi Isaiah answered. "Soldiers raided Japhia and Nain two days ago. They were hunting some rebels and crucified ten men on the road to Capercotnei."

Someone shouted at me. "Augustus should have chosen you instead of Tiberius as his co-emperor. Then we Jews would have a Caesar of our own." He spat.

Isaiah shrugged. "Jesus, what's important is that *you* know who you are."

We began walking toward my house. The day had been scorching, even for the end of the Roman month of *Julius,* and I had spent a long day carrying rocks for Joseph who was rebuilding a terrace wall. I was tired and dizzy from a terrible headache and a nagging fever.

Isaiah handed me a skin of water. "Jesus, a farmer sows his seeds with the wind. Some fall on to good soil but in a weary land, most land upon stone. Therefore some take root but most wither away." The old man bent over slowly to sit on the flat of a large rock. "You live on weary land. The village tongues wagged. They pity Joseph, but you...? It's been years since your infamous Passover and they still slander you about it. They will never hear truth."

Isaiah furrowed his brow as if his mind was grinding. "A man's mind is a storehouse of words, remembered. Memories are gathered and re-gathered from this storehouse like dried herbs gathered for the kitchen. Each gathering makes a new dish, something like the one before but not exactly the same."

"Why are you telling me this?"

Isaiah took a deep breath. "I've heard Joseph tell the story of your Passover four times, twice to me, once to his brother, and once to Daniel the potter. The flavor of each telling was different—each memory has been made more bitter."

I said nothing.

"It is the way of men, Jesus. Hearts steer memories like warriors turn chariots. All men's ears are false."

"Then is no man to be trusted?"

"The witness of many brings light. This is why no man can be put to death on the witness of only one man."[133]

"Cannot the witness of many be false?"

---

133 Numbers 35:30

Isaiah nodded. "Yes, this is true. And *Elohim* can also bear witness through a single righteous man. I'm simply saying that men's minds are rarely storehouses of truth."

"Then what say you about my father?"

"In the beginning, Joseph told the Story of your birth to me with a heart that longed to believe. But his spirit became weary long ago."

My throat was parched and I longed for a cool drink from the cistern. I looked beyond the edge of Nazareth where we sat. The wheat fields had been harvested and so they were little more than stony stubble, looking very much like the poorly shaved face of a sun-browned Roman. The olives and the vineyards were wilted and yearning for their harvest yet weeks away. The sheep dotting Nazareth's fourteen hills were lazy and sleepy like old men.

"So, Jesus, you must understand that the village is not a good place for you any longer."

We walked in silence until my father's house was in sight. Isaiah faced me squarely. His countenance fell and his words became firm. "Jesus, tell me again how old you are?

"I'm nearly seventeen."

He looked me up and down. "You are strong. Look at those hands." He took me by the shoulders and squeezed. "Yes, strong as Jeremiah's ox. You've a field of young grass growing on your face.

"Let me see your eyes," he said. "Yes, yes. You will make a fine husband and father. And soon. Does Joseph speak of it?"

"No one has ever spoken of it."

Isaiah shook his head. "Some say that a bachelor is not a man at all."[134]

I waited.

"Yes, well hear my counsel: Leave Nazareth for a season. Let the dark shadows that follow you in this place attach to something else."

"But Nazareth is my home..."

"Is it? Here you have become a plank in others' eyes. When they look at you they see what they don't understand. And for them, uncertainty is worse than death."

We walked quietly to Joseph's gate where I thanked Isaiah for his wisdom and assured him that I would consider his words. It was then that I

---

134 Bachelorhood in these times was seen as an unnatural condition for a man.

suddenly heard Salome crying from within the courtyard. I bade Isaiah a hasty farewell.

Salome, now with child, was kneeling alongside my mother, weeping. I ran to them. "What is it?"

"Oh, Jesus!" Salome cried. "Will you forgive me?" She turned away.

"For what?"

"How will he ever forgive me, mother?" she said. Salome kept her eyes from mine. "Why should he? And *Abba* will never forgive me either!"

"Sister, whatever it is I forgive you."

She faced me. Tears had made a web of stains down her dusty face and she wrung her hands. "I...I..."

"What? What is it? Salome!"

"Jesus, do not be angry with me...I lost one of your coins."

My jaw dropped. If the coin had somehow found its way beyond the gate, then the whole business of the Parthian gold would travel through Nazareth and beyond, no doubt finally to the Roman garrison.

James shouted from somewhere, "No, it's not here."

Joseph was frantic as he crashed into the courtyard. "Salome!" he shouted. "Count them again!" He turned to me. "Remember what I told you about these things!"

"Only five," sobbed Salome.

Joseph tried to control himself. "Then tell me again: where were you playing with them?"

"Just here, by the shop door. Simeon and I made two little chariots of wood scraps with four of these as wheels. The other two I set aside."

"Where's Judas?" Joseph roared.

Judas fastened his face to the stone threshold of Joseph's workshop.

Mary stood, slowly. "Judas?"

The boy reached into a small pouch tied to the belt of his tunic and sheepishly withdrew a gold coin. Mary groaned, but all eyes fell on Joseph. The poor man nearly collapsed with relief but rather then take the rod to my brother, he grabbed the lost coin from Judas and the rest from Salome. He then took several long strides toward me and opened his callused palms. "Get these out of my house!"

Mary rose and hurried to stand between us; it had become a place she had lately been taking all too often. "Husband, we should rejoice the coin has been found. Why are you..."

"No more. Not another word." He turned to me. "Take these coins to Zebedee. That's your plan, isn't it? Now just do it!"

I was sad. The truth I didn't wish to tell him was that I thought the coins might help him believe again. I remembered how they had once coaxed me and I had seen him holding them on his lap one night not long ago. So I had hoped for him. But I could see now that the coins had lost their power. I should not have been surprised. After all, my grandfather once taught me that signs, like symbols, have no life of their own. They are given life by belief—and Joseph's belief had greatly faded.

"Well?"

I looked at him and he at me. It was enough; Isaiah had been right. The time was fast coming for me to leave Nazareth, at least for a season.

CHAPTER XVIII

A FACE OF THE FATHER

"Yes, this is my decision."

"Have you sent word to your uncle?"

"I have, father."

James entered the courtyard. "This isn't right. You ought to march to the Temple and pour the coins into the thirteenth Trumpet!"[135]

Before I had a chance to say 'no,' Joseph turned against my brother. "You think that is the *righteous* thing to do, don't you? Well, it's not...it'd be the stupid thing to do."

No, we'd not be taking James's advice. He had a keen eye for precepts but was blind to spirit; he had always been one to fix his eyes on his feet and never on the horizon. Isaiah once told me that if James had been a Greek he'd have been a fine mathematician and a terrible poet!

I had a different plan.

Uncle Zebedee and Aunt Salome—my mother's sister—had moved to Capernaum where Zebedee had been traveling for business over the past year. He had negotiated a fishing license with the publicans who were agents for Herod and was now building a co-operative fishing enterprise with several men of the sea who actually knew how to throw a net. In the

---

135 The Temple treasury held chests, called 'trumpets,' into which people would put their offerings.

course of this business, Aunt Salome had met Parthian Jews who traded in silver and gold with the very same publicans in Capernaum.

It occurred to me that Parthian gold in the hands of these Jews would arouse no suspicion, especially since the new Parthian emperor had been educated in Rome and seemed less a rival to Augustus.[136] And I knew that Uncle Zebedee was shrewd enough to exchange the coins for Roman silver without putting any of us at risk.

I liked my plan and so did Joseph. He wanted nothing other than to rid himself of the secrets in his storeroom. So the matter was finally settled and I prepared to leave.

My mother filled my waterskin with a forced smile. She was bravely mourning the end of a season in both our lives. "My father told me that the face of the waters are the face of the Lord. He said that the lake is in the shape of a harp, so one should always listen for music there." She sniffled. "Now, you fill this skin whenever you can. And here, I've packed your satchel with bread and salted fish...But I should find some fruit, and..."

I took her arm. "I love you, mother."

Her chin quivered. Suddenly unable to speak, she kissed the tip of her finger and touched it to my chin.

Rabbi Isaiah burst into the courtyard with open arms. "Jesus, my son. Be blessed!" He kissed me on my cheeks and then held his hand against his heart. "Somewhere in the crocus and hyacinth, or in the amazing blues of the water you will see that beauty is rooted in love. Where one is, the other is." He wiped his eyes. "So, my son, go and find love." He blew his nose into his sleeve. "Now hear this:

> May your eyes search out the Lord's love;
> May your lips celebrate the Lord's song;
>> May your feet stand firm on the earth and your hands be
>>> lifted up, and be ready to serve the Kingdom of His
>>>> Glory."

---

136 Parthian emperor Vonones I. The Parthian Empire lay to the east of Palestine and stretched throughout Persia and beyond. The Parthians were a threat to Rome in greater and lesser degrees over time. Jesus' Galilee should be understood as near the frontier to this potential enemy of the Romans.

I was suddenly so happy that I nearly burst. I longed to set my feet in sapphire water and watch the birds dance in the wind above. *O, Chinnereth— Lake of Gennesaret! Sea of Galilee![137] I am coming.*

As you already know, the main route from Nazareth to Capernaum is about twenty-five Roman miles. It crosses to the north of Nazareth's basin before it leads eastward through the easy limestone hills of Galilee, through the lush Arbel Valley, to the oasis of the notch and finally to the busy town by my beloved waters.

With my six coins stitched carefully within my garments, I joined a caravan of wealthy merchants making their way from Sepphoris with a Roman escort. The half-dozen red-caped soldiers would ease the grasp of the toll-collectors and keep bandits at a distance. The road was smooth and broad and I very much enjoyed the color of those caravans coming toward us from the mountains of Phoenicia or from the farther expanses of Syria. A band of travelers from somewhere in Asia joined us, happy for the protection of the Romans. At mid-day of my first day they shared fine wine, bread, fish, and some bowls of sweet fruit that I had never seen. During our brief rest, these travelers sang and danced to the sounds of lute and tambourine. I clapped and laughed with them.

We prepared to camp near a rocky height. As others tossed their burdens down, I clamored up the mount in hopes of spotting the lake of which I had dreamed. I scrambled higher and scanned the rolling hillsides falling away from me. Then there it was! Oh, the wondrous water of Galilee's own sea—the great gathering of mournful, joyful tears that my Father had shed for his beloved Israel. *"El Abba!"* I wanted to sing, and so I did and with arms opened wide.

"He is majesty, may his Kingdom reign.

---

137 What many of us know as the 'Sea of Galilee' had many names throughout history. It is a large, harp shaped fresh water lake that receives water from the Jordan River and releases water into that same river, water that eventually finds its way to the Dead Sea in the desert east of Jerusalem.

May his will be done in mystery and in sight.

May he feed us from his bounty as we rest in his love.

May he never drown us in the deep but rather deliver us from tempests.

For to him belong all things, whether in the heavens or on the earth,

And we are forever held by the might of his glory! *Selah.*" [138]

A curious fellow traveler had followed me. He surprised me from behind. "If you love the lake so much just go to that place." He pointed downward toward two opposing cliffs that formed a notch in the distance. "Those are the cliffs of Arbel…Make your way to that one on the right. Be there for sunrise, my young friend. Hurry."

Grateful, I abandoned the others and made my easy descent. I arrived at dusk and was immediately welcomed into a poor man's house in the village of Arbel whom I thanked by sharing the rest of some Sepphoris wine that I had brought in a small skin.

"Are you going to pray at the cliffs?"

I nodded, eagerly.

He smiled a toothless smile. "Then you will be blessed, my son. But when you pray, don't always use words."

I stared at him, blankly.

Before first light I hurried to the cliff's edge and waited. In the blue darkness of dawn the air filled with the happy chatter of birds. I sat on a wide ledge and faced east, praying with eyes opened to the magnificent space below. Then I saw the first edge of the new day's sun slip above the dark, even ridge on the far side of the lake. I stood. The rising sun began casting pink light over Tiberius in the distance to my right. To my left the uneven mountains of Galilee stood as black silhouettes against a lightening sky.

I looked down to see the lake far below begin to reflect the yellow light of a new day. The sun tipped the water, then rose confidently, and as it did a golden path of light raced across the waters to the shore beneath my feet. I smiled. I wanted to walk that path to Heaven's gate. The strip of gold shimmered, and as the lake's face ruffled in morning breezes the sun summoned the spirit within me.

"I rejoice, oh my Father, and I give you thanks.

---

138 An adaptation of 'The Lord's Prayer.'

For you have sent the breath of your Spirit to refresh me
And you have shown me your face upon the waters."

As Isaiah had said, here was a place worthy of my Father's Spirit. It lies in peace far from the greed of the Herodians, away from the boasting prayers of the proud, and not stained by blood from either Temple priest or Roman. I tilted my head backward and drew deeply of freshened air through nostrils stretched wide. As I did, my tongue tasted of distant grapes and saffron spice, of salted fish and carob and wild honey. The land around me was fertile and generous; it was gentle and welcoming. The words of a prophet came to me and I sang to my Father again, and kept singing until the wisdom of the old stranger came to me. *Pray without words?* I sat on a flat rock overlooking the lake and thought about that. Finally, I took a breath and closed my eyes.

At first it was not easy to push words from my mind. I quickly learned, however, that a gentle nudge begins to move them. A breeze tossed my hair; I tried not to think about that. Instead, I simply let myself be with my Father and in the silence he made himself known--but not by words. Therefore, I've no words to offer you. All I can say is that when he came, love came. And with love came joy and peace... the stillness of *shalom*.

When the sun was finally full and my spirit well rested, I rose to begin my descent down the steep face of the cliff. I held fast to the rocks; they were smooth and even waxy to my touch so I knew that one slip would cast me to the bottom. I climbed carefully, eventually passing empty caves where I thought of Herod Antipas' father, Old Herod. That monster had lowered baskets of soldiers from above to drag out the families of Jews who once hid within these same caves in defiance of his treacherous rule. I looked far below to the bottom of the cliff and groaned. I could hear their cries as Herod's soldiers cast them to their deaths. I closed my eyes and prayed for them.

Before long I discovered a narrow goat trail that led me carefully to the bottom. That's when I first praised my Father for goats! I eventually rested by the deep pool of clear water that lay between the two cliffs and alongside the roadway that brought a steady stream of travelers from Galilee to the middle shores of my lake. I sank my face in the cool waters of the spring and drank deeply.

I then followed the easy road along the lakeshore northward, past the prosperous village of Magdala and through a widening valley filled with nut trees, olive groves and dates. Across the wide lake stood the rutted faces of the even ridge that marked the lands of Philip's Tetrarchy and Decapolis. I wondered about the people whom I had heard about in Tel Hedar and Hippos, the Gadarenes, and my relatives in faraway Kochaba in Batenea.

Did they love my Father?

I continued on, and not far from Capernaum I spotted a shallow cave that gouged the base of a high, rounded mount.[139] In the cool shade of that place--some say the very place where Job suffered--I thanked my Father for the many mercies he had granted to those who mourn and to those who hunger, and to those who endure for righteousness sake. There the Spirit whispered in my ear words of peace—more words of *shalom*.

Entering the dark stone buildings of Capernaum, I sought Uncle Zebedee's house and found it not far from the synagogue. My aunt, Salome, rejoiced to see me and quickly washed my feet. She fed me and soon my uncle returned home to share good wine with me. But before night fell, I was angry and so was he.

"I never said I would do this for free." Uncle Zebedee pounded his fist on a table.

"I didn't ask for anything to be free. But I'm no fool. Twenty percent is too much."

Zebedee folded his arms. "I've two boys to feed—they're your cousins, you know. My fishing business goes badly, Caesar's a thief and Herod's a bandit, my partners are cheats, the weather is poor, my boats leak, and my nets tear."

"So now you cheat me? I'm your nephew."

"Cheat you? Cheat you?" He grabbed me by my cloak like a guilty man. "Listen, Jesus. I'm taking a great risk in this. Do you think the Parthians don't wonder why I, a Jew under the Romans, have gold coins from their empire? I saw two of their spies lurking about my boats last night. They wonder if I work with the bandits in the Jordan Valley..."

"Did they say that?"

"No. But I'm sure they think that."

"I'm sorry you're afraid. I didn't want to bring you trouble."

---

139 The site of the Mount of Beatitudes. Travelers can still be inspired by sitting in this cave.

Zebedee spat and looked at me with a hard face. "Boy, I fear nothing. But you've brought us all trouble. If it weren't for your aunt, I'd be done with you long ago. The way you shamed your father..."

"Enough! I will speak of that no more. If you won't do this fairly, I'll just do it myself."

Zebedee grumbled. "You? They'll take your coins and flay you like a trout—or they'll summon a guard and have you crucified for treason."

"I don't think so."

My uncle cursed, then kicked at the ground. "I know your game. You know that my Salome would make my life miserable if this ends badly."

"It won't end badly, Uncle."

He paced forward and back, grumbling. "Let me see what I can do."

On a dark night two weeks later I felt both relief and regret as I finally released my six coins into Zebedee's hand. They had been both a blessing and a curse, sources of both belief and fear.

"What's the matter with you?" Zebedee muttered.

"Nothing."

He stuffed the coins into a small pouch that he hid deep inside his cloak. "And you'll get what you get. *Denarii,* shekels..."

"Tyrian..."

Zebedee grunted. "No promises."

"These should be worth no less than twenty *denarii* each...a Roman *aureus* is worth twenty-five."

"As I said, you'll get what you get. You can't expect full value from an alley-way deal."

"Remember that my parents suffered much to protect them."

"I don't intend to suffer for them at all."

I smiled to myself; that was something Zebedee would say. "I'm not asking you to suffer."

Zebedee grunted. "What will you do with the money?"

I had given that a great deal of thought. "The poor are always with us, but I will save much of it for my mother's care in old age."

"And if she dies young?"

I didn't like the question. "She won't."

"Ha! How do you know?"

"I know."

"You know? Then what about me?"

I looked at him carefully. "A dangerous question."

"I am a brave man."

"Then you have no reason to ask."

CHAPTER XIX

HANDS AT WORK

At dawn, my uncle tripped through his doorway where he dropped two leather bags to the ground and slammed his gate shut, hurrying to force the large locking beam into its iron arms. "Get what is yours out of Capernaum. Otherwise they may break my door down to steal it all back!" He was panting and sweated.

Aunt Salome hurried to get him some wine.

"I've made a dangerous enemy on your account."

"How?"

He took a long draught. "Because you made me bargain too hard."

"Me?"

Zebedee swore a terrible oath. "At my first price he threatened to summon the centurion." He took another drink. "He then gave his counteroffer. My mouth was dry but I managed to spit on his carpet. When I did, he threatened to have his servants cut my throat and sink me in the sea."

He drank more. "All I could do was warn him of lost honor for his family in Dora. What a pitiful threat. I felt weak. I don't like to feel weak."

I could see that he was frightened.

"You've only heard about men like these, boy. You've never sat across from them."

I watched his hand shake as he took another drink. He was right. I knew of tax collectors' ways, of course, and of bandits, and even of the sly lies my neighbors in Nazareth would use against one another. But what did I know of dark dealings in dangerous alleyways? "Thank you. My parents risked much to protect those coins and so have you." The spirit of my mind flew to images of the Magi and the night of my birth. *Is any of this what they had hoped for?* "Perhaps it would have been better had I never been given them?"

Zebedee grunted.

Aunt Salome whispered in my ear. "Those coins helped some of us to believe."

I nodded, but I also knew by then that things we touch can only help us to believe what we already want to believe.

Zebedee grumbled. "I'm glad they're gone." He drained the wine from his clay jar and commanded Salome to bring him more. He then looked at me, coldly. "I will take what I deserve from these bags."

"And what will you take?"

"Twenty-five percent."

I leaned close to him. "No."

Zebedee scowled. "No?"

"No."

Standing, he threw his jar against the wall of his courtyard. Salome grabbed hold of her youngest son, John, as Zebedee roared, "I will take what I will take. You didn't face the edge of a dagger."

I stood. "It is not good for you to steal."

"Steal!"

"I've heard you say that Caesar is a thief."

"Yes? What of it?"

"He takes twenty-five percent...as does Herod, the one you call a bandit. Should a man say the name 'Zebedee' in the same breath as Caesar and Herod?"

I thought my uncle might stomp himself into Hades. He jumped around his courtyard cursing my name and my father's name. He then jerked an amulet from beneath his cloak. "See this? I wear this when you are near because I fear you! Yes, I do fear you. Some say you have the power of darkness."

I was shocked. Where do such lies come from? "Uncle?"

Salome ran to him. "Shh, shh, my husband. You don't believe that!"

"Why would you believe such a thing…and without a single sign? You believe this foolishness and yet you don't believe the Story of the gold?"

"The gold proves nothing."

I took a breath. He was right and he was wrong. "I fear it proves your heart, Uncle."

Zebedee looked at me for a long, silent moment, then collapsed hard upon an overturned basket and closed his eyes. He sat in silence for a long time as Salome knelt beside him and stroked his hair. She began to whisper into his ear.

I picked my little cousin John from the floor and walked a short distance away. The child smiled at me and I at him. His older brother then ran to me and held my leg.

At last Zebedee opened his eyes and spoke. "Come close, boy."

I did.

"You confuse me and so I think the worst. Who refuses to sacrifice a lamb at Passover? Who divides his own family against one another? What boy teaches the doctors of the Law? Who are you?"

"I'm your nephew…and I love you."

The man tried to speak but he could do no more than release his breath and look at the ground. I laid a hand on his hard shoulder. I knew then that my Way would lead me along the treacherous edge that divides who should be known from things that are thought—that perilous brink where light clashes with darkness. *Father,* I prayed within myself. *May your Kingdom come. Lead us in the path of righteousness…and deliver us from the temptations of the Evil One.*

You ask about the money from the Parthians? I gave a generous portion—though not twenty-five percent—to my uncle for the great risk he had taken on my behalf. I gave another portion to Rabbi Isaiah as a special offering for the poor of Nazareth. I told Isaiah that I wished the rest to be held for my mother. He then instructed me that I should consider money as if it were a well-tended grapevine that yielded fruit so that others may be blessed. So I asked Zebedee where to invest it.

For another fee, my uncle recommended three men of business: a Parthian named Obeeta, a Roman steward named Petrus from the new city of Tiberius, and a trader from Gaul named Calvinius. My friend from Jerusalem—the lawyer named Jakob son of Joazar—eventually arranged a ten-year contract with each. I learned many years later that two returned the principal plus a profit, but one only returned the principle. My beloved John of Jerusalem is now the steward of it all and, as we speak, he uses it for the care of my dear mother.

In the year that Caesar Augustus died I was living in the northern region of my lake.[140] I was now eighteen and had returned to Nazareth only one time since I had left. This, of course, disappointed my mother but my absence was agreeable to Joseph. I thought it was good to honor the wishes of a man in his own house.

I was now a man according to the Romans who required me to pay my annual head tax—a sum that I would learn varied according to the state of mind of the collector. I had become a man on all counts, yet Joseph had sought no wife for me. James later told me that it was a matter of terrible conflict between Joseph and my mother. Dear Mary grieved for my loneliness but Joseph said that no virgin's father would speak to him since most in Galilee thought me to be a bastard. What sort of *Abba* would give his dear daughter to a bastard...or worse?

Some had even mocked Joseph, saying that he should search among the 'dogs' of Samaria to see if he could find a 'boil-spotted girl' with a desperate father. Others suggested that he speak to our former neighbor, the shamed mother of the red-haired *mamzer* named Susanna. It had been always believed that the girl was the unclean daughter of a Roman soldier...a claim that her unmarried mother had never denied. But Mary resisted this since it was now commonly believed that the poor girl was possessed by demons.

140 14AD

Joseph eventually said that he no longer had a hand on my neck and so it was up to me to find my own wife…or suffer the shame of a bachelor. As for me, I had begun to give more thought to the whole matter because of Leah of Bethsaida of whom I will speak shortly.

In this time I had no home in either Capernaum or its surrounding villages but I rented rooms according to where I was working. I mostly labored in stone near Chorazin, though sometimes in wood in Magdala, and I also spent many happy hours among the vineyards of Kinnereth. Then, too, in the cold mornings of late March —when the ox still shivers—I helped harvest fields of barley near Hukkok. In the late days of *Maius* I helped harvest wheat all the way from Arbela to Hammath. In the heat of *Augustus* I pulled weeds from among the fresh sprouts of next year's grain in the fields by Magdala, and in September I shook olives from their branches on the far side of the lake in Kursi.

I finally remembered that the Babylonian Jew, Zebulon (from my first journey to Jerusalem), had a brother named Enoch who lived in Bethsaida—a village of many fishermen set on a small rise not too far from Capernaum. So I eventually went there and rented a small shed from him where I rolled a blanket over some straw for my bed.

Enoch was an aged, furrow-faced man with close-set eyes and just a few wisps of grey hair on his head. He was almost toothless so his words often ended with a hiss, a whistle or—like my dear grandfather, Heli—a shower of spittle, all of which made it hard for me to pay attention to his wisdom.

Enoch called himself a 'dragoman.' He taught me from the Scriptures in new ways and showed me great respect by inviting my argument. So for many an hour the kindly mystic and I explored the visions of the prophets, even as I plied my trade. Yet I found that his instruction was not unlike my time with Moses in Sepphoris. Each of these men seemed to be more like porters than teachers; their instruction was like the opening of gateways in my spirit to things that I already knew. So, as I slid my plane over rough wood or as I chiseled joints, the man's words delivered my mind to distant images—sights and smells and knowledge that were vaguely familiar but not fully known. And so, too, did the hidden voice fill his words with so much more. Such had been the wonderful mystery of my learning.

While I was there, Enoch's nephew, a drunken, untrustworthy fisherman named Jonas, would sometimes abandon his two boys—Andrew and Simon—to me so that they could watch me work while he engaged in some debauchery. The two of them would linger for hours, listening from the corners until Simon—the impetuous boy that he was—would end our time by falling from a rafter or by carving gouges in my finished work!

In this same place I spent many an evening fashioning a gift for my mother. I decided to make her a small remembrance of our days with the dear Therapeutae of Alexandria by crafting a *shulchan*—a small round table with three curved legs upon which she could set small plates and a vessel.

On a cold day in the winter that followed, I slung the *shulchan* over my back and walked to Joseph's house. My mother was delighted with my gift and held her breath as Joseph inspected my work. He ran his fingertips along the smooth olivewood edge. "Fine work, Jesus." He looked at my mother. "It reminds me of our time in Egypt."

He ran his hands over the oiled wood again. "You have surpassed me. And that is as it should be."

James entered the room and Joseph quickly pointed to a cedar cabinet standing against a near wall. "James made this for me. He does fine work, too. Look, each door closes tightly. No gaps."

I smiled. *No gaps...that's James.* I paid a carpenter's respect to James' work by inspecting it carefully with my fingers. When I was finished, I looked at him and noticed that he was wearing a wood shaving behind his ear. "You are skilled, brother. I cannot find a flaw."

James frowned. "As my father taught us: what use is a flaw other than to a critic?"

What use is a flaw? His words made we wonder.

CHAPTER XX

LOVING LEAH

I remained near my beloved lake of Galilee and became friends with some young men, though all of them could think of nothing other than the girls to whom they had been betrothed. My favorite among them was Tobiah, a stout, learned fisherman and a righteous youth who was curious and wise. He was betrothed to the girl named Leah—a relative of my landlord and the one who had caught my eye some time before.

On a clear day in June, Tobiah woke me early and led me along the lakeshore through some thick marshland and finally to the mouth of the Jordan River where it flows muddy into the sea from the north. The land surrounding the junction was rich and green and generous with the shade of tall reeds that waved gracefully in the wind. Tobiah led me along the Jordan's soft banks northward to a spot where boys from Chorazin often played. He pointed to several of them climbing aboard a small raft. "Come," he said. We hurried toward the riverbank and asked to ride with the others. As with most in Galilee, they were welcoming and so we joined them atop the rope-lashed logs. With the help of two long poles we were quickly floating in the center of the narrow river. Tobiah pointed to a rock jutting into the water from a muddy bank. "Moses."

"What?"

"Moses. They call it the 'Moses Rock' and they call the part of the river between here and the lake, the 'Passage of the Law.'"

I was confused.

"From the Moses Rock the river has ten great bends, one for each commandment. Look, there." He pointed to the first wide bend just ahead. "The First Commandment." When he said that the boys of Chorazin recited from the words of the Exodus: "'I am the Lord your God who brought you out of Egypt, out of the land of slavery. You shall have no other gods before me.'"

And so it went as we floated our way toward my lake. But, as every good Jew knows, the speaking of the whole Ten in one reciting is forbidden. So the boys always chose to skip one and it was always the fifth! That made me laugh.

Floating under the summer sun, Tobiah encouraged me with the wisdom that he too, had learned from Enoch. "See all around how these waters bring life?"

"Yes."

He then pointed in the direction of where we had come from. "We entered the Jordan at the 'Moses Rock,' but its living water flows to us from far beyond that place. It comes from streams and a spring with no bottom."

I nodded.

"It's that water that carries us through this 'Passage of the Law' until it releases us into the lake."

"Yes?"

"Now, Jesus, I ask you: where will this same water take us from there?"

I turned and faced the horizon beginning to open as we neared the mouth of the river. *Where does living water lead?* I looked ahead and thought about my friend's question for many days to come.

"Have you heard, Jesus?" asked Enoch.

"Heard what?" I put my tools down.

The old man's eyes were red and swollen. He staggered toward a stool. "Your friend...dear Tobiah..."

"What?"

"He drowned with his father and brothers."

My belly rolled. I felt a cold chill run through my veins. I sat in disbelief...and then I thought of poor Leah. I had been so happy for her and for him. I had been building them a chest of cedar wood as a wedding gift. *Why, Father? Why!* I imagined Leah weeping and fearing for her future. I imagined Tobiah's mother grieving a whole family. I choked. I closed my eyes and wept. Deeply grieved, I threw my tools across the shop and put my hands in my face.

Hours later, I was helping Tobiah's suffering relatives carve out a sepulcher for their loved ones. And after they were buried I walked the shoreline for many hours. There I stared at the waters now lying flat and harmless. I peered into them and imagined Tobiah releasing his last breath as a terrible fountain of bubbles. I then imagined him floating limp and lifeless atop the waters until the wind landed him on the stony shore where he was finally found. I wept and I complained bitterly to my Father.

During all these years I had faithfully traveled to Jerusalem for each of the three great feasts (where I left the bloodletting to the priests.) Past my twentieth year, I was old enough to more deeply appreciate the friendship of my friend and former fellow student, Jakob, who was happy and prosperous and blessed with children. Jakob was a righteous man and was loved by many, especially some families in Bethany for whom he had provided honorable services.

In the year of the terrible earthquake of Asia—when *Simon bar Camithus* became High Priest—I found my father and Cleopas sharing a booth at the Feast of Tabernacles. [141] Joseph greeted me warmly and so joyful was my Uncle Cleopas that I thought he might die from snorting!

Joseph invited me to a celebration of James' delayed betrothal to *Judith bat Joshua* of Nain. I followed Joseph back to Nazareth and rejoiced to see my mother and the family. I was introduced to Judith but greeted her with some fear! My brother Joses, (now sixteen) had taken me aside to tell me

---

141 17 AD

that he, fourteen year old Judas and young Simeon, were frightened of the girl who they said screeched like a jackal. I suggested that the roof might be an excellent hiding place.

In these times my sister Lydia was desperately studying the faces of the boys of Nazareth in hopes of hurrying Joseph toward *her* choice of husband. My sister, Salome had recently given birth to a fine son—after having born two daughters in the years prior.

Salome's husband, Samuel, found me holding his fine son. He was a strong, direct man. "Brother, when does your kingdom come?"

I was pleased that Salome was still a believer and so was Samuel. "When my Father wills."

"And what sort of king will you be?" Samuel asked.

I had thought about that for some years. I had asked my Father the very same question and only once was I given a glimpse of the answer. It came in a dream about my poor Obadiah. "I believe that I am come to serve. More than that I do not yet know."

"What kind of king is that?" Samuel was sorely disappointed.

"What sort of king do you hope for?"

Samuel set his jaw. "One to set us free!"

I soon returned to my work in Bethsaida and sought my favorite resting place by the lake. Enjoying the evening horizon, I took a long draught of water and began to sing to myself when I heard a woman's voice call my name. I stood. "Leah?"

"May I sit with you?" It was a bold question for a shy virgin to ask an unmarried man, especially under a darkening sky.

"Yes, of course." I offered her a drink and could see that sadness had not left her face.

Leah brushed her robe flat against the back of her legs and sat in the grass. She said nothing for a long moment, but feigned happiness. "Jesus, do you remember that song you taught Tobiah?"

"Yes! Let's sing it together." I looked at her and she at me, and then together we sang:

"Set the round table and make ready the lamps,

Gather lute and harp, singer and horn,

So the women can dance and the men make merry..."

When we finished we were both laughing until Leah said, "Tobiah loved that song." We both fell quiet.

The two of us sat in silence for a long time, before I finally asked, "Tell me what's wrong."

She said nothing at first, but began to sniffle. Finally, she turned toward me. "This morning my father said that I'm to marry Phineas, the horrible son of that miserable fisherman, Babi."

I knew both Phineas and Babi. This was not good news. "You told your father you don't want this?"

She nodded. "But he tells me that a year is passed since Tobiah's death. He also tells me that he's been negotiating for a groom for months but many think that I brought a curse to Tobiah. Besides, who wants to marry a widow?"[142]

I thought about that as I watched water birds play in the wind. Finally I answered, "According to the law you are old enough to reject his will."

"Yes, I am. That's another problem, I'm *old;* I'm soon to be sixteen." She thought for a moment. "So you think that I should ignore my father?" She sounded suddenly hopeful.

"I didn't say that. How does one not do a father's will, law or no law?"

Visibly disappointed, Leah nodded and stood, slowly, as if lifting the weight of the whole world.

"Wait." I stood with her. "Please, sit again. Tell me more." I reached my hand toward hers and she let me touch it. When I felt the warmth of her hand on my fingertips my body suddenly filled with life. She must have felt the same for she withdrew her hand quickly. She sat again.

"I wish you hadn't said that, Jesus. You know Phineas; he's cruel and impious. He once cut the nets of some Gergesan fishermen who sought

---

142 In this culture, a 'betrothal'—what we would call an engagement—was considered a binding state of relationship. Though intimate relations were strictly forbidden until the actual marriage, the couple was considered already bound together. Thus, death would leave the survivor as something of a widow/widower.

cover from a storm. And he's violent. I saw him beating a dog with a stick while laughing, and..."

"Then why would your father..."

"He doesn't want to keep me any longer. He fears I'll cost him too much." She removed her veil boldly. "Look at me, Jesus. I really am getting too old."

Perhaps I should have turned away but I looked into her face, deeply. She was beautiful, especially in the blue light of the summer's evening. A thought leapt from my heart to my mind. *What if I went to Leah's father on my own behalf and... What if Leah could be my queen?* The whole of my body lifted at the thought of it. I found myself suddenly smiling.

"What are you laughing at?"

"Uh...no, no, I'm not laughing. I...I'm smiling because...uh..."

She shook her head. "I've said nothing to smile about."

I quickly stopped smiling and I studied her. Her skin was smooth and her form was such that pleases a man's eye. Her face was even and gentle. And the warmth of her heart and the kindness of her spirit made her all the more beautiful to me.

Suddenly self-conscious, Leah pulled her shawl forward so that she could sink more deeply into it. But she could not escape my eyes following her into that shy place. She lowered hers. Suddenly I blurted, "Your father is wrong to do this."

This surprised her. "Yes...but you would have me do his will."

"That's because I thought your father loved you."

"Loved me? Who loves a daughter? He only loves my brothers."

"My Father loves his daughters and his sons."

Leah's voice fell. "Then your father is a strange man. But what does it matter? Your father is not my father."

I wanted to tell her that 'yes,' he was. But the time for that had not yet come.

Leah then spoke softly, even submissively. "Tell me, Jesus. Truly, does the *Torah* teach that there is no limit to the honor I owe my father? Must I obey a father who hates me?"

Hates you? Who could not love you? I thought. *Dare I speak to her father?* Would that be *my* Father's will?

My eyes fell into hers, half-hidden by shadow but burning with life. How much I wanted to hold her, to comfort her, to let her feel the strength

PART I

of my body against hers. My mind imagined a wedding, there, on a hillside by my lake. We would dance and drink wine; our families would laugh together…and Leah and I would be one.

My breath quickened. I could feel my loins swelling as I felt my love for her grow. I was drawn to the beauty of her spirit and I wanted to touch her heart through the tenderness of her body. "A father ought not provoke a child to wrath…" I said with half a thought.

I could see that she had smiled—and in that fragile way that makes a man feel like a man. My chest rose; my chin lifted. I leaned close to her. She exhaled, slowly, and my nostrils filled with her breath. I inhaled the fragrance of a springtime meadow. *Leah, 'your eyes are doves; you are altogether beautiful; there is no flaw in you.'*[143]

Leah then said something so softly that I could not hear the words, but the sound of her voice was like the sweet music of a night bird. Everything within me longed to lift the shawl off her head and to touch my hand upon her cheek, to tell her how I loved the gentle arch of her nose, the light in her dark eyes and the smooth curve of her neck. A small bird flew near, chattering happily. O how much I desired her love, her touch. *Yes, I* thought, *I will ask her father to withdraw his arrangement with Phineas' family! Leah will be my queen!* I felt my hand begin to move toward her.

But at that very moment a breeze from the east cooled me, and as it did I felt a different feeling climb hurriedly within the whole of my body, one that soon washed through my spirit like the waters of a calming bath. A gentle gust of wind then spun some dust between Leah and me, and I felt a sudden, odd sort of distance from her. I lowered my hand. My eyes remained rooted in hers but my racing thoughts settled and my heart slowed. I could not speak…I felt myself fading away. Another moment passed, and a stronger wind tossed my hair. My gaze was then drawn to the black center of her eyes where I saw the images of children at an unhappy table, a small boat and a net of fish. Leah was serving and she was weary. I watched her staring blankly into an empty bowl.

That was when I knew my Father's painful will: Leah was not to be my queen.

A cramp seized my belly and I closed my eyes, but when I did my heart released her, even to her trials. I was saddened to let her go for I did love her, and I did not like the images that I saw. I expelled the volume of air

143 Song of Solomon 4

that had filled my lungs. If I truly loved her—and I truly did—I would trust my Father to treat her according to *his* will;.

Finally, Leah spoke. "I...I was hoping..." She gathered her shawl tightly to her face. "My father was going to ask you to take me but someone told him that you are a bastard. It wouldn't matter to me..."

My heart ached for her. How could I comfort her? What could I say to her? "Leah, I..."

She waited, hopefully, but no words came to me, and in that terrible silence she knew.

"I understand." Her chin trembled. She stood, slowly. "I must go."

My legs nearly failed as I stood with her. We looked at one another for a long moment until Leah finally said, "Jesus. I'm a woman. I am unable to oppose my father's will. We both know this. I'm not free. It is the way of the world and you are not able to change that." She turned away. "And I forgive you."

I watched Leah leave me through tear-blurred eyes. I wanted to say something that would give her hope, but I could think of nothing. So I remained in my place, silently staring at her. I stood there long after she had disappeared behind a clump of low trees, searching for her. Finally, I forced myself to turn westward and lose myself in the horizon now slowly yielding to stars. I hung my head. *She forgives me.* I knew then that I would surely argue her name before my Father more than once in the years to come.

CHAPTER XXI

PREPARING FOR WHY

"Jesus, poor Jesus. That looks heavy." Two young men that I knew were laughing as they squatted in front of the fire-pot keeping them warm on a bitter January day.

I grunted. I was bent low under an oak beam that I was delivering to a building site in Bethsaida. I eyed them each, warily. One of them was Phineas, the man now married to Leah. He walked toward me in the menacing way that was his and he gave the beam a shove, forcing it off my shoulder. It fell to the rain-soaked street with a splash, splattering me with mud. The pair laughed, loudly.

"Why don't you just go back to that polluted ruin you call Nazareth?" Phineas said.

I wiped mud off my face. "So *Phineas bar Babi* and *David bar Israel*...I see you decided to let go of your mothers' belts."

David spat. "I found work here. I wasn't driven out like you."

"Yes. I remember. Your father gave up trying to find you a wife, and I'm guessing that he supposed the fathers of Bethsaida to be...less particular?"

David cursed.

Phineas stepped closer. "You meant that for me."

"For you? Why for you?"

"Because you think Leah's father was a fool to choose me!"

"Was he?"

Phineas grumbled an oath. "You still want my Leah. I know it."

"You know nothing."

"I know this: she's mine and I will do with her as I please...until she falls from my favor."

My face twitched and my eyes penetrated his spirit. What I saw was a polluted darkness that was void of joy—a foul chamber filled with loneliness and sorrow. I held my tongue for a moment before finally saying hard words that might save him from himself. "Listen well, Phineas and try to hear me: If you harm her it would have been better for you if you were never born."

With a quick motion Phineas swung the back of his right hand across my right cheek, stinging my cold skin. My face flushed. What was I to do with this poor wretch? I kept my hands at my side. "You must mean to insult me, for your arm is too weak to harm me."

The man looked to David.

I smiled at them both. "I have no honor but what my Father gives me, and the honor my Father gives me you cannot take away with the insult of your hand." I turned my face. "Here, strike my other cheek."

Phineas stared at me coldly. "Just stay away from me." He lowered his arm. "And stay away from *my* Leah."

I stepped close enough to him for our beards to tangle. "Hear me and hear me well. As sure as the sun rises in the east, if you harm *your* Leah you will suffer the wrath of *my* Father."

Phineas leaned back. "You hide behind your father? He's an old fool with a bad back. I don't fear him."

I leaned forward. "Your heart is filthy, your tongue is a serpent and your hands do the Devil's work."

He took a step back. "My...my heart is no concern of yours and neither is Leah's."

I stepped forward and answered him with words that were not easy to say. "Yes, Phineas, even you are my concern."

Flustered, he sputtered, "Shut your mouth! You are a mad bastard and your mother is a whore!"

I felt my teeth clench. My jaw turned to stone and my eyes to fire. No, I cared nothing about being called a 'mad bastard,' but to speak of my dear mother in this way...

Phineas must have felt the heat of my wrath. He took another small step backward and I followed him. And then he took another step and then another, and I followed him step for step. With each tread of my sandal I could feel the rage of Heaven fill my limbs. Truly, this man was my enemy—as were all who would deny the Spirit's love.

Yet I did not hate him, and that surprised me.

A gust of wind ruffled my robe and I released him from the grasp of my eyes. I looked at the smoky fire-pot nearby and remembered some of Moses' teaching. An image that the Spirit once gave me then filled my mind. I pointed at the red coals. "Look and see Gehenna, *Phineas bar Babi.* That is the end of those who persist in rejecting the love of God. If you do not turn away from the darkness that you love, you will perish in the pit of wrath, gnashing your teeth in shame until your soul is consumed by everlasting fire, devoured from all memory by worms that never cease keeping death as death." [144]

Phineas was troubled with these words. He paled and fumbled with his hands. "Just leave me alone and stay away from my Leah."

I said no more as Phineas and David hurried away. Instead, my mind quickly went to poor Leah and I groaned for her. I bent over to pick up my beam and as I lifted it atop my shoulder I imagined her and so many others suffering the haughty wickedness of men like Phineas. Standing beneath the weight of the timber, I stared at my muddy sandals for a long moment. *I fear you will suffer many trials in this world, Leah, but be brave and of good cheer, for when my Kingdom comes, my Father will surely grant me the power to overthrow men like this.* [145]

---

144 Gehenna was the name for the valley outside of Jerusalem's walls where the city's rubbish—including corpses of animals and occasionally, of men—was consumed by an everlasting smolder as well as by worms that never ceased eating the organic waste. The gospels record eleven references to this place by Jesus. Sometimes interpreted as an image for 'hell,' it stands in contradistinction to the Kingdom of God.

145 From John 16:33

"Look deeply into the stars, my son," said Enoch. "They live to tell the story."[146]

I lay sleepily under a warm night's sky along the lake's wide shoreline far from the hilltop lanterns of Bethsaida. It was a night of the new moon, many weeks from my encounter with Phineas; I was fasting and so was Enoch.

Enoch let his bent finger trace a highway in the sky. "Our people named the star-beings and the gatherings of stars, and a few among us remember what they say to us. There, if you look carefully, you will see the Lion...the Lion of Judah."

I remembered a similar lesson from his brother, Zebulon.

"There are signs in the sun and in the moon and in the stars. They tell of the day when men's hearts will fail because they will see the powers of Heaven shake the earth, for then..."[147]

"...Then the Son of the Most High shall be revealed." I suddenly thought of the Magi, those Parthian stargazers who had come to find me in Bethlehem.

Enoch stopped. I could feel him staring at me in the darkness. "Yes. You know of these things?"

"A little."

He collected his thoughts. "The stars follow the sun in a circled path..."

"No. The stars *announce* the sun."

"What does it matter?" The old man drank some wine and then pointed once more to his stars. "So tell me, Jesus, where do we people of the Lord begin our journey?"

I laughed. "With the promise of God to Eve...they begin with a woman." I pointed my finger vaguely into the sky toward the shape of stars called 'The Virgin.'

"Yes, yes! 'The woman's child shall crush the head of the serpent.' [148]Yes, yes, you understand."

I stared into the night's sky, yawning. As I did, however, Enoch's voice suddenly faded from my ears and in its place came the sound of a terrible screeching. Immediately, all strength left me; my limbs failed me; my jaw seized.

But my eyes...my eyes were pulled to one side and then fastened to the star-form of the Scorpion. I could look nowhere else. Its stars then began

---

146 It was believed by most in these days that the stars were living beings.

147 Psalms 19:1; Genesis 1:14; allusion to Luke 21:25-27

148 Genesis 3:15

to pulse and throb, finally bursting into flames so bright that I was nearly blinded. I wanted to cry out for Enoch. Where was he? Where was I?

And then I knew.

The Terror had come for me, again.

The scorpion quickly became a single torch of black flame in a sky that turned orange. The other stars yielded to this terrible torch, slowly melting into red and dripping like blood from the second heaven. They began to fall into the black water as a hissing chorus, whispering, 'Y...e...s...h...u...a...'

I could not make a sound, nor move, and I could barely breathe.

It was then that I felt myself being carried over the waters of my beloved lake. My eyes were opened to the bones that lay strewn in the deep. I began to weep for all that had been swallowed up. When my tears splashed into the waters a great cry sounded and I saw the bones stir. Then I heard a mighty noise of chariots rumbling away from me, toward the east and the west, toward the north and the south. My joints began to scream in pain as I felt each limb pulled toward the four corners of the earth. My tongue was suddenly loosed and the echo of my lament sounded throughout the hills of Galilee. My body was rolled around to face the heavens. There I saw the army of Heaven raging against the black fire of the torch.

I awoke to the sound of the old man's voice.

"Jesus! Jesus!" Enoch was shaking me by my shoulders. "Jesus, are you with me?"

I ached. My mouth was cracked and dry. My eyes were blurred and my joints still burned. Enoch helped me to sit, then hurried to cup water in his hands and wipe my forehead. "Dear boy, dear boy," he cried. He cradled my face in his hands.

I looked into his wide eyes, and then into the sky where the stars had filled the night again. A warm breeze settled my heart. "Thank you, Enoch. I...I must have fallen asleep."

He was not convinced. "Tell me what you saw."

And so I told him.

Had the moon been shining I would have seen the color flee from the poor man's face. He fell to his knees and prayed, rocking urgently and begging mercy from my Father. "Keep him free from the snare that is set for him, for you, O Lord, are our refuge. Into your hands I commit his spirit; deliver him!"[149]

---

149 Psalms 31:4-5

Poor Enoch had been afraid to talk to me for many days after our time by the lake. He finally came to my shop. "What are you making?"

I was smoothing the end of a wooden peg that I had turned on a lathe. "This." I reached for a block that I had spent hours balancing. I inserted the peg into a hole in the block. I hefted it and handed it to Enoch. "A new mallet that will follow my hand."

Enoch took it from me and bounced it lightly. "Without the head the handle is just a peg of wood."

I waited.

He set the mallet down and looked at me. "Your mallet is like a wise man. A wise man is a man made of two parts. The first part comes in his youth when he learns *who* he is; the second comes after much struggle and teaches him *why* he is."

I liked that.

"Someday it will be so for you."

"And how will I know?"

"Your second part will urge you toward your path." The man moved around my workshop a little. I could see he was deep in thought. "Look at me, Jesus."

I did.

The old man took a bit of my bread and hummus, and then walked to my doorway where he stood washed in sunlight. "Where were you born?"

"In the city of David called Bethlehem of Judea."

He turned and faced me.

"Tell me of your mother."

Do I tell him my Story? "She is the handmaid of *HaShem*; she is a righteous woman."

"And what of your father?"

I looked at him, carefully. Was I to answer what he did not ask? I said nothing.

He walked to the dishes set on my small table and shoved a piece of bread into his mouth. He swallowed the bread with some water. "Jesus of Nazareth…" he muttered. He took a deep breath. "Magi from the east came to Judea about twenty years ago...To Bethlehem." Enoch sat, slowly. "Or so says my brother, Zebulon."

I waited.

"In Babylon it is said that the promised king has already come. He would be about your age..."

I said nothing.

The learned man leaned forward on his elbows. "Seventy weeks were once decreed for our people to put an end to sin, and to atone for iniquity..."

I finished the sentence: " '...to bring everlasting righteousness...to anoint a holy place.'"[150] We both knew of Daniel's prophecy.

Enoch sat back and closed his eyes. "The Pious Ones in the desert say that this is the generation of the promise...this is the day that the Lord has made. They teach that the prophecy was witnessed by the Magi." He opened his eyes. His hands were now trembling. "Go to the desert, my young friend. Find the Holy Ones near the Salt Sea for they are waiting for you."

"Why do you say they are waiting for me?"

He took my hands in his. "Go to them and present yourself. They will know."

"They will only see what they seek to see. The promise is not found, it is revealed," I said.

Enoch lowered his head. "Then go, my son...reveal yourself and... remember me in your Kingdom."

I drew a deep breath. "Tell me, who do you say that I am?"

He did not answer.

---

150 Daniel 9:24

CHAPTER XXII

CAST OUT

Enoch's command was rich in love and so I could not resist it. Indeed, the joy on his face the day I closed his workshop door was a treasure far greater than gold or jewels. With a smile as wide as the horizon, he embraced me and prayed over me, and as I turned for my final farewell he called faintly after me, "*Immanuel.*"[151]

With the image of his happy old face on my mind, I left the countless hills of Galilee with their clumps of terebinth and oak, seas of brushwood, myrtle and wormwood behind and made my way south through the Jordan Valley. This familiar highway of the kings had a beauty of its own as it lay like a dusty ribbon atop a wonderfully harsh countryside to the east of the Jordan.

I and the many other sojourners eventually came to the palm-shaded oasis of Bethabara and crossed the Jordan near Jericho not far from the boasting palace of Herod. Here the road to Jerusalem turned west and here I parted company with those pilgrims traveling to the Feast of the dedication of the Temple.

I kept southward and now made my way along the west bank of the Jordan and into the desert around the Salt Sea. The air was comfortable and clean as it so often is in late November. I breathed deeply of it and stepped lightly with my thoughts. I thought of my family in Nazareth and

---

151 The name means, 'God with us.'

especially of my mother whom I had not seen in many months. Zebedee told me that she was weary but well, but that Joseph was struggling with his health. On my last visit—Joses' wedding—I had noticed that he was no longer able to shoulder a ten-cubit beam of oak.

Zebedee recently had also informed me that Joses' wife and James' wife were now bitter enemies under my father's roof and their constant quarreling was not helping Joseph's sleep or my mother's. Lydia had given birth to a second child, Salome to another, and Judas had been betrothed. My uncle had also told me that Joses had begun to drink more wine than what was proper and that he had shamed us by committing some sort of theft with my little brother, Simeon. This was all grievous news to me. I prayed for them all, but especially for my mother.

I also grieved the recent death of Rabbi Hillel and considered the way he had read the *Torah*. 'Do not do unto another man as you would not want done to you,' was his summary of the whole of the Law. I smiled to think of it. Unfortunately, his death meant that the school of Shammai would ascend and that would greatly affect the majority of the Pharisees. Of course, all of this would make my brother James very happy and I expected that he would join them. I had little doubt that they would rejoice to have Camel Knees—James' new nickname—pray with them on the street corners where all can see.

Hillel's death troubled me for many reasons, but I was quite certain—and grew angrier with every step—that the new stewards of the Law would soon set aside my Father's gentle mercies; they would hide them securely behind the polished, granite walls of Shammai's teachings where the desperate might never know of them. And so I grieved mightily for the children of Jacob as I walked—as I do even now.

And I grieved for dear Jerusalem. Caiaphas had been made the High Priest just two years before and by now he surely had the Temple firmly in his grasp. What is one to say about a High Priest of Israel who is the favored concubine of Pilate?

And I also grieved for Galilee. In that same year, Herod made the new city of Tiberius the official capital, even knowing that it was a place defiled by its cemetery so that no Jew could set foot inside of it. What is one to say about a pretend-Jew who is Caesar's willing consort?

Eventually the Jordan widened, spreading shallow waters into reed beds before losing itself in the wide Salt Sea. At my feet was a stretch of white salt crystals that were sharp to my fingertips. The water lapping over my sandals was clear but felt thick on my skin. The place was terrible and yet beautiful—a watery desert that would one day be no more.[152]

I finally abandoned the salt-crusted shoreline and made my way across a rutted landscape in the direction of the mountains that followed the western side of the sea. There I found the roadway that hugged the narrow flats between the water's edge and the sharp mountains. At last I stood at the entrance to the community of the *Yishiyim*—the Holy Ones—set squarely between the Salt Sea and the lifeless mountains of the wilderness.

"Welcome, stranger." I shielded my eyes from the sun and saw a young man who greeted me warmly. His name was Simon, and he was a Galilean like myself though the son of a merchantman in Capernaum. He kissed me on both my cheeks.

"*Shalom.*"

"You are thirsty and you need a bath," Simon said. "Follow me."

I laughed. By his dress I knew that the youth was an initiate in the community. I was surprised to see such a young man in this place, for the much-maligned vow of chastity demanded by these Essenes (as the Greeks called them) discouraged most except for those old men whose loins had dried up. So I admired Simon for loving my Father enough to deny the passions of his manhood. Such restraint requires a gift that some may imagine but few are given.

Simon quickly led me to a *mikveh*—one of ten placed about the community—so that I might be immediately purified before I polluted the village. I removed my dusty robe and my well-worn tunic beneath. I then unwrapped my loincloth and stepped naked into the water made cloudy from others. I extended my arms and squatted until the water touched my armpits, and then hurried to wipe myself clean with a towel.

Simon fed me a modest meal of goat cheese and flat bread, a few olives, and gave me some water. He then sent me to a small room where I was given a bed of straw. Here I rested for several days until the community's three overseers and their twelve assistants were ready to meet with me.

I soon learned that these white-robed men were not ordinary Jews. I learned why it was that they rejected the Temple in Jerusalem and the priests, Levites, and Sadducees who 'defiled' it. I was particularly moved by their abandoning of bloodletting for sacrifice. One of their Elders taught

---

152 An allusion to Revelation 21:1

me that instead of shedding blood, their sacrifice was a chaste life of purity and service to others. I also learned of how their purity as 'Sons of Light' (themselves) would set the way for the coming Priest and King to defeat the 'Sons of Darkness' (all others,) and of how certain they were that their salvation was to be revealed in this very generation.

I was finally invited to eat in the refectory where the two hundred brothers ate in silence, but afterward I overheard one speaking of a certain man who had come to them not four years before as an initiate. When they said the name, *Yohanan bar Zachariah* of Bethany, my body shivered with joy. But then they told me that they had dismissed him in accordance with their particular requirements of purity and perfect righteousness that he challenged.

I will not put you to sleep with the many stories I could tell from my time with these earnest men, but allow me to tell you just this one, for it will help you to understand the nature of their teaching:

"Are you making a joke?" I asked one Sabbath.

"No."

"Are you sure?"

Simon shrugged. He had informed me that no one was permitted to go to stool on *Shabbat*. [153]When I finally believed that he was serious, I protested, lightly. The thought of it would have amused me more had I not been in some need, myself.

To stay pure these Pious Ones had built their latrine a great distance from their village. More then a generation before, a teacher had instructed them that such an abominable place should be at least as far away as the farthest distance a man was permitted to walk on the Sabbath. This, as every Jew knows, is two thousand cubits, or about twelve hundred paces. [154]But to be certain of purity, this community placed their field fifteen hundred paces away.

I came to learn that a latrine of fifteen hundred paces requires a certain amount of prophetic skill. Simon and I laughed often and loudly as we watched the poorest prophets among them sprint away or walk in such strange haste as to look like someone had inserted a great stick into them.

---

153 This discomforting but historical regulation is presented in the research of Robert Feather in the *New Dawn Magazine*, 12/23/2010.

154 Approximately 3,000 feet.

However, even laughable rules can become terrible masters. Many weeks later, Simon awoke on a Sabbath night with a terrible pain in his belly and a fever. I heard his cry and came into his room where I lit a tiny, hemp-wicked lamp. I held it over Simon's sweated face. His eyes opened, wide. "No, no, Jesus," he whispered weakly. "It is written,' You shall kindle no fire in all your dwellings on the Sabbath day.'"[155]

"Listen to me. The Lord loves mercy more than sacrifice and he loves you more than your rules." I reached for a rag and dipped it in a small pail of water to wipe his brow.

Simon groaned and bent himself nearly in half. He then released a terrible odor from his bowels.

"Enough of this." I lifted him into my arms. He was heavy.

"What are you doing?"

"You can't hold this in."

"No, no, you know the rule…"

"This is what I know: my friend is sick and I can help him." Against his feeble protests I carried him out of his small room and struggled just past the edge of the village where I lowered him on to the ground. "Here," I panted.

Simon moaned. "Oh, no. I cannot…and surely not here. The whole village will be corrupted…" He climbed to his feet, groaning in pain and bending over himself. "Take me back, Jesus. I need to wait."

"Wait? Your body won't let you wait, nor should it!"

"I beg you."

I stared at him in disbelief. "This is madness." I stooped low and lifted Simon with my shoulder like I was hefting a heavy beam. Over his protests I started walking toward the latrine again but was soon staggering under his weight. I finally collapsed. "Can you do it here, Simon?" I wheezed. "For my sake?"

"No…I must not do it at all."

"You'll not be able to hold your bowels the rest of this night and all of tomorrow! And if you try and plug yourself you will do great harm." With that, I took a deep breath and hoisted him once more. I tripped my way the final eight hundred paces and delivered him to my mercy. Unable to do otherwise, Simon finally obliged his body.

We returned to find the Overseer and more than a dozen others waiting under moonlight. I was severely reprimanded and Simon was threatened

---

155 Exodus 35:3

with expulsion. I listened patiently and said nothing and then finally led Simon to his bed where he slept like a small child.

Simon recovered from his fever within a few days and after sunset on the fifth day of the new week he was summoned into the common hall to sit before the brothers, as was I. The Elders began by forgiving Simon of his disobedience because of his being 'dragged' to the latrine against his will by 'the stranger.' I was happy for their compassion, but Simon would not allow them to pass blame on to me. "No," he said. "My friend did rightly."

The men grumbled. A temperate one spoke. "My son, when the Prophet reveals the truth you shall understand. Until then, you must believe in us."

"The Prophet? The Prophet is already come. His name is *Yohanan bar Zachariah* and you sent him away."

I leaned forward.

"You sent him away because you didn't believe him," said Simon. "Messiah King is here, among us…"

"No, *Yohanan* cannot be the Prophet for he seeks the repentance of *all* Israel. As you know, the promise of true repentance is only to the 'Sons of Light.'" The others murmured in agreement.

Simon stood. "You think purity is only found in this place? We hide here in the desert and we wrap ourselves in the Law as with leather bands. And then we sink ourselves in the *mikveh* so that the water draws the bands tighter still."

"Guard your tongue, young man. Few will enter the Kingdom of God. Few."

Simon then surprised us all by throwing up his hands and answering. "'Do not be over righteous, brothers, neither be over wise—why destroy yourselves?' [156] I am done with you."

A gasp went up. Many began to shout at my friend. So I stood next to Simon and raised my hands to speak. "I knew three men; one kept the Law but did not love his neighbor; another loved his neighbor but lit a candle on the Sabbath;[157] the last neither kept the Law or loved his neighbor, but he beat his breast in sorrow for his sins. So I ask you, who of these is pure? Who is righteous? Who pleases the Lord?"

The men grumbled. Finally someone answered, "'The one who may stand in the Lord's holy mountain is he who has clean hands and a pure heart;

---

156 Ecclesiastes 7:16

157 Again, a violation of Exodus 35:3

who does not trust in an idol or swear by a false god.' So I answer you this way: *None* of them are pure or righteous. Therefore, none are pleasing."[158]

I looked carefully at these white-robed 'Sons of Light,' and I marveled. They loved my Father more than the Pharisees, much more than the Sadducees, but perhaps not as much as a forgiven harlot. "So to be clear, this is the holy mountain of *Elohim* and your hands are clean, your hearts are pure?"

"You know who we are," came an angry voice. "No Jew in all of Israel keeps the Law as we do."

Another then cried, "And we are not defiled by women."

"Defiled by women?" I felt suddenly angry. "Do you not have mothers? How have your mothers defiled you? How can you say that and still 'honor your father and your mother'?" I shook my head. "Besides, without women, how will you produce your army of Sons of Light?"

Simon laughed, loudly.

Someone shouted, "Unlike you and your kind, *we* do not go to stool on *Shabbat*."

I was weary of this. "Hear me: The Sadducees who disgust you strain at the Law and so they struggle to stool every day. The Pharisees...for whom you have some compassion...bloat themselves with the Law and so they likewise struggle. But you Pious Ones clinch yourselves with the Law until what's in you bursts out and defiles you all the more. As for me, I will let stool pass as it should."

To that a great cry rose up. "Get out! Leave us!"

"Leave? I must leave this holy mountain? Why?"

"Because you are not one of us; you are defiled; you are not welcome in the Lord's Kingdom."

"And where is the Kingdom of *El Shaddai*, my friend?"

"Here. We have told you! 'The Lord has granted us a wall of protection in Judah.'"[159]

"Here? The Kingdom is here, fenced by you and your false gods?" I scowled. "No, the Father's Kingdom has no boundary. Not even the latrine!"

"False gods?" another shouted, "We have no false gods!"

I turned and fixed my gaze on him. "Look inside yourself."

To that someone hurled a cup at me. "We have shown you kindness; we have fed you; we have taught you. And now you mock us?"

---

158 Adapted from Psalms 24:3-5
159 Ezra 9:9

Am I mocking them? I took a deep breath and released it, slowly. "I do not mock you, friend. I pity you." I laid a hand on his shoulder. "You welcomed me kindly, even as one of your own. You have taught me much. But you say rightly that I'm not of you. *Yohanan bar Zachariah* knows who I am and you chased him into the desert. You have eyes and do not see."

The men began to whisper among themselves. Simon then leaned close. "Who are you?"

"Who do you think I am?"

He thought for a moment. *"Yohanan* prophesies of *you?"*

From nowhere another dish struck me, and then a jar and another. Simon shielded me until the men's wrath eased. He then shouted at them, "Stay here and hide close to your *mikvaot* and stay two-thousand cubits from your latrine. Look around. You think this is what purifies? You think this prepares the way for the promised Priest and King?" He wiped blood off his brow. "You watch the sky and wait; you do nothing but seek one another's blessing; your kingdom is no bigger than a few yokes of land and you make it smaller every day."

Simon retrieved a dagger from his belt and threw his robe into the dust. Standing in his thin tunic, he raised his dagger to the air. "If Israel is to be pure, she must first throw off the Romans!" He then pointed his dagger toward Jerusalem and tucked his tunic inside his loincloth. "Gird your loins...the battle is out there, not here." He then took my shoulder. "And here is the promised King!"

To that the men roared and began hurling more pottery. Simon and I fled from the room but they chased us through their village, now throwing stones. The two of us finally raced to safety in the darkness of the desert.

"I will not forget you, brave friend," Simon said, panting.

"And I shall not forget you either, Simon."

He looked at me carefully. "Where will we go?"

"I go to Nazareth. I must see my family."

"Will you lead us?"

"Us?"

"My father was a Zealot, a follower of *Judah bar Gamala*. The Romans crucified him when I was young. My mother wanted me to keep away from the rebels and so she begged me to come to this place. But I will return to Galilee where I should have stayed. So, will you lead us?"

I stared at Simon for a long while, wondering.

CHAPTER XXIII

TERRIBLE FAREWELLS

"Oh, Jesus." My mother took me in her arms. Her body was tense.

"What's wrong?" I asked.

Not answering, Mary led me across the courtyard and sat me down as she hurried into our pantry. She returned with bread, olives, cheese, some salted fish and some wine. My brother, Judas—now nearly eighteen— emerged from Joseph's workshop. For a man soon to be married I thought he might smile but he didn't. Instead he wiped his brow and took a long draught of water, saying nothing. I walked toward him and kissed him. "Hello, brother."

"Mother didn't tell you, did she?"

"Tell me?"

Judas swallowed another gulp of water. "Two weeks ago the Romans searched the whole region for rebels." He cast an uneasy glance at my mother now pursing her lips. "They crucified many..."

I felt my heart pumping.

"They sacked Cana. They killed Salome's husband."

My knees felt weak. "Salome is safe?"

Judas nodded. "She is unharmed."

"Unharmed? Her husband is dead..."

"Then the bastards came here. They killed Rabbi Isaiah and ransacked the synagogue..."

I groaned.

"Hannah was raped in front of her husband, and then they were both killed. The animals raped Rachel and she died the next day. One of them grabbed their daughter and said that he liked red hair. So he tied her up and threw her atop his horse."

"Susanna..." I groaned and fell on my knees. I threw my shawl over my head.

Mary knelt by me. "Praise to the Lord that Joseph was not here, or James or Joses..." I then noticed my mother's uneasy glance at Judas. I took her hand. "What?"

"Tell him." Judas turned away.

Mary answered, reluctantly. "Since you were gone our house has been visited with many troubles." She lowered her voice. "On your teacher's recommendation, Herod's own steward—a man named Chuza--hired your father to build a chest. Joseph and Judas worked on it together for many weeks before Judas loaded it on a cart to deliver it..."

I waited as my mother struggled for words. Her voice fell to a whisper. "Along the way a merchant from Caesarea tempted your brother with a handsome price for it..."

I waited.

"He sold it to the merchant...and then he bought a cheaper one and delivered it to Chuza."

I said nothing.

"The work was not fine so Joseph was summoned to the steward's house. He confessed that the chest was not the one that he and Judas had made, and so he paid the man back. But Chuza fined your father and the chest was burned. Now our family's name is stained and your teacher is dishonored." Mary took a long drink of water. "James demanded that Joseph go with him to appease the steward during Tabernacles. That's why they were not here."

Judas emerged, head hanging. "I sinned against our family, Jesus, and the whole of Nazareth." His face tightened and tears filled his eyes. "I'm unworthy to be in this house."

I felt compassion for him and I took his arm. "You are forgiven, brother."

To my surprise, Judas jerked his arm from my hand. "Forgiven? Who are you to forgive me? And what would it matter?" With that he left the courtyard.

Mary took my arm, firmly. "Leave him be, Jesus. Your brother would rather suffer for his disgrace than be released from it. You have seen this in men, Jesus. To be forgiven is to be beholden and Judas does not wish to be beholden to any man."

"No, to be forgiven is to be restored."

"That's not how most men see it. Judas would rather provide a feast for the village and pay for his sin." Mary said nothing more but sat again and handed me some cheese. I took it and ate it, wondering how it was that humility and honor had become opposed.

Ten days later, I was awakened by fists pounding on Joseph's door. I ran from the workshop where I now slept and threw off the gate's locking beam. James, Cleopas, Simeon and Joses burst threw the door carrying Joseph. "Help! We need help!" shouted Cleopas. All the men were bloodied, but Joseph worst of all.

My heart began to race.

Mary ran into the courtyard and Judas followed. Joseph's face was swollen and his scalp severely cut. He was barely breathing and his eyes fluttered. Mary shouted for them to carry Joseph into the bedroom where he was laid on the floor atop his mattress. "Simeon, go to Lydia, and then run to Cana and bring back your sister and their rabbi...he's a physician."

Judas raced away. Mary ordered Judith and Joses' wife to run for water. James and I undressed Joseph.

"What happened?" I cried.

Cleopas answered. "We were attacked by bandits just before dawn near Agrippina."

"This morning! Why didn't you get him help?"

"No one would help! No one."

"Would no one offer you water? Could no one lend a donkey!"

"Not for hours. We lay along the side of the road begging passers-by, but everyone hurried past as if we were lepers." Cleopas dug in his robe and retrieved a *denarius*. "A Pharisee tossed us this and kept going. Finally the wife of some Greek commanded her servants to load us into one of her carriages, and then she had her men deliver us to Nazareth. May she be blessed."

Judith crashed through the door with a heavy jar of water and Lydia ran in behind her. Mary quickly began bathing Joseph's wounds. I could see that fear was about to overtake her. At the touch of her hand Joseph moved slightly. My mother then looked at me with the same imploring eyes that she had on the day that Assia died. She said nothing but her chin quivered.

I fell to my knees and turned my face upward as I wrapped the cords of my *tefillin* tightly around my left arm. Begging my Father to heal my father, I then stretched out my hands onto Joseph's breast as if to press my life into him. I could feel his heart beat faintly; I could see his eyes fading.

He groaned and strained with what little strength he had. I prayed as the desperate man I was. *Who am I? You say I am your son, yet I have no power; you say that my Kingdom shall have no boundary, but my own weakness is a fence around me.* I was angry for Joseph's sake, and frightened. I pressed harder upon Joseph's breast and he groaned again as I muttered another prayer. I then heard Lydia say my name. I turned toward her; she was hoping, begging that I do something.

But James interrupted, perhaps mercifully. "Enough. Listen to me, all of you. Jesus can do nothing."

Jesus can do nothing. Was that true? It surely seemed true. I looked at Joseph and pressed my hands upon him yet more firmly. He struggled to breathe. But then I heard mother's voice whisper into my ear. "Be at peace, my son, your time is not yet come."

I turned and looked at her, blankly.

She took one of my hands in hers and lifted it lightly off Joseph's chest. "Jesus, you need to believe me." She then lifted my other hand off his chest. When she did, his breathing began to ease a little. Mary then spoke to me the words of Hosea. "'I will heal them and love them *freely...*'"[160]

I didn't understand. I looked at Joseph, and then at my mother.

"Are your hands demanding something?"

I stared at her.

Her voice began to crack. "Does he know that you love him, Jesus... that you love him *with or without* his doubts?" Tears fell from her cheeks. She lay gently across Joseph's breast.

---

160 From Hosea 14:4

I was confused. Was it possible that after twenty-six years he didn't know that I loved him with all of my heart? I quickly took hold of my father's face and leaned close. "*Abba*, I love you. I love you no matter what and I always have." Joseph's eyes opened, but his look of surprise deeply troubled me. "*Abba, Abba*, I have always loved you..."

Joseph lay still.

"Did you think I loved you less because you struggled with our Story?" I leaned over him and laid my forehead upon his halting breast. "Oh, *Abba*," I groaned. "How terribly have I failed you? I'm sorry...I have always loved you..."

I then felt Joseph's hand fumbling for mine. I took it and lifted it to my lips. It felt cold as I kissed it. With his other hand he reached for Mary. Summoning what strength remained, he rasped, "M...my...s...son..."

I could not answer.

My mother tried to hold her tears. She stared lovingly into his fast-fading eyes. "Egypt, husband...do you remember our time in Egypt?" Her voice trembled.

In a few moments Joseph's breathing became shallow and slow. His eyes fluttered, finally resting on my mother's strained face. I gave his hand to her and she clutched them both to her heart. I then raised my arms over dear Joseph, knowing that his time had come. I sang a hymn from the Psalmist and as I came to the end, my brothers and sisters joined me: "... Even as I enter the valley of the shadow of death, you are with me...and I will dwell in the house of the Lord, forever..." [161]

Joseph's eyes remained fixed on my mother's as he released his last breath. A silence followed, until Mary began to wail.

After an hour of much sorrow, the women hurried to prepare his body. They first gathered strips of linen for his shroud. My mother then asked me if she might anoint him with a portion of the spices that had been given to me by the Stargazers like she had my sister, Assia.

I could only nod.

After his body was washed and thus anointed, Mary closed his eyes with a kiss and two copper coins. When his body was then bound in his linen shroud, Judas retrieved Joseph's favorite mallet...a simple tool that would lie by him in his tomb to identify him as the craftsman he was.

---

161 From Psalms 23

As I watched, I remembered much about Joseph. I smiled a little, especially as I remembered the day that he found this very same mallet in Rachel's house. And I remembered how much I enjoyed his song when he fashioned wood or stacked stone; I remembered how kind he was to the lepers of Sepphoris. And then I thought of my other Father and I smiled again. An image appeared to me. *Father and father...together and in a better place.*

Perhaps it was my smile as Joseph's body was being prepared that forced me so quickly from what was now James' house. Joseph had barely been closed within his tomb when James proclaimed himself to be the rightful head of Mary's household and insisted that I leave at once.

"James," protested Mary. "Jesus is Joseph's oldest son."

"Woman, this is not your business."

Mary wiped an eye, but stood erect. "I know my place, son, but I am your mother and I love you too much to let you be double-minded."

James gawked and we all fell silent.

"If you demand our traditions, then you must also honor the law. And according to the law, Jesus is Joseph's eldest son; Jesus is heir." Mary took her daughters' hands in hers. Her chin still up, she said no more but left the room to the men.

I stood alone to one side thinking about all that was happening and all that had happened. I understood James' resentment of me; I did not judge any of my brothers for their doubts and unbelief. No, they had loved Joseph dearly and they truly loved my mother. But my mother was right--James should not be allowed to demand what was not his. So I finally spoke. "According to the law *I* am Joseph's eldest son and therefore entitled by law to lead this household and to be heir to all he possessed."

James puffed himself up. "We will prove to the court that you are mad...or a bastard. Either way, you're not entitled to the inheritance."

I darkened. "Is this what you want? Do you really want it said throughout Galilee that James, son of Joseph, accuses his own mother of impurity?"

James shifted in place, slanting his eyes among our brothers. I took a breath. "Listen to me. I am heir according to the law." James seethed.

A month after we had buried Joseph with loud wailing and the sad song of flutes--after my poor mother had begun to eat again--after I finally heard her sing a soft song in her bed--I summoned witnesses to stand before my brothers and me at the synagogue.

I raised my hands. "Let it be said that according the Law, I am the rightful heir to my father's house."

James squeezed his fists and my other brothers stood by him. I waited for a long moment to see what he might say, but he remained silent. I was pleased with him.

I lowered my arms. "But I surrender all my rights but one in favor of my brother James."

James stiffened in surprise.

"The one claim I will not yield is my authority over my mother." I could see that James might protest, so I walked close to him. "If you do not accept this, then I will simply reclaim *all* my rights." I folded my arms in the way that all my brothers recognized.

"This is not customary," he mumbled. Others agreed. "A man does not separate his inheritance."

"I don't care."

The Elders murmured. James began to bluster; friends of his did the same. Finally, James shouted, "You shame me, Jesus."

"I don't shame you, brother, but be careful that you don't shame yourself. I will not yield."

James gaped at me. Spittle formed around his lips but he finally accepted my terms. The nodding witnesses folded their hands, my brothers walked away from the synagogue. The matter was settled.

I hurried away to seek out Mary who was waiting anxiously with the other women. I embraced her with a smile. "May peace settle over this house." I took her hands. "You are mine to protect, and I will never abandon you. I must leave Nazareth again, but live each day believing my promise that I am yours and you are mine, forever."

CHAPTER XXIV

CAIAPHAS AND THE GOAT

I was welcomed in Cana by dear Cleopas and Miriam who were quick to tell me that the Romans had captured eleven of the bandits presumed guilty for Joseph's death. They had crucified them on the side of the road as rebels and their bodies would hang there for days as a warning. My uncle and aunt celebrated justice. "Does this not please you, Jesus?" asked Cleopas. He was still limping.

I imagined the men suffering on those terrible trees and the disgrace of their bird-ravaged bodies now rotting in the sun. "Please me?" I answered. "It can be a sorrow to see men reap what they sow."

"And sometimes it is a joy!" snapped my aunt. "You should be glad."

I looked at Miriam with some surprise. "It's true that they have sewn the way of the wicked and so they harvest wrath. But joy? No, such things may be necessary, but they are a necessary sadness."

In Cana I plied my trade and made new friends. My greatest happiness, of course, was to be close to Salome and her growing children. I loved to make them gifts with my hands, and to bring them honeycomb from the beekeeper. Most of all, I looked forward to my walks with Salome through the forest-covered slopes by Cana. She had the strength of my mother, and she had accepted the woeful loss of her husband with grace. But I suffered for her and I wanted nothing more than to comfort her. She would listen, and smile, but thinking nothing of herself, Salome would always seek to bless me.

Within a few months of my arrival, my brother Simeon walked from Nazareth to Cleopas' house where I was working. He called for me as Miriam washed his feet. When I arrived at the door he pointed to the *shulcan* that I had built for my mother. "James says he wants it out of his house."

I looked at the little round table fondly and remembered Mary's kind acceptance of it as my gift. I took it from Simeon and ran my fingers around its smooth edge, thinking of how Joseph, my mother, Salome, James and I had once gathered happily around the table of the Therapeutae in Egypt. I had always hoped that this little thing could serve as a remembrance of our wonderful communion in that place. Instead, my brother had rejected it and so I pitied him all the more.

My months in dusty Cana grew heavy over time. Salome was my joy, and my visits with my mother were wonderful. But I longed to return to my beloved lake and so I soon did. From there I continued to visit my family from time to time, but I spent most of my days working throughout the lakeshore villages. This I did for several years until I happily stumbled upon my old school friend, Jakob of Jerusalem.

Jakob was traveling through Capernaum with his wife and one of his three sons to attend to some business of his father, Joazar. The old Sadducee had recently died and left him with a large estate.

Jakob lunged at me with a kiss. "Oh, my friend. I'm so happy to see you! I have never been the same since your time with the teachers." He turned to his wife. "You remember Esther, and this is my youngest son, " he said proudly. "His name is John. He was born in the year that Caesar Augustus died."

"Hello, John."

The boy had a cheerful, winsome way about him.

Esther smiled. "He is my little dove, Jesus. He flutters above this messy world of ours."

I thought her comment to be interesting. Before I could respond, she said, "And he sings." Esther immediately told John to sing a song that he had sung to his grandfather.

The boy hesitated. He stared up at me, suddenly anxious. I squatted so that I did not stand over him. He seemed to like that. Relaxed, he cleared his throat and he began to sing.

"In the beginning
   Of all beginnings
Began the Beginner
   Who began to begin.
And his beginning began
With a word
   And the word was good
      And it was very good."[162]

I clapped for him and he liked that, too.

Jakob then took me aside and told me that he had inherited several houses near Jerusalem from his father, including some in the village of Bethany where family of my mother lived. The houses needed repairs and he wanted me to work there under the direction of a contract broker. I agreed, and a month later I traveled to Bethany where I was disappointed to learn that my cousin, John, had moved away.

I quickly became friends with the household of a young man named Lazarus. Lazarus was righteous, but more than that, he was gracious and compassionate. In the two years that followed I quickly came to love him and his two young sisters, all orphaned by the untimely death of their demanding father. They remembered a little about my mother's cousin, Elizabeth, but they told me much about my cousin John, now called, 'The Baptizer.'

I learned that John was preaching in the wilderness along the Jordan not far from Jericho. They said he lived like a prophet of old, wearing a hair shirt and eating honey and carob.[163] I laughed—that sounded like John to me. They also told me that many in Judea were answering his message of repentance and coming to him to be reborn, as it were, in a new baptism of water.

"What do you two think?"

Martha—the oldest of Lazarus' sisters—answered, "I think your cousin is a prophet that should be heeded."

"And what is being said about him in Jerusalem?"

---

162 Foreshadows John 1:1

163 Per author's research, the Hebrew word for 'locust' is nearly identical for the word 'carob.' Thus, many believe a more proper interpretation of John's condition was that of a man eating honey and carob rather than honey and locust as is commonly thought.

Lazarus entered the room. "Well, now that Sejanus—Rome's chief Jew Hater—has made Pontius Pilate governor of Judea, our people are flocking to your cousin out of fear. Many believe that Pilate is a sign of coming punishment."

"And you?"

"We are disgraced by Caiaphas and suffocated by this new governor. Our people need to be reborn but it ought not be out of fear. No, nothing good will happen unless Israel repents...unless she turns away from herself and to the Lord's purpose for her."

I listened to Lazarus and I was moved by his wisdom. He was certain that my cousin's time had surely come, and that his message was sorely needed. I knew then that I would soon seek John in the wilderness.

A month later—on the tenth day of the seventh month—and during the fifteenth year of the reign of Tiberius Caesar, [164]I entered Jerusalem for the many sacrifices of the Day of Atonement. Lazarus, Jakob, and his three sons joined me for this most solemn of all our holy days. We entered the nearly completed sanctuary as the first streaks of dawn lit the sky. This day, as you must know, was not like any other; the only blood to be shed was that drawn by the knife of the High Priest. And so the Temple would not be filled with the sounds of many panicked animals or of merchants selling them for profits.

I looked at the men now filling the sanctuary and I felt compassion for them. My Father loved his people, for Israel belonged to him. But Rome had burdened us with Caiaphas to lead as High Priest...a man who was happy to bask in the light that belonged to my Father.

How sad for Israel.

How sad for him.

Yes, he would follow the form of the ceremony according to the law: He was now bathing behind a screen. Seven days ago he would have moved from his luxurious house in the city to his luxurious quarters in the Temple;

---

164 In close sequence to Luke 3:1

The Sanhedrin would have spent yesterday rehearsing with him to be sure that he made no error; Twice this past week he would have been sprinkled with the ash of the red heifer to confirm his supposed purity. Young John—Jakob's son—had asked me how much ash that would require! His father laughed, but the boy had spoken a painful truth.

Yes, the form of my Father's will was being honored, but what of the spirit of his will?

Where was love in this place?

Caiaphas emerged from behind his screen. He faced east and laid his hands on a pure bullock that he would slay. "Oh, Jehovah; I have sinned—I and my house. I entreat you to cover over the iniquities, the transgressions and the sins which I have committed..."

The cleansing of the High Priest's household done, Caiaphas moved to the eastern side of the Court of Priests where two perfectly matched goats stood facing west. Next to them was the urn containing two golden lots--one inscribed as '*la-Jehovah*,' and the other as '*la-Azazel*.'[165]

Caiaphas shook the urn and then reached inside of it with two hands. He withdrew the lots and set one upon the head of each goat. Reading the inscriptions, Caiaphas then tied a scarlet cloth around one of the horns of the goat given to the lot inscribed, '*la-Azazel*,' and turned him around to face the people whose sins he would soon carry away.

I shuffled closer so that I could see the goats. Why? Of the many symbols of that day, why was I most drawn to this one? I didn't know. But I didn't give it much thought at the time so I pressed even closer. I felt sad for them both, and yet grateful. Like the lambs slain throughout the year, one of the goats would be slain so that men might see that the impurities of unintended sin is so deadly serious that it can only be washed away with the power of life—blood. The other goat would be laid heavy with the intentional sins of Israel and driven into the wilderness so that men could see that God would not abide with sin.

After preparing the Holy of Holies, Caiaphas came for *la-Jehovah*, the goat that was to be slain. He took hold of him and cut him, and gathered up his blood which he carried into the Holy of Holies and sprinkled atop

---

165 The goats were to be identical so that their separate sacrifices could be considered a unified event. This is of particular interest to those who see the purposes of each goat brought together in the sacrifice of Jesus.

the Foundation Stone of Israel...the rock upon which Abraham prepared to offer Isaac—the rock that once held the Ark of the Covenant.

My heart felt heavy for little *la-Jehovah* and all the many helpless animals that had been slain so that men might see the stain of Evil washed away. I turned my head away and considered the deep channels of blood cut in the Temple floor; I let my face feel the heat of blazing altar. I stared at the horns, the vestments, the golden cups, the trumpets—all symbols that my Father had given so that the people might see and hear and smell the hope of their freedom.

But did the people understand what these symbols meant?

I shook my head. I was becoming ever more certain that the symbols that filled my eyes no longer empowered the people of Israel to love mercy and to seek justice; instead, they empowered the leaders of Israel to hold the people in their grasp. I wondered if these things should continue as symbols at all?

Some noise to one side alerted me to Caiaphas' approach and so I abandoned my thoughts to watch him as he returned to *la-Azazel*. With great drama, Caiaphas placed both of his palms upon the goat's head and in so doing pronounced the transfer of a year's worth of Israel's intentional sins to the beast. "Oh, Jehovah, they have committed iniquity; they have transgressed; they have sinned..." When the High Priest finished his prayer, he then faced us. "You shall be cleansed!" The people believed and so his words had power, *real* power for them. I could feel those around me release fear from their bodies with sighs and clapping; their consciences had been loosed and they *felt* freedom fill their limbs.

I kept close to the goat as priests now led him out of the sanctuary and toward the Eastern Gate. I wondered if the people felt the love of my Father through these goats. Did they understand how it was that he longed for them to delight in being clean? Did they understand how merciful he was to exile the memory of their sin so that they could delight in his presence?

Did they understand anything?

At the gate, the goat was handed to a Gentile who was hired to lead the unclean animal into the wilderness. He took the rope with a shrug and then followed a priest away from the city along with several scribes.

I trailed them across the Kidron. The crowds of people grew and at the sight of the scapegoat they began to jeer and curse the frightened animal. As the procession continued, the people pressed closer to the goat and soon kicked at it and spat, pulled its hair and threw stones. The animal...and the perplexed Gentile...were terrified.

I was amazed at the wrath poured out upon this innocent sin-bearer. After all, he was carrying the sins committed by the very same men who were now casting stones! I began to shout at those who were abusing him. "Stop!" I stepped between the goat and a shrieking woman. "Stop! Let him pass!"

"Move away," shouted someone. A stone struck me from behind; the priests began to scold me.

"No! Leave him alone!" I pushed one man aside and then caught the arm of another who was stabbing at the goat with a stick. "Stop! Enough! This goat is the Lord's mercy...have you none for him!"

Someone shouted, "That goat is covered in sin..."

"Yes. *Your* sin."

That outraged the man who then proceeded to curse me before throwing some dust in my eyes. No sooner had I wiped my eyes than a woman spat into my face. I looked at her, sadly. "What has become of Israel?"

Saying nothing, she turned away and threw a stone at *la-Azazel*.

By the time the procession had reached the bend in the road on the Mount, I was exhausted and bleeding. Thankfully, here the crowd began to turn back, satisfied that the goat had suffered enough for their sin. I shook my head in disbelief. "*HaShem* forgives." I cried.

I was soon alone with some priests, a few scribes, the goat and the Gentile. "Who are you?" one asked. I didn't answer. I was comforting the goat with my words.

"He is unclean...you should keep away."

I turned an angry face at the man. "You did not tell that to those who pulled his hair or punched his head."

"They were striking at sin, not handling uncleanness."

I marveled. "You make the law what you want it to be."

The priest ignored me, but a scribe walked in a wide circle. "If you touch him you are unclean. You are a Jew...you must know this!"

"You who deny mercy would call me 'unclean?'"

The scribe turned his back on me but I followed him and the others for the entire half-day journey that ended by the edge of a cliff at a place the scribes called 'Azazel.' A rabbi began instructing the Gentile on what to do next.

While the man was listening, I walked to the goat. He was trembling and thirsty. I looked into his slanted pupils and I felt such compassion for him. So I knelt by him and a scribe warned me again. "He is unclean."

Was that true? Was he *really* unclean?

I looked up and began to pray for understanding and for wisdom. As I did, a scalding wind blew suddenly from the south forcing me to cover my eyes from stinging sand. The wind then stopped as suddenly as it had come. Everyone shook dust and debris from their clothing and the Gentile began positioning my goat at the very edge of the cliff.

I was confused. "What are you doing?"

"I'm doing what I'm paid to do."

"And what are you paid to do?"

CHAPTER XXV

TURNING

The Gentile spat. He pointed to the rabbi who had instructed him. "I'm supposed to push this miserable goat over the cliff. You people are insane."

"What?" My mind raced. The Scriptures that I remembered simply said the goat should be *released* into the wilderness. Letting him go was the whole point! The wind blasted us again and as it did I knew what to do. I snatched the rope from Gentile's hand and pulled *la-Azazel* away from the edge. I jabbed my finger at the alarmed scribes and quoted from Leviticus: "'The scapegoat shall be presented *alive* before the Lord to cover iniquities by *sending it into the wilderness*...the appointed man shall RELEASE him into the wilderness...'"[166]

The astonished men were confused by my challenge.

"This is the way we do it now," answered a scribe. "He is unclean."

I immediately thought of the little leper girl in Sepphoris from all those many years ago. "Unclean? And what do you do with unclean things? Do you *kill* them?" I knelt by the goat. "No, the only reason he is unclean is because my Father says he is unclean...and my Father says it only so that he might show Israel his mercy."

---

166 Leviticus 16:22. The entire chapter 16 is instructive when considered within the typology of Christ's atonement.

193

I took the water skin from my belt and pulled the cork from it. The scribes fell silent. Hesitating, I looked toward Heaven. *Is this what you want of me, Father? Will you protect me? For if I do this, nothing will be the same.*

I turned my face toward the scribes once more, and when I did I saw hatred in their eyes. *There, I see it, Father.* "And surely, if love has been lost then nothing *should* remain the same."

I stared at *la Azazel*, very much aware that what I was about to do would mean much…it would mean far more than my day in the Temple as a boy.

But love has been lost, I thought.

To the dismay of the scribes, I then laid my hand on the goat's head and gave him water. At the touch, however, my hand began to tingle and sting. I kept it in place, even as a great lament rose up from the scribes who began to fall to the ground, beating their breasts. "Fool! Fool! Must we throw you over the cliff as well?"

I looked at *la-Azazel* and I remembered that he did, indeed, bear the sins of Israel because my Father said he did…and I believed my Father. And so my hand felt the pain of sin. In that moment I also felt as if the face of my Father had suddenly turned away. A chill went through me and I quickly removed my hand.

Had I done wrong?

My heart pounded but a breeze cooled me. Still holding the goat's rope, I begged my Father to return to me. To my great relief, I felt as if he then returned…

but something had changed.

The scribes and rabbis were now outraged. They began throwing stones at the goat and at me. I dodged a few, then considered again what I was about to do. Still certain that it was what my Father had willed, I quickly fled with the animal toward the side of the cliff.

The descent was steep and treacherous. My feet slipped on the gravel beneath me several times, but my goat kept from tumbling to my certain death. Above me the scribes shouted, calling me all manner of blasphemer.

And why would they not? I had turned the day against them.

When the goat and I were finally beyond the throw of the scribes, I leaned my head backward and said a prayer for them. They were blind men who needed sight. I then waved to them and followed my goat eastward into the wilderness.

The Judean desert was what it is...naked. Sprawling before me like a baked lion skin were red-silt basins and rocks stripped of all life except for a few broom trees and lonely clumps of tamarisk. For some, its horizon was desperate, but for me its boundlessness felt like a wondrous gift of what might be.

But since I had believed that the sins of Israel had actually been put upon my goat—according to my Father's word—I continued to feel them stinging my hand. I shook it, but I supposed that I would continue to feel the stinging until I could bathe in a *mikveh*. The deed had surely seemed like my Father's will...but why did it feel like he had turned his face from me?

Troubled, I walked with my goat, praying. At last, the cool air of evening began to refresh my skin and I found a dish of soft sand into which I lay, keeping a slight distance from my little friend. The sin he bore was not his sin, and so I felt all the more compassion for him. Yet I knew that I could not keep him in my care; the law said he was to be released in the wilderness. So I stood and loosed the rope from his neck, carefully. "Now, *la Azazel*, take the sins of Israel into the wilderness. Let them be forgotten as far as the east is from the west." He bleated three times and stared at me under starlight before trotting happily away.

The next dawn a rising sun cast color over the black hills of distant Moab. I rose to hear the colors sing, but no sooner had I rested my eyes on pleasing purple than a vision of Herod's vile haven—the stronghold of Machaerus—appeared in my mind from its haughty hill in the faraway land where the spies of Joshua once trembled. I could see within its walls. Drunken men of Israel were falling over the women of Rome and dancing the dances of serpents and of demons. Herod was toying with a young woman; the young woman pulled her heart from her chest. It was rotted. She placed it on a silver tray and laughed.

I pressed the heels of my hands into my eyes and cried out. The vision left me and the morning's sun edged into the sky. I stood and took a drink from my water skin. My hands were trembling. Why had I been shown such a vision as that?

Then I realized that the sin of Israel was upon me...the goat was clean. Now even more troubled, I made my way home to Nazareth where I plunged into the village *mikveh* three times.

"What?" James was not happy to see me. "We have heard of your madness...All of Galilee has heard! Get out, get out, you are unclean."

"Don't worry, James. I baptized myself."

"We've not enough water in all of Israel to make you clean!"

My mother embraced me. "Let me feed you," she said. "Lydia, bread, water, cheese...olives. Judith...!"

I was tired and I sat down in the courtyard and wiped my face with a cool rag. James seethed. "We know...we all know what you did. Caiaphas covered it up during the last days of the feast lest there be a riot, but news came to us from everywhere. You could have upset everything. Some are calling you a rebel..."

"The Temple does not honor the Law, brother. Do you know that the priests have the scapegoat *killed*?"

James stared.

"Yes. They have the Gentile lead it away from the city but then they throw it over a cliff instead of releasing it as the Scriptures require. "Think as you will, brother, but know this: the Law is corrupted by men who squeeze it too tightly. They press it like grapes under feet of stone and so they crush the seeds. Their wine is therefore bitter."

"You make trouble everywhere," said James. "You need to leave."

Now it was me who did the staring. I finally took a deep breath and nodded. After all, this was the house of James. So I called for my mother and the two of us took a walk to the edge of a low cliff at the edge of Nazareth where we sat under a late day sun.

"Why do you bring me here?" my mother asked.

Hers was a good question. Nazarenes had thrown sinners from this cliff and stoned them to death. "I...I don't know."

She took my hand. "You are thinking of the scapegoats who have been murdered. I love that you love mercy."

"I'm not sure how that all happened. One thing that followed the next, and then..."

"I'm pleased with you."

"But I touched it. When I did I felt as if my Father had turned away."

Mary thought for a long moment. "His holiness cannot look upon sin..."

"It seemed that he was abandoning *me*. I felt a chill..."

"You might have *thought* that he was abandoning you, but he was turning his back on the impurities that were upon you. *HaShem* will never leave you. Besides, think of how pleased he must be...you caused upset in the Temple because of mercy!"

"When I felt that his face had returned to me, something seemed different."

"In what way?"

"Something about what he expected of me. Do you think my time is now come?"

"Listen to your heart and do not be afraid. When your time is come you will begin turning from *who* you are to *why* you are." My mother's eyes were shining. "Think of a key. To unlock a treasure a key must be turned." She took my hand and looked at me carefully. "Your cousin, John, has turned to his 'why.' He's baptizing many in the wilderness." She squeezed my hand. "Perhaps John's baptism is the way for you to begin a turning of your own."

Two days later I began another journey south, through the harvest-shorn Jezreel Valley and then across the Jordan at the easy ford just below the lake. From there I followed the eastern bank of the river south along the Perean highway where numbers of spring-fed oases gave shade and refreshment to many a caravan. I was excited. I had spent so many years waiting for what my mother would call 'the fullness of time' for me. Now I wondered whether it was upon me.

Would my Kingdom begin today?

As I neared the village called Bethabara, the crowds were large and excited. I knew that John was close. [167] I followed many others along the road as it split away from the highway to Jericho. Now hurrying toward

---

167 See John 1:28. Sometimes translated, 'Bethany,' the village may be better known as 'Bethabara.'

the river, few spoke. All faces forward, we looked past the flat, rutted desolation of the plain and soon saw the green band of the riverbank. Just beyond the trees would be the narrow river, and in that otherwise quiet place would be my cousin. I could barely keep from running to him.

I pressed with many others toward a small clump of softwood trees, finally elbowing my way past the rest. I stopped. There he was... *Yohanan bar Zachariah*! The Baptizer was standing in waist deep water just beyond the tall reeds of the river's banks and helping an old man out of the river. I laughed for joy. For a man just over thirty years old, he looked strong and powerful. I could barely wait for him to see me.

I looked about. This was a good place. Here the narrow river had cut a deep channel of green in the earth so that all who stood here felt as if the wider world had disappeared. I removed my sandals, my robe, and my loin-cloth. I then slipped down a short, muddy bank and stood amidst a large crowd of other naked men at the river's edge. Shaded by towering reeds and surrounded by the songs of birds, my ears filled with the thunderous voice of the Baptizer.

Hearing him again I remembered how he and I had walked the lamp-lit streets of Jerusalem as boys. Neither he nor I had understood our calling, yet as I looked at him there, surrounded by opened ears, I knew that he now understood his.

I stepped farther into the chalky-brown Jordan. With my eyes fixed on John, I made my way through the crowded river, slowly. My mind turned to my forefathers who had crossed this river to leave their exile behind and begin life anew in the Promised Land. I began to believe that my Father would likewise use this same river to begin my life, anew.

I made my way slowly into deeper water. As I drew closer to John, how-ever, I began to feel concern for him. He looked thin and wild; his beard was untrimmed and his head had not been shorn for a very long time. He wore some sort of hair shirt belted by a leather cord. It seemed to me that he could have been Elijah. I paused and stood silently to watch.[168]

---

168 Matthew 3 and John 1 offer detailed accounts of John the Baptist's ministry and the baptism of Jesus. The author has used reference in this section primarily from these sources.

"Herod, that fox, has poisoned Israel!" John pointed his finger at a huddling group of Pharisees and priests on the opposite bank. "You and you and you…" He jabbed his finger like it was a dagger. "You generation of vipers! Yesterday I warned you, today I warn you again."

A Pharisee whom I recognized from many years before answered, fearfully. "What then should we do?" His name was Nicodemus.

"Were you not here before? Day after day I say that you must produce fruit that is worthy of repentance." He squatted in the water and lifted some rocks from its bed. "Woe to you who depend on Abraham as your father. For I say to you, *Elohei Avraham* [169]is able to raise up sons to Abraham from these very stones!"

I marveled and moved closer.

Someone cried out, "Tell us what to do."

John answered like thunder answers lightning. "You must turn from your selves and to *Elohim*. He who has bounty should give to him with less." He pointed. "You, tax collector…cheat no one. You…hear me: do not deal harshly with those weaker than you. Every tree that does not bear fruit will be cut down and destroyed in the fire that does not go out!"

A Levite shouted, "Who are you?" Another priest shouted, "Tell us plainly, are you the Messiah?"

Whipping his head from one side to the other John finally raised his fists to heaven. "I say again: I am not!"

John was angry with them, but I felt sudden compassion. *Men are made of dust,* I thought. *Israel needs more than a return to former ways. She needs to turn to mercy and truth.* I cried out to my cousin, "From where comes the power to believe?"

John turned, slowly.

My heart began to race and I opened my arms.

He squinted and moved toward me, shielding his eyes with a hand. Not certain of who I was, he hesitated until I saw his face turn upward. He then smiled a smile such as I had never seen! *"Yeshua?"* He began to splash toward me. *"Yeshua!"*

---

169 Hebrew for 'God of Abraham'

I hurried toward him, laughing. And when we were upon one another, I lunged into his arms and he into mine.

"Jesus, Jesus!' Tears fell from his face.

"Oh, cousin. I have missed you," I said.

He couldn't speak. He nodded, happily. Then he wrapped his arm around my shoulder and spun me toward the silent crowd waiting in the river. "Hear me! I baptize with water but there stands one among you whose sandals I am not fit to loosen."[170]

I wanted to say something, but I could not speak. I let John lead me into deeper water where he took me by the shoulders. "You've come to be baptized?"

I nodded.

"We both know that I am not worthy to baptize you; you should baptize me."

I stared at him but thought of my mother. *Was this the day that the new Kingdom would come?* I loosed my tongue. "No, John, I need you to do this."

He stared.

"Do you love me, John?"

"I love you with all that I am."

"Then believe me. This is the day that the Lord has made…"

His face brightened. He rested his thick hand on my head and said, "Who you have been, is who you will be again. Rejoice…"

He released his hand and when he did, I, son of Mary, readied myself to leave behind all that was. I lifted my eyes to Heaven. "Let me be according to who you say I am."[171] With that I bent my legs and lowered myself beneath the Jordan. [172]

Leaving the world of breath, I found the world of water to be cool and silent.

I felt *welcome.*

---

170 From Mark 1:7. Note, the interested reader may enjoy the differing emphases of detail offered by the various gospel accounts found in Matthew 3, Mark 1, Luke 3 and John 1.

171 This is an adaptation of conventional Jewish ritual baptismal practice which refers to Exodus 16:7 by asking, 'What are we?'

172 Note, according to Leviticus 15:16, 'all flesh' needed to be bathed in water for ritual cleansing. For this reason, the witness to one's baptism (John the Baptist for Jesus) did not cover any part of the person's body by touching them during the act. Nor was the repentant to be clothed. Further, immersion was considered the only way to fully obey the command. For most Christians, of course, three dips are generally associated with the Trinity.

I lingered, but then I returned upright into the sun and took another breath before sinking myself for a second time. As I did, my mind flew across the years that had passed; the life that I had lived suddenly became warm memories that comforted me. I felt gratitude and peace. The currents of living water now ran over my limbs and filled them with strength.

I then stood and I breathed clean air before submerging myself for a third time. This time the water stirred my heart for a desire to become more of *who* I already was…and more of *why* I was; I felt the Spirit exciting me to become *all* that I was ever meant to be. My limbs stretched like a waking lion. My ears filled with the river's song.

I sprang from the water singing, my smiling face turned upward into the light of the Light. The sky then split above me and I looked into the third Heaven where I saw a chorus of angels without end. It was then when the Spirit descended upon me like a little dove, and as the dove rested on me the angels fell silent and the world was still. I felt her fill me to overflowing.

I then heard the proud proclamation of my Father's voice fill my ears like thunder from a mountain: "Behold, this is my beloved Son. I am well pleased with him!"

My beloved Son! I bowed my head, weeping.

When the sky was sealed once more, I faced my cousin and embraced him. He laughed for joy and pointed at me. "Look and see, this is the Lamb of God who takes away the sin of the world!" [173]

Many in the crowd gasped and some Sadducees on the far bank began to object, loudly. "How can this be the lamb of God? How can a man take away sin?" Many began to rush out of the river. "Blasphemy," shouted several. "You will be arrested!"

But John only looked at me and I only at him. I could feel every part of my being awakening; my limbs warmed and my heart raced. I began to sing and to laugh with my cousin. I closed my eyes and thought about what had just happened. *My* Father and *my* Spirit had come to *me*, and not just in love

but *as* love.

Surely, my Kingdom had come.

---

[173] John 1:29 Note: The author recognizes some difficulties in harmonizing the various Gospel accounts of Jesus' baptism.

Other than myself, only John had borne witness to the dove. So I listened carefully to him when he instructed me. "The Spirit of God is now with you in every moment until the end."

"The end?"

He shrugged. "I don't know. It was given to me to say."

We laughed, loudly.

I then felt the Spirit urge me to begin my journey. I reached my hands toward my cousin's face and held him for a long moment before kissing him on each cheek. The farewell was difficult for us both, and I made my way out of the Jordan's chalky waters slowly.

When I came to the water's edge, I dressed and then made my way up through the thick-reeds of the steep bank where I turned to look at John. Standing quietly in the water I thought he looked suddenly small and even weak. I waved to him and forced a smile, but he could barely lift his hand above his belt. My throat thickened. "May the Lord be with you," I whispered.

CHAPTER XXVI

KINGDOM COME

I turned away and followed the Spirit into the wilderness until I could walk no more. In the morning I found myself wakening in the shadow of Mt. Nebo. I reached for my bag and retrieved some bread, but I knew that I was to begin a fast and so I spread my bread for the birds.

The Spirit then compelled me to rise and begin my journey deeper into the wilderness. You ask how I knew her voice? I had heard her whisper all my life, though I did not always know whose voice the whisper was. I had also felt her when she would come near me in the breeze, and I felt different when she drifted away. It took many years to understand, but now that she was dwelling with me...*in* me...her voice was plain to my mind; the beat of her heart was alongside my own. So I obeyed the Spirit, happily, as did the angels whom she used to help lead me over the many days that followed.

One morning I awakened alongside a tiny spring that formed a circle of green in an otherwise desolate place. I was thirsty. I cupped some water to my mouth and then looked about the endless desert. I took another drink, and then stood slowly. It was then when I realized that I was the object of interest for a host of wild animals.[174]

---

174 Mark 1:13. Interestingly, Jesus' first encounter after his baptism is with angels and wild animals. Wild animals are always mentioned in contrast to the regular 'beasts' that would have been domestic animals such a donkeys, oxen, horses, etc. Some scholars suggest

I stood still as stone and slid my eyes from one to the other. As I did, I remembered my Father's words to Job: 'Do not fear the wild animals… for they shall be at peace with you.'[175] I smiled and released my breath. Standing before me were four long-legged jackals, three nervous hyenas, and more. They were not exactly the sort of company that I had hoped for, but I enjoyed watching them. "Are you hungry, too?"

I heard a noise to one side and so I turned slowly to face a small thicket. Within a dry tangle of weeds crouched a leopard. I stared at him for a long moment. He was a beautiful beast, wild and unruly like the world that surrounded us both. He stepped forward, silently, and as he did his mate emerged, restless and shy. "*Shalom,*" I said.

I took a slow breath and then noticed a slender, reddish-gray fox sniffing the air to another side, and not far from him was yet another fox—this one with large ears and a pale coat. I thought of Herod and imagined him scenting the air to plot his next step.

I shifted in my place and when I did I stirred the attention of a whole group of unseen watchers. A half dozen little martens scampered for cover; I had seen their skins sold in Jerusalem so I had sympathy for their fear. Three gazelles lifted off the ground from behind a nearby boulder and dashed to a safe retreat. A horned ibex—who, unseen by me, had been in full view all this time—planted himself firmly. So defiant was his look that I laughed out loud.

But I wondered why they were here. I looked from one to the other. Most I had never seen before. A magnificent Oryx with an unbroken set of long, twisted horns trotted across my view from behind a rock shelf to my right. A nervous sentinel for a nearby daman community scooted near my feet. And then of course, a handful of gray geckos and a lizard or two scattered away. Above, curious birds had begun to circle.

The words of the prophet, Hosea, came to me: 'I will make for you a covenant with the wild animals, the birds of the air, and the creeping things of the ground…and you will lie down in safety.' [176] I then thought of Eden and I remembered of the prophecy of Isaiah where the world would be restored…when men and wild beasts will share in the *shalom* of my Father.

---

that this is an important acknowledgment of his care for both the angels and the wild animals, and that his eventual Kingdom is universal.

175 From Job 5:22,23

176 From Hosea 2:18

PART I

Moved by these thoughts, I raised my fast-weakened arms slowly. "Peace be upon you all, for though the whole of Creation groans in wait; you will be surely welcome in the coming Kingdom."

A serpent then slid from behind a heated rock. An asp, perhaps? I stared at it and it at me as it slowly disappeared. *Will there be room enough for a serpent in my Kingdom?*

I continued my fast and the Spirit pressed me deeper into the wilderness. My belly began to cramp, desperate to be filled. *Why no manna?* I wondered. *Moses and the people were fed in this place, but no food for me? How long must I fast? Forty days and nights?*

Too weary to press on, I crawled into the shade of a merciful rock and fell into a deep sleep where I dreamt of my friend, Tobiah. In my dream he and I had climbed atop a raft in the Jordan's waters at the Passage of the Law— and we laughed our way past the Moses Rock and the Commandments, and then through the mouth of promise and into my lake where we drifted south through the middle way of my beloved waters. The water birds cried above and we threw bits of bread to them. In this dream I then counted exactly 153 large fish that swam close to us.[177]

We soon came to the place where the river was about to leave the lake and there the wind held us for a moment. We both looked at the shoreline and marveled. Tobiah said we must have drifted to Eden. Waiting for us were cool oases of date palms and figs, olive groves and magnificent fields of red anemones and purple crocuses, hyacinths and gladioli. I saw a lion grazing on grass and a little lamb dashed about playing with a leopard.

But in this dream a boat came alongside of us and four men urged us to pass by this new Eden: A Pharisee shouted, 'Sail on, sail on! 'Go and build up the walls of Jerusalem!'[178]A Sadducee in a fine turban quickly moved the Pharisee aside. 'Sail on, sail on! 'Blessed are those who remain in the Temple!'"[179]An angry Zealot then drew his knife, 'Sail on, sail on! 'Rise up, the Lord will give the city into your hand.'"[180] Finally, an old man of the

---

177 Allusion to John 21:11 Numbers have symbolic importance all through the Scriptures. The ancient world was more familiar with their meanings. The reader may find a study of '153' to be a fascinating though confusing adventure.

178 From Psalms 51:18

179 Ps 65:4 adapted

180 From Joshua 8:7

Essenes shook his head. "Sail on, sail on. 'Be without blemish so that the Lord God will not turn away from you.'"[181]

In my dream Tobiah then asked what we should do. I told him that because I loved him he could choose, but that I hoped he would choose wisely. I was not surprised that he chose to sail on. So a wind came to our back and pushed us away from this Eden, past Jericho and finally delivered us into the Salt Sea.

Tobiah stared at the lifeless mountains rising from the east and the west in that place. He desperately searched the heavens for a single bird. No fish swam in those waters; nothing lived here. Finally Tobiah said to me, "Too far. We've sailed too far!" He dipped a finger into the water and licked it, only to quickly wipe his tongue on his sleeve. "Too much salt!" He shielded his eyes from the blazing sun. "Too much light."

Finally Tobiah turned to me sadly and repented of his error. He then asked me how we might return to Eden. I smiled and asked if he truly believed that I could return us to that place. When he smiled, a great wind blew us backward, against the river's flow.

I awakened, happy.

I was refreshed by my dream, but more days passed slowly as the Spirit continued to lead me. I soon staggered for hunger and for thirst, falling twice into deep ravines where I was blessed with a few drops of water. My lips were badly blistered and my dry eyes were nearly blinded by scorching sand. *What is wanted of me?* I thought. I dragged myself forward to the base of a great mountain where I found shade. I struggled to climb upwards a little distance from the desert floor and lay upon a flat rock. I groaned aloud, "Spirit? Why am I here? What do you want?"

I then heard a woman's voice answer. "Jesus?"

I squeezed my eyes to clear them as I strained to see. "Who comes?"

"Jesus?"

The voice sounded familiar. "Mother?"

---

181 From Deuteronomy 23:14

"Oh, Jesus," the woman said. "What has happened to you?"

"Mother?"

"Look at you. You are little more than dry bones. You haven't eaten?"

"No, mother." My heart began to race.

"I have no food with me but look around you. See these stones, they look like loaves of bread. If you are the Son of God you can command these stones and they will become bread!"

I stared at the woman. 'If?' I thought to myself. *My mother would not say 'if,' for she knows that I AM the Son of God.* I prayed for the Spirit to awaken within me and she quickly filled the whole of me. I stared at the stones. *They were made to be stones and so it is good that they remain according to how they were made.* I took a breath and spoke by the Spirit. "Man does not live by bread alone, but by every word that comes out of the mouth of God." [182]

I waited for the woman to answer but she said nothing more. Instead she faded silently away, leaving me staring into the empty desert from my flat rock as if she had existed only in my mind.

I went to my knees in my sorrows. It was then when Wisdom taught me that I had been tested so that I would remember that I had been made as a man. A gentle voice filled my ears. "You must therefore remain according to how you are made—you are made to be dependent on the Father for all of life."

I lay on that flat rock for some time considering who I was, until I felt the urge to press on. I climbed along the face of the high mountain and tried to find a way around it. I then realized that it would easier to be a beast than a man; beasts do not battle with temptation.

I had no sooner thought this than my feet slipped on sharp stones. Thorns clawing at me from a crevice cut at my badly worn tunic. I held fast, clutching my faithful prayer shawl with one hand. At last I could go no more and I paused in the deep shade of a cliff where I sat against a cool rock wall to ponder my struggle. I soon sensed someone was near so I abandoned my shade. "Who's there?"

"Jesus?"

"Yes."

"Ha, ha! Jesus the Son!"

---

182 Deuteronomy 8:3, Matthew 4:4

"Who is it?" I strained to see. There before me was the image of a familiar man. "Jakob of Jerusalem? What…what are you doing here?" He was smiling and looked freshly bathed. He wore a fine, striped coat and a silk headdress covered his head.

"Oh Jesus. You look weary, but why not? You are a man—and men grow faint. It is how they are made. Ah…but you also claim that you are the Son of the Most High!"

Confused, I leaned forward. "Jakob, why are you here?"

"My friend, I want you to show me that you do believe your claim to be true."

I said nothing.

"Come, come with me for a moment." He took my arm and I felt dizzy at his touch. The world spun and a rushing wind nearly tore my *tallit* from my shoulders. I then felt my feet land hard upon some sort of tile. I fell forward and caught myself.

"Where are we?"

"You don't know?"

I stood slowly. "Jerusalem?"

"Yes. We are standing on the Pinnacle. Below us the scribes are still talking about you. Remember when you came as a boy. Oh, how they marveled. Now they whisper angrily about you and the goat."

I said nothing.

"Look and see, Jesus. Below you is the Valley of Kidron. If you are the Son of God, throw yourself down. For it is written that your Father will command the angels so that they will bear you up, not allowing your foot to strike even a stone! Then the whole city can believe that the Messiah has come!"

"*If* I am the Son of God, Jakob?"

"Just show me that you still believe, Jesus—show all of us, and then we can follow you."

Show you? I stared into the valley below me and felt faint. I closed my eyes. *Ask my Father to prove his own words? I will not.* I opened my eyes. "It is also written, 'You shall not test the Lord your God!'"[183]

A loud hiss rose from the valley below like a red coal had been thrown into water. As the sound filled my ears, the image of Jakob vanished and I felt as if I was falling. I cried out and at the sound of my own voice I felt

---

183 See Deuteronomy 6:16, Matthew 4:7

my fingers digging at the walls of a desert rock. I collapsed to my knees, disoriented. But there, in my terror, Wisdom taught me a second thing: No man must sin so that grace might abound.

I collapsed for a time, considering how a man should live when a deep sleep came over me. When I awoke I began to wander away from the rocks where I had been lying. But the moment my foot touched upon some loose stones I felt as if I was suddenly thrown upward, high into the blue sky until I found myself atop a summit. From there I could see the rooftops of faraway Jerusalem...had I flown to Pisgah? But wait, I could see yet farther. How was it that I could see across a wide ocean to behold another city? *Rome?* I spun to my left. *Alexandria?* I turned to my right. *Babylon?*

A gentle voice turned me around. It was Leah's. Her face was downcast, empty. My heart seized in my chest; I ached for her.

"Oh, my dear Jesus, only you can help me. I'm poor; my husband oppresses me. You are a Son of Man so you understand my suffering. But you are also the Son of God so you *can* save me. Please, Jesus, have mercy."

Tears filled my eyes and my throat thickened. The image of Leah began to blur. A sudden gust of wind then nearly blew me over. I staggered to keep my feet but the wind's force had cleared my mind. I clenched my jaw and narrowed my eyes. "Lucifer. Confront me!" I commanded. With a shriek, the image of Leah rent in two.

The Beast now stood before me.

A lifetime of memories sickened my belly. Horrid images of my days in Egypt, my mother's sufferings, and the many nights of terror found my mind. The Beast abruptly transformed into a beautiful angel of light and breathed a sweet fragrance. "You are wise, Jesus of Nazareth." The dazzling figure smiled at me. "Look around you. Look and see all that can be yours, *now.*" With a gentle command, the atmosphere opened wider and I saw yet more cities and more kingdoms. "I yield the authority of these kingdoms to you, for they have been given to me in this age to give away as I wish." He smiled a kindly smile. "I've heard you speak of love...why can't you love me? Just show me a little honor, and then it will all be yours to rescue... now."[184]

I was sorely tempted for I thought of Leah and all those many who were like her. Oh how love filled me! As long as this monster was permitted to

---

184 Per Luke 4

rule the air, suffering would find them. The whole of me longed to heal the sick, comfort the broken and set the prisoners free...*now*. I knew that my Father yearned for my Kingdom to come...I craved to see Evil cast into the lake of fire...now!

But ought things be changed before their time?

The Spirit quickly filled me with her power. *Worship the Beast?* My jaw pulsed. *Never. Not for anything. May my Father's will be done on earth according to his will in Heaven.* "Away with you!" I shouted. "As it is written, 'You, *Satana,* should worship the Lord our God and *you* should serve *him!*'"[185]

At the mention of my Father, the Beast screeched such a terrible cry that the heavens cracked and the mountains shook. I crouched to hold my feet fast to the quaking rocks as lightning fell like rain from the sky. The Spirit then hovered over the sky and the earth until the Terror flew away.

I felt sudden pity for the Beast and for all things that evil had polluted with its miseries. So I began to weep so loudly that the stars began to rattle. But in my sadness, Wisdom taught me a third thing: In the fullness of time, mercy and compassion will cover the earth.

I felt myself falling but I landed softly atop a mound of desert sand where I rested for a long while, considering what meant for a man to live a life inside of Wisdom's promise. Such a constant hope quickly eased my heart and I sat up, smiling. Soon I felt as if many unseen hands were helping me to my feet. The hands felt kind; they were comforting and so I stood, obediently. I was then led around a low hill and to a small spring. There, flowers that bloomed among lush plants; date palms offered shade. Numbers of restful animals lay about, some of which I was quite sure I had met before.

I hurried toward the green where I saw a pool of crystal water and I drank deeply. I undressed and washed my body and then my clothes. I laid my clothes to dry upon the heated rocks and laughed as I beheld a heavy-laden fig tree by a generous pomegranate. Nearby was a bountiful a citron[186]tree and a sagging pear tree. Naked, I began to pick any fruit that I wanted, unashamed.

The Spirit then opened my eyes and I saw angels all about me. I laughed, loudly, and welcomed them. Their names came to me oddly—as if I was

---

185 Per Deuteronomy 6:16 added, *Satana,* Matt 4:10

186 Sometimes translated apple (Song of Solomon, etc.)

somehow remembering them. "Thank you, Nith-Haiah and Nelchael, Iabamiah and Vasiarah. And you, Lauviah and Michael…blessings…And Gabriel!" I thanked each and every one for delivering me and they, in turn, spoke words of encouragement to me.

Then, to my astonishment, I heard bleating. I looked about to see a little goat trotting toward me from the desert with the Temple's weathered red cloth still hanging from its horn. I ran to him and he to me. "Ha, *la-Azazel*! Run free, I took the sins off you." I then lay back and I allowed the Spirit to unloose my mind so that I might know again of things that I seemed to already know. But she suddenly filled me with images that were deeply troubling and I began to tremble and shudder so violently that she quickly comforted me with a wondrous vision that I did not fully understand.

Confused, I asked aloud, "I don't understand. Tell me, what do you want of me now?" A breeze nudged the thick leaves of a fig and I listened carefully as the words of the prophet Isaiah came to me:

'The people who were sitting in darkness
    Have seen a great light;
    A light has dawned to them who sit in the land
    By the way of the sea,
    Beyond the Jordan,
        In Galilee of the Gentiles…'[187]

I stood and prepared to return to Galilee. For I knew that the Kingdom of Heaven was surely at hand.

---

187 Adapted from Isaiah 9:1-4

PART II

"I have come so **they may have life...**"

JOHN 10:10

Dear reader, patient listener, I—Adlai—must interrupt the words of *Yeshua* for just a moment. You see, when the rabbi finished telling us of all the things that had prepared him for his Kingdom, he simply stopped talking. He reached for a wine skin and drank a little wine, and then he ate a rather great deal of fish. He hummed a song or two and when he took his seat again, he said nothing more until the impatient Gaul urged him to go on. He then looked at us, carefully. "First, answer this: *why* I have come?"

We shifted in our seats.

"I've come to set my Father's world free; I've come that all people might have abundant life within the peace of my Father's love." He leaned toward us. "So what use is my Story if it doesn't live on in the lives of others…of you?" He pushed a little stick into the fire. "Do you understand?"

We didn't.

He sighed and fell quiet for a long time. Finally, he said, "It's not possible to tell you all that I did after my preparation in the wilderness. However, I will tell you of my times with some others--others in whom all people can be found." He lifted his burning twig and smiled. "Listen and you will find yourselves."

CHAPTER XXVII

BEGINNING

After my difficult days in the wilderness, I returned to the site of my baptism where I stumbled into the water to embrace my cousin once again. He held me up, joyfully, and prayed for me, then carried me to the riverbank where he summoned others to get me food and drink. "Eat and be strong, Jesus," he commanded. "The Kingdom is begun."

I nodded.

"And I am telling everyone that it has," he said. He bent close to my ear and lowered his voice. "You are ready, aren't you?"

"I am. The Spirit is upon me."

John exhaled, slowly. We studied one another for a long, silent moment. I could see his face beginning to twist in sorrow; his lower lip quivered beneath his matted beard. He then took my shoulders in his powerful hands and squeezed them, knowing that this was the end. Saying nothing more, he wiped his eyes, stood upright, and strode away.

I watched my cousin return to the river where he started to shout at others about the 'Lamb of God.' I smiled a little smile and began to pray for him when a cracking voice turned my head. The distraction annoyed me, but my cousin was right..the Kingdom had begun.

The voice was that of another John...young John of Jerusalem, the son of my friend and former classmate, Jakob. I was surprised to see him at all, and especially surprised to see him adorned in bright colors. I say that because an ungrateful tenant had recently murdered his parents. I stood, weakly, and greeted the youth with a kiss. "*Shalom,* John."

"*Shalom,* Rabbi."

I rested a hand on his shoulder. "I'm so sorry. Your father was a dear friend of mine. May the Lord grant you peace."

The young man's smooth chin quivered. "The world is dark, just as my mother taught me." He quickly changed course. "Rabbi, all of Jerusalem is still talking about how you laid hands on the scapegoat. Why did you do that?"

I took a breath. "The Temple has been killing the goats in violation of the Law."

"So you touched an unclean beast in order to fulfill the Law? Isn't that..."

"Your father told me that you might be a lawyer someday, or a priest."

John shrugged. "I had many dreams when I was a boy. My grandfather spent hours teaching me every detail of the Temple."

"Well, you would sing a fine song. I've never forgotten listening to you in Capernaum."

"I remember." John wiped his hand through his neatly cut hair. "My mother often begged me to sing to her. She said that singing kept us apart from the darkness of the world...where love is hard to find."

We sat and I considered his mother's words. "Then a song would be a lonely thing," I said. "And love would not be love." I decided to say nothing more but waited as the young man cast his eyes toward the nearby Jordan. A woman finally delivered a basket of food to us just as a familiar voice turned both our heads.

John seemed relieved. "Andrew. Where have you been? Here's the rabbi."

I studied the young fisherman and then greeted him with a kiss. "*Shalom,* Andrew. It's good to see you after all these years. You've grown into a man. I still remember you playing in my workshop."

Andrew laughed. "Yes, yes. I remember it well. Simon and I did our best to annoy you!"

I told John of the times in my Bethsaida workshop with Andrew and Simon, and when I was done I took each of the young men by the shoulder. "So, it seems that you two are following me? What is it that you want?"

Andrew answered. "We want to learn from you. The Baptizer says that you're the One."

"Eat with me, then come and see."

It was about the tenth hour of the day when the three of us were led to a small house in Bethabara where I had been invited to stay. My host brought us some wine, bread, oil, and fish, and so we ate a little before Andrew stepped out of the house to find his brother.

I took a bite of bread and dipped it into the clay bowl of oil. "Tell me, John, why do you follow the Baptizer?"

"One of my uncles told me that I needed to repent for the family, otherwise the sins of our family would strike us all...like they did our parents."

I took a drink of wine and passed the skin to him. "Your parents did not die for their sins."

"Then why?"

"Because Evil prowls the world...it crouches at the doors of sinners and the righteous alike."

John leaned close. "Why?"

I picked at some fish. "Men are meant to be free to choose between Light and Darkness."

John measured my words, carefully. "Then the cost of freedom is too high. I've walked past too many sick by the Pool of Siloam. I've walked past too many children..." His eyes filled. "Men are prisoners of darkness. What freedom do they have to make choices?"

I knew then that he would be my perceptive witness. I set my hand lightly on his forearm. "The blind shall be healed; the prisoners shall be set free."

"When?" His voice was hard.

I removed my hand. "Perhaps when others stop walking past them?"

John winced and took a draught of wine. "My father loved you since the time you studied together in Sepphoris. And my grandfather was confused by you."

I remembered his grandfather from my three days in the Temple when I was just two years younger than John was now. "I loved them both." I took some bread and dipped it. "Now, I must ask you something: why is it that you grieve your parents in such bright colors?"

"Because as I've told you, the world is dark enough. My mother taught me that color and music keep us safe." He looked away from me. "She taught me to use these things to keep the darkness away..."

I waited.

His face fell. "But the darkness found her..." He wiped his eyes. "And sadness fills my heart."

We sat together in a long silence. Looking at him, I admired how much he opposed evil, but I also pitied him. Finally, I said, "Beauty and song are not meant to be walls, my son. Walls don't defeat evil...they can only hold it back for a season."

The youth stared at me like a starving man stares at a basket of bread.

I leaned close to him. "Like beauty, John, a song keeps joy alive...but only when it's sung *to* this suffering world." I waited as he chewed some bread, thinking. I then asked, "Now tell me again, my young friend, what is it that you want?"

He thought carefully and then answered, "I want the whole earth to be beautiful and good..."

Before he could finish, Andrew burst through the door with his clumsy brother. "See, Simon...it's Jesus, like I told you!"

Annoyed at the interruption, I began to stand when he ran at me and lifted me off my cushion. "Rabbi! Remember me? Ha! I watched you chisel wood in Bethsaida!"

"Yes, yes, Simon, let me go." I struggled to hold him at arms length. "Let me look at you." The stocky boy I remembered had grown into a burly fisherman. His bearded face was eager and bright. "It's good to see you again, Simon." I then pointed to the slender John who had faded warily into a corner. "That's John—my friend from Jerusalem." I then called to John. "Don't be afraid, but this is Simon of Bethsaida..."

"I live in Capernaum now." Simon pushed past me. He reached for John and yanked him into his embrace with a kiss. "If the rabbi loves you, I love you."

"You stink like fish," complained John as he pulled away. "And look, you've stained my robe with your dirty hands!"

"Stink?" Simon began to laugh, loudly. "Of course I stink!" He grabbed John's head and smelled his oiled hair. "And you smell like a Greek! Let me see your hands." He grabbed both of John's wrists and forced his palms up. "Not one callus! Not one speck of dirt! Who are you?"

I was unable to finish my conversation with John because of the days of bickering between him and Simon that followed. The pair eventually made an uneasy peace and agreed to come with me to return to Galilee when I was ready. So, before long I led them away out of Judea and to Cana along with Andrew and two new followers—one named Philip and the other, Nathaniel. There, my sister, Salome, welcomed us into the household of her father-in-law to celebrate the wedding of her eldest son. "Oh, Jesus!"

I embraced her, joyfully. "It is so good to see you again, and on such a good day!

She wiped a tear from her cheek. "I only wish my husband would have lived to see it. You look thin."

I walked her to a donkey we had borrowed and asked John to throw the blanket off our cargo. "For you. Do you remember?"

Salome clutched her hands, happily. "The *shulcan* you made!"

A familiar voice turned my head. "Jesus!"

"Mother!" I lunged toward Mary. "Woman, dear woman!" I kissed her cheeks and held her, tightly.

She then took me by the shoulders and held me at arms' length. She wrinkled her nose. "You look thin."

I shrugged.

She called for someone to bring me bread, and then finally asked me to introduce my followers. I began to do so until a loud snort behind me turned my face. "Cleopas!"

"You're too thin, Figgy Face!" He snorted again and kissed me. "Mary... get this man some bread." He looked at John. "And who's this bony shoot?"

The youth lowered his eyes.

"Look at me, boy."

"I...I'm not a boy..."

Cleopas circled him as he tested the fabric of John's robe between his fingers. "Fine work. Very fine work." He studied the cloth more carefully. "But what's this? There's dirt on it."

John grumbled.

"So, you're the son of a rich man?" Cleopas asked. "And you have a Judean accent. Hmm. You're from Jerusalem."

John shuffled, suddenly uneasy. He nodded. "My father was much blessed. And yes, I'm from Jerusalem."

Mary had been hovering. She took John by the elbow and pulled him lightly away from Cleopas. "Now, John, come with me; we need a *man* to carry some things."

I watched the two of them walk away and I was happy; John needed to be loved and Mary loved to love. But before they disappeared in the growing crowd, John turned and shouted back to me, " 'Figgy Face?' "

Sometime around the ninth hour of the second day of the celebration my mother took me aside. "I like your friend, Jesus, but he won't dance. He likes to keep a distance."

I searched the crowd and saw John standing to one side, alone. "He's afraid."

"Of what?" Mary asked.

"He is a dreamer who fears more about what could be than what is." I went on to tell my mother all that I knew of the youth. "And he sings like a songbird when he finally feels safe."

Mary smiled one of those knowing smiles that I so loved to see. With a twinkle and a wink she made her way to my young friend.

For the next three days I watched my mother and John. At first he offered polite smiles, then real ones, and by the fifth day of the celebration he was laughing loudly with her and Cleopas.

On that same day, the bridegroom bravely invited me to stand before the canopy of the bride and bless her. I say that my nephew was brave because many there were still unhappy with me from the time of my first sacrifice, and some quietly hated me for whom I was said to be. I picked a pomegranate from a basket and held it high overhead. "Woman, may your womb be as fruitful as the seeds of this fruit!" I then dropped the pomegranate and smashed it with my foot. "*Selah!*" Seeds burst from the fruit and flew in all directions.[188] The bridegroom clapped; the bride blushed.

---

188 An ancient Palestinian custom

My mother then led John closer to the canopy and, to his surprise, turned his shoulders to face the families. She whispered something into his ear, kissed the tip of her forefinger and touched it to the point of his dropped chin. She then handed him a wineskin. Terrified, John drank generously as everyone fell silent.

I walked to my mother's side. "What did you tell him?"

"I told him to sing a blessing to the bride and groom. And then I told him that fear is a kind of darkness that he could drive away with a song."

I squeezed my mother's hand. "You love him."

"I do."

I kissed her cheek. "Love drives out fear."

She smiled. "Yes. Love and a song." We both turned toward John. The youth was wiping his hands on his robe and swinging his eyes from face to face. I felt my heart begin to race. I spotted Uncle Cleopas encouraging the youth with a smile, and I saw my sisters doing the same. Simon gave him a hearty slap on the shoulder and walked to one side. At last, he looked to Mary one more time. She nodded, confidently, and mouthed, "Now." The young man was pale. He drew a deep breath.

I held my own.

When he released his breath all of Cana fell suddenly still. His voice was sweet and soothing:

> "We rejoice and delight in you,
> We will praise your love more than wine.
> Eat, my friends, and drink;
> Drink your fill of love..."[189]

When he finished, the families praised him loudly with happy cries and clapping. Flushed, John shyly received many embraces until he was able to seek out my mother. She squeezed his cheeks. "See! John of Jerusalem! You have blessed us all!"

The delighted wedding host made a special effort to take John by the hand and lead him around. When he returned, we laughed freely until the sun was nearly set. However, as lamplight filled the courtyard I knew that something was bothering him. I waited as he pushed some lentils into his mouth.

"Rabbi...over these days I've heard more than one say that you are a disgrace because you never married."

---

189 A collection of various excerpts from the *Song of Solomon*

I bit some bread and chewed, slowly. "And what do you think?"

"You're no disgrace! But I think you must be lonely...especially at a wedding."

"Lonely? I'm not lonely, dear John," I said. "A family is waiting for me."

He tore some bread from a loaf and dipped into the lentils. "I don't understand."

"In time, little brother."

On the final day of the party, the courtyard became quiet except for Simon's loud belching and his constant releasing of air from his bowels. He laughed about it but John was disgusted. "What's wrong with him?" asked John.

I shrugged. "He's content to be who he is."

"Well, maybe he shouldn't be." John shook his head, but then noticed my mother and my sister. "Look."

I stood as my mother came to my side with Salome close behind.

"Jesus, we have no more wine," Mary said. She was anxious. "Your sister is ashamed..."

I shrugged. "Well, what business is this of ours?"

My mother was shocked. "This is *our* family's wedding...and *we* are failing to serve as we should!" Her eyes flashed. "Your father would have understood."

I looked at John. "You Judeans know the ways of hospitality more than any of us. What do you think? Is it our problem if the host runs out of wine?"

John wouldn't answer.

I wiped my hand through my beard. "Mother, so what do you think *I* can do?"

"You told me that the Spirit of *Elohim* was preparing you in the wilderness. What better way to introduce your Kingdom then at a wedding? And what better than with wine?"

I scratched my chin. "But how? And is my time *now* come?"

My mother had just decided that, yes, my time *had* come. "Why not now!" She boldly summoned two servants.[190] "Do whatever he tells you to

---

190   John 2:4,5

do." She then folded her arms and looked at me. "Do you love your sister? Do you love me?" She set her jaw.

I stared at her and then at the blank-faced John. "Of course, but..."

"Then do something."

What was I to do? Defeated by my mother, I closed my eyes for a moment. When I did a rush of images quickly filled my mind—a few memories of what was coming came over me. I trembled, lightly. Yes, the Spirit had begun to show me things in the wilderness, but would this be the beginning?

Here, in Cana?

A wedding?

Wine?

I opened my eyes and looked carefully at my mother. I remembered how often she had calmed me by telling me that my time had *not* yet come. She had been so sure then...and she seemed just as sure now. My belly fluttered. "Woman, you believe that my time is truly come?"

Her eyes swelled with hope. She took my moist hand, softly, and waited.

"Is Israel ready for me?" I stared at the unhappy guests now grumbling about the courtyard.

Mary squeezed confidence into my hands. "Remember love, and do not be afraid."

I looked deeply into her face, marveling at her faith. I then met the wide eyes of my dear sister. She clutched her heart. Oh, how I loved her. I took a breath. I then faced the courtyard and my gaze rested on a cluster of purification vessels standing in a corner.

My mother saw what I saw. She smiled, knowingly. "Go and see that Israel is ready. See that *you* are ready. " She kissed the tip of her forefinger and touched it to my chin. "Believe."

I felt my heart begin to race as I stared at the large vessels. I then looked at the confused servants and finally at John. His face was filled with excitement. "Do not be afraid," he whispered. A light breeze toyed with my hair. I took a prayerful breath, and when I released it I knew that *El Abba* had, indeed, prepared Israel for me--and he had prepared me for her. Yes, the world was about to change, and I was not afraid.

I kissed my mother's cheek and then directed the servants to the stone vessels. "Fill them to the very top with water."

They ran off and one soon returned. "We have done as you have said."

"Good." I licked my lips and closed my eyes. "Now go back and dip a clean cup into one of them. Take it to the wedding steward."

My mouth went dry as the obedient servant trotted away. I remembered the crushing disappointment that my family suffered when I had failed to heal our little sister. I never wanted to see that look in my mother's face again. I took a breath and fixed my eyes on the steward as he received the cup. I felt John shift his feet next to me. My mother took my hand.

The steward lifted the cup to his nose. He then sipped from it once and then once more. Startled, he gulped a great swallow. His eyes widened and then he lifted the cup high overhead. With a huge smile he shouted, "I have never drank better!"

A wind rustled the dust at my feet. Strength filled my limbs. My mother clutched my hand to her heart and tears of joy ran down her face. "My son! Do you see? Your time *has* come…and the Lord *has* surely prepared Israel for you." She grabbed my bearded cheeks and pulled me close. "And you are surely ready for Israel!"

My heart was pounding. *All these years, mother. And you have been faithful…*

John began laughing. "Look! They're dancing and singing again. Is this how your Kingdom will be? I would belong to a Kingdom like this!"

I wiped my eyes. "Yes, John, yes. Now go and dance, little brother, for this is why I have come."

CHAPTER XXVIII

NEW DAUGHTERS
FOR THE KINGDOM

Happy to begin the work of my Kingdom, I left Cana to make my way into Judea. By my side were young John, Andrew, Simon and my cousins— James and John of Zebedee. With each step my feet felt lighter; the Spirit filled me to overflowing with her joy, and she began to enlighten me with her sight. So when I found a child with fever near Samaria, I immediately knew what to do. "Give me your little daughter," I said to a reluctant woman.

She passed her limp infant to me. As I received the child, my arms began to burn but my heart raced with joy. I breathed over the little girl and she opened her eyes. The heat left both of our bodies. I smiled and the astonished woman grabbed her child with a happy cry.

My followers clapped and we all praised my Father until vile words from a shrieking woman turned our heads. Staggering toward me was a threadbare woman with an uncovered head. Her sallow skin clung tightly to the bones of her face and hands; her hair was faded red and blowing wildly in the wind. She was clutching an empty sack of some sort to her breast and a little cat crouched on her shoulder.

"You, healer!" she shrieked. "You, teacher of lies. You are the Fool of Nazareth! Jesus...bastard of Nazareth. Imposter...*mamzer!*"

I knew her at once, and I felt a heavy weight in my belly. "Susanna."

The woman lunged at me and tried to scratch my face. Simon took hold of her, but her strength was unworldly. With a hiss, she pushed him aside and then crouched like her cat, ready to pounce. Her eyes were wild and she slid them from one side to the other as she slowly rose, still clutching her bag.

Dear Susanna, the poor child of Nazareth. What has happened to you? Again, the Spirit opened my eyes and I knew what to do. I raised my hands over her. "Out, out, come out of her."

Susanna shuddered. She threw her head back. "No."

"I name you Greed and Hatred and I command you to leave this woman!" Susanna was thrown to the ground where she coiled like a snake. I raised my voice. "Leave this woman, now!" At that final command, the demons abandoned their prey and cut through me like hot knives. I clenched my teeth in pain and staggered. Catching my breath, I then kneeled by Susanna now lying limp in the dust. "Woman?" I said.

Susanna opened her eyes, but she did not smile. Climbing to her feet, she muttered, "Jesus. You are Jesus of Nazareth."

"Yes."

She began to walk away. "Nothing good comes from that place. Nothing."

My followers—which now included my cousins, James and John of Zebedee--continued to travel throughout Judea, and there I met Mary of Magdala. On that day, everything began to change.

We were resting by a spring as a Roman carriage rolled to a stop close to us. Inside, the passengers were laughing, loudly. I recognized the laugh as false joy. I left the others and approached the carriage to find it being tended by three Nubian eunuchs. A wealthy Jewess emerged from behind a curtain and climbed awkwardly to the ground. I looked at her bloated face and a rush of images suddenly filled my mind's eye.

Once seated on a thick pillow, the woman turned oddly wrathful and shrieked at the slaves in many voices and many languages. I was able to understand two of the tongues: "Hurry up with my wine, you ungrateful fools! After all I've done to spare you the whip!"

The trembling slaves brought her wine in a tall vessel and set two clay cups in her ring-jeweled hands. One slave nervously filled both cups. The woman drained the first cup and then the other. The slave refilled them and while he was pouring she began to shout for food. Another slave scampered toward a large chest from which he removed several platters heaped with fine wheat breads, fruit, and some sort of meats.

She stuffed her mouth and began to chew, but the faraway look in her painted eyes told me that Mary of Magdala had been buried deep within and long ago. The woman yawned. "Find Cassius and tell him that I'm bored and I want to go home." She belched, staggered back to her carriage and retrieved a fine silk veil and a golden necklace that she draped over her ample bosom.

I moved closer and she saw me. When she did she turned hard as stone and began to tilt. A slave caught her and held her, not knowing what to do. Her lips parted without making a sound, and her eyes fluttered. Then, as quickly as she had been seized, she was released. "Take your hands off me!" she shouted at the eunuch, this time in Greek. "Who do you think you are?" She stood and slapped the poor man with such unworldly force that he toppled backward.

I walked toward the fallen man as the woman pushed a bit of graying hair beneath her scarf. Then, as if nothing had happened, she smoothed her purple robes over her broad body and turned her face away from me. I lifted the slave to his feet as a Roman nobleman approached the woman with two Herodian friends. All of them were drunk and laughing loudly.

The Magdalene pointed to some naked young men splashing in the spring. "Cassius, I want one of them to take home."

"Ah, but Mary, you have me," the nobleman slurred.

She toyed with his hair. "I have your money." She giggled.

Images of the woman as a sad little girl filled my mind. I closed my eyes to see her in the tiled courtyard of her father's wealthy house in Magdala. Starved for love, she was serving him in terrible ways. Rage filled me. I pitied this woman for all that Evil had done to her. The Spirit then opened my eyes further to see what else clung to her heart. I stepped forward. "Enough! Leave this woman!"

The rich men were offended, but I was not commanding them. Mary lunged at me with a fist and I grabbed her wrist. At the touch I felt as if I might vomit. Her face darkened. She threw her other fist at me and I caught it and held it firmly. Foam began to pour from her nose and mouth; her eyes swung wildly from side to side and she began to curse me in many voices and in many tongues. The rich men ran away.

Then Mary's body clenched. "We know who you are, Jesus of Nazareth!" Breaking my hold, she curled into a ball. "Leave. This woman belongs to us."

I bent to one knee and grabbed hold of one hand. "I command you..."

"Hear us!" several voices shrieked. "The spirit named Sloth found her first but the woman wanted to sweep out Sloth with her own strength. We let her so that Pride could enter her...and Pride opened the door for us all."[191] Laughter shook the earth below my feet. "She is ours!"

The seven were right and the seven were wrong. With a wave of my hand I threw them each from the poor woman. But as they passed from her they scorched my hand with seven stripes as if red coals had brushed me. I cried out.

My followers came quickly, and when John saw my hand he ran for water. Simon helped Mary to her feet.

"Who are you?" Mary was weak.

I looked into her heavy-painted eyes and I felt for her. "You need to go home, Mary of Magdala."

She was startled and she held a blanket to her body, tightly. "How do you know me?"

"I saw you under the shade of your father's porch when you were a little girl. I saw you weeping at your child's grave when you were a young mother, and I saw you grieving your cruel husband."

"How do you know these things?"

"I know."

She stared for a long moment. "You are a seer...And if you've seen these things, then you have seen the rest." Her face reddened and she looked down.

"Mary, I know you. You are clean, sister, now go home and be well."

---

191 Allusion to Matthew 12:45

In the days that followed, I continued teaching my disciples...my students. "You see me cast out demons and I see fear in your faces. Never forget that we do not make war against flesh and blood, but against the forces of the unseen powers. These powers move around you like the wind. You don't see them, but you must learn to see their effect, for they are mighty enemies who lust for every manner of misery and destruction."

I had barely finished teaching when John pointed to a woman lingering under a tree not far off the road. "Rabbi, it's Susanna again."

Excited to see her, I quickly walked toward her. She was weak and frail, helpless and in grave need. As I approached, she hurried to pack something in her sack and picked up her cat. "Susanna!" I cried. "Stay. Sit with me."

The woman yielded. I came close. "Will you speak to me?"

She nodded, obediently, and set her cat on the ground.

I began by asking her a few questions about her cat that she answered, warily. I then spoke of Nazareth and of her miseries as a child. To that she fell silent. Eventually I told her of my sorrow for her mother's death and finally asked her what happened when the soldiers stole her away.

Her body tightened. "Rabbi Jesus...thank you for casting out the demons." She started to weep. "Forgive me. Even after you saved me I was afraid of you."

I took her hand. "I've come to set people free, Susanna."

She wiped her eyes. "Free? Who is free? I was a slave of soldiers at the garrison for six years. I escaped during a party for Pontius Pilate when he arrived as governor. I thought I was free, but the demons found me somewhere in Samaria when I was near death from hunger. They taught me how to steal but I never could steal enough." She pulled her sack close to her body and fell silent.

I let her be still for a long while, and then pointed to her sack. "Tell me about that, Susanna. It's important to you."

She clutched it tight, firmly. "This and my cat...they are all that I have in this world."

I took a breath. "I'm sorry that Nazareth failed you as a child."

"Everybody fails everybody. Look at me. I'm a skeleton with rags…like my mother before me. No one has provided for me…except the soldiers who gave me three children." Her throat filled. "But they took them from me and sold them."

I groaned.

"My mother hated me, Jesus. I was her ever-present shame."

It was true.

"I've learned that the world does not have enough for all of us—not enough food, clothing, money, wisdom, or even love. So I gather for myself what I can. I live to keep my bag from being empty and I hope to make my cat happy."

I took her face in my hands. "Susanna, will you follow me?"

She hesitated.

"I will not force you, but you are welcome to follow as long as you will."

"No one has ever welcomed me."

"I do."

Susanna wiped her nose and fell into my embrace.

I said that the day I met the Magdalene everything began to change, and so it did. I led my followers back into Galilee where I taught and healed and cast out demons, now with ease. The news spread and the crowds following us began to grow. One morning I looked up to see Mary's face standing boldly in front of me.

"*Shalom*, Rabbi."

I stood. "Mary."

"I want to follow you like they do." She pointed at the men and at Susanna.

"Why?"

She didn't hesitate. "You need me." She pointed to my *tallit*. "That needs to be washed."

I laughed, loudly. I had made sure that the urine stain from my dear Obadiah had never been washed away. "And what do *you* need, Mary?"

"I need to understand who you are."

I took her hand. "No one can understand unless they are first set free."

"Then I want to be free."

Susanna looked hopeful, but Simon started complaining. I lifted my hand. "Don't you see? This is why I have been sent." I turned to Mary. "Come and follow, sister."

Simon growled, "No. It's not decent, Master. Women without escorts in our company? It's...it's shameless..."

Susanna retreated, but before I could answer Mary the Magdalene stepped between us. She blew strands of hair off her forehead. "Who are you, fisherman?"

Simon cursed; Mary barked; Simon kicked stones; Mary stomped her feet. And so it was until the troublesome day that the Spirit urged me to return to Nazareth.[192]

We entered my village as a long parade of weary, heavy-footed men and Mary's dusty women. I ran to embrace my dear mother and my sister, Salome. My mother then happily greeted my followers—some she knew, of course, like my cousins and Nathaniel of Cana. But when I introduced her to Mary of Magdala she had such a look of shock that I almost laughed out loud.

Eventually, we received the reluctant hospitality of my brothers. James, of course, now occupied Joseph's house with his wife and children. My mother lived with him as did my brother Simeon and his family. Joses lived nearby and Judah had built a small house near the Gentile baths. The contempt that all of my brothers now held for me made for an awkward greeting. But more importantly, it was very apparent that my arrival had made life especially difficult for my poor mother who loved them, even as she loved me.

Wanting to bring peace to her family, my mother had always tried holding my hand in one of hers, and theirs in the other. But rather than bring us together, this seemed to tear her apart, and so I realized that my presence with her was putting a great strain on her heart; I knew that I would need to leave my village, soon.

Mary Magdalene recognized my mother's agony quickly and did her best to comfort her. But the Magdalene also knew that Nazareth was not

192 Luke 4:16

safe for me. She warned me that that I, like Elijah, would be given no honor in my own home. She was right. The disbelief in that place was so heavy that in the days that followed I could barely heal a person.

However, the Nazarenes were curious, and so I was invited to teach in the synagogue. There I taught the Scriptures and they marveled. But when I repeated the story of Elijah's rejection and how I would give them no signs, they became insulted and therefore outraged. The men whom I had once played with as a boy then set their hands upon me and began to drag me toward the 'Cliff of Justice,' as some called the place.

Midst shouts and curses, my disciples were shoved to the margins as I was driven out of Nazareth and up the steep slope of a low cliff. Spat upon and accused by the men of Nazareth, I could hear my mother's wailing not far behind. I thought of our time talking with one another on this very spot. I smiled. We arrived at the edge of the rocks as many voices cried for my death. But I was not afraid. The images that the Spirit was showing me were not of rocks and spitting Nazarenes, but of things more terrible.

Somehow, Simon pounded his way close to me by striking down several men in my name. My cousins, James and John, did the same. The slight, young John of Jerusalem was tossed aside, but Nathaniel and Andrew fought their way toward me, bravely. I feared for them and I cried out to Heaven.

A hard hand jabbed from the mob and nearly knocked me over the cliff. My feet slid on the crumbling limestone and I fell to my knees, catching myself. It was then that the Magdalene suddenly emerged. Elbowing others aside, she offered me her hand to help me stand. I took it, and at the touch I knew that the hand of the Spirit was upon her own hand.

However, our touch infuriated the mob all the more and men began shouting all manner of vile things. But Mary was not shaken. With me now standing behind her, she faced my sputtering neighbors and began to remove her many rings. She yanked a jeweled brooch from her hair. Holding her jewelry high over her head, she began to shout at the suddenly silent Nazarenes. "Are there poor in Nazareth?"

The men stirred.

"Yes. I think so." Mary then turned her back on the people and tossed her jewels over the cliff, crying, "For the poor of Nazareth."

At that, the crowd scattered down the slope in a mad frenzy. And as they did, my bruised disciples and I were able to pass through them with ease and I found my mother and sisters, weeping. I kissed them each, then took my mother's hands. "I must leave, but I will surely keep watch over you."

Unable to speak, my mother fell into my arms.

I then turned to embrace my sisters. Salome, however, refused to accept my farewell. "Brother, my husband is dead, my daughter is married and my son apprentices for my father-in-law. I am ready to serve your Kingdom."

"Then return to Nazareth and be with mother."

Mary shook her head. "Lydia is enough. Salome wishes to follow you."

I looked into my sister's face. "Then come."

Simon groaned.

CHAPTER XXIX

WRESTLING WITH SONS

Simon the fisherman was loyal and brave; he bore the bruises of Nazareth to prove it. Surely, no man could rule him, but he was afraid to abandon himself--so he was not free. That same day, he led us away from the wrath of Nazareth and toward his house in Capernaum where we could rest. A couple of days later, his wife was preparing another good meal for all of us.

"Simon, show me your hands." I was happy that the man loved me, but I was tiring of the man's stiff-necked belief in himself.

The fisherman put down his bread and sat up with a grumble. He reluctantly held his thick paws toward me. "Yes, what now?"

"What do you see?"

"Hands."

"*Strong* hands. Hands that are scabbed for your sake."

I nodded. "Your hands trust their master."

Simon belched. "Of course. *I* am their master."

"Now show me your feet."

"Why?"

Simon's wife, Emanuh, set her bowl of hummus and cloves hard on top of a small table. "'Why?' You always ask 'why.' You're like some wary wolf." She cast a look at her nodding mother and then added, "Really, Simon, you are the most miserable scoffer in all of Capernaum."

"No, that's not..."

"Yes, you are." Emanuh pressed. "You don't believe anything unless you see it yourself. This morning the centurion believed that the rabbi could just say a word to heal his servant and he was healed! Jesus said he was a man of great faith. Think of that, Simon...*a Gentile* of great faith.

"And then there's you. You insisted that the rabbi come here to prove himself in *your* home by healing *your* mother-in-law in front of *your* face."[193]

Simon stuffed his mouth with some bread. "The world's full of trouble, woman. I don't trust it."

I dipped my bread in the bowl of Emanuh's hummus and leaned toward the blustery fisherman. "It seems that you have great faith in *your* hands."

"So what? I know what I'm doing." He folded his arms and looked at me. I smiled to myself. Sitting there with his shaggy hair, his broad head, and his thick neck, he reminded me of my teacher's dog, the Molossian named Petrus. "Now, Simon, once more: tell me what you see when you look at your feet."

"I see two thick feet...that go where I send them."

"Yes." I leaned forward and took hold of his feet. "Now, let me tell you what I see. I see feet that are not washed...like your hands."

Simon looked at his wife.

"Wait here." I left the table and returned with a bowl of water. "Now, let me wash your feet."

Surprised and suddenly embarrassed, Simon stood. "No, no. That's what servants do! Let me wash *your* feet *and* your hands."

I knelt before the confused fisherman. "Simon, Simon, tell me again: who is the master of your hands and your feet?"

He struggled for his answer.

We left Capernaum and eventually found our way to Jerusalem. We had no sooner made our way into the city than an old Pharisee greeted me with a kiss. "*Shalom, Yeshua* of Nazareth. I am Rabbi Nicodemus of the

---

193 Matthew 8:15, Mark 1:30

Sanhedrin."[194] He reached a handful of bent fingers toward me, kindly. "I heard you speak with the Elders when you were a boy."

I remembered him.

"My son, news of you finds us every day. Complaints come to us from all over Judea and Galilee. We are confused because you've broken the Sabbath...again. And again by healing someone."[195]

I looked deeply into Nicodemus' baggy eyes. "Tell me, friend, is loving my neighbor breaking the Sabbath?"

Nicodemus cleared his throat. "According to the Law..."

"Tell me, do you want to be healthy?"

The Pharisee paused. "I'm not sick."

"No?" I turned to my disciples. "See. We should leave. It's not the healthy who need a doctor." I faced Nicodemus again. "I have not come to call the righteous to my Kingdom, but the sinners."[196]

Nicodemus strained. "I don't understand you."

"I do not ask you to understand me; I ask you to believe me. Understanding may or may not follow..."

"But..."

"You search the Scriptures because you say that you trust in them for eternal life. But you deceive yourself. What you actually trust is *your own understanding* of the Scriptures." I shook my head, sadly. "You are like the rest of your kind. You believe in yourself. If you really understood the Scriptures you would see that they point to me."[197]

Nicodemus lowered his face and turned away.

"We will speak again, Rabbi," I said. "And soon."

That same day I met Judas Iscariot on the Damascus Highway just beyond the city walls. His eyes were black and close-set; his bearded jaw was square. When he spoke, he spoke boldly, raising his shoulders behind his neck in such a way as to make him appear like a desert cobra about to strike. At his side were his fearful wife and his two young sons whom he

---

194 The Sanhedrin in Jerusalem was comprised of seventy-one revered rabbis and functioned under the Romans like a Supreme Court for Jewish affairs.

195 From John 5

196 From Mark 2:17

197 From John 5:39

had named Samson and Saul. If I told you nothing more of this poor man you would know much.

Judas followed me in and out of the city that day and for many days thereafter. He clung to my side and listened to every word—though never actually hearing. I came to learn quickly that the man was happiest on the days that I raged against the Pharisees—and sadly, those days were many. So it could be said that Judas was happy when I was sad, and so he was particularly delighted on the day that we learned many of the Pharisees had begun to conspire with the Herodians to destroy me.[198]

When we left the city, Judas bade his family farewell and followed us back to Galilee. Along the way I learned that he thought of himself as a mighty guardian of truth and a champion of Israel. But he made me uncomfortable with his heated language, and the women did not like him. Therefore, it was not easy for me to say what I had to say on a warm morning in the Jezreel Valley.

"Come, all of you." I suppose there were about twenty-five men and as even more women now following me wherever I went. I led them all to the shade of thick-leafed carob trees where I bade them to sit in the dust. Once they were comfortable I said, "Like the tribes of Israel, twelve of you will be my chosen ones to serve as special witnesses to my Kingdom. You are the first of my elect that I will authorize to cast out demons and heal the sick in my name."

I surveyed their excited faces; each looked hopeful. I opened my arms and said to the first, *"Simon bar Jonas,* fisherman, come and stand by me.[199]

With a happy roar, Simon came running.

"And you, *Andrew bar Jonas.* And...and James and John of Zebedee, come." As my cousins approached I thought how each of them were blustery and bold like their father, my uncle. I smiled. "I now name you two, 'Boanerges'...sons of thunder!"

The crowd laughed.

I took a drink of water and then called Philip of Bethsaida and Bartholomew. "Come, be blessed and bless others."

I looked about the rest. A gentle breezed rippled through their robes. "You, Thomas the Twin. Come. I need a careful thinker."

---

198 Mark 3:6

199 From Mark 3:13 and forward. Note Levi and Matthew are considered to be the same person.

He laughed.

I then pointed to another. "And Levi, come."

To that, Judas immediately stood, protesting. "No, Lord. Not him! He profits from the misery of others..."

Judas angered me. "You call me 'Lord,' yet you do not accept my choice?" I took a drink and a bite of bread, then surveyed the hopeful faces still staring back at me. "My beloved." At the word, 'beloved,' I found John of Jerusalem's earnest face. I could hear him asking, *'Is it I, Lord?'* But I had to force my eyes past him and I sought out my other cousin, James the Little, son of Cleopas. [200]"You, cousin, come."

James snorted like his father and I smiled. I then called Thaddeus, and after him I pointed to our very own Zealot, Simon--the one whom had lived with the Essenes. "Come, come. And you never need to fear the Sabbath in my Kingdom!"

Eleven men now stood behind me and I faced an anxious press of faces waiting breathlessly. My eyes fell on humble Nathaniel... the one who was the first to call me the 'Son of God;'[201] But the Spirit nudged me past him. Then my eyes rested on young John. Oh how I loved him. But it was not to be. A breeze rustled the carob trees and I drew a deep breath. I felt my head pivoting away from John and toward Judas. I stared at him for a long moment, and he at me. At last I forced my lips open. "Judas, son of Simon of Kerioth, come."

"I don't understand, Rabbi," John of Jerusalem snapped. His face was filled with hurt; it was as if I had cast him away like some unwanted fish. "I was a fool to dance! Your Kingdom is not safe."

"John..."

"No. Andrew and I were the first to follow you...yet you take Andrew and not me?"

"Should I not have chosen Andrew?"

---

200 The names Alphaeus and Cleopas are interchangeable

201 John 1:49

John spat. I had never seen him do that before. When he did, I groaned, for if my beloved John could fall back into himself, then all of my followers surely would.

"I am here to do my Father's will."

John backed away. "But why them? They...they are ordinary men."

I answered him harshly. "Happy are the poor in spirit, John, for theirs is the Kingdom of Heaven.[202] I need every kind of man, John, and women, too. Even ordinary ones."

He looked away. "Who would want..."

I then took his shoulder, firmly. "You once told me that your mother thought the world was broken and empty. Didn't you say that you wanted to bring goodness and beauty into the world?"

"So?"

"To do so is to bring *love* into the world."

He stared at me.

I took a breath. "Not long ago I watched you hold the hand of a paralytic at the pool. And I heard you plead for the demoniac in Capernaum. You prayed for that deformed child in Samaria, and I haven't forgotten the little goat with the broken leg you brought to me by night. You want to bring love *into* the world, John."

He looked down.

"Listen to me. When you...you, John...walk *close* to the world it becomes a better place. Remember how you blessed all of us at the wedding? I need your feet here, by mine, right here where darkness tries to destroy us." I took hold of his shoulders. "Don't set yourself apart from me. "Sing my song to the broken and to the empty...and do it *with* me...with *us.*"

John fell silent.

"Do you love me, John?"

He paused. "Yes."

"Because you think I set myself apart?"

John's face filled. "No. Because when I was just a child, you squatted in the dust to hear me sing."

I felt my throat thicken. "Friend. You are right to say the world is dark, but we can still be happy...for I have overcome the world."[203]

---

202 Matthew 5:3

203 From John 16:33

John turned away from me. I let him be still in silence. When he finally faced me again I could see that something had changed. He removed his colorful robe and tossed it to the ground. "Lord, I don't wish to hide behind these colors anymore." He wiped his eyes. "But let this Kingdom of yours come, quickly." My beloved disciple[204]then kissed my hand, and my heart was glad.

---

204 While tradition identifies John of Zebedee as the 'beloved disciple,' strong scholarship suggests that this is unlikely. Instead, a John of Jerusalem is referenced by the early church, a young man probably from the priestly class and well-schooled in the symbolism of the Temple. Thus, he also becomes a candidate for the writing of the Book of Revelation. The interested reader should research the work of Dr. Richard Bauckham, particularly his book titled, *Jesus and the Eyewitnesses*.

CHAPTER XXX

LIGHTING SHADOWS

We arrived at a lakeside mount near Capernaum where a great crowd had gathered.[205] I taught many things to them, but when I began to speak of those who seek love from others, Mary Magdalene drew close.

I looked at her carefully and thought about her and the ways that she sought love. I then raised my arms. "Some of you fear sorrow so you try to win the joy of others by giving them much. But I say, don't fear sorrow. " I then looked directly at Mary. "Happy are those who mourn, for *I* am come to be the one who comforts them. And I do so, freely."

Mary smiled but I knew that she still did not understand.

I continued to teach until the ninth hour of that day when the crowd grew weary and began to drift away. The Twelve, Mary and her women, and some others finally found shade by the lakeside where we went into our bags for food. Mary summoned two merchants who were selling food and wine to the people. She tossed them some silver. "Figs if you have them, bread, olive oil, honey and fish. Wine, too." Mary then handed me a purse filled with silver coins. "This can buy us what we need, at least for a season."

I looked at the coins and then at Mary. I suddenly remembered old Rabbi Isaiah from Nazareth. I considered how the village gossips had

---

205 See Matthew 5:1 and forward; also Luke 6:20 and forward

accused him of serving others in order to command them. "Mary, why do you give me gifts?"

"Because you saved me."

I took a bite of honey-soaked bread. "Mary, look at me."

She poured me some wine. "Yes?"

"You have lived your life as a merchant."

"I don't understand."

I stopped chewing and set my wine down. "When you give you expect to get, so when you get you think you must give."

She was not pleased to hear those words. She looked at the others, red-faced. "May I tell you a story?"

"No."

I smiled. "Then don't listen. I will tell the others." I turned my back to her. "A man saw three children walking through his village. To the first child he gave a kind word, to the second a bushel of grain, and to the third a silver coin. After three days he received no praise from any of the children but he lay on his bed and died happy.

"The first child came to his burial and sang; the second baked bread for the mourners, and the third paid flautists to play. Tell me, who was most blessed?"

No one understood.

"The Kingdom of Heaven is like a man who loves for love's sake, for *HaShem is* love." I handed Mary back her money. "I love you, Mary. But I don't *need* your money and you don't *need* to pay me for loving you."

Mary stood to leave.

"Another man saw the same three poor children walking through his village. He offered the first a kind word but the child said nothing and the man cursed her. He offered the second a bushel of grain but the child likewise said nothing so the man put weevils in the girl's little storehouse. The third did not thank him for the coin so he robbed her house of what little she had.

"That same night the man died and the village rejoiced." I looked carefully at Mary. "Serving others in order to rule their love is not love, at all."

Mary stared at me stone-faced. "I just wanted to be thankful."

I knew Mary's wounded heart and I knew it well. "Yes, in part. But hear me, your sufferings have blinded you. You seek love by serving because you think you are not worthy to be loved."

Ashamed, Mary protested, loudly. "I've heard you say that a person reaps what he sows? What of love? Don't we sow service to others and harvest love?"

"Dear sister, do you still not understand that I love you because you *are*, not because you serve."

Mary turned and ran away.

A few days later we were resting along the road with my growing number of followers, a woman named Joanna ordered her carriage to stop. I stood. A rush of images filled my mind. Looking at the luxury surrounding her, I greeted her with a blessing. "Happy are the meek, for they who don't oppress others with ambition will be given much..."

Joanna ignored what I said. Escorted by two female servants, she walked toward me, boldly. She lifted a veil from her face. Beneath the cover of rich man's silk was a young woman terribly marred by boils and oozing scabs. "My husband tells me that you are a great healer."

"Where is your husband?"

"He's not here, for he is working in the palace of Herod Antipas in Tiberius."

The way she raised her voice about her husband's position told me much about her. "He should have brought you," I said.

She raised her voice again. "Chuza is not sick, I am. And his position requires that he stay by Herod's side."

I asked to see her hands. They were scabby and red. She winced when I touched them. I looked into her young face. "Why do you want to be healed?"

"What? Look at me."

"Is your husband repulsed by you?"

Joanna covered her face with her veil. "Yes."

"Do you repulse yourself?"

"All a woman has is her appearance and her cunning. I cannot advance my husband at court when people turn away in disgust."

"I have not turned away from you, Joanna. You do not disgust me."

"How do you know my name?"

"I saw you at your father's grave. The mourners were many and you inherited such great wealth that all of Galilee knows of you. Your father was a powerful Jew who loved Herod's house. You married a Jew who also loves Herod's house. Do you love Herod's house?"

Joanna was astonished, but she lifted her chin. A servant adjusted a gold shoulder pin and fussed with her hair. "You have many questions for a penniless man from Nazareth."

Simon came to my side. "What do you want, woman?"

Joanna turned to Simon. "You stink."

I steadied Simon with a touch. "Enough." I returned to Joanna. "Come close, woman. Do you believe I can make you well?"

"Of course."

"Some think I'm a fool."

"Then they are fools."

"Ah, but you said that I'm only a penniless man from Nazareth."

"My husband met your father and brothers."

I was suddenly curious.

"One of your brothers tried to cheat him with a wooden chest. Your family was shamed, but your father returned to show remorse. Lesser men would have hid away in their forgotten village. Your eldest brother came with him. He's a clever one. This tells me that you come from those who are wise like serpents but harmless as doves."

I wondered about that, but saying nothing more, I laid a hand on the woman's shoulder. She winced. Beneath the silk her skin was tender, hot, and moist with pus. I commanded the disease to leave the young woman. When I did, the skin of my own hand erupted into a boil and I cried out.

Joanna stood still as death for a long moment. She then threw her veil back. Her servants faced her, wide-eyed. Daring to believe, she lowered her face to see her hands now smooth and clean. Speechless, she touched her fingers lightly to her clear, soft cheeks. Tears fell along her smooth skin and she fell at my feet.

Oh how time passed! With each new day I marveled at the power of my own Kingdom! Truly, the blind were given sight, the oppressed were set free...the Spirit was upon me and I was blessing many with the good news.[206] We sailed back to Capernaum and had barely left our boat when Jairus, an elder of the synagogue, found me and pleaded with me to come to his house. [207] When I arrived, however, the musicians had been called and the house was filled with weeping.

"You are too late!" someone scolded. "She is dead."

The girl's mother was wailing and a dark gloom chilled the edges of my spirit. I turned to the musicians. "Go away. She is not dead; she is only sleeping the sleep." To that the crowd began to laugh, mocking me. But my disciples didn't laugh, nor did Jairus and his wife. And neither did Judas. He moved by my side and defied the crowd with his folded, muscled arms.

"Amaze them, Lord," he said.

I was surprised at his faith. I went inside the house with the girl's parents, Simon, and my cousins, James and John. There, the Spirit filled me with the breath of life and I leaned over the girl, blowing life into her. *"Talitha cum,"* I said. "Little girl, get up!" She stirred, and when she did, I trembled. *Death, defeated!*

Her astonished mother lunged for her, squealing, and so I stepped away. "Get her some food. She's hungry..."

Astonished, Jairus shouted out for joy and began to cover me with kisses. I took his face firmly in my hands. "Tell no one."

Then, weak from all the strength that had been taken from me, I left the house of Jairus and hurried to Simon's house. There, Judas took me to one side. "Well done, Master. Well done! This is exactly what we need to throw out the Romans. Wait until news of this spreads to Judea..."

"No! I want no one told about this."

"Why?"

"It is not yet time."

Judas growled. "It is time, Lord. Let's get to Jerusalem and take your Kingdom...now."

I looked carefully at the man. He was sure of himself—a trait not unknown amongst Judeans. "You think this is for you to say?"

---

206 See Luke 4:18

207 See Mark 5:35 and forward

Surprised, he stared at me. "I'm a Jew. Yes, I have a right to demand justice for my people."

My eyes fell on Mary the Magdalene and Suzanna and my sister, Salome. I then looked at the waiting face of Simon and the hopeful faces of the others. "A Jew knows that his people belong to God and not to himself."

Not long after this, I sent the Twelve into the villages and the towns of Galilee, and when they returned Judas boasted. *"I am building our army, King Yeshua! I gave strong men sight and took fevers away and... "*

"You?"

"Yes, Lord, *me!*"

What was I to do with this man? I rebuked him and walked away. My sister followed me. "He heals, cruelly," she said. "He heals with a lust for power, not compassion."

Judas overheard her and came toward us. Salome set her face and squared her body. "You use the brokenness of the weak to make yourself feel strong. And ever since you became our treasurer, you bounce coins on your lap like they're your keys to the coming Kingdom."

"Are you accusing me of something?"

"Should I?" snapped Salome.

The blustering man turned to me. "What should we do with her, Lord?"

I shook my head. "You have more to learn than you will ever know."

Young John suddenly ran toward me. He had been talking with a messenger. He whispered terrible news into my ear.

I sat, broken. "It would be better for him had he not been born. Tell the others."

John raised his hands and all fell silent. "Herod has beheaded the Baptizer."

A gasp went up. My disciples collapsed to the ground; the women began to sob. Salome took my hand in hers. "I'm so sorry, brother."

I wiped my eyes. Not long before I had sent a message to John assuring him that I was who he thought me to be.[208] I hoped that had given him peace before he faced the butcher. I sought young John of Jerusalem. "You see? Evil still crouches at the door. But I tell you again, I have already broken its power. My Kingdom is come...and is yet to come."

Unable to grieve for my cousin as he deserved, we went to Bethsaida where thousands of eager listeners had gathered. But as the sun began to set beyond the lake, I realized that the people had no food and were hungry.[209]

"Send them away, Lord," said Judas. "We've not enough money to buy what they need."

I turned to Joanna. "Go and see how much food we have."

While she went to count our baskets, I ordered the others to organize the people in groups of hundreds and fifties. Soon Joanna returned with a basket. "Here...two fish and five loaves. That's it. And I'm almost out of money so I can't buy more."

I took the basket into my hands. "It is more than enough." I then prayed and felt the Spirit fill me once again. I blessed a fish and a loaf, and as I did I felt the Spirit's hand through mine as the fish and bread multiplied at my touch. I filled one basket and then the next, and I noticed Joanna, gaping. I laughed. "Sister, go and tell Herod's court all that you have seen."

---

208 Per Matthew 11:2
209 See Luke 9:12 and forward

CHAPTER XXXI

FAMILY LIFE IN THE KINGDOM

Simon's drunken father once told me that Simon was an awkward ox. I suppose there is some truth to that, but whether as a boy in Bethsaida or on the day that Andrew dragged him to see me by the Jordan--or to this very day--I have always thought of him as *my* awkward ox and I love him.

After we had fed and dismissed the people, I sent my disciples ahead of me on a boat to the other side of the lake so that I could rest, alone. I quickly fell into a deep sleep. But before dawn, a violent wind began to churn the waters of the lake. I awoke to imagine my friends being tossed dangerously about in those winds and I knew that they were terrified. I also knew that they had been so overwhelmed by my feeding of the many thousands that some of their hearts had hardened toward me...they simply could not understand what was happening and so they had begun to close their minds.[210] This led me to worry for them all the more, for how could they endure a storm such as this if their faith was weak?

Fearing for them, I stepped from the stony lakeshore on to the waters, and searched for them beneath fleeting moonlight. Seeing a distant silhouette, I began to walk within the waves toward the little boat. As I drew closer, I saw that their shredded sail was snapping uselessly in the wind. I could also see that the men were holding fast to the rails with faces filled with fear.

---

210 Mark 6:52

I drew closer still and I heard Simon shout some orders to one of them, but the man couldn't move. *What will they do when I am gone from them?* I wondered.

The winds howled but the sky allowed the moon to reveal me. My cousin, James of Zebedee, was the first to see. He was terrified. "A ghost!" I came toward them, waving. "It's me! It's me!" It was then that poor Thomas fainted straightaway. I shouted again, "It's me…Jesus!"

At first, no one moved. I waved again. Then I saw Simon suddenly climb over Andrew's back. He peered forward with two hands clutching the rail.

"Lord?"

"Yes, Simon." I was now close enough for him to see my face.

I waited. The racing waves splashed over my knees. I held fast to my shawl. Simon set his broad jaw as he so often did, and then cried to me, "Say the word and I will come to you!" He began to remove his robe.

I was so proud of him. "Yes, Simon. Come!"

I wasn't certain that he was happy to hear those words, but the brave man threw his robe into the boat and turned to swing one heavy leg over the side. For a long moment he stood facing the boat and gripping the rail. By the look on their faces, I was quite sure that the others thought him mad. *Yes, Simon, yes. You can trust me.* He slowly swung his other leg over the side, and then released his grip. He turned toward me, white as death. "Look at me. Look only at me." I said. "Now come." I moved closer.

His face fixed on mine, he lifted one leg forward, timidly, and then the next. Each step delivered him farther from himself and closer to my joy. A grin began to spread over his face. *Yes,* I thought. *Oh, Simon! I'm happy for you!* Ah, but then…then he took his eyes off me, and he turned his thoughts back toward the tempter within.

"No, Simon, look at *me!*"

Simon had already returned to those false places within himself and so he began to sink. "Lord?" His body began to sink like a barrel swamped with water.

I splashed forward and stretched my hand for his. At the touch, I clasped it firmly and held him fast. I pulled his sputtering face to the surface. He gasped and then lunged desperately away from me and toward the boat. I snatched his tunic with two hands and turned his body to face me. He started flailing.

"Look only at me."

The poor man was terrified.

"Why so little faith in me? Why so much faith in yourself?"

Simon wasn't listening. He only wanted to feel wood under his feet so I helped him into the boat and I ordered the wind to stop.

Simon struggled with shame for the next days...a shame I tried to take from him. His pride wounded, he kept to the edges of our company where Susanna was usually found.

Through all that time, dear Susanna continued to follow me even though she kept to the margins of my company where she clutched her sack tightly to her body. Salome had taken a special interest in this woman, for she had never forgotten her from our days as children in Nazareth. Nor had Salome forgiven herself for not being more compassionate in those days. Perhaps that was why Susanna continued to reject her. But Mary Magdalene had also taken an interest, and Susanna was suspiciously grateful. The match was good: Mary was a giver and Susanna was happy to take.

We entered Capernaum again and I began to teach in the synagogue. [211]I said many things that day to many people, but when someone said, "Master, share with us this bread of life you talk about so we can always have it." I noticed Susanna move closer.

I answered the man. "I'm like the manna that came down for Moses. But Moses' bread will leave you hungry and you will die; I will fill you forever." I looked squarely at Susanna as the crowd murmured. I then raised my hands, "Those who eat my body and drink my blood will have eternal life."

This, of course, caused an outrage. "Does this offend you?" I shouted over the crowd. "You doubt me, like I was some kind of fool. Hear me: My words are of *spiritual* things and they give life." This was all too much for many. Furious, the people rushed out of the synagogue, including many who had been my followers. I watched them leave, sadly. But my beloved

211 From John 6

John, my Twelve, and my faithful women came to my side and we began to make our way to Simon's house.

As we walked among the dark stones of Capernaum, the people shouted at us or vanished behind slamming doors. "They hate you," Susanna whispered. "They are full and fat and don't want to hear of hunger and death. I'm empty and already dead."

I stopped walking. "Do you believe in me, Susanna?"

She looked at me, shyly. "I know that my bag is full whenever I am near you."

"Then believe that you are filled and very much alive."

Sometime later, I was resting by the lake near the border of Decapolis when I turned to see Judas dragging Susanna toward me.

"She stole money from us!" Judas held up two silver coins. "These. I found her taking these from my purse while I was resting..."

I groaned.

Then the Magdalene held a gold brooch for us to see. "And she stole this from me. After all I've given her!"

I sat up. "Susanna?"

Salome came running. "No, no. Listen to me, Jesus. Susanna thought we were going to abandon her. She heard Thomas and Judas talking..."

"That doesn't matter," said Judas. "She's a thief."

I held up my hand. "Susanna, is this true?"

She nodded.

I studied her for a moment. "Tell me, sister, what are you afraid of?

Her eyes swung between Judas and Mary. "I...I'm afraid that I'll be left alone and hungry again..."

"Why would we leave you..."

"I heard Judas counting our money. He told Thomas that we've only enough left for those who deserve our help. And those who deserve it are the righteous...I'm not righteous."

I looked at Thomas, John and the others. I asked them each what they thought about Judas' teaching. Only young John seemed to understand what I was searching for and so he answered, "Who is righteous?"

"He who has clean hands and a pure heart," snapped Judas.

"Do you?" I asked the man.

Judas looked away.

I faced Susanna. "Can you answer John's question?"

She shook her head.

John then spoke, kindly. "*Elohim* walks with the one who is lowly in spirit in order to restore them."[212]

I turned to Susanna. "Did you hear the good news? Do you believe that I would abandon a wounded lamb?"

Susanna shrugged.

Judas interrupted. "She's a thief."

"Enough!" I fixed my eyes on Judas. "My sheep are righteous *because they are my sheep.*" I faced Susanna again. "Now, you saw with your own eyes that I am able to feed any who is hungry, yet you believe Judas?"

She looked down.

I sighed. "Susanna, in this world some will always have more and some will always have less. I come so that no man will have everything, and that all men will have enough. Do you understand?"

"Is this really possible?"

"Believe *me*, Susanna. Follow me and you will have enough, for my Father has given me all that is needed." I turned to Mary and Judas. "Now, will you forgive this woman?"

Mary nodded but Judas hesitated. "She didn't ask."

I closed my eyes.

On a very hot afternoon in late May we came to a mount by my beloved lake and here we remained for three days to teach and to heal many whom were laid at my feet. I noticed that Susanna continued to guard her satchel,

212 Isaiah 57:15

but that she was giving more of herself to others. Near the end of the third day I was very weary. I had healed all who had come to me--and many had come. I was about to teach the people when two women hurried a group of sick children toward me like hens mothering chicks. One of the little ones was a red-haired little girl whom Susanna immediately lifted on to my lap.

Simon scolded Susanna, and the other men began to chase the children away. "Don't bother the rabbi with these," said Simon. "He's about to teach men..."

"No! Leave them come to me." I held the little girl. "Look at these little lambs. Unless you are like them, you'll not be part of my Kingdom!"

Simon was confused, but Susanna knelt before me. "She's so hungry." She opened her sack and gathered up all that she had stored away. "Feed as many as you can."

"Are you willing to give up what you have for the sake of others?"

Susanna smiled, and I was filled with joy.

We were traveling near the border of Tyre and Sidon when Joanna found us again.[213] Mary Magdalene led her into a rented room where she slept with the other women that now included my Aunt Miriam of Zebedee who was the mother of James and John. (My aunt came and went like the moon depending on her concern for my cousins' status in my Kingdom.) At dawn, the women made us a good breakfast of hummus, bread, yoghurt, and some fine tea that Joanna had brought along.

"Joanna, it's good to see you again," I said. "Your husband doesn't object?"

"Oh no. My husband was very happy to see me healed. He even ordered a feast and invited Herod. Of course, Herod wanted to know all about you. I told him how you cast out demons and healed the sick. And I did as you said: I told him about how you fed the thousands from just a couple of fish and a few loaves of bread."

---

213 Matthew 15:21

We all laughed as we imagined the look on Herod's face! Salome asked, "Did he ask what my brother teaches?"

Joanna turned red. "Yes, but all I could remember was the rabbi saying, 'Happy are the meek.'"

I laughed with the others, again.

"And I suppose Herod liked that?" Salome giggled.

"No! He called it 'nonsense.' Then he said that it sounded like a clever thing for a secret rebel to say. Then he asked one of his priests if you were John the Baptist returned to life."

At the sound of my cousin's name I hung my head. I grieved him nearly every day, and the images of his beheading continued to wound me, deeply. Before I spoke, a Gentile woman burst into the courtyard. "Have mercy on me, Son of David. My daughter is oppressed with a demon."[214]

I looked at her carefully and walked away. But the Gentile kept crying after me. Finally, Simon shouted at her to be quiet. "Get rid of her, Master. She's not of your Kingdom." He and the other men folded their arms, angrily.

"It is true, Simon, that I've been sent to the lost sheep of Israel." I cast half an eye at the woman, interested to see the earnestness of her faith.

She persisted and fell at my feet. "My Lord. Please help me."

I handed my staff to Joanna and squatted before the woman. "Sister, it isn't right to take food from the children and give it to the puppies."[215] I waited, hopefully.

The woman countered, believing. "But even the puppies eat from the crumbs that fall to the floor...this is how they find life."

"Ah!" I stood, smiling, and lifted her to her feet. "Woman, great is your faith. I give you what you want...your daughter is healed."

Overjoyed, the woman kissed my hands and hurried away. I turned to my followers who were now gawking at one another. "You can learn from her," I said.

The men grumbled and Simon folded his arms. "You want us to learn from a Gentile woman?"

I put my hand on his shoulder. "Listen to me, Simon...all of you. I've been happy to see you begin to love *what* I love--things like mercy and

---

214 Matthew 15:22 and forward.

215 Mark 7:27,28 'dogs' is better translated as 'puppies' and the effect is significant.

justice. But you struggle to love *whom* I love--people like this Gentile. Until you learn to love both, you do not love at all."

This was a hard teaching for them. Most shrugged and walked away, but Joanna stepped forward. "Well, I can see why you love her. She's a fighter. Her persistence healed her daughter."

"Is that what healed her? Is that why I love her?"

"Yes. You were going to send her away but she pressed you. She won your blessing...and your love."

"And winning is what's important to you, isn't it?"

Joanna tightened. "Everything is won or lost. Blessings come to those who win."

I leaned close to hear. "And love, too?"

She nodded.

The Magdalene had been listening, carefully. She pointed a finger at Joanna. "You don't have any idea what the Master teaches." She began to circle. "So tell me, why are you with us?"

Joanna's eyes quickly searched out her servant who came and stood by her. He was a large Persian with golden earrings and powerful arms. With him at her side, she answered Mary with crushing force. "You are the glutton of Magdala—a lazy, greedy, envious woman who gives anything to get what she wants." Joanna pursed her lips. "Anything. However, in a way I admire you. You worked hard to become...this." She smiled, cruelly, and waved her hand over her. "Well, this..."

Mary reddened and clenched her jaw.

Joanna continued. "So here you are telling *me*, the wife of Herod's steward and a close friend of the court that *you* don't trust me." Joanna then aimed her flashing eyes at me. "So, since I don't know anything, tell me, Jesus of Nazareth, why are *you* here?"

I answered Joanna softly, "Woman, what good is it for you to win the whole world and lose your own soul?"

CHAPTER XXXII

EARS THAT DO NOT HEAR

By now, Simon was the clear leader of my chosen Twelve. Perhaps that's why I so wished for him to be less the wary wolf, the stubborn ox, or the resolute Molossian. Often I longed for him to be still and to *listen* to my words like John the Beloved. But my Simon was a man of hands and feet. He trusted little that he could not handle, kick, probe, or tear to pieces—and he didn't understand how words could do any of that. So as I continued to teach throuhout Galilee, Simon struggled.

"How are we supposed to know that?" he shouted one day. "All I said was that we forgot to bring the bread and somehow you turned that into some big lesson about the Pharisees!"

"You never listen." Like the others, I was tired and out of sorts.

Ignoring me, Simon looked away and cursed at Levi (my disciple whom some of you call Matthew). "And you, Tax Man. Your tax whores at the Capernaum toll are assessing me and the Zebedees higher taxes because of us following Jesus."

"*My* whores?" snapped Levi. "They're not mine."

"No? Well they're your friends."

I stood. "Simon. Do you never listen to me? I told you that you can still be happy even if you are persecuted on my account."

Simon spat.

"Look at me. Are you willing to be persecuted for my sake?"

Simon lifted his chin. "I would die for you."[216]

"Then what's all this about?"

"I'm tired. I'm a fisherman...not educated like John. Your teachings are difficult for me, yet I get punished because of what you say."

"I know. But tell me, why do men want to persecute you? Who do they say that I am?"

"Some say you are Elijah; others say you are Jeremiah."

I kept my eyes fixed on him. "But Simon, who do *you* say that I am?"

He paused, and then answered with fire in his black eyes. "You've not said it plainly, but I believe you are the Messiah, the Son of the living God!"

"Ha! Yes! You see? The Spirit teaches you what you cannot understand. Simon...you are my rock." I laid my arm over his shoulders and led him to the others. "Listen, all of you. From now on his name is *Cephas*—'Peter'— the Rock, and I will give him the keys to my Kingdom!"[217]

Beaming, the Rock lifted me off my feet as he recited some poorly remembered promise from Daniel. Then he kissed my cheeks. "Messiah! I knew it!"

You knew it? I began to laugh.

Excited, the others began to clap and dance, but when they were done I gathered them into a circle. "Now, little flock, hear me and hear me well: Tell no one that I'm the Messiah. For now, this mystery is for you to know and for others to seek."

In the week that followed, Simon Peter did something that reminded me of a day in my youth when I walked my teacher's dog through a wild field just outside of Sepphoris. The animal chased a hare into a tangle of weeds where his leg was snared by a creeping vine. The harder the poor dog jerked his leg, the tighter the tangle held. He was frightened. I approached him, slowly, inviting him to trust me. He knew me and he knew that I loved him. But when I reached for the vine he suddenly lurched *at* me,

216 From Luke 22:33

217 See Matthew 16:18

still more certain of himself than me. Disappointed, I rebuked the dog and walked away from him until he was ready.

I tell you this for a reason: As Peter and the others walked with me I began to tell them of the tangling snares to come. I told them that I would eventually be rejected by the Temple and then killed. To this there was a great outcry. I quickly added that I would be raised on the third day, but I think few either heard or understood what that meant. So great was their fear and disappointment that most of them raged like madmen; they expected my Kingdom to be of this earth. No matter what I had ever taught, these men and women (except for Salome and the Magdalene with whom I had talked alone) heard only what they had hoped to hear: that I had been born to take the throne of David and thus overthrow Rome.

What other purpose would the Messiah have?

I understood their outrage; I remembered the confusion I suffered over what it meant to be who I was. I had complained many times in secret prayer and I groaned to my Father over this same agony. And it was not until the Spirit gave me faith that I was able to believe.

So I did not judge them.

But now I thought that Peter might lose his mind. He stormed about our camp throwing stones at Heaven and tossing dust over his head. Finally, he lunged at me and took hold of my robe. The others fell mute and still as death as Peter leaned his face close to mine. I could see that his mind had turned inward again, for my Light had left his eyes. "You are the Messiah. You are sent to overthrow the proud, to correct the Temple, to rule from David's throne. You will *not* be killed. Stop speaking these things. Who could believe in a Messiah that is to die!"

I pitied him.

"Listen to me, Rabbi: these things you say should never be, never."

I had enough. Until this stubborn vessel was broken open, the Spirit would not be able to fill it. My tongue turned into a sword and I loosed it. "Simon Peter, you've become my adversary! Get out of my way. Your faithlessness is a stumbling block to my Father's will. You are leaning on your own understanding...again."

I turned to the others but pointed at the stunned Peter. "He who wants to save his own false life will perish!" I let the Spirit's sword sink deeply. My eyes went from face to face until I hung them on Peter once more. I felt my tongue soften and I took a deep breath. "But he who will abandon his own self to follow me in faith will find true life."

Peter closed his eyes. His chin quivered and he fell to his knees. "My Lord and my God." He bowed his face to the ground and began to weep.

I fell before him and embraced him. "Stand, Peter. Stand with me." He did, slowly, and my heart was filled with gladness, for Simon Peter was nearly free from himself.

During all this time, Joanna bickered with the other women day and night and so she finally abandoned us. Her leaving made me sad, and added to the weight I was feeling from my four brothers whom had sent me a message daring me to accompany them at the Feast of Tabernacles. They wanted me to present myself to the very Judeans who sought to kill me so that I would be forced to answer their charges. I declined, of course, for my time had not yet come.[218]But, when they left for the Feast, I did dare enter Nazareth to see my dear mother again. Oh how I had missed her.

"Jesus!" My mother rushed to my arms.

I held her tightly for a long while, and then began to ask her questions about her well-being. She ignored those questions, of course, instead pressing Salome and me about our own travels. We said nothing about the plots to kill me--she did not need to bear that pain just yet. Instead, we told her the good news of the blind that see and the lepers made whole.

"I know that many hate you, my son, but they will soon understand. The Kingdom is here."

"Yes, mother." I stroked her hair, now all gray. I thought her face had many more wrinkles than I remembered, but her eyes still sparkled.

She was happy to hear that, so she kissed the tip of her finger and touched it to my chin. "Then you must go, my son. Go now and save our people."

---

218 From John 7:6

After bidding my mother a heavy-hearted farewell, I led my followers toward Jerusalem by way of the less busy highway that led through Samaria. But just before crossing into that sad land, a detachment of soldiers from Herod caught up to us near Jenin. Chuza had ordered our detainment so that his wife might join us again. We were escorted to the edge of the village where we were given hospitality under the welcome shade of an ancient grove of olive trees. There we waited for two days while the Magdalene and Peter murmured against our former sister, still believing her to be a spy. Finally, I spotted the young woman with two maidservants and a company of soldiers coming toward us. I thought that it was very strange to see Joanna leading a donkey.

"*Shalom*, Joanna," I said as she approached.

"*Shalom,* Rabbi." Joanna was deeply troubled. She beckoned Judas to come to her and when he did she poured a bag of silver coins into the common purse that he carried. "I want to help you," she said. "I was angry but I want to follow you again." She cast a wary eye at Mary Magdalene as she pulled two rings off her fingers and added them to the bag.

"Why do you want to follow me, Joanna?"

"I'm grateful that you healed me, and my husband wants me to be a spy."

I raised my brows.

"May I come or not?"

I shrugged. "Of course. Come and spy."

In a few moments she changed her clothes and took the lead rope of the donkey from one of her servants. She handed it to the Magdalene who grunted and handed it to Peter who handed it to Andrew. She then bade her servants farewell and found her place in line, just behind Mary Magdalene.[219] In this way we crossed into Samaria and began traveling toward Jerusalem, again.

As we walked, I sought out Joanna. "Sister, you are ashamed of something?"

She nodded.

"You dishonored your house."

"Yes."

"Chuza has threatened to put you out."

---

219 Order of women per Luke 8:2

"I failed him and now he's in danger." She stared into my face. "My father was right."

I waited.

"He told me that failure is the greatest shame."

"Do you believe that?"

"Yes. Have you ever failed, Rabbi?"

I thought about whether I had failed Assia and Joseph. Had I failed in not believing my mother as a child? Had I failed to give Leah hope? Then I wondered whether it would be possible to fail my Father? These thoughts troubled me greatly and so my heart opened wider for Joanna. "Joanna. I'm like you in many more ways than you know."

We walked in silence for a long time. Joanna began to play with a coiled, golden wristband, and then adjusted a jeweled hairpin. "Chuza promised Herod that he would learn everything about you. But I came home without learning anything new. I told him that you wanted to save Israel but that your kingdom was not a real one. Chuza thought that I must have misunderstood you because that made no sense. Then my eunuch told him that you are far too clever for a woman like me. But Chuza had already promised Herod a report. So he had to go to Herod with lies. Now we are completely out of Herod's favor and in fear of everything."

Joanna looked at me, carefully. "We could have had advantages in court by knowing you better. But I was angry and I left you. This is how I failed." Her chin trembled. "I have seen you do marvelous things. You make my world seem false. My father left me with many talents of silver and my husband is rich. But I tithe, I help the poor..."

"So now you see yourself as a righteous woman in a false world?"

She released a breath. "Maybe."

"And yet you are ashamed."

"As I said, I failed my husband and now he is dishonored."

"Does your husband love you, Joanna?"

"He says there's no greater thing for a man than to claim his honor, and there is no greater thing for a woman than to guard her husband's house from shame."

"That's not what I asked."

She thought for a moment. "I don't know. How would he love me if I've failed him?"

Some days later, we crossed into Judea near Shiloh and made our way into Jerusalem where crowds pressed on all sides for the Feast of Tabernacles. Donkey's and carts laden with heaps of long sticks and palm fronds crept along, bringing building supplies for the thousands of tiny booths that were already covering the hillsides. Peter and John led us to a spot on the upper slope of the Mount of Olives that was close to the deep tombs of the prophets, Haggai and Malachi. Here we began to build our booths.

That evening I took a walk with Joanna to look over the Kidron Valley and into the city. The Temple stood before us in all the gleaming splendor of the Jews; the Antonia Fortress boasted the magnificence of Rome. I pointed past all of it and to the deep ravine just beyond the southwest walls where the city's rubbish was endlessly burning. "The day will come, Joanna, when all false glory will be destroyed. Selfish ambition, greed and gluttony, murder and abuse, injustice...all of it, will perish. As Isaiah has written, 'the fire that consumes them will never burn out.'"[220]

"Why do you tell me this?" Joanna asked.

I turned her face toward mine. "You are ambitious, like your father before you and your husband. And you are hard on those who stand in your way."

She waited.

"I can see that you want your husband to have a favored place in my Kingdom."

"Yes, Lord. Like Judas and..."

"Do not listen to Judas."

"Why? He is a loyal follower."

"Is he? Some follow in ignorance, some are confused, some are curious, many doubt...and most are desperate. I welcome them all. But others are false followers. They want to use me to serve themselves. These do not love me. Which are you?"

I knew Joanna's heart. It was divided against itself and so a part of it could not forever stand.

"I'm all of those people. I am confused and desperate...but I do want you to honor my husband. I want him to be great in your Kingdom."

---

220 See Matthew 13: 49, 50, and Isaiah 66:24. These references are generally associated with Gehenna as previously noted.

"Do you know that in my Kingdom the least are the greatest and the greatest are the least?"

"You see, I'm still confused." She sighed. "So, tell me. When will this Kingdom come?"

I opened my arms. "It is here."

"I don't see it."

I took her hand. "I know."

CHAPTER XXXIII

LOVING THE LEAST

Oh Bethany! Tall, thick figs and broad-branched oaks shaded the busy village in summer, and because it lay on the southeast side of the Mount of Olives, the sun warmed it in winter. Yet Bethany had a comforting warmth of its own, for it was here that the alms house provided for the poor, and here sick-houses shielded those suffering from the scorn of Jerusalem. Indeed, even lepers could find mercy in Bethany and I had always loved my time there, especially with my friend Lazarus and his two sisters.[221] I had known that family since the days before my baptism when I did work for their father. So I was delighted to lead my followers out of the city to again find rest in Lazarus' house. We arrived at dusk, and after a small meal and a few happy songs, I went to bed. However, deep in the night, old Rabbi Nicodemus found me.

"I'm looking for Rabbi Jesus of Nazareth."

Lazarus hesitated and lifted his lamp close to the aging Pharisee's face. "What do you want? It's late."

"I need to speak with him."

"He's sleeping."

"I have important business with him. He knows me."

---

221 The reputation of Bethany as a place of healing is attested to by Jerome who calls Bethany the "House of Affliction."

The men's voice wakened me, so I pulled on my tunic. "I'm coming, Lazarus."

I wiped my eyes and walked into the courtyard where I was surprised to see Nicodemus. The old man quickly kissed my cheek. "I've come to warn you that you are in danger."

I said nothing as I led him into one of Lazarus' rooms. Lazarus lit some lamps, set us wine and bread on a table, and left us as we reclined on couches.

"Some of the rulers want to kill you," Nicodemus said. His voice was strained.

The Spirit had long since revealed to me the end of my beginning. "I know. And you don't have to whisper."

This surprised the Pharisee. "I've been defending you to the Sanhedrin."

"You don't need to defend me."

"No? Joseph the Arimathean and I were the only ones to speak on your behalf."

"Thank him for me."

Nicodemus shook his head. "Did you *have* to point to the teachers and say that 'no one keeps the Law?'"[222]

"Yes. Happy is he who hungers and thirsts for *true* righteousness. The rest are miserable...like you."

Ignoring me, Nicodemus drank from his cup and took a bite of bread. "And then we have the unending problem of your healing on the Sabbath..."

"We talked about this many months ago. Tell me, Nicodemus, why can a boy be circumcised on the Sabbath but a man not healed? Does my Father love one more than the other?"

The Pharisee took another bite of bread and chewed it slowly. "You once told me that you are the Lamb of the Lord. Now, let me ask you directly: Are you the Messiah?"

I took some bread of my own as I searched Nicodemus' heart. "What say you?"

"I'm divided, like the people. I sometimes think that you are, but it is said that no man will know where the Messiah is from.[223] So then I wonder how it can be since I already know where you're from."

I nodded. "So you have a problem."[224]

---

222 John 7:19

223 John 7:27...a reference to a non canonical source

224 John 7:27,28

Nicodemus struggled. "You will not answer me directly?"

"Would it matter? Like all men you will believe what you want to believe."

He thought about that.

"What do you *want* to believe, Rabbi?"

The Pharisee grumbled. "You see, this is what divides the people and makes the rulers angry. Why must you confuse everyone?" He took a drink of wine and tore some bread with his few teeth, then changed the subject. "Today I reminded the Sanhedrin that the Law does not allow a man to be condemned without first hearing from him. They scoffed at me and asked if I was from Galilee, too."

I looked carefully at Nicodemus. "Tell me, friend, do you love me?"

"What?"

"Do you love me?"

He took a long drink. "You are a Jew, and so you deserve to be treated justly." He took another long drink. "What does love have to do with it?"

I laughed, loudly. "Oh, Nicodemus, what am I to do with you?"

"I believe you are a good man...and for that I love you."

I looked at him carefully. "Tell me, Rabbi, does not a sinner deserve love?"

Nicodemus wiped his brow. "You mock the righteous. I tell you, it's better to be right than be loved."

To that I gawked. "Surely, you must see your error."

Nicodemus fumbled with his fingers. "No, I don't."

I believed him; he was blind to himself. I filled his cup with more wine. "You think of yourself as a man who is right and therefore a righteous man...so you think you don't need love?"

Nicodemus hesitated. "I didn't say that, but what about you? Do you need love?"

I smiled. "Tell me, do you know why you don't laugh very often?"

He grumbled.

"Because your desire for joy is choked by your fear of error. And this is why you're always tired!" I leaned close to him and took his hand. "Friend, you think too highly of yourself."

"I only seek to be righteous."

I laughed, lightly. "What you really seek is to be right. Listen to me. You deceive yourself; No man can be so right as to not need love. Be at peace; *all* men are unclean...no man is truly right before the Law or the Lord on his own. Yet the Lord so loves the world..."[225]

"Enough of these riddles," grumbled Nicodemus. "I defended you today and I came to warn you tonight...and you say these things to me. No wonder they want to kill you..."

"And I will ask my Father to forgive them. Unlike you, I dine with gluttons and drink with drunkards. My friends are prostitutes and thieves. Among my followers are liars and adulterers, tax collectors and bastards. They've sought my love and I've granted it to them, happily. Such is the Kingdom of Heaven."

"What about the Law!"

"My Kingdom is ruled by love, and love rules the Law."

Nicodemus stood, deeply shaken.

I embraced him. "Surely, Nicodemus, goodness and mercy will find you."

The next morning I was preparing to leave for the city once again when Lazarus' sister, Martha approached me. "Jesus, are you thirsty?"

"Yes," I said. The fifteen-year-old smiled, yet I pitied her. Lazarus had not been able to negotiate a husband for her.

Martha pointed to her sister, Mary, who was two years younger. "Look at her."

I did. Young Mary was a beautiful girl. She already had the shape of a woman. Her face was even and she had amber eyes that could melt a man.

Martha set her heavy pitcher of water down and wiped her brow. "She was betrothed, you know, until her shame was found out. Nobody wants her now. I warned her, but she always gives in to the demands of others. She was always afraid of being unwanted that she grew up to become nothing."

I raised a brow.

"She's like a cup of rich wine poured down a well. She's lost herself into everybody else, just to be accepted...now more than ever."

---

225 Isaiah 64:6

Mary's voice came from behind. I turned and Martha slipped away. I could see that the girl had been crying. "Tell me, Mary, what troubles you?" I asked.

"Martha. She orders me around like I'm her slave. She's miserable and so she never stops working. She's angry and won't forgive me."

I waited.

Mary shook her head and then faced me, shyly. She faltered for words and then she stared at me like a frightened little doe. "You know of my shame?"

"Tell me."

"I...I just wanted to belong...to be loved by my betrothed. His family was wonderful...Lazarus was so excited. They were important and popular in Jerusalem." She fell quiet and gathered her thoughts. "Some weeks before the wedding he took me for a walk and he...he began to do what men do." Her voice fell away.

I said nothing.

"He was on top of me like some...some beast and I cried out in pain. A shepherd and his sheep broker were walking near and heard me. The two came running. Oh, Rabbi, it was terrible. They told the families and the wedding was canceled. Now all of Jerusalem knows that I am spoiled...and my brother can find no husband for me." Mary hung her head and wiped a sleeve across her eyes.

I stood and asked her to walk with me. "Mary, you want nothing more than to be loved. So it is with all of us. And how is it that we are loved?"

Mary thought. "People love others who don't cause any kind of trouble. I know that because my father was a trouble-maker and nobody loved him."

"So, you'll be loved more if you're an empty pot?"

"What?"

"Empty pots cause no trouble. They make no noise, they stay in their place—they can be used as others will."

Mary fell silent.

"Are you nothing more than an empty pot?"

She didn't like what I asked. "I am more than that."

"Of course you are. You have a voice and you dance and you are filled with wonder. So why do you think you are unlovable?"

"I've offended everyone."

"Oh." We stopped walking. "So what will you do about Martha?"

"I don't know. She won't forgive me. And without her and my brother, I'm nothing at all."

"Nothing?"

"Not without being forgiven." Mary thought for a moment, and then clutched her hands to her heart. "Rabbi...you have the power to forgive sins. You've forgiven harlots and tax collectors, thieves and adulterers..." She dropped slowly to her knees. "I am no better than any of them. Will you forgive me, too?"

I stooped and looked into her young face. "Can you believe that you are loved even before you are forgiven?"

Mary returned to her brother's house, singing. Happy for her, I sought out my followers and led them out of Bethany and toward the storm now gathering in Jerusalem. Others around me sang, but before long my heart was heavy with dread.

We entered the crowded Temple where Judas announced that he needed to go to the treasury to present our tithe. Most were happy to see the back of his robe disappear in the crowd. Others scattered to find old friends. The women stayed with me, as did Peter, John and a few others. They followed me as I walked quietly across the great courtyard under a pleasant September sun.

We paused alongside some scaffolding to admire the repairs of the masons, but from the corner of my eye I saw angry fingers pointing at me. I took a breath and said a prayer. But Joanna tugged on my sleeve and pointed to a group of common people rushing toward us. I greeted them with a blessing and they begged me to teach them and heal them. But I had only begun to teach when a group of Pharisees and scribes dragged a woman through the crowd. They delivered her to me by shoving her to the ground at my feet.[226]

Though barely dressed, the woman had the bearing of wealth and dignity. I stooped alongside her as a Pharisee shouted, "Rabbi, this woman was

---

226 See John 8:3 and forward

openly caught in the very act of adultery. The law says she is to be stoned. We want to know what you say."

I looked up and studied the man. I knew that he loved the Law and that he loved my Father. If only he would love his neighbor. I turned to the woman. She feigned bravery but I could see her trembling so I sat down with her and began to draw my finger through the masons' dust.

The impatient Pharisees demanded my answer. "Should she be stoned or not?" Some began to gather stones from the workers' pile, but I kept writing so that the crowd would grow ever larger; many needed to hear what I was about to say. Finally I stood and lifted the woman to her feet. All fell silent. I turned to the Pharisees. They stood there knotted together like a fist and eagerly waiting to honor my Father by stoning a broken sinner. I prayed that the Spirit would give them sight, and then I took a breath. "Whoever is without sin may be the first to throw a stone at her."

The woman stood still as a Roman statue, whimpering lightly. I could hear her breathing quicken. As the men considered my words, I squatted at the woman's feet and wrote more in the dust.[227] I heard a stone drop and then another and then another. I kept drawing. More stones dropped and then lips began to drip grumbles and a few oaths. I heard sandals padding away. Saul was among the last to leave. Still squatting, I watched him as he stared at me hatefully. At last he turned and joined the others.

The Magdalene and Joanna hurried toward the woman and me as I stood and took the woman's hands. They were moist and she was quaking. "*Elohim* is merciful; our God is compassionate. Blessed be the name of the Lord."[228]

She bit her lip.

I then asked her, "Where are those who are without sin?"

She turned her face toward the ground.

I put my dusty finger under her chin and lifted it. "Does no man condemn you?"

---

227 Many have wondered what Jesus was writing in this Gospel scene. As previously noted, the dust of the Temple was used as the primary ingredient in mixture that women accused of adultery would sometimes be forced to drink in order to establish guilt or innocence. Therefore, perhaps the writing was not the issue, but rather his doodling in the very dust that would have been used to test the woman. On the other hand, a death sentence needed to be written so some believe Jesus may have been writing out such an order in dust to further press the woman's accusers.

228 Adapted from Psalm 116:5

"No man does, Lord."

"Neither do I. Now listen to me, go and do not return to this sin."

She kissed my hand and collapsed into Mary's embrace.

I then took Joanna aside. Pointing to the two women I said, "Truly I tell you, little sister, this is what makes up the Kingdom of Heaven."

Joanna stared at the adulteress and the glutton with eyes that I'd not yet seen. "They once had everything and now they are nothing. I pity them."

"No. You're wrong. Do you never listen to me?" I took Joanna's face firmly in both my hands. "They've no need of your pity, for they are everything to me and to my Father. Do you understand?"

Joanna pulled away. "I'm trying."

CHAPTER XXXIV

LAUGHTER AND
TEARS IN JUDEA

Two men could make me smile just by being near. One was my Uncle Cleopas and the other was Joseph of Arimathea—a well-fed, wealthy young Pharisee with a gentle spirit and a heart yearning for happiness. Something about Joseph made everyone around him smile. When Joseph laughed, his fleshy face pinched his eyes shut. With his eyes therefore nearly always closed, I pronounced him to be the happiest blind man I had ever known— and the only blind man to whom I was reluctant to give sight!

Many months after blessing the woman caught in adultery, I met young Joseph at a Sabbath feast on the edges of Jerusalem.[229] Our host was a member of the Sanhedrin and a good friend of both Joseph and Rabbi Nicodemus. I had just come from healing a poor beggar whose body was swollen with water. The Pharisees around me were very unhappy that I would do this on the Sabbath. They were beginning to press me on all sides when Joseph appeared on top of a struggling donkey led by a grinning servant.

"Look," said John, pointing. *"Joseph bar Samuel*, the youngest member of the Sanhedrin...and the fattest!"

---

229 Beginning Luke 14:1

The seventy-one rulers of the Temple were typically aged scholars of the Law made wise by time, yet here was a man younger than myself. I watched him dismount, awkwardly, and land hard atop his sandals. "He looks like a rich man."

John laughed. "Rich? His family provides every drop of oil to the Temple and has for three generations. I've heard that he's also a broker of dye to the Romans in *Britannia*."[230]

I thought that surely accounted for the man's purple silk and his jeweled, crimson turban. I smiled as the large young man chortled and adjusted the wide sash that circled his broad girth. He then opened his arms and welcomed himself to his many friends among the Pharisees. "Ha, Isaiah and Samuel and Lazarus and Judas and Manaen and Jonathan…I'm here!"

The Pharisees welcomed him with a cheer and a great deal of laughter, and then stood in a long line to greet him with kisses. An old Pharisee shouted, "I'm told that you already bought a tomb…in the finest garden outside the walls! At your age, why do you think of death?"

Joseph answered with shining eyes. "Happy is the man who knows he'll wait for the resurrection in comfort."

Nicodemus called out to him. "Joseph, tell me, is it lawful to be so happy on the Sabbath?"

Joseph took hold of his robes and tilted back on his heels as he stroked his beard. "Lawful? Hmm. I think it is unlawful to *not* be happy on the Sabbath, Rabbi!"

The men clapped.

Another shouted, "Tell us, why are you so happy on *this* Sabbath?"

Joseph's eyes pinched shut and his round cheeks swelled with a huge smile. "Today I worshiped the Lord." His lips tightened.

"No, no! That's not it."

He laughed and sang and began to wiggle his rump, wildly. "Then just call me Elkanah!"[231]

Someone answered, "But is your wife smiling, too?"

Joseph spun around. "Ha! Her smile dwarfs the sun, my friend." He then lifted a large bag of coins that were tied to his belt. "And unlike you, *Samuel bar Ezra*, I don't need to give her money to give her pleasure." This, of course, caused a great deal of elbows and howls. Joseph eventually

---

230 His trade per Church tradition

231 From a story in I Samuel 1:19

spotted me. "You. You must be the prophet of Galilee. Nicodemus talks about you…actually, everyone is talking about you."

We exchanged a kiss of greeting. "I am."

He looked at me kindly and then turned his eyes to my disciples standing close by. "And these are your followers." Our host interrupted us with his invitation to enter the large dining hall. Joseph held my elbow and tugged on Nicodemus' sleeve as we then made our way through the gate. Giggling, Joseph then led me to a seat by him at the very farthest end of the room. "Watch this."

I waited.

The host rose and surveyed his room. Turning to the Pharisee at his left, he said, "*Samuel bar Yakob*, why are you sitting there?"[232] He immediately waved Joseph forward to the seat of favor.[233]

Joseph whispered something in the host's ear and I was summoned to sit at Joseph's left hand. Then my young disciple, John—who many of these Pharisees knew from the Temple—was given the seat by my left hand, and Nicodemus by his left. When the host was finally satisfied, he blessed the food and we began to eat.

I was eventually asked to teach. So I stood from my couch and proceeded to speak of my Kingdom. "Everyone who seeks the highest position will be humbled, and those who humble themselves will be lifted up."

This caused a low murmur. Joseph, however, listened carefully and then asked questions that revealed his interest in justice and mercy. [234]Eventually another Pharisee challenged my healing on the Sabbath. My answer brought a great deal of woe into the room.

Joseph finally stood and turned a smiling face to the angry Pharisee. "Rabbi *Ezra bar Lazarus*, I'm surprised that you never joined the Essenes." Joseph folded his arms. "Shall I tell you why you never did?"

Ezra waited.

"Because I'm told that you love to go to stool on the Sabbath."

---

232 According to Jewish custom, the places of honor at a table were to the right and to left of the host, the *left* being the highest honor. See Alfred Edersheim's, *The Life and Times of the Messiah,* vol 2.

233 From the parable beginning in Luke 14:8

234 From Luke 23:50

The surprised diners howled…as did I. Even poor Ezra couldn't help but laugh. The tension gone, the room gradually fell quiet again and we all sat with our wine until the host urged me to tell more of the Kingdom. I looked about the room. *How do I teach them?*

I stood. "Once a king invited rabbis from Jerusalem to a great banquet. The first told the king's messenger that he couldn't come because he had just bought a new field and needed to see it."

The men nodded.

"Another said that he had just bought new oxen and needed to try them out."

The men leaned forward.

I smiled. "And the last said that he had just taken a wife and…well, he just couldn't come."[235]

Surprised, Joseph blew wine out of his nose with a roar. "Ha, Rabbi! Good one!" The diners roared and I laughed with them until it was time to say more. I took a deep breath and sharpened my eyes. "Now, yes…who could blame the last one? But the king was actually very angry and he sent his servant to fill his feast with the wretched of the city."

The room fell silent.

"The king, seeing his servant's surprise then said, 'Not one of those men who scorned me will taste of my feast. Not one.'" I took a breath. "So it is in the Kingdom of Heaven."

On a cool January morning that followed, I was resting near Jericho. My followers were nervous about the latest news from Jerusalem that revealed the Temple leaders' increasing wrath against me. So here we sat for safety's sake.

I was watching workmen throw their pruned branches into an angry fire when a messenger found me to deliver the news that my dear friend,

---

235 From Luke 14:16 and forward

Lazarus, was near death.[236] I already knew this and had been suffering quietly. Now it was time to tell the others.

Salome loved our friend and so she said, "Hurry, Jesus. You must heal him."

Others prepared for the short journey to Bethany, but I hadn't commanded them to do that. "No," I said. "Not yet."

They were confused. "Why?" shouted one of them.

"I want you to trust me in this." I turned away, sadly.

On the morning of the third day of my delay, Judas disturbed my thoughts. "You're sad."

I knew that Judas hated sadness—and weeping, and lamentations, and all manner of things that he thought were weak. "Yes, I'm sad. What of it?"

"A sad King is not a strong King."

I stood. "Why do you speak such foolishness?"

"The Romans do not respect weakness!"

"Someone I love is now sleeping the sleep. What do I care about the Romans?"The man growled. "Who cares if he's sleeping?"

"Enough of this! My friends are suffering..."

"Then why didn't you go before? The truth is, we could have used another healing."

I clenched my teeth. "As I said, he is sleeping the sleep. 'Many who sleep in the dust of the earth shall awake, some to eternal life...and some to everlasting contempt'."[237] I eyed the man, and then stood. "Enough of this. It's time to wake him up to life."

Judas was confused.

Others overheard us and came close. I quieted them and said, "Lazarus is dead. It's good that I was not there to heal him, for I need to help you believe in me."

Thomas answered, but then Judas shouted, raising his fist. "Good! This will set our enemies' teeth on edge!"

I led my followers on a hurried walk to Bethany, and when Martha heard that I had finally come, she greeted me outside the village with an

---

236 See John 11

237 Daniel 12:2

angry word. "Where were you? If you had been here he would not have died!" She took a deep breath. "But I know that *Elohim* can give you whatever you want."[238]

I was pleased.

"Woman, your brother will rise...Now tell me, where is Mary?"

"She's at the house, mourning. But..."

"Go and bring her."

I waited with my anxious followers. They were whispering among themselves when Mary came running toward me with a host of breathless friends. She fell at my feet and clutched them. "Rabbi, if you would have been here you could have saved him."

I could feel her suffering through her hands and I felt nauseated. Deeply distressed, I looked about at the twisted faces, the wringing hands and the ravaged hearts. All of it summoned a deep well of grief within me and I felt my eyes fill. *Must my witness always bring such sorrow?* I looked at poor Mary once more. I stooped to be close to her and I burst into tears.[239]

To that, Judas was aghast. He cursed under his breath and stepped away from me. He surely did not approve of a weeping Messiah. Finally, I stood with the young woman. "Dear Mary, where have they put your brother's body?"

When we arrived at Lazarus' tomb, Mary took my hand. At the touch I could feel the hope now filling her broken heart—and I knew that she had forgiven me for my delay. I squeezed her hand and then commanded my disciples, "Remove the stone."

Unlike Mary's, Martha's faith had failed her. "What? No! By now he stinks! It's been four days." The woman's voice was shrill.

Again, I was greatly distressed. "Didn't I tell you that if you believe me you *will* see *Elohim* honored!"

Peter, James, John and Judas quickly lifted the stone away as I cried out to my Father, thanking him for what he was about to do. I then looked at Mary once again. Her amber eyes were glowing...for she knew.

And she believed.

I put my fists on my hips. "Lazarus, come outside!"

---

238 John 11:20 and forward
239 John 11:34,35

The air became still; the birds fell silent. I felt my breath leave me to fill Lazarus' lungs with life. In a moment, the shrouded body of my friend began to stagger awkwardly toward us. Others gasped, but I laughed. "Unbind him. He is alive!"

All of that sadness and all of that joy had made me so weary that I thought I might sleep for a week. I was awakened from my bed in Lazarus' house by Peter's voice at cockcrow. I stood and rubbed my eyes. "What is it?"

"They are plotting to kill you."

"So?"

"This time it's the High Priest Caiaphas, and the Sanhedrin," said Peter. "A messenger just came to Lazarus. News of his being raised has spread all over Jerusalem. The leaders fear you now more than ever. Caiaphas said that it would be better for one man to die rather than the whole nation perish."[240]

I climbed to my feet. "He's right."

Judas was pleased. "When the leaders realize they *can't* kill you, they'll follow you...and so will the people!"

Simon the Zealot joined us. "No, Judas. Listen to me. Caiaphas will always fear the Romans more than Jesus. He and the rulers know that the Romans would smash the Temple if they ever joined a rebellion."

Judas spat. "*I* don't fear the Romans or our own leaders and you shouldn't, either. The way of Israel is not the way of fear."

"Enough. Enough." I turned to Judas. "My Kingdom is come...but are you really willing to follow?"

240 John 11:50

I withdrew with my disciples toward the walled city of Ephraim that lay in the direction of Samaria. [241]This city was near Ramatha, the birthplace of the prophet Samuel and the home of Joseph the Arimathean who was happy to see me, again.

"Rabbi!" Joseph led me into his house and ordered fine wine and wheat bread, some olives and a plate of expensive cheese. "Tell me that you are well."

"I am."

"Good, good." I noticed him begin to fidget with the rings on his left hand. "But it's not good for you at the Sanhedrin."

"And you?" I asked. "Are you well?"

"Yes, yes. I'm blessed, to be sure, though one can always have more."

I raised an eye. "More? More what?"

He took a drink and then bit some cheese. "More of everything. More pleasure, more money…" He eyed me. "More righteousness."

"What do you say to those who do not have more, Joseph?"

"I pity them. I really do. I want no man to suffer."

"And you do not suffer, Joseph?"

He stared at his hands. I thought he might cry, so I asked him, "Joseph, what is it that you seek?"

"Joy."

"And where do you seek it?"

The man tapped his chin. "A king had a room with three windows. From the first room he could see the peace of his garden, from the second he could see the power of his courtyard, and from the third he overlooked the dreams of his treasury. Which window led him to joy?"

I let him answer.

"The garden was too easily filled with weeds; the courtyard too easily filled with complaints. But his treasury was a quiet source of tithes and alms, of feasting and gift-giving." He turned to me and looked at me squarely, waiting.

I picked more cheese off the plate. I chewed it and swallowed it, then held up my empty hand. "My friend. Don't believe in things that do not endure. Instead believe only in that which leads you to eternal life."[242]

---

241 John 11:54
242 Adapted John 6:27

CHAPTER XXXV

PEACEMAKER IN
A TROUBLED HOUSE

I remained in Judea for a time, though out of the easy reach of the Temple authorities. I was teaching near the Jordan where I had healed numbers of children when I heard a familiar voice. [243]I turned to see Joseph the Arimathean once again. "*Shalom,* friend." I kissed him.

He feigned a false smile that quickly faded; I knew that he was deeply troubled. Though well fed, the young man was starving.

Joseph wasted no time. "Tell me, Rabbi, how does a man overcome his sorrows?"

"Sorrows? I thought you said that a man might simply open the window to his treasury?"

"You use my words against me."

"No, friend, I use your words to set you free." I studied his face. His eyes were no longer hidden away by laughter. "Joseph, do you see those little children?"

He lowered his eyes.

"I have healed each one of them, but many others are sick and lame. Look, there. More are coming. They endure the pain of a world that is tortured by the Evil One."

---

243 From Mark 10:13 and forward

He would not look at them.

"No, Joseph. Look at them. They suffer because sorrow preys upon this world and no amount of laughter will keep it at bay."

He still refused to look.

"Are you not willing to weep with me for the little ones?"

His eyes now filled with tears. He wiped them, hastily.

"I tell you this, happy are those who weep. In this world there are many who suffer for all to see." I laid a hand on his shoulder. "And others suffer in secret, bound to false joy."

His shoulders sagged. "You are a good teacher."

"Tell me, Joseph, what makes a man good?"

"The Law."

I winced. "Unless a man can keep the Law better than you Pharisees, he cannot enter into eternal life."[244]

Joseph paled.

"You do know the commandments, don't you?"

"I have kept them."

"Yes? Then give all that you have to the poor. Once you have done this, find me and follow me."

I held my breath. I wanted him to abandon his belief in his own treasury so I could fill him with mine. Instead, he wrung his jeweled hands and bit his lip. "These are hard words, Rabbi."

"The world is a hard place."

Joseph took a deep breath and turned away.

Early in the month of April in the fifth year of the governorship of Pontius Pilate, my followers and I returned to our beloved Bethany where my mother was visiting with Lazarus' family. We arrived just six days before the Passover and after spending some time with my mother, I was soon reclining with the happy dead man in the house of a grateful Pharisee whom I had healed of leprosy. Martha and a servant served us a wonderful

---

244 Adapted from Matthew 5:20

meal that included milk-boiled fish, roasted sheep tail and pink wine that was spiced with crushed iris.

The meal (and the haircut that preceded it) had put me in better spirits. I had been annoyed with Judas for much of that morning and so I was delighted to turn my heart toward my host and my happy friend, Lazarus. Of course, we all kept one eye on the doorway in hopes of seeing the laughing Arimathean join us.

When the meal was done our host began singing from the Psalms. It was then when I heard a sound behind me. I turned and saw young Mary--the sister of Lazarus--moving toward me with an expensive box held reverently in the palms of her hands. She was smiling and unusually confident. Caring nothing about others, she dismissed the surprised grumbles of the men reclining near me.

"Mary?" I sat up.

She opened her alabaster box behind me and began to anoint my head with oil. She then knelt at my feet.[245] The powerful aroma of spikenard quickly filled the whole room. Saying nothing but fixing her eyes into mine, she quickly poured a generous amount of the perfumed oil over my feet.

Someone grumbled, "Get out." A guest stood and pointed his finger. "This woman is a fornicator, get her out of here." Lazarus stood and rebuked the man, but others were still grumbling. Finally Judas stood, growling. "What are you doing?"

Mary ignored him.

"What's wrong with you? Do you know how much that perfume costs?" He looked at the many nodding heads of my other followers. Filled with wrath, Judas turned to me. "Master, you speak endlessly of feeding the poor. We could have fed many with what she's wasted here!"

I looked past him. "You will have the poor forever, but you won't have me for much longer." I then directed my words to Judas. "She understands my Kingdom. And she will be remembered for this deed long after you are forgotten."

The man's face flushed; his dark eyes flashed. He clenched his fists and tried to speak, but only spittle sprayed from his mouth. He swung his arm heavy across the table, casting bowls and goblets into broken pieces on the marble floor. "She understands nothing!"

---

245 Matthew and Mark indicate that his *head* was anointed, John says it was his *feet*.

"Hear me, all of you. This woman has decided to honor my body for burial *before* my death. The treasure she has poured over me is the treasure of herself." I pointed my finger at Judas. "Now, you, get out of my sight."

Cursing, Judas stormed out of the room.

All the while, Mary kept her face on me and only at me. She continued to anoint my feet and wipe them with her hair. I closed my eyes. I could feel her love run through my body as her hands and hair smoothed over my feet. I opened my eyes and looked at her, amazed at her faith. With a song in my heart I then said, "Young woman, your sins are truly forgiven. The faith you have been given has set you free."

Singing softly, Mary kissed my feet and held them tightly to her cheeks. She then stood and calmly closed her alabaster box, saving some of her oil for my coming burial. Holding the remaining perfume against her heart she smiled at the diners. She understood that I did not love her because she was lovely or because she belonged or because she was not troublesome. I loved her because I *wanted* to love her.

And believing that had set her free.

Despite my annoyance with Judas, I worried about him over the next hour and after Mary had left the room, I took my leave of the table to seek him. Peter followed. We found him in Lazarus' courtyard where he was sitting in the dust. His beard was spotted with white bits of foam that had dripped from his lips. He was cursing to himself and drinking much wine.

Judas stood as Peter and I approached. "You say that I will be forgotten and that...that shameless woman remembered! How dare you. You trusted me as our treasurer; I thought I was to be your right hand in the Kingdom." He tossed the bag of coins at my feet and gripped his dagger. "Why do you hate me?"

I looked at the man, carefully. "I don't hate you, Judas. I pity you."

"Pity? Pity? You pity me?" he hissed. "I would rather you hate me!" More foam fell over his lip. "You should be glad to have me, Jesus. I make us stronger... And we are safer when we're strong."

"Your might is an illusion. Like Israel, you are blind to your weakness and seduced by power. You are a prisoner of these deceptions."

I thought the man might burst. He took his wine jug and threw it hard against a cistern. He then staggered about and quoted from the Writings, "May the Lord give strength and power to tread down all who hate you.' Rabbi, I was ready to fight for your Kingdom!"[246]

"I know, Judas."

The man stopped. "But..."

"Do you really think I hate you, Judas? I tell you again: I do not hate you. I love you."

He eyed me, warily, and I could see that he was conspiring to quickly restore his imagined place. His tone softened. "My Lord, I have worried about you. Sometimes you seem...like you are a madman."

Peter stepped forward, angrily, but I raised my hand to keep him quiet. "Go on, Judas."

"You don't act like a King. You serve the weak; you make enemies of those who can help you, and you make friends of commoners and whores. Listen: you need *me* to help your Kingdom come...but I don't think you have ever understood what I can do for you..."

"Judas. You do not know what you are saying..."

"Yes, Lord, I do..."

Peter then interrupted by snatching the moneybag off the ground and bouncing it on his palm. "I thought it would be heavier."

"What? What are you accusing me of, fisherman?"

"I'm wondering where the rest of our money is."

Judas clenched his fists and turned to me for rescue. "Tell him, Lord."

I knew the man's heart. "You do not think of yourself as a thief, do you?"

"Of course not. Whatever I do, I do for Israel."

I took the moneybag from Peter and weighed it in my hand. I closed my eyes and the Spirit revealed more of Judas. His heart appeared like an opened gate, and crouching before it was the Beast ready to enter.[247] I felt the blood drain from my face as I handed him the moneybag. "You choose to be bound by your own desires. You shall have what you wish."

---

246 *Book of Jubilees* 31:18 adapted

247 Adapted from Luke 22:3

I rested for a day, but my spirit became restless for I knew that everything was about to change, once again. After a hurried breakfast, I sent my cousins to find a particular colt tied alongside his mother in the nearby village of Bethpage.[248] They were to bring both animals to me. While waiting, I reclined anxiously in Lazarus' house and listened to my now famous friend as he complained about the outrageous taxes Rome was collecting from the Temple to pay for Jerusalem's new aqueduct.

"Our people protested and Pilate had them clubbed," he said.

"Water and blood…two fluids that mean much for two opposing kingdoms." I looked out of the window to see if James and John had returned.

Judas grumbled something and then said that Rome's endless goading had at least prepared the nation for my coming. "The people will follow whatever you say. The rulers of the Temple will have no choice but to join us in pushing the Romans out." Many of the others agreed.

Peter stood. "Master, you will drive out the Romans and set Israel free."

I chewed some bread, slowly. "Do you believe that *this* Israel is to be the coming Kingdom?" I waited. "Has *this* Israel been a light to the world? Has Jerusalem been a city of *shalom*?"

Peter shrugged.

"I tell you this, friends: It may be that not all who have been born from Israel are to have a place in the coming Kingdom."[249] I knew that they didn't understand. How could they? Did I? I bit off another piece of bread and tried to swallow but my throat was suddenly thick with sorrow.

Peter scratched his face. "So what about *this* Israel, as you call it?"

I turned. "All that I have done, I have done for the *shalom* of *this* Israel. I pray that she receives me so that she can become the way of peace for the whole world."

"Then smile, Master, and enter the city as the King," Peter said. "Your time is surely come and the children of Jacob are ready for you."

I smiled. *Peter, my rock,* I thought. *How I long for your words to be true.*

---

248 The inclusion of both mother and son in Matthew 21 may be a significant point to consider in light of its potential symbolism.

249 Allusion to Romans 9:6

PART III

"For God so loved the world..."

JOHN 3:16

CHAPTER XXXVI

ENCOUNTERING THE KING

"Blessed is the King who has come in the name of the Lord!" shouted the hundreds of people now pressing close to me on the descent toward Jerusalem. "*Shalom* in Heaven and glory in the highest!"[250]

The colt stepped lightly atop the garments and the cut branches that were spread across the road to honor me. On all sides, people sang 'Hosanna' and chanted the *Shema*. Many reached to touch me and many more shouted words of thanksgiving and praise.

As I bounced lightly along my way I looked at their faces, beaming with hope. I remembered my own struggle to believe in who I was. Now I wondered who they believed that I was. Was who I was really what they were hoping for?

I then thought of my mother and I strained to see if she was there. *Mother Mary, you are truly blessed among women!* I wished that I could have found her. I waved and I smiled as I rode my little colt down the Jericho Road. Directly behind me was my cousin, James of Zebedee, leading the colt's mother. I turned to look at the moody mare; I could see that she had once been strong and fit, but she was now weary and her time was past. I spoke to her. "You've born a good son who will carry Israel's King into Jerusalem." James laughed.

---

250 Luke 19:38

I was sure that somewhere in the cheering crowd must be Uncle Cleopas, snorting. And what of my brother James…would he have come? If so, my other brothers and my sister Lydia would have followed…they always did. I strained to sort through the faces. I then remembered my father, Joseph, and wished he could be there. I remembered my grandfather, Heli, and old Rabbi Isaiah…and Leah. Voices of children then turned my head from side to side and I laughed with them. Together we sang of hope and of promise. A little girl handed me a bunch of wildflowers and I held them to my nose. Their fragrance was heady and my spirit lifted higher still. Indeed, my time had come. *This* was the day that the Lord had made. *I* was my Father's hope for *this* Israel to be Israel! Oh, how I wanted to serve her…

…but did she want *me?*

I began to think it could be so. The dark images that the Spirit had once shown me were lifted away and I suddenly imagined Israel repenting of her self-love. I closed my eyes and I saw the Temple as the seat of mercy…and I saw living waters healing the sick. I suddenly beheld a vision of Israel filled with my Father's Light. *Oh that Avi HaRachamim*[251] *would open their eyes!* I quickly prayed that what I was once told would be…

…might not *have* to be.

The roar of the crowd became so great that I turned my eyes upon them once again. Women were dancing with tambourines and men were singing. I thought of the words of Jeremiah: 'Young women shall dance, old men and young me*n shall make merry.'*[252]My disciples were shouting my name as '*Yeshua* Messiah,' and 'King of Israel.' It was as if the whole world had joined in song. As far as I could see were palms waving in the air and the hands of the hopeful stretched toward Heaven. I laughed. I was happy!

I then heard the voices of several Pharisees shouting angrily into my ear. "Stop them!"

My colt sidestepped and I nearly fell. "What?" I cried over the crowd.

"You. Rabbi. Stop them. Tell them to stop!"

I was confused.

---

251 Hebrew for 'Father of Mercies.'

252 Jeremiah 31:13

"Can't you hear what they are saying? They are calling you, 'Messiah' and 'King of the Jews!' Some old teacher is even telling the crowd that you are the Son of Man from Daniel's vision![253]"

"And?"

"Blasphemy!" they shouted. "Make them stop!"

I shook my head and laughed, gently. "Even if I commanded the people to be silent, the very stones would cry out!"

The Pharisees tore their clothes and fell away, and as they did, my shoulders suddenly sagged. The rage in the Pharisees' red eyes revealed that my Kingdom was likely to come in the painful way the Spirit had revealed after all. To that, my belly twisted and cramped. I wanted to vomit. I urged my little colt through the crowd with a light kick of my heels.

I hurried my colt to the very place where Uncle Cleopas had once uncovered my eyes so that I might see the city for the first time. In this same place, my parents had laid my prayer shawl over my head. I stopped my colt and asked my disciples to wait with me as I dismounted. "And keep the people away for a moment."

I then took the lead of my colt and the lead of his mother, and led them both to the ledge. I removed my shawl and ran my fingers over the faded stain that Obadiah had left on it all those many years before. I covered my head again and stared at the glistening jewel called Jerusalem. The gleaming white of the Temple, the tall towers and the mighty walls, the rooftops and the tombs, all now seemed to cover the silent hills and the valleys below me as if they had imprisoned the whole of the earth. "Oh Jerusalem," I whispered.

I stared at the city in silence as my disciples kept the press of the crowd away. My sister Salome moved near to me and took my hand. Her touch was love and it lifted my heavy spirit for a moment. I said nothing, but I squeezed her hand, lightly. Dread still filled my belly and I finally fell to my knees. "Oh Jerusalem," I muttered. "Oh Jerusalem. If only you knew that I have come for your peace...if only..."

In that moment I was shown a sudden vision of the destruction that would soon fall upon the city. Enemies would press it on all sides; stone would not be left upon stone; the people and their children would be cast down to death. I wept, loudly. "Oh Israel! 'You have forsaken the fountain of wisdom; if you would walk in the way of the Lord you would dwell

---

253 Daniel 7:13,14

in eternal *shalom!*' [254]If only you would believe that *I* am the way of your deliverance!"

I returned to Bethany from Jerusalem wondering what had just happened. It was true that the people of the city had received me with jubilation, but *who* did they think that I am? *Why* were they so overcome with joy?

What do they want from me?

Did they want *me*, Jesus of Nazareth—the one who taught them to love their enemies, to feel blessed in their sorrows, to find happiness in their poverty? Or did they want a son of David to lead the chariots of Heaven against Rome?

The truth was plain to see for eyes willing to see. I knew the truth—but I did not want to believe—that *this* Israel wanted another King David and *not this man of sorrows.* And so I did not sleep well that night, nor did I eat the breakfast that Martha had prepared before the dawn. Instead I wanted to hurry back to the city where I would teach the rulers and the people again and again until they either finally opened their ears to hear... or rejected the gift that had been sent to them.

At cockcrow, my grumbling disciples trudged behind me as we once again ascended the Mount of Olives from Bethany and then descended the other side toward Jerusalem. None said anything, for they knew that I was deeply troubled. Deciding we should rest, I led them toward a large fig tree that I saw at some distance in the early light. I approached the old tree hopefully, marveling at its age and the many fresh leaves it boasted. My mouth began to water as I prepared to pick some early fig-buds to eat.[255]Relieved to see my mood change and happy to rest, my followers ran ahead to fall under the tree's shade. I arrived, smiling, and took a drink

---

254 From Baruch 3:12,13

255 Beginning Mark 11

from Susanna's water skin. "I'm sorry that I've been out-of-sorts today. My heart is heavy for Jerusalem. Now, shall we nibble on some buds?"[256]

I turned my eyes to search out the branches, expecting that I would happily pluck and share a bounty of little fig-buds. However, the first branch was bare and so was the second. My hands flew along the next and then the next. "This can't be. The tree *looks* healthy enough."

I took hold of another branch and lifted myself deeper into the tree where I could climb and reach yet higher. Starting to grumble, I climbed higher and then higher still. The tree confused me.

Its leaves flourished;
Its branches stretched wide,
    Its roots were deep.
    This old fig boasted of its greatness
And stood taller than the rest.
    But it bore no fruit;
It yielded nothing to another
    And so living, it was lifeless.

I dropped to the ground and I stared at the tree. Anger quickly filled my limbs and so I began to shout at the worthless fig. My disciples moved away, anxiously watching. Finally, I pointed at the thing. "Now and forever will no man eat fruit from you!" I turned to my followers. "Everyone get ready. We're going to the Temple...there we'll have to climb another boasting tree with no fruit!"

---

256 In this season, little buds from productive fig trees could be eaten. When present, these fig-buds signaled good fruit to come.

CHAPTER XXXVII

WRATH

My followers and I entered the Temple. I surveyed the Court of the Gentiles and watched the business transacting in the cool of every portico and once again, anger filled my limbs.[257] "This place is a den of thieves. Peter, get the women to safety!"

I grabbed cords from a vendor and began to braid them when I felt a trembling hand suddenly take my arm. I turned to see my old friend, Nicodemus. "Rabbi?" I asked. "What do you want?"

"Friend, you are wrong in what you are about to do. A child could see that this is blasphemous."

"Look around, Nicodemus. The blasphemers are those who oppress the poor in our Father's house."

The Pharisee guarded his response. "I understand, but this is not in keeping with the Law...and so it is not good."

I swung my whip overhead, letting the cords sing in the air. "Goodness, my friend, is found in a song." I began to walk away.

Nicodemus nearly wept. He wrung his hands and followed close, shuffling desperately to keep up with me. I finally stopped and faced him, squarely. "Nicodemus, I must once again be about my Father's business."[258]

---

257 See Matthew 21:12 and forward.

258 The Gospel of John records the scene of the moneychangers in the beginning of Jesus' ministry, though Matthew, Mark, and Luke record it near the end. Therefore, some

Leaving the old rabbi behind, I marched toward the moneychangers' tables with my disciples at my heels. I grabbed hold of the first table and set my jaw. With a loud cry I threw it over, dumping loose coins atop the courtyard marble. I then turned to the next and did the same, and then sent my disciples after the merchants selling sacrifices and all manner of trinkets and amulets. Together we kicked over the seats of the outraged sellers, loosed sheep and goats, spilled merchandise and broke open the cages of doves and pigeons.

I swung my whip wildly, cowering the angry merchants. "By whose authority?" they shouted. "Did the Sanhedrin send you?"

"You ask the right question!" I threw a scale into the crowd now gathering. The police came running, but only stood and stared as they waited for orders. Priests went scampering for help. I spotted young John and Andrew scuffling with several merchants; my cousins James and John throwing over another table. On the other side, Peter was flailing and Judas was charging a merchant. At my command, they all came to me and we stood together like a tight knot.

Over my shoulder I saw a group of raging Pharisees rushing toward us with a company of the Temple police. When they were upon us, I faced their flaring nostrils with a scalded eye. "Let justice roll down like waters, and righteousness like an ever-flowing stream.'"[259] I folded my arms.

Nicodemus licked his lips, anxiously. "Rabbi, can you show us a sign that proves your authority?"

"Of course. Destroy this Temple and in three days I will restore it."

These words stunned the people but infuriated the Pharisees. One of them shouted at me. "Re-building this Temple has already taken forty-six years and it's not yet finished!" Another cried, "He will raise it in three days? He is a fool! He has no authority...arrest him!"

Nicodemus bravely answered him. "I say who shall be arrested."

The Pharisees pressed me. "By whose authority?"

"I will answer you if you can answer a question of mine."

The group scowled. "Then go ahead and ask," shouted one.

I spoke loud enough for the people to hear. "Is the baptism of John from Heaven or from men?"

---

disagreement remains as to whether there were one or two such events.
259 From Amos 5:24

The teachers looked warily into the crowd now gathering very close…a crowd that had loved my beheaded cousin. They knew that if they answered that the Baptizer was only doing the work of a man, the people would be outraged. But if they answered that he was doing Heaven's work, then they would have to accept my authority because John had declared *me* as the promised One.

Finally one of them answered for the rest. He took hold of his robes and leaned back on his heels. "We don't know."

The crowd burst into laughter.

"Then I won't tell you by what authority I do what I do."

Nicodemus shuffled close and leaned toward my ear. "This is why they hate you!"

I took a breath and eased my tone. "Let me tell you a story."[260] I told the Pharisees about the owner of a vineyard who sent his son to collect the harvest from the farmers who tended the vines. "The farmers rejected the son and killed him to keep the harvest for themselves. Now what is the owner to do?"

The teachers stared at me, thinking.

A few voices from the crowd offered some answers but I waited for the rabbis who had no answer. So I said, "The owner will come and destroy the farmers and give the vineyard's care to others."

The rabbis were not happy with this answer. "No. Never."

"No? Then let me ask you about something similar. What do you think the Psalmist meant when he sang of the stone that the builders rejected?"

The switch confused the men.

I opened my arms. "The stone that has been rejected is a gift from God; it is the cornerstone of a new Kingdom. Because you reject this cornerstone, the Kingdom of God will be taken from you and given to a new people… like the owner did with his vineyard."[261]

I watched them struggle with my words. *Hear me; believe me,* I thought. Instead, they began to rage about, tearing at their robes and wailing. Yes, they had heard me…clearly. But because they wouldn't believe, I knew that they would want to have me arrested. Finally, shouting words of woe and wailing lamentations, they turned and hurried away. Only

---

260 From Matthew 21:33
261 Psalms 118:22, 23; also Matthew.21:42 and forward, Luke 20:18

Nicodemus remained, and he took my hand and placed it against his tear-soaked cheek.

Exhausted, I returned to Bethany with my men. Here we were safe and welcome, and I was overjoyed to find my dear mother who greeted me with a happy kiss. "You look hungry, my son, eat!"

Our host had provided a fine calf that the women prepared in a stew that was flavored with leeks, salt and cumin. Alongside were dishes of chopped eggs and fava beans, goat cheese, and a bowl of date honey. None of us said a word as we filled ourselves.

When we finished, I decided to walk alone and find a place to pray. So I abandoned my friends to their stories and their wine, and made my way to a secluded fig orchard just beyond the crest of the Mount. There I sat under my shawl and I spoke with my Father until a noise turned me.

"Hello?" My mother stepped from the shadows that were now growing long. She came toward me and lowered her eyes. "I didn't wish to bother you…"

My mother had grown old. Her skin had become weatherworn; her teeth were beginning to leave her. "Come, sit with me." I said. I took her hand and helped her sit on the flat rock where I had been praying. Soon, we both were looking over Jerusalem. I thought of all the many years that my mother had been faithful to my Father…and how deep her love was for me. A small flock of birds suddenly scattered from a tall tree overhead. The silence broken, I asked, "Are John's stewards managing your money well?"

She nodded, but then blurted, "I worry for you, my son."

"Worry? Don't worry for me." My throat thickened. "Look at those birds. They don't plant or harvest…they don't even store grain in their nests, yet our Father takes care of them…"

"And you are worth more than birds," Mary said. "I know. But I listen as you teach. When you talk to others you believe in them…you hope for them. But they don't hear you; they do not believe you. I watch the joy fade from you when they turn away."

I picked up a blade of grass. "I have been shown what is to come and I tremble for them." I stared at the distant Temple and pointed. "Do you see it?"

"Yes. It is magnificent."

"You think so?"

"I do. See how it shimmers in the sunset. It's the very heart of Israel, my son. It's the house of your Father, *HaShem*--or as you like to say, *El Abba*." She smiled and touched my hand. "It's where all the sins of Israel are collected and washed..."

"The day is coming when not one stone will be left on another. It will all be broken down."

Tears formed quickly under Mary's eyes. "But..."

"Listen to me, carefully. When I'm gone from you, false teachers will come in my name and..."[262]

"Gone from me?"

I took my mother's hand. "Dear woman. The Spirit has shown me that I will be handed over to the Romans..." I hesitated. *Is she ready to hear this?* "And I will be crucified...but then I will rise again."

Mary never heard those last words. She grasped at me, angrily. "No! I want you to live, my son, you did not come to die..."

I held her, tightly. "But I will live again."

She wiped her nose. "You will live again? This is a hard teaching." She struggled. "I don't understand this."

"I know."

My mother sat quietly for a long time, sniffling. "But what happens after you live again...? Your Kingdom must come!" She took hold of both my hands and spoke with sudden confidence. "Israel must do what is right; she must love mercy again and walk humbly with *HaShem*."[263]

She drew a slow, trembling breath. "I don't understand about your crucifixion...perhaps that cup will be taken from you." She thought for a moment. "But however the Lord wills, I think it's too small a thing that you only restore Israel. Your *El Abba* has promised to use Israel to save the whole earth." She took my hands. "Jesus. You must be the Light to *all* the

---

262 From Matthew 24:5

263 From Micah 6:8

nations…' Your Kingdom will have no boundary. This I believe with all my heart." [264]

I was astonished.

Mother then squeezed my hands and lifted me to my feet. She raised her chin and removed her scarf. "Let the Beast hear me and let Evil listen: Because the Lord of Israel has chosen my Jesus, the kings and princes of the earth will bow down!" [265]

I was awestruck. My legs felt suddenly rooted to the earth and I was happy to stand firmly on the Kingdom that was mine. I parted my lips and began to sing to my mother:

"See, the river of life, clear as crystal coming from the throne of God.

See the fruit gathered from its banks.

See the new Jerusalem coming down from Heaven.

Here the wolf will dwell with the lamb;

Here the leopard will lie down with the young goat;

Here the baby will put his hand on the viper's den.

Truly, none will come to harm in my holy mountain

For the earth will be full of the knowledge of the Lord,

And his resting place will be glorious!" [266]

Mother Mary then answered me: "Blessed be the name of the Lord." She kissed the tip of her finger and touched it to my chin.

---

264 From Isaiah 49:6

265 From Isaiah 49:7

266 Conflation of excerpts from Revelation 22:1,2 and Isaiah 11: 6 and forward

CHAPTER XXXVIII

CITY OF WOE

The next day I taught in the Temple again. But soon, the same Elders who had run away from me on the day before sent scribes and some Herodians to try and trick me on matters of money and marriage. I answered them with stories, with shocking exaggerations, and even with the Law taken to its perfection. Oh, how I yearned for their eyes to see.

Among the eyes that did not see was one pair that I remembered from my youth. "Saul, son of Tish," I said. "It's good to see you again."

The man gawked. He was just a boy when I was almost a man. I remembered him standing alongside his father on his crooked legs as I engaged the scholars in Solomon's Portico. I had seen him and his unbroken eyebrow a few other times at the fringes of the Pharisees when they would gather against me. This time he stood in the fore with a shaking fist and a balding head.

Saul asked me some question about Caesar, but the crowd laughed at him and he became furious. He stomped and screamed at me, and as he did the Spirit filled me with images both terrible and wonderful. He finally turned his back on me and stormed away, but I knew that I would speak with him again.

The Pharisees and Sadducees proceeded to tirelessly set their traps, but the harder they tried the more they entertained the mocking crowd with their foolishness. I felt sudden pity for them and for their desperation.

Finally, a wise scribe stepped from the shadows. By his side stood Nicodemus and I spotted Joseph the Arimathean just beyond them. The scribe waited patiently for a Sadducee to finish challenging me on matters of the resurrection, and then he stepped forward. "Rabbi, what is the most important commandment?"[267]

"To love the Lord your God with all you heart, soul, and mind."

The scribe waited.

"And the second goes with the first. You should love your neighbor as yourself. There is no commandment greater than these."

He spoke again, and loudly. "Your words are true, my Master. These commands are more important than all the burnt offerings and all the bloody sacrifices in this place."

I nodded. "Friend, you are not far from the Kingdom of *El Shaddai*, for on these commandments hang *everything* that is taught in the Scriptures." I noticed that the remaining Elders were gaping at me in both wonder and fear. Some were beginning to walk away. Were not any of them able to listen? Had this truth not pried open the ears of anyone? A breeze played with my *tallit* as I waited. Then a few more began to leave. I felt desperate for them so I decided to invite them to consider who I was one more time. "Tell me truly, what do you think about the Messiah? Whose son is he?"

Several voices from the people answered, "David's."

I took a breath. "Yet David called the coming Messiah his 'Lord.' What man calls his child, 'Lord?'"

The people laughed.

I shouted after the scribes again. "If David called the Messiah his 'Lord,' how could the Messiah be David's son?"

The people seemed to understand and they approved of my words. Many clapped but the few scribes still standing nearby shifted in their places and whispered to one another. None of the wise rabbis would answer me. Their faces hardened. They simply refused to open their hearts to a new Kingdom. I tried opening my arms toward them, hoping...praying...begging the Spirit to soften their hearts. But they said nothing. Instead, one by one the last of the Elders of Israel turned their backs to me and walked away. From that day forward none of them questioned me again. [268]

---

267 Mark 12:28-30

268 This important exchange found in Matthew 22 and in Mark 12 marks the end to the interrogatory dialogue that Jesus had with the Pharisees.

As I watched them leave, my heart broke for each of them and for the Israel that they kept tightly in their grasp. For what hope remained? I pitied them for their pride, but I also pitied all of Israel for their pride. Would their stiff-necks not bring judgment upon all? I had seen the visions…and they were terrible. So I turned to those around me and said, "The teachers speak for Moses, so seek the truth that is found in their words. But Moses words do not contain all truth, so do not do as they do!"

Finally, in desperate anger for all those they would harm, I called after the teachers again. "Woe to you! You pile heavy burdens on the people but you won't lift a finger to help another. You close the doors of heaven's Kingdom to keep any from entering. You are blind guides who tithe herbs and forget about mercy—you honor gold and dishonor the altar. Your hands are red with the innocent blood of the Prophets. Look around you, you serpents…you children of snakes. You have abandoned your people!"

The rulers who opposed me would not turn, they would not look; they would not listen. I knew then that I had been right to tell them of the cornerstone—that I had been right to rebuke the fig tree. So I fell to my knees and raised my hands. "I am done with you. You will not see who I am unless you are finally able to say, 'blessed is he who comes in the name of the Lord.'" [269]

I returned to Simon's courtyard in tears, but noticed my beloved John hiding in deep shade. I walked to him. "What's the matter?"

The youth was pale as death and was trembling. "It's Judas. He…he seems filled with darkness. I can feel it."

I knew that John spoke truly. I asked Mary Magdalene to get him a drink.

"He was in the city doing something wicked."

"What kind of wicked?" I bade him to sit.

---

[269] These final words to the Pharisees underscore the final rift in any relationship Jesus would have with them as a group. Matthew 23:39 is something of an exclamation point to that sad fact.

"I don't know. I just feel it."

I looked up to see Judas glaring at me from across the courtyard. I turned my body toward him and waited for him to speak. The man scowled and turned away.

John shook his head. "You see? Something's wrong."

"He was very angry that I rebuked him about the perfume."

John took a drink of cool water from the Magdalene. "Yes, I know..."

"He hates you both," blurted Mary. "I heard him tell Simon that Jesus is weak and that he lacks the will to take the throne. And John is soft."

I turned to the woman. "What do you think?"

"I think that I don't understand what's happening."

"In time you will. In time we all will."

"I do know something, though," said Mary. "The city is not safe for you any more. Maybe it's not safe for any of us. You sent the Elders away in disgrace..."

"But the people love the Master," said John.

Mary turned to him. "You, more than all of us know how the powers of Jerusalem work. The people's will doesn't matter..."

"I know that the rulers fear the people. So does Rome." John faced me. "Our hope is in the people."

I corrected John, lightly. "Our hope is in *Avi-khol*.[270]" The two fell silent. I heard voices beginning to come from within the house...and I heard another voice whisper to me—it was that of the Spirit.[271]My throat tightened. "John, have you made the arrangements with your friends in the city?"

He nodded.

"And they are not afraid?"

"The rumors are not good."

"Rumors?" asked Mary.

"They say that Caiaphas and many in the Sanhedrin want to have Jesus arrested, now."

"For what?"

"Blasphemy."

Mary shook her head. "What will that get them?"

---

270 Hebrew for 'Father of All'

271 John 13:1 from this point forward begins what is 'Passion' of Jesus Christ.

John shrugged. "They're embarrassed by the people's love of the Master and their dislike of them..."

Peter's voice suddenly filled the courtyard. "Are we staying here for Passover?[272]

"No, Peter."

"No? Then where?"

Others gathered around me. I closed my eyes as my heart filled with both sadness and hope. I breathed deeply and as I did, the Spirit taught me more of what was to come.

But would my brothers and sisters understand?

I opened my eyes and looked at Peter, "Now listen carefully. Take John of Zebedee with you to the city, and when you go through the gate you'll see a man carrying a water pot..."[273]

"Ha! What kind of man carries a water pot?"

"The kind you'll follow! Just do what I say. Follow him through the streets until he enters a house. Then tell the owner this: 'The Master asks about the guest room where he may eat with his disciples.' Can you two fishermen remember that?"

They nodded.

"He'll show you an upstairs room with all that we need. Take the women with you; they know better than you what we need for supper." I looked at Judas and I felt sick; he was fast filling with darkness. "Give them some money."

The man grunted.

---

272 Note: The synoptic Gospels (Matthew, Mark and Luke) appear to disagree with John's Gospel as to whether the Last Supper was a Passover meal. The former accounts suggest that it was. (See Matthew 26:17, Mark 14:12, Luke 22:8,15, etc.) However, John seems to place the supper on the Thursday night *before* the Passover that would have begun after sunset on Friday (see John 19:14, etc.). According to John's Gospel, the various trials of Jesus occurred after the Thursday evening meal and into Friday, resulting in his crucifixion about noon on Friday. Thus, Jesus would have died at the same time that the priests were slaughtering the sacrificial lambs in the Temple. The author leaves the resolution of these apparent differences to the scholars.

273 Luke 22:7

CHAPTER XXXIX

BODY AND BLOOD

A group of my disciples entered the city at dusk and followed young John to the upstairs room of his wealthy friend where Peter, John of Zebedee, and the women had helped prepare all that we needed for our meal. Our host greeted me with a kiss, and then left us. I looked about the generous room, well lit by lamplight and carpeted with fine rugs from Persia. When my eyes fell upon the table, however, I was disappointed. For some reason I had imagined a large, round table, like that of the Therapeutae. Instead, our host had provided a short-legged, three-sided table known by the wealthy as a Roman *triclinium.* Alongside it were positioned a number of firm cushions, and scattered about the room were mats for those who would find no room at the table.

Peter began joking with Andrew and Philip, and the Zebedees began to push and shove their way to the seats of honor that their mother wanted them to claim. I shook my head. "Listen to me, cousins, the greatest should be the least! Go, sit there." I pointed to the right wing of the table. "And Peter, join them."

I raised my hands over the rest. "Am I not your host? Then *I* shall seat you." I looked carefully at each of them and they at me. I loved them so— all of them. My seat, of course, would be on the left wing, with a person of honor to my right. That would be my beloved John. He smiled.

But all were wondering who would be given the seat of highest honor to my left. Once again, I studied their faces. They had served me well. There stood Nathaniel—though not among my chosen Twelve he was still much loved by me; indeed, he was the first to recognize me as the Son of God. I looked at Levi the tax collector who had taken so much chiding from the others for these years, and Philip of Cana and dear Andrew and Bartholomew, my cousin Little James of Cleopas, and Thomas—the thinker. Finally there was quiet Thaddeus and then, of course, Simon our Zealot—my old friend from the latrine of the Essenes. In the shadows stood others who had been faithful through Galilee.

But there was still another.

Was it too late for love to rescue him?

Indeed, was it too late for love to rescue all of Israel?

"Judas," I said.

He stiffened.

I walked close to him. "I would like you to sit on my left." The man's face twisted; the others gasped. Silence followed. I laid a hand on his shoulder. At the touch, my fingers felt a familiar heat…a terrible, stinging singe like red coals on tender skin. I did not remove my hand but Judas pulled away from me.

Suddenly sweating, he muttered and wiped his brow. "As you wish, Rabbi."

The women filled our clay cups and I blessed the wine. But the room was quiet and full of trouble because of my seating Judas to my left. So I soon left the table and removed my outer clothing. I then wrapped myself in a small towel and poured water into a large bowl. "Come. Each of you."

Confused, the men obediently formed a line in front of me. I knelt by the bowl. "Come." Young John understood. He stepped forward first. I removed his sandals. "Little brother, happy is he who is poor in spirit." I began to wash his feet. "Sing for us, John."

The youth took a breath and he began to sing:

> "I will gather you from the nations
>> I will sprinkle clean water on you
>>> And you will be clean
>> I will clean you,
>> I will remove your heart of stone
>>> And give you a heart of flesh.

You shall live in the land..."[274]

John's song went on as I welcomed the next to my bowl, and the next, but when Peter stood before me he would not remove his sandals. I looked up.

"No. This isn't right, Master. You are our Lord."

"You'll understand soon enough."

"No. You won't ever wash my feet!"

"No? Then you will not be a part of my Kingdom."

With that Peter tore off both his sandals and splashed one of his big paws into my bowl. "Then wash all of me!" [275]

I laughed and used his words to teach the others. But as I dried his feet I felt a sharp pain cut my heart. I looked up at my dear Peter. "Happy is the one who will suffer for my sake."

Judas finally stood before me. I looked into his face but I could not smile, for as I removed his sandals I knew that his feet were purposed on great evil and that his heart would not turn from stone.

But was there no hope for hearts of stone?

I emptied my bowl and had Mary fill it with clean water so that I could wash the feet of Judas well. He stood, awkwardly, shifting his weight from leg to leg, discomforted at the thought of a king acting like a slave. I then asked for a fresh towel and wiped his feet, even between his toes.

But the feet of Judas were not clean.

He stepped away quickly and so I called after him. "Happy is he who is merciful."

I then asked for another fresh bowl of water and looked at the women waiting to serve us our meal. They had faithfully given of themselves, some for a long time. I loved them and my Father loved them and my Spirit loved them. When the bowl was filled, I invited the women to come.

They were shocked and the men fell utterly silent. I could hear Peter begin to breathe hard as he did when he was about to complain. The Magdalene stepped forward first. She removed her sandals without a word and lifted a foot into my bowl. I cupped it gently and prayed for her. I washed that foot and then the next. I lifted my face to see that her eyes had swollen. "Happy is she who is able to mourn for others' sake."

---

274 Adapted from Ezekiel 36:24-28

275 See John 13:1-20

Susanna followed, shyly. I washed her feet. "Happy is she who is willing to remain hungry for others' sake."

Joanna hesitated and then placed her foot in my bowl. I smiled at her and said nothing until I dried her second foot. "Happy is she who is meek."

Martha followed, then a woman who had just joined us, and then another. Then Mary of Bethany removed her sandals. She stepped forward lightly and I took her foot in my hand. "Happy is she who makes true peace."

Finally, my mother came forward. She was hesitant. "My son…"

"I know."

"But…"

I reached for her foot. "Take this easy burden upon yourself, for I have humbled myself for your sake…and you will find rest for your soul."[276] I washed her feet, and she was clean.

The women quietly served us a course of vegetables and some lentil stew with bits of fish into which we dipped our bread. During the meal we talked of many things and I told my disciples how happy I was to know each of them. I passed the wine and changed the subject. "I will not drink of this again until the Kingdom is come." [277]

The room fell silent.

I then lifted a large piece of unleavened bread into my hands and gave my Father thanks for it. I broke it. "This is my body. It will be broken for you." I passed the pieces along the quiet table. "Eat, and when you do, do it as a remembrance of me."

The men slowly bit their bread and chewed. I could see that my words had confused them. I then filled another cup, but before I gave my Father thanks for it I stared into what seemed to be a bottomless well of red wine. My hand trembled, lightly. "And this cup is my blood; it is my promise of

---

276 Adapted from Matthew 11:29

277 The story of the Last Supper can be found in Matthew 26, Mark 14, Luke 22, and John 13. Paul references this as well in I Corinthians 11.

the forgiveness of sins. I will pour it out for you and many others." I passed
the cup and watched each man and each woman hesitate before drinking
from it. I knew that they were struggling. [278]

The room remained quiet as I reached for a piece of bread. I dipped it
into the bowl of herbs at my left. As I did, Judas dipped his bread with
mine. I looked into him and then said to the others, "One of you who is
eating with me will betray me."

John fell on to my breast from my right. "Is it I, Lord?"

Oh, dear John,

Then another asked the same, and then another.

I finally answered, "You will all stumble. Satan has asked for each of
you..."[279]

Peter then stood. "Even if everyone else stumbles, I will not!"

My heart sank for my well-intended friend. He still clung to the power
of the self within him. *Oh, Peter, why won't you believe what I'm saying? Where
is your faith in me?* I stood and faced him from the far side of our table.
"Peter, a rooster won't crow again until you deny me three times!"

My skin became cold and tight. "I tell you again that one of you will
betray me. Woe to that man, for it would have been better for him if he had
never been born." I then broke bread and dipped it. "He is the one to whom
I give this piece of bread." I handed it to Judas the Iscariot.

Judas feigned surprise. "Is it I, Rabbi?"

I looked deeply into his strained face. *Is he mocking me? Does he think that
I don't know?* "It is." The room fell silent as a tomb. "Do what you must do,
and quickly."

Judas stood abruptly and collected himself. His black eyes fell to the
ground and I groaned within myself. Saying nothing, he hurried out of the
room.

---

278 Matthew 26:28, Mark 14:24, and Luke 22:20 all report this unusual statement by
Jesus in similar ways. Drinking blood was a clear violation of Jewish law and custom, as
was eating flesh. Therefore, Jesus' offer of his blood—even symbolically—was surely a
troublesome one. If, however, it is remembered that the prohibition on blood ingestion
was because of its sacred status as representing life, then perhaps this act could be understood as Jesus' invitation for his followers to take his life into their own. In so doing, they
would honor the Law even as they transformed it into what Jesus calls 'the new covenant,'
(the new relationship) with God and his people, one based on Jesus' own life and death.
279 Luke 22:31

My friends were distressed and so I stood. "Listen carefully: you will soon have trials of many kinds...you will soon grieve and you will be scattered. I will not be with you...and then I will be with you again."[280]This confused them of course, but I knew that they would soon understand. So I continued. "I want you to love one another so others will know that you belong to me. And be happy! Be daring! Yes it is true that the Evil prowls about but I have conquered Evil."

After our supper, most of us made our way out of the city and over the night-covered Kidron Valley to the lower part of the Mount of Olives. A press and a small field named 'Gethsemane' lay there, surrounded by the gnarled silhouettes of old olive trees. I embraced each of my friends, one by one, and bade them rest while I would pray. I then asked Peter and my cousins—James and John of Zebedee—to follow me away from the others and deep into the olive grove.[281] (I had often invited these three to join me when I needed the others to be emboldened. Peter was my great, shaggy, bear of a man, and my cousins were my 'Sons of Thunder,' like their father. The others took heart from the strength of each of them...and there were times when I did, as well.)

When we had walked about a stone's throw from the others, I felt a weight begin to pull on my spirit like an iron chain wrapped around the legs of a man in deep water. I started to struggle for breath again and I felt suddenly afraid. I fell to one knee and Peter ran to me. "Grief is filling my chest," I gasped.

As the words left my lips, my eyes darkened. I nearly fell over. I took hold of a tree and tears began to stream down my face. I thought death was upon me and so I seized Peter's arm. "Stay here...and keep watch, for Evil is circling in this place to tempt you."

I said no more, but staggered a little further, alone, until my legs grew so heavy that I could not take another step. I fell to both knees and then

---

280 See John 16:16 and following verses.
281 See Matthew 26, Mark 14, Luke 22, and John 18.

on to my hands. I opened my eyes and stared at the earth where a terrible vision filled me: I saw a pool of corruption began leaking up from the dark soil and soaking my hands and knees with the poisons of greed and lust. A stench of rotted corpses slain by haughty power and shameless oppression filled my nose.

I retched.

I shut my eyes but when I did my mind filled with lurid images and vile deeds. I opened them to escape, but then they burned with endless tears from those who had suffered through the generations of men. My own tears began to flow from me like a waterfall into the pool of corruption below my face. So great were my tears that I began to drown in the sorrows that had flowed over the earth from the beginning. *Where is mercy?* I cried within myself. *Where is salvation?*

The tears that I had shed then turned into a lake of blood that began to congeal. My hands and knees began to stick to the earth. I tried but I could not lift them. I opened my mouth to speak but I could say nothing as my ears now filled with the mocking laughter of the Beast. I tried to cover my ears but my hands remained fixed to the ground; I tried to turn my head away but it was weighted in its hanging place as if a heavy crown was now pulling it forward.

The edges of a spiked whip flew toward me and bit at my flesh; I saw red robes and a huddle of silk turbans. The men in the red robes mocked me, and the men under the turbans laughed at me. And then I saw hatred in an endless parade of people…and I watched flocks of frightened sheep tethered to great gold rings on a field of marble, waiting to be slain.

My body shook. A cold chill spread over my skin.

And I felt so terribly alone.

The weight then left my head so that my head flew upwards, and I saw the Temple rise over me; its mighty blocks began to separate and lift as if floating one above the other. The blocks spun in the air, slowly, and moved away from me. Yet as they did they grew larger and larger until they began to entomb me within themselves.

A voice then hissed at me: "Leper, sin-bearer, filthy-one…unclean…"

I collapsed on to my face. "Father, help me."

CHAPTER XXXX

THE TRIALS OF MEN

An angel appeared to me. His face was sad yet comforting. I felt his hand upon my shoulder. "Gabriel?" I groaned. "Michael?" His presence gave me the strength to pry my hands from the dried blood and the fouled earth. I quickly covered my head once more with my *tallit* and gripped its corners with all my might to pray. "Father, if it is possible take this cup from me, for to bear this burden is too great...I am not able..."[282]

I fought to free myself from my knees, but I was too weak. I fell forward again. Desperate but not abandoned, I gave the whole of my hope to my Father. "Yet do not do as I want, but as you want..." I released all words from my mind, and the images faded.

The angels gave me words of peace.

And I rested in the *shalom* of my Father.

Staggering, I returned to my three disciples whom I found sleeping comfortably. Peter was snoring. "Peter, James, John...you didn't believe me? You couldn't even stand watch with me for this short time?"

Peter rubbed his eyes. "We...saw that your spirit was in need of prayer. So we let you be alone. Then...then we fell asleep."

---

282 Luke 22:42, 43, also Matthew 26:36 and forward.

I was too exhausted to scold them. "Listen to me. Keep watch and don't stop praying. Danger is all around you." I took a breath. I know your spirits are willing but your bodies are weak. Pray."

Once again I walked a little distance from my sleepy disciples and I covered my head. I prayed to my Father even more earnestly. This time I saw a dark plain covered by armies that had no end. To another side I saw mountains of Light-bearers preparing for a terrible battle. My heart began to pound so that I thought it might burst. My mind pressed against the walls of my skull; I began to lose all sense of life and death—of being and un-being. The Spirit then showed me yet more plainly of what was to come and I groaned in terror...terror for Israel, for my followers...and for myself. *Is there no other way?*

Feeling faint, I collapsed to my side and I lay still until the angel comforted me again. But then the Beast began to whisper in my ear and to that I recoiled. I sat up and pressed my fists together. "Not my will, Father, but yours..." I heard the Beast fall away, laughing. I opened my eyes and drew breath, then dragged myself to my three disciples who were fast asleep, again. I looked at them and knelt by each of them. I touched them lightly and said a prayer, then returned to my place.

The angel was waiting. As I approached him he stood and rested both his hands on my shoulders, squeezing strength into my body. "Jesus, son of Mary, the end has come...and also the beginning."

My mouth was dry. I nodded.

"Judas is bringing the guard now. You will be delivered into the hands of sinful men."

My belly turned.

"May the Lord bless you and keep you; may the Lord make his face shine on you and be merciful to you...and give you the deep peace of *shalom*."

The angel's words filled me with new power and my spirit began to lift. I thanked him and blessed him and watched him leave me. I then sat alone deep within my shawl, waiting.

I thought in silence for a long while until I felt fear rising within me. I begged my Father for the third time to take this cup away. After all, if he would only just open the eyes of Israel; if only he would just fill their ears with truth and bend their knees to follow in his ways. If only...

But had my Father ever forced his way on his people?

When had he denied them the desires of their hearts?

Would he enslave them...even to his will?

And so I said for the third and final time, "Father, my desire is that your desire be done on earth, even as it is in Heaven. *Selah.*"

"Wake up you three."

My sleepy disciples stirred.

"Wake up!" I kicked Peter.

The first of many voices then came from the darkness. "There! There they are."

Peter, James, and John suddenly jumped to their feet as hundreds of men with clubs and swords rushed toward us under torchlight. [283]Peter drew his sword, as did James.

Judas emerged at the front of the mob. His eyes were shining with ambition and zeal. He walked quickly toward me and kissed me on the cheek. At his kiss others rushed toward me.[284]

"No!" cried Peter. He swung his sword wildly, shaving the right ear from the head of Caiaphas' servant, Malchus.

Malchus cried out like a baby...and pressed his hand hard against his head. Blood ran freely down his neck. "What have you done!"

I pitied the servant and rooted around in the darkness for his ear. I found it and blew the chaff off it. "Come to me, Malchus, and be healed."

The servant looked about, warily, and then took a few cautious steps toward me. I was happy that he believed. I then pressed his ear lightly to his head where it remains to this day.

No sooner had I healed Malchus than some of the others began scuffling with my three. One held John as Peter and James began swinging their swords, wildly. *What are they thinking? They'll be cut to pieces!* "Enough!" I cried. "If I wanted, I could summon armies from Heaven to protect me."

---

283 Note: in Greek, John 18:3 says that Judas came with a *'speira'*...a battalion of about 600 men

284 See Matthew 26:47 and forward

I faced the mob. "You come after me like I'm a bandit...or some kind of rebel. And look how many of you come!"

One of the soldiers barked a command but then we heard a sudden commotion on all sides. My other followers had heard me and had awakened to see the torches. They were now racing for their lives through the orchard. At the sound of their cries, Peter panicked, as did James, and they pushed their way out of the grasp of the guards and disappeared. Peter thundered for me to follow.

A thin figure then raced past me. His hand brushed me and I caught his eye but not his face. By his slender figure I thought he must be a mere youth. Was it my beloved John? Was it another? I couldn't see clearly, but a soldier lunged for the lad and caught hold of his robe. With a couple of grunts and a cry, the youth then slipped out of his clothing and dashed away, naked.[285]

I looked after him until a hard hand slapped my face. The Pharisees at the fore of the mobs then quickly laid their hands on me. At their touch I felt the sins of Israel begin to weigh on me; my knees bent under the weight. Soldiers then bound my arms with a thick rope as Judas watched from one side. Our eyes met for the last time. He turned from me and he slowly faded into the darkness.[286]

As many hands pushed me forward I prayed for him, and I began to feel the anxiety that was upon him. He was wondering whether the people would now rise up.

As was I.

A policeman from the Temple punched me in the belly and I gasped for air. "You're nothing special." The policeman spit into my face and shoved me backward. I fell into the limbs of a low-branched olive tree where I felt sudden comfort as if I was being embraced by many arms. But I was jerked out of the tangle and an unseen hand snatched away my *tallit*—my beloved prayer shawl from the Therapeutae. "No! Give that back to me!" I shouted. My mind flew to my parents and Uncle Cleopas, to my many prayers in

---

285 This rather odd detail is found in Mark 14:51,52, leaving some scholars wondering whether the youth was actually Mark, himself.

286 We are told in Matthew 27:3-5 that Judas was later remorseful and returned the 30 pieces of silver (the value of a slave as per Exodus 21:32) that he was paid to betray Jesus before hanging himself. Acts 1: 18 describes his end somewhat differently. In any event, Judas life ended in tragedy.

the wilderness, and to the children who touched it. I fell to my knees and begged. "No!" An image of my Obadiah came to me.

But the thief was gone

and I would never see my *tallit* again.

I was soon kicked and dragged into what I thought was the courtyard of Annas, the former High Priest.[287] Though the Romans had appointed his son-in-law, Caiaphas, as High Priest more than a dozen years before, all of Jerusalem knew that Annas was the power behind the vestments. A Temple policeman shoved me into a dark corner as soldiers and servants hurried about. A column of wakened Elders snaked their way through the gate. A stinging slap on my face turned my attention away.

"You're coming with us."

I was delivered into a large room adjacent to the courtyard and waited as about half the Sanhedrin silently took their seats on cushions strewn informally along three walls. Annas walked toward me and studied me with a finger covering his lips.

"Untie him," Annas commanded.

A Temple guard released my bonds. I rubbed my wrists but did not thank him. Annas walked around me three times muttering to himself. He moved to a throne-like seat that a servant had set directly in front of me. "I remember you as a boy in Solomon's Portico."

I nodded.

Annas paused to receive a message from a servant. His face twitched and I knew that something had agitated him. He returned his attention to me. "Tell me about your sayings."

I waited. Annas was an old man and I knew that he would soon begin reciting all that he wanted me to say. And so he did, beginning with rumors of what I said and finishing with those teachings of mine that he had actually heard with his own ears.

I answered him. "You know that I have spoken openly. I have said nothing in secret." I pointed at the many new faces arriving. "Why don't you ask them? They know what I've said."

Annas shifted in his seat and looked away as a guard fell on me with his fists. "Is this how you speak to the Chief Priest!" he shouted. He knocked me to the ground.

---

287 See John 18:13 and forward.

I pulled myself to my feet and wiped the blood off my face with my sleeve. "If I lied to you, then judge me for that. But if I spoke the truth, why do you beat me?"

Annas stood and walked away.

As I was dragged from Annas' courtyard, I overheard some conversation about Caiaphas and I heard the word 'Pilate.' At the sound of that word I felt a cold dread begin to creep over me, for every Jew in Judea knew what Pilate could do.

I was hauled through the night-hushed neighborhoods of the city until I was eventually pushed through the gates of the house of Caiaphas where I waited as more members of the Sanhedrin gathered. I spotted the figure of my own young John pleading with someone in the household whom he must have known. The sight of the youth lifted my spirit. I strained to see him more clearly and when I did I also saw what seemed to be the broad shadow of Peter crouching nearby.

Before I could react, a guard shoved me against a wall with such force that I fell over. A kind servant then gave me a drink of water before I was hurried through dark corridors and into a large room. As I entered the room, I saw Caiaphas situating himself and arguing with this one and that over details of the Law. As I waited, I turned my head to peer between the marble columns and into the adjacent courtyard. I saw several fires and around them many had gathered to keep warm. Servant girls were scurrying back and forth with bread and wine. *Is John here? Is that Peter squatting near a fire?*

"You." Caiaphas' voice turned my head.

I said nothing.

He began by telling of our time in the Portico when I was a boy. His memory had changed many of the details, but he quickly dismissed all of that and began to question me. I chose to not answer. Why should I? What he sought was testimony that he might twist into a public pronouncement supporting what he wanted to believe…that it would be better for one man to die than for all of Israel to be crushed by the Romans.

Since I wouldn't speak, Caiaphas proceeded to boast his knowledge of truth and flaunt his supposed wisdom. He challenged those many things that I had taught, but when he finally exhausted his own treasury of knowledge he realized that he hadn't actually provided the evidence that he needed to have me executed. He began to tap his fingers together. Finally he stood. "Now, I need to hear the testimony of the Elders."

Among the seventy-one judges now gathered were my dear friends, Nicodemus and Joseph the Arimathean. They looked frightened and angry. I watched them argue against others in hoarse whispers, but when I saw Nicodemus finally wipe tears from his eyes, I knew that there would be no justice. Two of the Elders then stepped forward and accused me of saying that I could destroy the Temple and rebuild it in three days. That testimony pleased Caiaphas. He stood and pointed a stiff finger at me. "How do you answer such a charge?"

I said nothing. What could be gained by repeating myself? Yet that prophecy was truly at the heart of all their hatred. After all, what would they have without Herod's Temple of stone?

Red-faced and blustering, Caiaphas then finally asked me what I needed him to ask. Spitting in fury, he shook his fists. "Before the living God, tell us plainly: are you the Messiah?"

I studied the man and I saw the fear that filled the cracks of his face. *He should be afraid,* I thought. For what would it mean if I were the One whom Daniel saw—the Son, coming in the clouds and presented with a Kingdom for *all* peoples?[288]

What if *I was* the Lord whom David had foreseen as the eternal Priest?[289]

Then what of this man's Temple? And what then of *this* Israel?

I felt the Spirit near. I had missed her and was glad to feel her presence again. I cast a quick look into the courtyard where Peter looked troubled. I turned to Caiaphas. "You have said it for yourself. Soon you will see me sitting on the right hand of the Almighty and coming in the clouds of Heaven."[290]

To that the Elders cried out, angrily, as the delighted Caiaphas fell to his knees, tearing his clothes. "He has insulted the God of Israel! He has blasphemed! Oh, what then shall we do with this man?"

"Death! Death" the others answered.

Many hands began to pound me and I was spat upon and thrown about. Driven to the edge of the courtyard, I was struck so hard with a cane that I fell backward.

And then I heard a rooster crow.

---

288 From Daniel 7:13, 14

289 From Psalms 110

290 See Matthew 26:64

THE LAST SCAPEGOAT

As you know, the Sanhedrin needs to make their judgments by light of day, so immediately after the Temple's priests sounded the dawn trumpets, the Elders of Israel pronounced their formal wish to have me put to death. You already know that only the Romans are permitted to execute a prisoner, so I had to be dragged away to the governor's palace where I was thrown at Pilate's feet.

Standing, I looked at Pilate closely and I felt anger rise within me as I considered the harm he had caused my people. Neither of us said a word as a messenger handed him a note from his wife, a note encouraging him to show me mercy.[291] While he was reading it, I looked to my right and there I saw my beloved John, again pleading with the rulers of the Temple who were well known to him. Next to him was Joanna--a friend to Pilate's wife and still an influence among the wealthy of Judea. I was pleased to see her; she was risking much to be my follower.

Pilate rinsed his face and then looked at me carefully. "Come inside, away from the Jews."

I was pushed behind him into his courtroom where he sighed as he took his seat. "You've heard all the accusations. If we would allow it, they would put you to death. He belched, indifferently. "What do I care about your

---

291 Matthew 27:19

blasphemies?" He settled into his seat and then looked at me, carefully. "But rebellion is another thing. So tell me, do you claim to be a king?"

"You say I am."[292]

Pilate darkened. He wiped one hand over his smooth face, and looked at his wife's note still hanging limply in the other. With a nod of his head, he had me dragged back into the courtyard where the Elders were waiting. Pilate followed, indifferently, and took a seat in front of my accusers. He raised a hand to command silence, then said, "I find him innocent."

This was not good news to the Elders. They began to shout at him with such wrath that his face twitched. Perhaps they knew what he knew: Caesar Tiberius in faraway Rome wanted no more trouble from Judea.

I then heard a voice cleverly cry out that I had started my teaching in Galilee. I searched the crowd. Was that John's voice? Nicodemus'? Joseph's?

"Galilee, you say?" Pilate asked. He brightened. "I see." He turned to an aide. "Herod would like to be our friend." He stood and silenced the crowd. "Then take him to Herod…he's staying in the city."[293]

I will not bore you with Herod. Let me just say that since I wouldn't do tricks for that clever fox he promptly returned me to Pilate with a set of bruises and wrapped in a mocking, purple robe.

Morning was still fresh as I was marched through the streets once again. The sight of me chained in royal colors drew the attention of the people. I studied their faces, hoping to see some desire in them to rescue me. But I could see that they were confused…if I was the Messiah, why would the Elders now be promising my death?

Will they lose heart? I wondered. *Might the Spirit use them to rise up?* Were the visions of my death of what *would* be, or what *could* be?

Pilate was not happy to see me.[294] He met me in the courtyard of the palace where the guards had now allowed the people to enter. He threw

292 Luke 23:4.

293 Luke 23:6 and forward

294 John 18:28 and forward

himself atop his seat, cursing. "You again." He summoned the leaders of the Temple forward. As they were coming he turned to me. "So you are or you are not King of the Judeans?"

"You have said it. But my Kingdom is not of this world, for if it were, my soldiers would defeat any who oppose me. I was born to be a king of truth; those who follow truth, listen to me."

Pilate took another breath. I saw that his mind was occupied with many struggles. "What is truth?"

I considered how to respond. He might have been interested to hear that neither my words nor my deeds were Truth—for no word or deed can contain the whole of me--but that *I am* Truth. I could have told him that to know Truth is to know *me*.

But to what end? No. I knew his heart and I knew that he did not *want* to believe me. So I remained silent.

An officer whispered a warning into Pilate's ear. "The Jews are coming from everywhere."

"Why?"

The officer shrugged. "Who knows with these people? But be careful."

Pilate nodded. He was well aware that Rome's greatest Jew-hater—a wicked man named Sejanus—had fallen from Caesar's favor and had been recently executed. He'd have no ally if he disrespected these people. But he also needed to respect the laws of Rome.

The priests, the Pharisees and the Sadducees began to shout questions at me. But I said nothing. Pilate spoke to me from behind. "You will not answer them?"

I said nothing.

Pilate finally stood and addressed the raging crowd. "Silence! Silence! Neither I nor Herod find any crime in this man that deserves death."

This was not good news for the people or the Elders. A loud protest echoed throughout the palace. My spirit sagged; who had bewitched them?

"But I'll see that he's punished for causing you trouble."

"No!" shouted one. Another cried, "Release Barabbas for us, instead."

Pilate turned a troubled eye to one of his advisors. "Barabbas? Barabbas the rebel? They want me to release a rebel and keep an innocent man. What are we to do with these people!"

"Give us Barabbas!" the crowd began to cry.

Why Barabbas? I wondered. The people began to chant his name over and over. "Barabbas! Barabbas!" Then I understood: they wanted a leader with a sword, not one in chains.

Wary, Pilate sought the advice of his councilors. I watched his jaw pulse and his fists tighten as anxious words were whispered in his ear. Disgusted, he finally stood and raised his hands over the crowd. All fell silent. "Hear me. Hear me! In the name of Caesar Tiberius, I release to you...Barabbas."

The crowd thundered their approval.

Pilate returned to his seat with unsympathetic eyes fixed on me. Perhaps he felt a certain pity—perhaps not, but it was known that he had contempt for any who called themselves 'Jew,' and surely, I was a Jew.

My arms weighted heavily by my chains, I faced my people. Their prior love had, indeed, given way to hate.

After all their fathers' hopes

And all their fathers' longing,

I had become their humiliation.

And they would have no more of me.

So my ears now filled with the cries of the Elders *and* the people gathered in that place: "Crucify him! Crucify him!"

Everyone knows that Pilate yielded to the will of *that* Israel —not to the remnant who mourned for me in secret on that awful day, or even those who just pitied me—but he yielded to those who desperately wanted to restore an Israel *of their own making*. So he filled a large clay bowl and washed his hands as if to blame others. But truly, he had abandoned justice to serve himself. No amount of water would make him clean.

Pilate turned away and when he did the soldiers of Rome laid their hands on me. At their touch, I suddenly felt the sins of the Gentiles weigh heavy on me like they had when the Jews did the same. My legs buckled. I was dragged through the screaming crowd and into the scourging pit of the Praetorium where the soldiers stripped me naked and tied my hands to the flogging post.[295] Laughing, one soldier taunted me with his short whip. "See those?" He gingerly fingered the rows of metal bolts and sharpened bits of bone that he had tied along the cords. "They're about to eat your skin."

My heart was racing; my mouth was dry. *Thirty-nine strikes?* Squeezing my eyes tightly shut, I tensed, waiting...waiting...ready to count. When the first scourge hit me I shrieked in pain and lurched. My legs danced wildly around the base of the post, but there was no escape. Immediately, another hit me and I wailed again. Then alternating from one side to the other, two soldiers reared back and swung their whips with all their might. I cried out, again, and then again, and then came more. With each strike I felt my skin tearing away from my back, buttocks, and legs.

All sounds began to fade except for the panting of the soldiers. My body hung limply from my wrists still fastened tightly to the post. I turned my head weakly to see the soldier's blood-splattered face. He seemed so young.

How many more? Is no one counting?

Must I say more? Is there a reason that I should recount all those terrible things?

No. Some of you have seen the raw meat of other men pulsing wet from their scourged backs. So, too, was mine. And you've smelled the stench of blood and sweat and urine and dung that fill the air around a man so cruelly abused. So, too, did I stink.

I need say no more.

When they finished, they pressed a purple robe flat against my open wounds, and then twisted a mocking crown of thorns deep into my scalp, mocking me as "King of the Jews." Two soldiers then set the splintered beam to which I would be nailed on top of my shoulders. A whip stung the back of my legs, and I was driven into the streets once again.

"Father?"

I listened, but all I heard was the rough commands of the soldiers around me. I felt faint as I shuffled along crowded streets where merchants paused to spit on me and women threw stones. I marveled at their hatred.

---

295 Matthew 27:26. Note: Roman law required scourging (flogging) as a prerequisite to crucifixion with the exception of women, senators, and some soldiers. Jewish law limited the number of strikes to thirty-nine.

This was nothing like that day not long ago when these same people waved branches over my head and laid down their cloaks before my donkey.

Then a child called me by my name. *"Yeshua?"*

The sound was sweet like a little bird in springtime. I turned and faced a little girl. I remembered her; I had healed her near Jericho and seeing her whole filled me with joy. I opened my mouth to speak, but my ears filled with the sound of the Beast hissing my name.

The stench of Evil filled my nose.

My eyes failed me,

And I tasted the first fruits of Death.

A whip snapped more skin away from my neck and I cried out. "Move away, child..." I said. Mercifully, the crowd swallowed the little girl to safety and I did not see her again. A stone hit my leg, and then one stung the side of my head. Someone threw a brick and I fell forward and landed hard on to my knees. The heavy beam bounced to one side. It was then that the Spirit sent a soft breeze to cool me—one that was enough to help me stand, but not enough to set me free from the searing heat sliding beneath what little skin remained on my back. I took a step, and then another. I thought I heard angels hovering near, weeping. But was that the sound of angels...or was it the song of the women whom I now saw following close? My heart began to race. "Mother?"

Did I imagine her, or was she there?

"Salome? Mary...Susanna..."

I then heard my mother's voice alongside me as clear and kind as it was when I was a child resting on her lap. "Lord, you have given your angels charge over my son.[296] Send your hosts."

I turned my head toward her and opened my mouth. A soldier struck me and pushed me flat atop the ground. My mother loudly protested, but another impatient soldier shoved her away. My jaw clenched.

Then a second child ran toward me with a cup. He touched warm water to my lips. I swallowed a gulp and then another. The dust washed away from my throat. "Mother!" I cried. The little boy was swept away by a Roman boot and I was whipped.

Two soldiers then lifted the beam from my back. My shoulders felt suddenly light. They jerked me to my feet and snatched some poor passer-by

---

296 Psalms 91:11

with rough hands. "Carry it!" they shouted.[297] The frightened man obeyed without a word.

I looked behind to see my mother being helped forward by the Magdalene. I reached an arm toward her but a soldier jammed the butt of his spear into my armpit. "Forward!" I stumbled alongside the grunting man now bearing my burden. Soon the two of us made our way through the shadow of the city gate where I turned my head at the sound of a goat, bleating. My eyes lingered on his slanted pupils, and I remembered my little friend with the red cord that I had led into the wilderness.

A breeze blew freely through the gate and my lungs opened to draw a fresh breath. I was suddenly glad to have borne the sins of Jew and Gentile alike beyond the walls of my Father's city. I turned to see the goat again, and I smiled.

When I smiled, a soldier clubbed me to the ground. Struggling to my feet, I cleared my eyes of blood and I saw the fingers of the Magdalene stretching toward me from one side. "Jesus, you are not alone..." she cried. Hers was as soothing a song as I had ever heard.

"Mary...Mary..." I gasped. But she was quickly jostled out of sight.

The walls of the city were now behind us and the stranger and I were driven to the shoulder of the crowded Damascus Highway. There, my failing eyes fell upon a row of wooden posts standing like a narrow strip of branchless trees in front of that terrible place called 'The Skull.' I stiffened. *Here I die? Here, along this road...Father?*[298]

It was then that a third child cried out my name. "*Yeshua! Yeshua!*" I turned. Running toward me was a little girl with something in her hand. *A flower? A piece of fruit? A sponge of water?* At the sight of her, my fear passed. I could see that she was weeping for me. I fell to one knee. "Child..."

---

297 Luke 23:26 identifies this man as Simon the Cyrene, most likely a Jewish pilgrim to the Passover Feast. Cyrene was a city in what is now known as Libya. It had a large Jewish population.

298 'Golgotha,' or 'the skull,' is believed to be the remaining limestone rocks that form the image of a skull's face in a cliff still visible today. The site was a stone quarry during the time of Solomon.

The Romans crucified their victims along a roadway to instill terror in the passing public. It is most likely that Jesus was crucified alongside the busy Damascus Road that paralleled the city walls, and probably in front of the cliff known as 'Golgotha.' Victims were usually not very high off the ground, leaving them barely above eye-level with those who looked upon them.

I reached for her as she raced closer, but a soldier snatched her away and tossed her into the crowd with an oath. The soldier pushed me forward. "There...that's for you." He pointed to the post that was waiting for me.

I stared at it. *How long, dead tree, how long have you been waiting for me? How many others have hung on you?*

"Now, Jew!" Another soldier kicked me and I fell at the foot of the post. I looked up, and I began to tremble.

Friends, I don't wish to speak of every terrible thing that happens to a man when he is crucified...and I was surely crucified as a man. You have seen men die this way, but none live to speak of it. So I will tell you some of what happened so that you will have pity on the next man whom you see hanging on a Roman cross.

I will tell you first that my heart raced with terror. And I will tell you that I was nauseated by shame as four soldiers disrobed me, roughly. The cloth had dried within my opened back and buttocks, so as they tore it from me, more of my flesh came loose. I cried out. Laughing, they then threw me on my back, naked. I closed my eyes and wished that my Father would clothe me like he had clothed Adam.

But he didn't.

And so I lay naked for all to see me as the man I was, even my mother, my sister, and the other women who loved me. [299]I did not think about this for very long, however, for my head was pulled forward by my hair and the beam inserted behind my neck. Two soldiers leaned their knees hard into my shoulders to hold me fast. I groaned. But when I saw them take hammers and spikes in hand, my chest began to heave.

I clenched my teeth.

They probed the soft skin of my wrists with the blunt tips of their spikes. I filled my lungs with what air I could and held it...My heart raced; I began to whimper. I then saw their hammers rise and I shut my eyes.

The hammers fell.

---

299 Victims were usually crucified naked, which was a shaming posture for most, but especially for Jews because of their moral codes of modesty. The Gospels refer to the Romans taking five items of clothes from Jesus, one of which was his inner tunic. (See John 1919:23, etc.) Typically, a Jewish man would wear sandals, a belt, an outer robe, an inner tunic, and a loincloth. The Gospels go on to describe his tunic as 'seamless,' and so rather than ruin it by tearing it, the (presumably) four soldiers cast lots for it...done by putting marked stones, etc., into some kind of cup or jar which was then tipped over, the first stone to fall out being the winner.

I shrieked.

And I kept shrieking as the hammers rose slowly and then fell again, driving the spikes between the bones of my wrist and deep into the wood.

Then the world went white.

THE FINAL SACRIFICE

When I awoke, the beam to which I was now fastened was being attached to the standing post. The weight on my wrists was so painful that I began to sob like a little boy. A soldier then wrapped his arms around my waist and lifted me enough to drop my loins atop the curved horn that was mounted on the post like a saddle.[300]

I cried out, again.

I began to twist and writhe. The agony in my loins was so terrible that I ignored the sound of my wrist bones grinding against their iron spikes. I might have ripped my arms free from their hands if it wasn't for the laughing soldier who now held my body fast against the post. It was then that I noticed how mercifully smooth the wood of the post felt against my raw back. Its splinters had long since broken away into the bodies of those

---

300 Historians are uncertain as to the exact way in which the beam was affixed to the post. Some argue for the traditional image where the post is positioned slightly higher than the beam, thus providing a convenient place for the sign noted in the Gospels. Others believe the beam had a hole in the center of its underside into which a pointed post top was inserted, thus forming the shape of a 'T.'

In drawings of crucifixions of this period, and in some records of the early church, it also appears that a small, painful seat was attached to the post upon which the weight of the victim was also suspended. Curving upward, it was intended to inflict additional pain and to prolong death that eventually came by suffocation.

hundreds of others who had perished on it. But the suffering of each of them then entered me, and I vomited.[301]

In moments, hands began clawing at my legs. The men pressed my heels hard against the sides of the post. I struggled, but a cursing soldier tied my legs fast with a rope. Two others approached with hammers and more spikes. Again I felt the blunt tips of the iron spikes probe my skin, this time searching for the gap between each ankle and heel.

I lurched, I wiggled, and I writhed. I called out to my Father as the whole of my body struggled against the ropes. *Do you see this? Do you hear me? Will you answer me?* From each side I saw the hammers swing back...and then toward the dreaded spikes.

I screamed.

Another strike, and another.

And then again...

I sobbed and I wailed. My bowels released whatever was left within my body. Warm, watery dung slid over my pointed saddle and down my trembling legs. I felt dizzy. I vomited but could not cast the bloodied liquid beyond my own beard. I gagged and I coughed and I sputtered, and...

I will say no more of it.

I awakened to feel the body of man looming above me. "There." He pointed over my head to something I could not see. "By order of Pilate you are now, 'King of the Jews.'"[302]He spat into my face and stepped off his stool. All ropes were taken away and so my wrists, heels, and loins now suspended me. Pain filled every joint; agony punctured all my inward parts. I cried out, but I quickly learned to not move...yet how could I not? My teeth clenched. My shoulders were tearing; I thought the base of my buttocks would be crushed on the point of that terrible saddle.

---

301 The shortage of lumber in Palestine called for the re-use of the timbers used in crucifixion. It is generally agreed--though not absolutely proven--that crucifixion sites kept posts fixed in place and the condemned would be required to carry or drag the crossbeam to the post to which he was assigned.

302 Pilate had ordered a sign to be placed over Jesus' head that mocked him as King of the Jews in all three languages spoken commonly in Judea: Hebrew for the Jews, Latin for the Romans, and Greek for all others. (Greek was the common language of the empire.) See Luke 23.

I could not breathe enough to weep. Suddenly aware that I might suffocate, I felt a rush of panic race through me. My skin tightened; my belly seized. I began to pant, drawing short, shallow breaths as quickly as I could. I then heard some mocking words from the man being crucified on one side of me. The one on my other side answered in my defense. I turned my head, slowly, to look at each of them. My defender's eyes were so sad. I looked into his spirit and I loved him; I promised him that we would be together in Paradise. Peace filled his face, and for that brief moment I felt joy, even there on my cross.

It was then that I felt a terrible scratching on my skin. A cloud of black flies had fallen upon my many wounds and they were burrowing through the pus and water leaking from my body. They swarmed over my dung-stained legs, and climbed into my nostrils. I tried snorting them from my nose.

"Away!" shouted a voice. "Away!" My beloved John began waving a branch in front of my face. "Leave him!" He began to curse at them and swing his branch, wildly.

Oh, how sorely I was tempted to come off that cross and comfort him. I dropped my head forward and stared at the ground that was just two hand widths beneath the bottoms of my feet. *So close...If I could just touch the earth again...for even a moment? Father?*

The Romans quickly shoved John onto his back. I closed my eyes. But then I felt a hand on my side. *"Ama..."* I began to whimper.

Soldiers grabbed for her, but John dug into his purse. "Here, you animals!" He tossed coins all about the ground, and as they scurried to pick them up, my mother leaned her body against mine. I could feel her warm breath; I could smell her hair. She was clutching the tiny scroll that the sisters in Egypt had given her a lifetime ago. "Mother..." I wheezed.

Mary feigned calm and let tears run down her face. She spoke softly to me. "My sighing is not hidden from you...blessed be the name of the Lord." [303]

I then felt warm hands cupping my heels. I looked down to see the Magdalene sobbing. "Be at peace, dear woman," I sputtered. My sister, Salome, and my Aunt Miriam began to sing. I stared at each of them—and I marveled. *Love,* I thought. *This is what love looks like.*

---

303 Psalms 38:9

The world outside of me fell away and I felt myself lurching about the world within me, desperately running from memory to memory...from face to face, until I rested on one.

Judas?

His skin was yellow.

His heart was crumbling stone.

He mind was an empty cistern, hollow and cold.

"Judas?"

I remembered that my Father was not willing that *any* should perish. "The day will come, Judas," I mumbled to myself, "When every knee shall bow to me...even yours." *What might that mean for him?* I wondered.

My worlds began to blur. The one within began to fill up with a fast-creeping darkness that frightened me. I retched, and in the retching I opened my eyes to the world without where the sky was turning black. The passers-by saw it too, and they turned away from me and looked upward, troubled. Even the soldiers around me became anxious and I felt their fear as it if were my own.

I noticed a young soldier side-step toward me. I could barely see him, but he looked frightened. I also could see that he was fair—a Gaul, perhaps? *So far from home,* I thought.

I struggled for another breath.

A small pack of wild dogs slinked toward me, and my mother chased them with a stick. I then heard a Pharisee throw the words of the Law at me as if they were stones. I groaned. "Blind. Are they all blind?" I fainted.

Sometime after that a cool breeze summoned my spirit. I awakened to the touch of a soft hand on my chest. *Ama?* I sucked breath weakly past the flies hovering near my nose, and I thought that I could smell her. My mother reached up to stroke my face. Her hand was red with my blood. She, my beloved John, and the other women were trying to be brave.

"All the others are afraid, Jesus. They are watching from afar but they love you."

I nodded, weakly. I then strained for another breath and said, "Dear woman... look there..." I slanted my eyes toward John. "There is... your son." I panted a few breaths and then looked at John. "Protect her...She is now...your mother."

John took my mother's hand.

My lungs burned as I struggled for another breath. My joints, once numb, began to awaken and as they did I felt my shoulders rip. My belly cramped with a nauseating agony. I tried to pray to my Father but my throat was so dry—and the flies were filling my mouth. I gagged. John swung his branch in front of me again. I then heard the slow flapping of wings as the birds came closer. *Will they take my eyes before I die? Will they blind me? Father? Where are you?* I let my head drop forward to face the small, red-black puddle of my blood congealing just below my feet. *No. John will not allow it.* My ears suddenly filled with the words of my cousin, the Baptizer: "Behold, the Lamb of God."

My mother pressed herself against me; I heard my sister singing. I then fell away again and mercifully began to dream of my little lamb playing in green grass and nuzzling his mother. *Obadiah...* A rush of noise filled my ears and I awoke to a fresh surge of pain in my buttocks and loins. I strained against my cross.

My mother quickly calmed me with a touch and a word: "The spotless Lamb who..." She faltered. "...Who takes away the sin of the world." She had always understood how it was that I was different from other men.

The words of the prophet Isaiah came to me: *'Our sorrows weighed heavy on him...he was bruised and beaten because of our evil ways...we are healed by his suffering...*[304] Words of other Scriptures washed over me. My heart lifted. I looked past my mother and at the people again...the blind people. I felt sad for them and I was glad that I had carried their sins out of my Father's city. The blood that ran out of my body would cleanse their new Temple. *No more animals to be slain; no more goats driven to Azazel...*My task on earth was almost finished—and men would soon be free. *Good...it is very good.*

In the midst of this unexpected joy I heard voices cursing at me. I saw a scribe and a Roman scowling at me with contempt. I turned my face to see others pointing at the sign over my head and laughing. I lifted my face toward Heaven. "Father, forgive them," I said. "They don't know what they are doing..."

I had no sooner spoken than sudden panic filled my pores. *Something's changing... Father? Father?* Terrified, I strained against the cursed spikes; I began to thrash and heave. *Where are you?* My terror was so great that I forced myself forward on the curved saddle-horn, dropping off the bone at the bottom of my loins; The point of the horn penetrated deeply into my

---

304 From Isaiah 53

bowels and I screamed. I felt my mother's hands desperately trying to lift me upward. She was sobbing. John joined her, but the soldiers threw them both to the ground.

Such pain...

My mouth opened, but no breath would enter.

A dark gloom then swallowed me and I felt as if my body was sinking into a deep pit of cold death. I struggled to cry out but no words would come. *El Abba! Where are you? Where are you?*

I could not escape the void. I sank deeper into that forsaken place. *What is this?*

My mind was flooded by a rancid pool of vile images and my ears filled with the whispers of evil desires. My tongue tasted the blood of men's innocent victims, and my nostrils filled with the stench of the oppressors' sour wine. Heavy blocks of men's corruptions pressed down on me: gluttony, murder, lies, adulteries, unspeakable cruelties...all the handiwork of self-love. I struggled against the spikes and against the puncturing horn. I felt the bones of my wrists and my heels grinding on the stubborn iron; blood dripped from my bowels.

Then something more terrible found me.

The millstone of men's false righteousness began to press down on me so hard that I thought it might rip me off my cross and crush me. I heaved my chest upwards; my mouth opened wide, desperate for a breath of life that might lift these burdens off me: envy, lust, greed, arrogance, hatred... all the desires of self-love. Breath, enough, did not come to me.

Falling faint, I then felt other sorts of agony ravage through my veins. The nauseating misery of men's regrets, the leprous decay of their shame, and the crippling shackles of fear turned my blood to vinegar. A chill came over me and my body began to quake. A sharp pain seized my chest and the world went dark.

In some black cavern I heard a chanting song of the Evil One. I tried to close my ears but I couldn't. The song was wicked and the terror of it was so great that every sinew that was not yet torn began to rip. I awakened to desperately snatch a precious bit of air, and with nearly all that was left of life, I cried out, *"El... Why...why have you abandoned me?"*

The world fell silent. No man, no bird, no dog, no hooves...nothing. I could not even hear my own parched throat gasping for air. Even Evil paused to listen for the answer.

I waited.

But no answer came.

Instead, the words of the Psalmist found me. *I will fear no evil, for you are with me...*[305]

Was he?

My mind was thick and slow like sliding mud. A breeze cooled my body and I then heard a woman's voice as crisp as a snowbird's: *Though he slay me, yet I will trust him.* [306]I gathered all that I could find within myself and I stole a bit more air from a sudden gust of wind that swirled dust over my eyes. I tilted my face upwards toward the now Unseen. "Father, I... yield...myself...to...you..."

As those final words left my lips, what little breath remained behind rattled upward from my lungs and passed quickly through my throat and over my now slackened jaw. A rising numbness followed, running from my toes, through my legs and loins, into my belly, and through my chest until it finally filled my head.

I felt life begin to fly away.

The world went white, and I then began to tumble, wildly. I could feel the whole of the cosmos quaking. I fell away, farther and farther, and I heard a deafening sound, like the tearing of a huge cloth. Then—as if I was now watching from some other place—I saw the poor Gaul soldier shove his spear into my side; blood and water poured out.

I then saw the earth cracking below me.

And I saw Satan laughing.

---

305 Psalms 23

306 Job 13:15 Note: Most translations agree with this rendering, though the NRSV reads differently.

CONQUERING KING

Time is not present in the realm of the dead and so time left me. All sense of old things vanished. Instead, I felt like I was being sucked into the belly of the earth where the power of Evil began to draw me deep, deep and deeper still.

You cannot bear to hear more.

I will simply say that my Father allowed Evil to bind me. He permitted every hissing sin, every curdling blasphemy, every corrupting and corroding perversion of his love from all time past and all time to come enclose me like a weave of writhing serpents. With that shroud of bondage wrapped tightly around me, my Father allowed me to be thrown to the undying maggots and the eternal flames of Gehenna.

There I was consumed.

And there I became as if I *was* no more.

The chambers of evil echoed with laughter. The demons swooned for joy, and the Evil One danced.

But then El Abba roared!

I was startled out of nothingness by a blast of trumpets. Breath rushed into my lungs; my limbs loosed with new strength; my mind was abruptly jolted by all knowledge; my spirit so filled with Heaven's joy that I sat up and tore the shrouds away, laughing!

I stood. *"El Abba...El Abba!* I am alive; I am free!" I opened my eyes wide and breathed deeply of the tomb's air. It smelled fresh like a forest after a thunderstorm. I stretched my arms and my legs. I felt light as Light; I knew that old things had passed away...all things had surely been made new. Humming, I walked around the large tomb, my Light filling every crevice. "The Arimathean's very own tomb! Thank you, Joseph. You denied yourself comfort in death for my sake." I laughed. I then thought of my dear mother and the joy that would soon fill her. I was happy; I began to dance when one of my angels appeared.

"Welcome, Lord."

"Shalom, Michael!" I said. The soldier was weary and battle-worn. "So... here I am."

He sat on an unfinished sepulcher across from my own. "Yes, Lord. Here you are. Did you hear the noise? It was quite a battle. Your Father crushed Death and Evil was not happy about it."

I laughed. "But you are exhausted." I began to fold my shroud.

He nodded. "Very."

"You fought well."

"We all did, Lord. You should have heard us at the end...just after our Father roared. That's when Raphael raised his hands and led us all in a warrior's song while Lucifer and his bunch fell away, shrieking."

Gabriel then appeared along with several others including Vasiariah and Nith-Haiah. I greeted them, warmly, and then Michael led us out of the tomb. He pointed to the large, round stone that had sealed the tomb. "The Romans were terrified," he said. "One crack of thunder, a little earthquake, some heavenly grunts...one big stone rolling away and off they went."

We all laughed and then we walked together into Joseph's fine garden, lit only by starlight...and us. Together, we sat on a large rock and breathed deeply of the sweet Passover air. "Lord," said Gabriel. "Thank you. Your name be praised."

Vasiariah then said, "We suffered with you, but the Father and the Spirit suffered *as* you…"

I nodded. "We are One."

Nith-Haiah turned my head. "This was all a terrible thing for us to watch…yet it was wondrous. You *are* love, my Lord, and your Father must love humankind very much to have you to suffer as one of them."

Gabriel then stepped forward and bowed. "Lord, you took upon yourself everything that Evil could throw at you--even death--and you conquered it all. May men and angels praise your name above all others under Heaven."

I looked at each of the angels. It was time to teach them. "Yes, you have spoken truly. But you must understand that my Father did not *need* to slay me—it was men who did, and for their sake he allowed it so that they might understand his love. Nor did my Father force me to the cross. I went because he wanted me to go. And, so that there is no confusion among you or among those of your kind who follow Lucifer, understand that he had no say in any of this. Nothing was done on his account."

The angels considered my words.

"And know this too: The *authority* of the Evil One is defeated and chained, but *he* has not yet been destroyed. His reach will continue to press the whole of the cosmos as long as we grant liberty to men--and we grant liberty to men as long as we love them as men. Therefore, the chains I have thrown around Lucifer do not keep men from his temptations and his lies."

I looked at my chief warrior. "Michael, do you understand? Men are still in danger, for I will not bind men's love to us. Love is only love when it is free."

I turned to the others. "Listen to me: the war is won but the battle still rages. Your work is still much needed."

They understood and began to sing a song of Heaven, and the *shalom* of my Father settled upon us all.

Soon, we began talking about the days before, and the angels marveled about how the Arimathean had convinced Pilate to release my body to his care, and how he and old Nicodemus had lifted me off the cross.[307] "They

---

307 Matthew 27: 57-60. Importantly, the Romans typically let the corpses of crucified victims be destroyed by birds and wild dogs, which is why few remains have been discovered. It is significant, therefore, that Pilate released Jesus' body for burial. This was

are to be blessed," I said. "And Joanna did her best to help. She risked everything for me."

Then Michael spoke of Nicodemus' generosity in his provision of spices for my burial. "He bought more than a young man could carry."[308] Another told of how Nicodemus and Joseph were being threatened by the whole of the Sanhedrin for believing in a 'dead Messiah.'

"They are willing to abandon themselves for me because they love me. And so they are free." I then turned to Gabriel. "Now, I want you to keep watch over my mother. She is in Bethany."

"Yes, Lord."

I turned to Vasiariah. "See that Salome is comforted." I looked about the circle. "And Susanna needs to understand that my love is sufficient for her...always."

"She's mine to watch," answered Nith-Haiah.

I gave more instructions, and then I heard a cock crow. "Michael, see that Peter is protected in Jerusalem...John and the others, too."

When I was finished, I left the angels behind and I walked into Joseph's fine garden remembering how it was that I became who I had been all along. I marveled. I knelt to thank my Father, and as I did I felt his presence and the presence of the Spirit come alongside me. We began to speak of what was and of what could be...

...of what should be and of what would be.

And there, in the Aramithean's quiet garden, we once again walked as if we were in search of Adam and of Eve. We groaned for all men and all women because of the sorrows yet ahead, but we also rejoiced for them; we knew of the glory that awaited our children and so we laughed and we sang. Eventually, we left the garden of my tomb and entered the wilderness. There we summoned the wild animals to encircle us as they had encircled me on that difficult journey I had made some years before. We blessed them each, by name.

The hyena laughed,

The ibex leapt for joy,

---

probably because of a generous bribe by the wealthy Joseph of Arimathea and perhaps because of the dream that Pilate's wife suffered (Matthew 27:19).

308 About 100 lbs of spices per John 19:39, an astonishing amount and of great expense.

The martens danced.

And the whole of my Father's world sighed happily at the sight of me For their redemption had begun.

I then thought of the other beasts not privileged to run wild. I thought of all the suffering they endured at the hands of evil men. But I rejoiced for them as well for their salvation was near. Yet the salvation of all would be worked out with fear and trembling:

For the Serpent still lived
So that men might be truly free.

I then returned to the tomb after a group of women had already come to anoint my body. Since I was no longer there, they had run to tell the men. The angels were waiting for me. "They think someone stole your body."[309]

We turned to the sound of feet running toward the tomb. I pointed my finger. "There. Ha! John and Peter...look at them."

The two men were racing through the lush garden toward us with slender John in the lead. Far behind, Mary Magdalene was trying to keep up. John arrived far ahead of clumsy Peter, and when he did he leaned into the doorway. Gaping at the bandages, he cried to Peter. "The women were right!"

Peter then forced his way past John and burst into the tomb. "There... there are his bandages...and over there...there's the cloth that covered his face. But where is Jesus? Who has taken his body?"

John was troubled. "Who would take him? What of the guards? The stone? It was none of us. Who would dare? The Elders paid to be sure no one could..."

The angels pitied them. Vasiariah leaned over to me: "You already told them that you would rise on the third day...how stupid are these men?"[310]

"They need to hear it from a woman," I said.

As I watched the two men hurry off to Bethany, I felt deep compassion for Peter, my Rock. I knew that he was suffering for his denial of me during my trial. But I also knew that the day was soon coming when I would eagerly invite him to declare his love for me, and he would offer it to me, gladly.

---

309 John 20:2
310 John 20:9

Mary Magdalene did not leave with the two men. She lingered in the garden, weeping loudly. Oh, how she loved me. She angrily pushed aside a basket of oils that she had brought to anoint my body, and then stepped into my tomb again. When she did, her breath quickened, for sitting at the head and at the feet of where I had lain now sat two of my angels.

"Do not be afraid, Mary, but tell me, why are you crying?" asked Gabriel, tenderly.

"B...b...because someone has taken the body of my Lord and I don't know where they put it." She began to back out of the tomb.

I then came up behind her. She turned but didn't recognize me. I said to her, "Dear woman, why are you crying?"

Mary darkened. "Tell me, gardener...where did you put him? I need to know so I can get him."

I said nothing and so she turned away from me, weeping.

I then called her name. "Mary."

She stopped crying and turned slowly toward me. I watched her eyes open a little, and then a little more until she knew. "Oh, my Lord!" She fell to her knees.

I squatted and looked at her and remembered how she had cupped my feet as I hung on that cross. "My dear Mary."

Her eyes were wide.

"You...you from whom I cast seven demons...you who were despised by the religious men of Israel...you, my dear Mary of Magdalene, go tell the others that *I am alive*! Good woman...be the *first* to bring the good news to the whole world!" [311]

---

311 It is impossible to overstate the significance of Jesus appointing a female to be his first witness. In that time the testimony of women was considered utterly unreliable.

ALL THINGS MADE NEW

The following days brought a great deal of confusion to my followers. They were distressed and arguing among themselves. One said, "The Magdalene insists that he lives, but who cares what she says...the witness of a woman means nothing!"

Another said, "All of Jerusalem says that we stole his body! What's going on?"

And many complained, "We thought he was going to throw out the Romans!"

No, I did not blame them for their confusion. These things are hard for men to believe. Even I had been confused during my time in time.

As a boy I wondered who I was.

As a youth I wondered what a Messiah would do.

As a young man I wondered what kind of Son I was to be.

As a teacher I wondered why I did not know all things.

As a dying man I wondered why this was my Father's will.

As the sin-bearer I lost all sense of wonder.

And then I was given to remember who I had always been,

And I was at peace.

It was true that my resurrection defeated the authority of the Evil One on the earth, but it remains true that the war rages on. And so I longed for my beloved followers to be at peace, even as I am. Filled with joy, I began to delight in revealing to them the Mystery of my Kingdom.

The same day that I had risen I took a walk with my Uncle Cleopas and my Aunt Miriam as they left Jerusalem.[312] They didn't recognize me, but Miriam proceeded to tell me of all their sorrows in the death of this one who was the supposed Messiah. She told me that 'this good man'—their nephew—was a great prophet, and though they were disappointed that he hadn't liberated Israel, they would always love him. I smiled to myself.

"But wait until you hear this," Cleopas said. "Certain women who were followers of his..." he tilted his head toward his wife, "...say that his body is gone."

"It is," said Miriam.

Cleopas wrinkled his nose. "Dear wife, if I ever find out who deceives those who love him, I'll..." He lost his voice.

I marveled. Had they forgotten everything? Did they think my teaching was that of a madman? Did they think they could sift my words like wheat...keeping what they understood and disbelieving the rest?

I interrupted my uncle. "Oh, you are just not thinking clearly! Don't you understand how it is that the Messiah must suffer *before* he comes into glory?"

The two fell silent.

I looked at him. Indeed, he had spent his life pretending that suffering didn't exist, but I could see that he had wept in secret for most of his life. My aunt stood patiently, waiting for me to say more. She was a woman of great faith and little understanding. So I began to teach them both how to find the Son of Promise from within the very beginning of Moses' words, and in the writing of the Prophets, and the songs of the Psalmist. They listened, carefully, and I spoke for nearly two hours as we walked.

We finally arrived at a house they had rented in Emmaus and since it was getting late, they begged me to come in and join them for a meal. I did, and what a happy sight was waiting for me...a little *round* table with wine and unleavened bread, fish, and a basket of dried figs.

---

312 The author's speculation that Uncle Cleopas and Aunt Miriam were the two disciples Jesus met on the road to Emmaus is supported by some scholarship though admittedly cannot be proven.

"Here, friend," said Cleopas kindly as he handed me the bread. "Would you bless this for us?"

I took the bread from him but I paused to enjoy the sight of the two of them. Only three of us were gathered to enjoy the goodness of my Father, but here, where even two are gathered, is my Kingdom come to earth. I smiled and I gave thanks for the bread, and I broke it. I then handed a piece to each of them and as I did, the Spirit opened their eyes.

The look of joy in their faces makes me smile, even now. But, as the Spirit opened their eyes, she called me away, and so I faded from their sight, even as I heard Cleopas begin snorting, wildly. Truly, the two of them were so happy that they turned around and hurried all the way back to Jerusalem that very evening. [313]

I ached to see my mother who was in Bethany with my brother, James. I knew that her faith was strong, but I knew that she longed to see me. And I knew that she longed for James—or 'Camel Knees' as many now called him—to believe.[314]

Poor James was so miserable because of his wife that nearly everyone avoided him. But I had always believed James to be a good man and I assured my mother that he would someday be a champion of my Kingdom. Hoping to comfort my mother after my crucifixion, James had joined her in Bethany along with my brothers. My mother's claims of my resurrection had so frustrated him, however, that on the third day he told her that he would never eat bread again until he saw me.

"I do not fear for you, James," Mary answered. "You won't go hungry for long."

I laugh to think of it.

Her answer didn't please him or his wife. "If you love your son," said Judith, "you'll just tell him to eat."

---

313 See Luke 24: 13-34

314 Early Church records record this nickname that was given because of his famous piety that kept him on his knees in prayer.

"No. He can wait until he sees his brother. He won't starve."

To that, I'm told, Judith kicked dust all over Lazarus' courtyard and shouted so loudly that my followers in the upstairs rooms hid themselves.

I came to James by night with a basket of bread and a smile. Hearing a voice, he quickly lit every lamp in the room and wakened Judith. "Who goes?" she said.

I didn't answer, but gestured with the bread. To that, Judith fainted straightaway on the wooden floor. But James did not bother with her. He fixed his wide eyes on me. So, I held out one of my hands and let a lamp fill a spike hole with light. I thought my brother might fall down, too. But he studied my wrist and then lifted a lamp toward my face, slowly. Our eyes met and I knew that he had been given sight.

James then fell at my feet, weeping. I stooped before him and lifted his face toward mine. "Brother." I kissed him and he kissed me.

Crying out for joy, James summoned our mother, Judas and Joses and Simeon, Salome, and Lydia. "Come! Come! Come and see!"

My siblings and my mother raced into James' room where they cried out for joy. My mother clutched her heart and sang. I ran to her and held her as she sobbed her song of joy. Oh, friends, look at me…even now I tremble for happiness as I think of that moment. Then, when we had all greeted one another and sang a song together, my mother looked at Judith who was still sprawled across the floor. "Jesus, do you think we should wake her?"

In the days that followed I appeared to more of my followers, but still there were those who would not believe. Even some of the Eleven who had seen me with their own eyes wrestled with doubt! [315] What was I to do with

---

315 Matthew 28:17, Mark 16:14, and Luke 24:41 are all in agreement that an element of doubt persisted among the disciples. Perhaps because the first reports came from a woman?!

them? I rebuked them, I encouraged them, and two days ago I ate fish with them…like we are doing now.

Then, at yesterday's dawn, I met someone whom I have loved for a very long time. I had built a small fire like this one along the lake's shoreline not far from here. I was staring into the coals when a familiar voice turned my head. A woman approached me, shyly.

I stood, smiling. "Leah."

She was startled. "S…someone said it…it was you, but…" Leah fell to her knees. "Then the rumors are true. But how can it be!"

I knelt before her. "Don't be afraid."

"But…but…can it be?" She stared at me, saying nothing. After a long time, belief began to spread over her face, but as it did she quickly withdrew within her shawl. "Oh, Jesus. Don't look at me. I've become ugly. I'm old and my life has been hard…"

"Dear Leah, don't hide from me."

She shook her head.

"Tell me what's wrong."

She hesitated. "My life is not what I had ever longed for. I used to laugh, Jesus. You remember. And I once danced. Now…" She sniffled. "I wish I was free from my shame, free from my fears…" Her voice fell to a whisper. "I want to be free from my husband…and I am ashamed to say it."

I sat close to her.

"This lake once gave me hope. I woke early to splash in it in summertime; I sang with the water birds. Now…now I hate it."

I looked over the waters of my beloved lake wonderfully lit by the very first hint of light in the east. "Are you sure that it's the lake that you hate?"

She struggled. "Yes. It took Tobiah from me but delivers my terrible husband home to me every night. And so I don't trust it."

I understood. Why should she trust it? I said nothing for a long time but the woman's sobs wounded me, deeply. "Dear Leah, you want to be free…but you will not be free until you trust the lake again."

She stared at me.

I leaned toward her. "Do you trust me?"

Her face fell. "Why should I?"

"Because I love you. I have always loved you."

"Then why didn't you marry me?" Her tone had a brave bite. She was right to ask.

"Would you have married me?" I asked.

"Yes." A tear slid down her cheek. "Of course."

"Why?"

"Because I loved you. Because...because I trusted you."

I took her hand. It was moist. "Leah, trust me again. Look at our lake. Its face is the face of *El Abba.*" We sat side by side for a long time until I said. "The lake is a mystery, to be sure, even a fearsome one. But in all its mystery, it is still the face of love. Look, see how the waters reflect the beauty of all that comes near. See the clouds, see the passing birds..."

"Love is hard for me."

"Of course." I looked at her." You have not been loved by others, Leah. But listen: where beauty is, love is...and beauty is surely here."

We sat quietly for a time. Finally I said, "Now, stand with me."

She did.

I took her hand and led her into shallow water. It felt cool and fresh over my ankles. "Look out there." The gentle colors of a magnificent sunrise had painted the lake, brightly. Fish were dappling the surface. Birds swooped low. I could feel the excitement suddenly filling her spirit. "Tell me, Leah, what do you see?"

"I see many things." She was quiet again until she whispered, "It *is* beautiful."

I let her eyes open wider, and as I did I let my mind fly to the many memories I had of this lake. I thought of my first sight of it from the cliffs at Arbel; I remembered sailing with Tobiah, of sitting by it with Leah, of praying along the shoreline, of teaching and feeding and healing others nearby--of Peter walking on top of the water with me!

I looked down at my reflection and in it I saw the face of my Father and the Spirit. I then pointed to Leah's reflection in all our faces of love. "Do you see yourself?"

She nodded.

Leah and I stared at each other looking back at ourselves. I took her hand in mine. "You are beautiful, sister, and much loved. Trust me and be free."

She sniffled, but her face began to shine.

I turned to her and took her other hand. "Leah, I tell you today, you *will* be with me in the Paradise to come."

My dear sister squeezed my hands; She could not speak.

"Now, Leah, I leave you with this song that we once sang together. Sing it often in remembrance of me...and of who you are becoming:

"Set the round table and make ready the lamps,
>   Gather lute and harp, singer and horn,
>   So the women can dance and the men make merry.
For Death will be no more.
>   Nor will there be mourning or weeping,
>   For all things will be made new,
And the joy of my rest will be upon you forever,
>   The light of my Light will guide you,
>   In the eternal *shalom* of my Kingdom now coming. [316]
>   *Selah!*"

---

316 Adapted from selections of Jeremiah 31, Revelation 21, and Revelation 22.

Shabbat Shalom[317]

So ended the Story as I— *Adlai bar Ammitai*—remember it being told.

When *Yeshua* finished his song he blessed us each with a light touch upon our eyes, lips, and hands. At his touch the women became still as eve-tide doe, but I trembled. I tried to choke out a clumsy word of thanks but my mouth wouldn't work and my legs lacked strength. I had to lean on the gibbering Gaul in order to find my feet and stand up. To that *Yeshua* laughed, though kindly. "Love one another, even as I love you," he said.

These were the last words that I ever heard my Master speak.

Yeshua then walked to the edge of the shoreline and lingered for a moment. I marveled at how he loved his lake. He then faded away like the easy drift of a sea-borne mist.

About a week later, *Yeshua* announced to his disciples that his Kingdom would be one without borders and so he commanded them to bear witness to his name even to the most remote parts of the earth. After saying this, he ascended into the clouds not far from his beloved Bethany on the Mount of Olives.[318]

When I heard the news, I left Capernaum and returned to the city where I joined with the brethren to consider all that had happened. There I began to write down all that I remembered.

Soon the rulers of Israel set upon us with a fury. Among our persecutors was Saul, son of Tish, whose eyes the Lord later opened. Such testing of our faith lasted through the many years that followed and so I hid my scrolls.

Years later, I was given the courage to retrieve the Story. When I read it again, my spirit lifted. Yet as I considered what I'd written, it was clear to me that I did not write these words with the same breath of the Spirit that some others had been given. I knew that my ears had been curved with the inclinations of my heart; how I had listened along that lakeshore was no less tainted than how I later remembered. So how reliable was my witness?

Did I dare share these words with anyone else?

A brief rain then began to fall. I climbed to my roof where I let it wet my face, and there I prayed about my writings. When I opened my eyes I saw a wonder appear over the rolling valleys of Galilee. Before me arced a glorious rainbow from one end of my world to the other. My eyes filled

---

317 Means 'Peace of the Sabbath'

318 See Acts 1:8,9

with the glory of its splendid colors; my lips murmured a song, and my feet felt suddenly light as air. I danced! I marveled until its colors faded slowly away. And when it was gone I thanked *El Abba* for such a gift as this.

I hurried to my room and opened my scrolls again. I read a few lines and then a few more. As I did I felt a warmth come over me. A breeze wafted through my window and I drew its fresh scent into my spirit.

And I was given peace.

Patient reader, I implore you to consider what I have written with care. As in all things, I beg you to invite Wisdom to teach you how to see and how to hear, for only then can words—like broken men—be used as if they are whole.

May the Grace and Peace of our Lord Jesus Christ fill you with all joy until he returns, and then forever and ever in his world without end.

The End

AUTHOR'S POSTSCRIPT

I suppose that I'm stating the obvious when I say that this was not an easy book to write. From the time the idea was hatched in October 2007, I recognized that something unusual was happening. Having written six other novels I was no stranger to the nature of the work, but this one was the most exacting project of them all. Four years later I leaned back in my chair and exhaled, finally prepared to type 'The End' though knowing that I will forever wonder what more or less should have been said.

You may have noticed that this is an 'author's edition.' Publishing professionals with whom I had worked on other projects warned me that this novel had little chance of publication. For one thing, the expectations related to this subject are rarely attained. And, if that were not enough, they said that the book would simply cause 'too much trouble' unless controversial elements were removed.

Their first concern seemed reasonable to me, but I decided to take the risk. However, their second concern did not seem reasonable at all. Therefore, I chose to set out on my own and offer this story directly to you in its intended state. I ask you to forgive imperfections in the text that may be the result of this decision.

I do understand the delicate nature of this topic, and I respect those who may find particular offense at the autobiographical approach. I would simply answer that the Christian faith is premised on God's desire to be in relationship with humankind--a desire so profound as to mysteriously overlap identities. As one example, Jesus said, "...I am in my Father, and you in me, and I am in you." (John 14:20). Additional comment on this and other issues can be found at my website: www.cdbaker.com.

I appreciate all of those who have taken this journey with me, whether reader or contributor. I would especially like to express my deep gratitude to Dr. Bruce Longenecker, a former professor of mine at the University of

St. Andrews. Bruce urged me to write a Jesus novel (though he ought not to be blamed for the autobiographical approach!) and his tireless, corrective encouragement was invaluable.

I also want to recognize the young artist/poet/mystic Akiane Kramarik (www.artakiane.com) for her immeasurable contribution of insight, especially in regard to the character arc of Jesus who, as she so wisely recognized, 'became who he already was.'

Amer Nicolas, the historian for Nazareth Village (www.nazarethvillage.com) in Nazareth, Israel, was a deep well of knowledge. Amer escorted me through the rather misty history of first century Palestine by spending hours in patient instruction. His knowledge of the times and of current historical scholarship proved to be invaluable.

Some years ago, Dr. Jeffrey Thatcher introduced me to the practical value of the ancient enneagram, a personality model that became an invaluable lens for the presentation of a number of the biblical characters.

A hearty 'thank-you' to David and Anna Landis whose wonderful 'Jesus Trail' (www.jesustrail.com) opened my senses as I experienced boots-on-the-ground research through Galilee, Israel, with my patient wife, Sue, who endured much over these years.

Courage is always deserving of mention, so I would like to commend Taras Boyko for his. The founder of Knigonosha Publishing in Kiev, Ukraine (www.knigonosha.com), Taras—with the talents of our meticulous translator, Yuri Shpak—has introduced this book to the world of Russian language.

My hope is that all of us will learn to regularly challenge the impressions of Jesus Christ that we have been given—even those in this book—so that we may encounter him in ever more meaningful ways. To that end, I hope we become more comfortable in asking questions, more adventurous in considering possibilities, and truly free to explore the deep wonders of mystery.

May the Spirit enliven our imaginations as she guides us into all truth.

Grace and Peace,
C. David Baker, Christmas 2011

P.S. On June 14, 2011, I typed the last pages of my first draft during a furious rainstorm. When I finished the final sentence, I sat back in my chair and exhaled, uncertain of what I had done. Then, within moments, my wife began calling for me to hurry outside. I rushed from my studio to find her pointing into the fast-changing sky. I looked up and saw a full rainbow arching boldly over our little farm. Each of the rainbow's legs stood on our green pasture—and *exactly* on each property line.

Coincidence?

You may decide for yourself. As for me, I took a deep breath…and I smiled.